THE IVORY DUCHESS

"The plot of *The Ivory Duchess* is unique and steady, with Kate and Philip's turbulent love story skillfully fashioned and well-tuned, like the pianoforte of a master craftsman. *The Ivory Duchess* promises to be Delia Parr's breakout book, and Ms. Parr is one bright star on the rise to watch!"

—*Romance Forever*

"The lead characters are superb as they grope with an unwanted relationship, and the support cast are top rate. Sprinkling elements of suspense and intrigue, Ms. Parr makes the mid-nineteenth century seem to come alive in this excellent historical romance."

—*Affaire de Coeur*

BY FATE'S DESIGN

"Delia Parr vividly depicts everyday Shaker life, and *By Fate's Design* showcases both triumph and anguish for the human heart and soul. Ms. Parr's star is definitely on the rise."

—*Romance Forever*

"Delia Parr has given us an intriguing historical, laced with delightful characters, passionate romance, and a heartwarming tale of love, growth, and trust—an incredibly beautiful love story."

—*Rendezvous*

"An excellent tale."

—*Bell, Book and Candle*

"*By Fate's Design* is an exciting Americana romance that brings alive the Shakers, an interesting part of our heritage. The lead characters are both superb and the support cast adds the right amount of spice to make Delia Parr's par excellence novel well worth reading."

—*Affaire de Coeur*

More . . .

St. Martin's Paperbacks Titles
by Delia Parr

The
Minister's
Wife

DELIA PARR

St. Martin's Paperbacks

THE MINISTER'S WIFE

Copyright © 1998 by Mary Lechleidner.

All rights reserved. No part of this book may be used or reproduced in any manner whatsoever without written permission except in the case of brief quotations embodied in critical articles or reviews. For information address St. Martin's Press, 175 Fifth Avenue, New York, N.Y. 10010.

ISBN: 0-312-96650-4

Printed in the United States of America

St. Martin's Paperbacks edition / September 1998

St. Martin's Paperbacks are published by St. Martin's Press, 175 Fifth Avenue, New York, NY 10010.

10 9 8 7 6 5 4 3 2 1

Dedicated to
Jeanne
my "partner in crime" and
the sister of my heart.

Acknowledgments

I am deeply grateful for the assistance of Harold F. Worthley, Librarian, at the Congregational Library in Boston, Massachusetts who provided the details of clerical garb for nineteenth-century ministers through correspondence including the Internet and snail mail.

I would also like to acknowledge the help of Mrs. Dale Green, Historical Research Assistant at the Chenango County Historian's Office in Norwich, New York, who guided me through a multitude of resources on county history and the impact of the building of the Chenango Canal on the surrounding region, just a day after the spring blizzard of '97 had nearly shut down the entire area. Yet, there she was—on duty and ready to help, as most other businesses struggled to reopen and foolish travelers who had disregarded weather predictions, like myself, were digging out of motel parking lots to make their way home, or to historical societies for a day of research!

My thanks go to my sister, Carol Beth, her husband, Robert, and their boys, Brian and Jeremy, for sharing their seashore home with me summer after summer so I can write while enjoying the sunshine along the peaceful Toms River. I am also blessed with a most understanding daughter, Elizabeth, who never once complained about being stranded in a blizzard on spring vacation (well, maybe a little), and two sons, Matthew and Brett, who offered long-distance encouragement I treasure. As always, my seashore friend, Linda Opdyke, has offered support that surpasses exceptional while my "partner in crime," Jeanne Seybold, continues to amaze me with her unfailing loyalty. To top it off, I have the best agent ever—Linda Kruger!

Finally, I wish to acknowledge my deep regard and respect for my editor, Jennifer Enderlin. She inspires me, challenges me to stretch and grow as a writer, and continues to guide my writing career with uncanny, professional wisdom. Her creative genius had a profound impact on THE MINISTER'S WIFE, for which I am indebted.

Prologue

April 1833
Western New York

What the Creator, in His infinite wisdom, has blessed and joined together as one, let no man put asunder.''

Emilee's new husband gently squeezed her left hand, and she felt the slim gold band on her finger—a symbol her long and arduous transformation into a righteous woman was now complete. She glanced at the gentle, soft-spoken Reverend Mr. Randall Greene, the man who had chosen her above all others to share his life, and her heart swelled with joy and pride. She straightened the white lace Geneva bands, the symbol of his ministry, that graced the collar of his waistcoat and smiled at him.

"Shouldn't you kiss your bride?" whispered Reverend Burke.

Randall blushed, and he gently tipped her face up to his. She stared into his deep-set brown eyes and watched as reluctance gave way to the older minister's prompting. He leaned toward her and pressed a passionless kiss to her forehead that evoked no fear of the marriage bed that awaited her this night or any other.

Mutual goals, expectations, and deep Christian faith, not love or a desire for physical intimacy, had brought them together as man and wife. Their marriage, he had assured her, would serve as a living example for others to follow with only one goal: eternal salvation.

"You have brought great joy to my life today," he murmured as he urged her against his portly body in an awkward embrace. "You are forevermore my wife and helpmate. Together, we will do the Lord's work." He set her aside as though suddenly mindful of the few guests who had braved the incredible spring blizzard that rendered the small village of Surrey in the foothills of the Catskill Mountains nearly impassable today.

She turned back to face Reverend Burke, who was more the father she had never known than her spiritual advisor. Leaning forward on tiptoe, she planted a kiss on his wrinkled cheeks. "Thank you. For . . . for everything," she gushed quietly, keeping her gaze centered on his still-handsome face to avoid any glimpse of the wasting disease that palsied his limbs and would force him into retirement in a few short months. Feeling a gentle nudge on her elbow, she turned and embraced his wife, Olivia.

Eyes red-rimmed, the tiny woman twisted a damp handkerchief in her hands. "My dear, dear Emilee. We're just so happy for you," she managed before a waterfall of joyful tears cascaded down her cheeks.

Emilee brushed away the tears and kissed her mother-by-affection on both cheeks. "I don't know how I can ever—"

"You were a joy. Always a joy. It was our privilege to raise you and watch you grow in your faith."

The hasty reply, so typical of the quiet woman who preferred the shadows to the limelight of her husband's ministry, did not belie the courage it had taken to defy an entire community and take Emilee to home and hearth twelve years ago when she was only eight years old.

"You should greet your guests," Olivia urged as she joined Emilee's hand with Randall's. "I'd best see to serving up some coffee and warm cider to our frozen guests." She escorted her husband to an upholstered chair before making her way to the kitchen.

Emilee edged closer to her husband until they were shoulder to shoulder. Ready now to welcome the few stalwart well-wishers, she blinked back tears of joy. Maryam Shale and Rozilla Hopkins, identical twin sisters, edged forward, each claiming a kiss from the groom. Now unencumbered by morose spouses, who had succumbed to an outbreak of dysentery a decade ago, the two women had been among the very first villagers, after the Burkes, to accept Emilee, thus giving each of them a very special place in Emilee's heart.

"You look radiant and oh so lovely, Emilee," Maryam gushed, giving Emilee a sidelong glance as a huge grin deepened the crescent-shaped scar that dimpled her right cheek and made it possible to tell the silver-haired sisters apart.

"You look right dapper, too," Rozilla teased, nudging Randall's shoulder with the tip of her bony finger.

Randall blushed again and mopped his brow with the back of his hand. Emilee looped her arm with his, a protective gesture that seemed to come as instinctively as caring for him when he suffered occasionally from debilitating headaches. "How did you ever get through the drifts of snow today?" she asked, commandeering the topic of conversation.

"Ansel and Hester," came the chorused reply.

As though announced at a formal gathering, Ansel and Hester Woerner joined them. Ansel grinned and reached out to shake Randall's hand. "Hitched up the sleigh and figured I'd best pick 'em up. Otherwise, I'd never hear the end of it," he grumbled good-naturedly.

The twin's sister, Hester, giggled, her eyes mirroring the devilment known to all to be a family trait. "We found them both stuck knee-high in a drift just outside their door."

Ansel winked at Emilee. "Shudda left 'em as bear bait, 'cept I knew you'd want to have 'em here."

"Bear bait!" the twins protested in unison, setting the other guests into a round of chuckles that lightened Emilee's heart.

Encased in a blur of renewed happiness, she greeted the rest of the small assembly. Felicity and Caleb Rogers, a town selectman and leader of the Board of Relief when the first bid for Emilee's care had gone unanswered as the entire community turned its collective back. Eliza and Richard Fenton. Both had witnessed Emilee's public conversion and acceptance as a full member of the church four short years ago.

Emilee's confidence grew with each hug and glowing compliment. Nearly giddy, she glanced at the final pair of guests who stepped forward: Mercy Traymore and her husband, Ezra. Merchant, landowner, postmaster, and local justice of the peace, he was the voice of secular authority; she was the village gossip. As he engaged Randall in conversation about continuing fund-raising efforts for the new church, Mercy stared at Emilee, and a tepid smile touched the corners of her lips. Her eyes hardened with warning and a reminder that while she had kept watch and ward over Emilee for twelve long years, she had no intention of abandoning her vigil now that Emilee had become a married woman.

When the Traymores left to join the other guests, Emilee took a deep gulp of air as chills tingled down her spine. "I am my mother's daughter," she whispered softly, "but I am *God's* child, too." Taking comfort in the phrase Olivia had repeated over and over until Emilee herself had believed it, she turned to her new husband.

Within the next few months, when Reverend Burke retired and Randall began his duties as pastor of the First United Church of Surrey, Emilee would step into a role that would be more demanding than being any other man's wife. She would be the minister's wife, a model of virtue for women of the congregation to follow.

Responsibility weighed heavy on her shoulders, but she was certain that Providence had designed and created this man to be the one and only helpmate she would need if she stumbled along the way.

ONE

September 1834

Primal fear propelled Emilee out the back of the parsonage. Even as the door slammed closed behind her, the muffled echo of her husband's angry words followed her. She stifled her sobs with a fist pressed hard against her lips and ran away from him as fast as her shaking legs could carry her. She crossed the rear yard, rounded the barn, and leaned the full length of her body back against the wall.

With her chest heaving, she gasped for breath. Her heart pounded so hard she thought it might burst, just as her husband had exploded only moments ago. Again. No one in the village, however, would ever believe that beneath Randall's gentle exterior lay an unpredictable temper that was growing uncontrollable. He kept it well-hidden from everyone except the one person who would never reveal his faults: his wife.

New tears filled her eyes. After nearly one and a half years of marriage, she still did not understand Randall. One minute he was the placid, even-tempered man she had married; in the next, he was like a long-dormant volcano that suddenly erupted, without warning or provocation, spilling out his frustrations in venomous words that scalded her very soul.

Randall had never attempted to strike her. Never. Until today. She turned and pressed her forehead against the aged, splintered wood and slammed her eyes closed, trying to block out the image of his clenched fist as he raised it against her. Just the memory, however, was vivid enough to spawn a deep groan that began in her heart and escaped through her lips.

"Emilee! Come back inside!"

Her husband's screeched command, evidence enough that he had followed her outside with his fit of temper not yet spent, inspired immediate, self-preserving disobedience. She raced to the rear of the small property and prayed he would not follow her further, if only to avoid the chance someone might witness their argument.

Taking shelter in the thick grove of sugar maples that separated the property leased by Ezra Traymore to the church from the Ives farm, she had to slow to a brisk walking pace to accommodate the stitch in her side.

The knot of hair at the nape of her neck had come undone, and tendrils of russet hair lashed at her cheeks. Oblivious to the dawning display of fall colors that surrounded her, she paused long enough to repin the long tresses into a simple knot and dry her cheeks.

Randall needed time to calm down, and she needed to compose herself before a horde of guests arrived for Donation Day, an annual event when church members and their families brought foodstuffs and a small purse of cash donations to tide the minister and his family through the coming winter months. The day had dawned with dazzling sunshine and crisp autumn air, and the promise of a picture-perfect picnic after the barrels and tins of flour, pork, fruits and vegetables, and sundry homemade offerings had been carefully stored away, but had disintegrated into the worst moment of her life as the minister's wife.

With her heart still pounding and her mind racing with questions about her husband's combustible nature, she ambled toward the one place in a small town like Surrey where she could be alone—the cemetery. Mt. Zion Cemetery crested a gently sloping hill less than half a mile away. Following the natural path she often used to reach the Ives farm, she stopped along the way to gather a handful of late-blooming bluebells as her thoughts traveled back over the morning.

She shook her head and kept up her pace as she tried to put this very troubling aspect of their life together into perspective. Randall's outbursts were as infrequent as they were frightening, she reminded herself as she skimmed past the rear of the construction site where workers were busy shingling the roof of the new church. Honesty, however, forced her to admit that her husband's outbursts were becoming more frequent and more intense.

She hurried her steps up the steep cindered roadway that led to the entrance to the cemetery only vaguely aware she was walking in sync with the clip of hammers as the laborers continued their work. Entering the cemetery, she hurried beneath a wrought-iron archway and made her way toward the rear past simple flat-stone markers, granite slabs with inscriptions weathered away by time and the elements, and beautifully sculptured memorials that marked the resting places of the genteel elites, forefathers of the town's wealthier families.

As the narrow roadway curved, she passed a child's grave marked by a simple wooden cross and finally sighted the impressive monument that had drawn her here. Next to a pair of small markers, a marble angel with his wings outstretched and his hands lifted in supplication glistened in the bright morning sunshine that bathed him in a heavenly glow. With her footsteps softened by deep green grass still kissed with summer, she approached the gravesite as yet another wave of tears escaped from her eyes.

Her hand trembled as she placed her meager offering of now-wilted flowers at the base of the statue. She gazed at the chiseled inscription, partially obscured by a cache of debris that had blown from a nearby stand of trees that blocked a full view of the village below. She knelt down and brushed away the dried leaves until each word of the inscription was visible:

BENJAMIN ALOYSIUS BURKE
AUGUST 17, 1777–MARCH 5, 1834
BELOVED MINISTER, HUSBAND, AND FATHER
HE LIVETH WELL
HE LOVETH WELL
HE SERVETH WELL
HE AWAITS US BEYOND

She bowed her head to offer yet another prayer for the repose of this sweet man's soul. Death had separated her from the man who had guided her into a life of faith and respectability, but she often found comfort in visits to his final resting place, where she could pour out her heartaches without risk that they might be revealed to others.

She sat down beside the monument, rested her head against the angel's robes, and let out a deep sigh. The sun warmed her body. A gentle breeze caressed her tear-stained face, and she replayed the morning's events over and over again in her mind to determine how she might have prevented Randall's explosion and how he might regard her sudden, disobedient flight away from him.

In the middle of her mental journey back through the past few hours, she stiffened. The skin on her arms dimpled with gooseflesh. No sound alerted her, yet she felt certain she was no longer alone. Had Randall followed her here? If he had, would he dare risk continuing his diatribe outside of the privacy of their home? Or had he come to her, just as he had done on a handful of occasions, repentant and asking for forgiveness, now that he had ridden the crest of his angry outburst?

She lifted her gaze and visually searched the cemetery. No one approached along the roadway. No visitor had arrived to tend the grave of a loved one. She nearly dismissed her intuition as paranoia when the nickering of a horse sent her head twisting sharply to the right.

A man. Not ten yards away, he sat lounged against the base of a tree where his horse, burdened with travel bags, was tethered to a low-hanging branch. She gasped out loud and brought her hand to her heart. With the influx of laborers and contractors who had invaded Surrey to construct the canal along the Chenango River, she was much less nervous around strangers than she had been in the past, and she was more surprised than frightened by his presence. She squinted against the sun to see him more clearly, but his expression was hidden by shadows. When he nodded stiffly to acknowledge her and stood up, her heartbeat tripped and skittered in her chest.

He was tall, very tall, with dark, wavy hair cropped just shy of his shoulders. Attractive, classical features hardened with a shallow smile. He looked oddly familiar, yet she was certain she would never forget meeting a man so distinctively handsome. One quick study of his expertly tailored traveling suit cast him as a contractor or investor rather than a mechanic, exactly the sort of man she would expect to be associated with Ezra Traymore, who frequently entertained wealthy strangers.

She took a deep breath and scrambled to her feet. Her hands brushed away leaves and dirt from her apron and the hem of her skirts. Her troubles with Randall, at the moment, were the least of her concerns. Unless she wanted to add fuel to Randall's fire or risk being caught in Mercy Traymore's gossip net, she had best make herself presentable and make a hasty but polite escape before anyone saw her here. Alone. With a man who most definitely could never be mistaken from any distance for her short and rather portly husband.

Acutely aware of her role and her place as a married woman, she carried an added burden. She was the minister's wife, and she was determined to keep her reputation unsullied. Even if it meant returning home to an emotional storm that had yet to abate.

She took several steps back as the stranger made his way toward her. He moved with the confidence and ease only wealth and self-reliance would inspire, yet his posture was stiff, even forbidding. A gentleman, she noted, but quickly erased that notion when he stopped just a few feet away and flashed her a smile that sent every bit of common sense and propriety she had ever possessed to the four corners of hell. The floodgates of sinful physical attraction opened wide. Dark, heavy, lashes framed pale gray eyes that seduced her. Charmed her. And gave her a glimpse of the kind of man charismatic enough to tempt even the most reluctant or determined of women.

"I'm sorry. I didn't mean to frighten you. Or . . . or to intrude." His gaze softened, and he nodded toward the marble angel. "You've been crying."

Shame burned her cheeks, and she swiped at the few remaining tears on her face. "He was our minister," she offered lamely, allowing the stranger to credit her tears to grief rather than reveal the truth behind her misery.

"So it says." His words were clipped, even cold.

"Are you just passing through?" she asked, praying he would soon be far, far away and taking every one of her body's sinful and traitorous reactions along with him.

He stiffened. "No."

With her will already weakened by the morning's disastrous beginning, she trembled and fresh tears welled in her eyes. Fear that she was her mother's daughter, after all, left her head spinning, and she swayed on her feet.

Immediately solicitous, he gripped her elbow. "Maybe you should rest a bit," he suggested as he led her back to his resting place in the shade. She was leaning back against the trunk of a tree, his waistcoat protecting her skirts and softening her seat, by the time she regained her senses.

He had taken a seat a respectable distance away. A tuft of dark hair peeked through the open neck of a fine white linen shirt that covered a well-developed chest. A paisley cravat lay on the ground where he had heedlessly tossed it next to several apples of assorted varieties.

She studied the fruit and smiled nervously. "I see you stopped at Ansel's orchard for apples."

"Just for a pocketful," he said defensively, as though she might think he had stepped beyond the boundaries of country custom that allowed every traveler a pocketful of fresh fruit as a courtesy.

Sweet memories surfaced, and her smile widened. "When I saw his orchard for the first time as a child, I couldn't believe my eyes," she offered, to fill the awkward silence that hung in the air. "He convinced me for ever so long that he grew magical trees. I still like to think they're magic—"

"And not just ordinary trees Ansel grafted with limbs from others. He was always quite a character," the man commented with a genuine smile that softened his expression. He picked up a bright red apple and reached over to hand it to her.

When the dark hairs on the back of his hand brushed her fingertips, her body began to tingle, and his offering suddenly symbolized the forbidden fruit which had led to Eve's downfall. She dropped the apple onto her lap.

Seemingly too preoccupied to notice or too polite to comment, he bit into a golden apple and closed his eyes as he chewed.

"You've . . . you've been here before. Or perhaps lived here," she stuttered as his remark about Ansel sliced through the physical attraction that had consumed her thoughts and piqued her curiosity.

He stiffened, but very slowly opened his eyes. "A long time ago." Glancing through the trees, he stared down at the village that rested on a bluff overlooking the river. "A lot has changed since then," he remarked with an odd blend of nostalgia and excitement as the distant chorus of workmen's hammers, saws, and shovels accented the truth of his observation. "It looks like it's about to change even more."

"The canal," she commented, and he turned to face her. Rendered speechless by aqueous gray eyes and a teasing grin that deepened the cleft in his chin, she dropped her gaze, stunned by physical attraction so palpable her skin tingled and her heart leaped into an incredible somersault. "Progress. Or so they say," she whispered as she glanced toward the village and noticed several wagons heading toward the parsonage.

"And what do you say?"

She stumbled to her feet, ignoring the apple as it rolled from her apron to the ground. "I—I have to get back. Home," she whispered as she backed away from him. "I—I thank you for your courtesy and your concern."

Without hesitation, she turned and half-ran back through the cemetery, hoping to arrive home and set the kitchen to rights before guests arrived. By now Randall would probably be himself again. While she hoped for an apology and a quick reconciliation, it was not his image that filled her mind and tripped her heartbeat as she returned to the parsonage. That image belonged to the stranger on the hill, and she prayed fervently that the man's visit to Surrey would be short. Very, very short.

Her steps were quick, her horror at her weakness deep. One chance encounter with a handsome, virile stranger had been enough to prove to Emilee she was indeed her mother's daugh-

ter after all, and it would take all of her courage to prove to
herself she was more than that: She was the minister's wife.

A cool gust of wind interrupted his dream, and Jared reluctantly stirred awake from an unexpected but much-needed nap.
He flexed his stiffened legs and arched his back as he
stretched. A knot in the trunk of the maple tree pinched his
shoulder blades, and he leaned forward, his gaze focused
straight ahead on the marble angel.

Bone-weary from weeks of travel that had brought him back
from Europe to his birthplace, he had finally completed a journey that had lasted seventeen long years. He stood up and
brushed at his trousers, but never lost sight of the statue. With
a glance up at the quickly setting sun, he took a deep breath.
It was time to go home.

He bent down, shook his waistcoat free of dirt, and dressed
quickly. When he picked up the cravat, his fingers brushed
against a red apple, and he frowned. "So it wasn't a dream,"
he muttered to himself as he picked up the apple his mystery
woman had taken and then left behind.

He closed his eyes and brought her image back into his
mind's view. Slender, yet womanly, her oval face stained by
her tears, she had obviously been crying for much longer than
the few moments she had spent at the gravesite before she
sensed his presence.

A lover's quarrel, perhaps. One that had sent her here seeking the same privacy he had enjoyed before her arrival. He
paused and ran his hands over his brow. At first perturbed by
her arrival, he had grown intrigued when she had stopped and
knelt at the marble angel.

Although he was anxious to complete the last leg of his
journey, he could not resist reliving the moment when she
looked up and studied him as he approached her. Crescent-
shaped green eyes, swollen from crying, were flecked more
with surprise than fear, and he caught his breath again, just as
he had done the first time he had recognized the glint of physical attraction within the depths of her eyes that mirrored his
own spontaneous and compelling fascination with her. The

downward curve of her lips labeled the experience as most unwelcome, and he chuckled to himself, knowing she had no idea he felt exactly the same way. Even more so when he noted the slim gold wedding band on her finger.

"A woman with morals," he murmured, "but very much a woman." Precisely the kind of woman he had yearned to claim in the idealism of his youth, but accepted in one blinding moment of truth as he approached adulthood, the very kind of woman he did not deserve.

He kicked the red apple aside and strode to the grave he had traveled thousands of miles to see. "Isn't that right, Father?"

He waited for an answer from the minister whose flesh and bones rotted below the ground that supported the marble angel, but no answer whispered back from eternity. He did not expect that it would. He had never once gotten the courage to ask that question while his father was alive, and now that he was dead, it was too late.

Jared had returned to Surrey ready to face the demons that had sent him away from home with a secret so vile and despicable his chest tightened, but only a strong will would continue to block the memories that simmered deep within his soul. He forced himself to read the epitaph once again, slowly, although he had already committed it to memory. He sighed, resigned to keep as silent about his father's sins as he had been all his life. His shoulders slumped beneath a heavy burden. People's lives and faith would be destroyed if he weakened. Innocent people, including one he loved more than life itself, the most innocent of all: his mother.

Disappointed and embittered that even the man's death did not release Jared from his burden, he refused to believe the final phrase chiseled into the marble which assumed the Reverend Mr. Burke was safe in the arms of his Creator.

Jared knew better.

He also knew that the moment he left the cemetery and made his way to his mother's home, he would have to keep his demons well-hidden as he cared for his widowed mother with a willing heart. He would keep his father's secret stored in the deepest part of his soul along with a lifetime of broken dreams and shattered hopes, and the fleeting image of a beautiful, green-eyed woman who had reminded him, in his first few hours home, he was truly his father's son.

Two

"Forgive me. Please forgive me."

Randall's plea touched Emilee's heart, but the remorse and misery in his eyes reached deep into her soul, soothed the hurt, and eased the memory of his violent outburst to sounds and images that would join the others she had stored away with the hope one day they might slip away forever. "You frightened me," she whispered, the closest she could get to admonishing him, as she stepped into his waiting embrace and accepted his apology.

"I'm not myself when I get these headaches. I'm sorry, Emilee. I need your strength and your wisdom as much as your forgiveness. I've been so worried. You've been gone for over an hour," he murmured as his arms encircled her.

Guilt flushed her cheeks as her face pressed against his. Could he feel it? She eased away from him and twisted her apron strings in her hands. It had not been easy for Randall to take Reverend Burke's place or to bear the recurring headaches. As his helpmate, she should have stayed home and helped him through his anger. "I'm sorry. I—I was selfish to leave."

"Where have you been?"

"At the cemetery," she admitted. She was as reluctant to tell him about her encounter with the handsome stranger as she was to break her promise always to be truthful.

"It's not safe to travel about with so many newcomers." His caring eyes softened his rebuke, and he smiled as he brushed her tear-stained cheeks with his hand. "The church members will be arriving soon. Perhaps you should freshen up. Tonight we'll pray together," he suggested.

She nodded, her expectations about the pattern of their reconciliation fulfilled and her decision not to mention meeting anyone at the cemetery affirmed. She escaped to her upstairs chamber, and once inside, she closed the door and leaned back against it.

The sound of voices and an approaching wagon sent her scurrying to the open window. She pulled aside a panel of the crisscrossed curtains, watched the wagon carrying yet another group of laborers proceed down Main Street, and dropped the panel back into place with a soft sigh of relief.

Reminded that their guests were due any moment, she stripped off soiled apron and gown and poured a generous portion of water from the pitcher into the washing bowl. After she repinned her hair into a soft knot on top of her head, she bathed her face with cool water. She did not have to glance into the mirror to know that her eyelids were still puffy, but her spirits rose when she noticed her eyes were not as red as she feared they would be.

A quick study of her features satisfied her that no one would guess Randall had frightened her to tears. She had no desire to expose his temper or to subject their private troubles to public speculation Mercy Traymore would gladly spread throughout the small village.

Emilee merely looked tired, a common enough state not to arouse anyone's curiosity now that the influx of newcomers multiplied her work. Between her home visits delivering Bibles to new families in the area and serving as a watcher for those facing death, she had to squeeze in her duties as homemaker and wife as best she could.

Her hand slid down her chemise to rest on her flat stomach. Wistful hopes for a child of her own threatened to bring new tears, and she dropped her hand away. It would take a miracle for her to conceive a child. Physical intimacy between herself and Randall was as rare as it was blessedly quick. Except for their wedding night and a few moments of weakness, he had resisted the temptation of her bed, just as he had promised he would before their marriage. He viewed each of her monthly flows as a testament to his virtue, but she wondered if his pious disinterest and the separate sleeping chambers he had insisted upon had more to do with his very private nature than the depth of his faith. She accepted her childlessness as a small price to pay to keep her own private demons at bay; her limited and unhappy experiences in the marriage bed had done much to dispel her fears of wantonness.

Images of the stranger's handsome face and his virile body peeked through the curtain of her most private thoughts. She blushed. That man would likely bed his wife twice a day and again at night, filling his home with enough children to fill a whole bench at meeting—assuming his wife could coerce him to attend.

Emilee doubted he would embrace self-restraint with the same enthusiasm as Randall, although the poor man's wife would try to rely on the Word and the minister's sermons to temper her husband's lust and give her a respite from child-bearing, like many of the women who had swelled church membership in recent years.

A soft rap at her door sent her bustling about the room and tossed thoughts of the stranger flying out of mind's way. "I'm almost ready," she sang out as she donned the pale green gown she had worn for her wedding day and every special occasion since then. With a final check of her appearance in the mirror, she opened the door.

Dressed formally, with his Geneva lace bands in place as a visual reminder of his status as a minister, Randall smiled and offered her his arm. "The Traymores have just arrived," he informed her as he guided her down the narrow hallway that led to the staircase.

Not surprised that ever-vigilant Mercy had been the first to arrive, Emilee knew the woman would also be the last to leave. With head held high, Emilee descended the steps and held tight to her husband's arm.

Jared sat astride his mount and studied the village again from afar. Main Street, once only two squares long, now extended to five without losing the free-sprawling country character he remembered so well. Dwarfed by an impressive new church nearing completion, the meetinghouse sat in shadows now.

He swallowed the lump in his throat and shook his head to

chase away the echoes of long-winded sermons and visions of his father standing tall and proud in the pulpit while his mother sat beside him in the first bench.

The white-frame, green-shuttered parsonage where he had been born and raised stood in the next square. Another rush of memories. Another exercise in self-control that refused to allow sweet childhood memories past the wall he had built to contain them.

His gaze skimmed past a farmhouse and the general store and settled on the impressive Georgian mansion that stood where he remembered an orchard had been. He looked farther down Main Street past the town square and a bevy of newer buildings that stretched northward. He held his gaze steady the moment he saw the cottage huddled in between two small cabins, an arrangement that had been well described in the letter he carried in his vest pocket.

He had no desire to ride down the middle of Main Street and risk meeting anyone who might recognize him. Before he had ridden a single square, word would spread fast on the winds of gossip, and the very private reunion he had planned with his mother would become a town event.

He shook his head as he eased his way back through the cemetery toward the rear entrance. He had spent years first at Oxford Academy and then Yale and had found one excuse after another to avoid coming home to Surrey. Visits to his ailing grandfather in New York City whose wealth sponsored an education far beyond the means of a country minister's son. Invitations to visit his new circle of friends whose old-money families opened up the business opportunities Jared needed to establish himself far away from home.

His duty now, however, was clear. With his mother a widow, he would fulfill his role as her provider and protector.

With the cemetery at his back, he turned north and followed a narrow roadway that would skirt the village proper and wind back toward the cottage, but his thoughts still hung in the past rather than the present. With important business contacts and a trust fund established by his grandfather's will, he had copartnered an important business with his best friend, Will Cooper.

After the first few shaky years experimenting with different goods and wares, they had stumbled into the nursery business, importing varieties of old roses from England. Finding the business far more lucrative than either of them had imagined, he and Will eventually had settled on an arrangement that suited them both well. Will had remained in New York City to run the business; Jared had traveled through Europe to expand and cultivate contacts beyond England.

He had taken his secret with him.

A vagabond of sorts, he had wandered through the countrysides from the Netherlands to Italy searching for unusual varieties of roses. He had established small nurseries, hired experts to propagate them and develop hybrids for export to the United States.

A fascinating life. Satisfying. And one that allowed him to justify not returning home.

He shivered even though bright sunshine splayed across his face and form as he approached the cottage. Guilt pressed heavy as he quietly dismounted and glanced at the travel bags, where inside, every one of his mother's letters rested in a leather case. Most, if not all, were still sealed, but he knew that the letters he had written home had been read and reread until the paper thinned and yellowed with age.

As he approached the cottage door, he realized how very little he knew about the past ten years of his mother's life, while he had been in Europe. He was grateful his partner had notified him of his father's death, although the letter containing the news was already several months old by the time it had reached Jared.

The letter had remained sealed for nearly two weeks before he garnered the courage to open it. When he did, finding details of his father's final hours and references to the lingering illness that preceded them in a letter already months old filled him with guilt and shame.

He had arranged for passage home that very night.

He knocked once and then again. The world seemed to be

suspended in slow motion. His heart began to pound. Muffled footsteps approached the door. He stepped back. The door creaked open. A woman peeked around the opened door. He squared his shoulders and fought a most uncommon well of tears that filled his eyes, and an emotion that tightened his throat when he gazed down at the beloved face that looked up at him.

Surprise and then joy lit her face and, for just a moment, erased the passage of so many years. "Jared!" she cried. "You've come home! My Jared. My Jared."

He embraced her, swiped the single tear that ran down his cheek, and held her close. "Yes, Mother. I've come home," he whispered, vowing no matter how hard it might be, he would guard well the secret he had carried back home with him.

Donations filled the pantry shelves. Boxes and barrels lined the root cellar. The small purse in Randall's pocket bulged with coins, and nearly all the church members feasted on the final remains of a picnic supper as Emilee made her way back into the house to fetch one last pie.

Mercy met her at the kitchen door. A tall woman with a sturdy frame, she nearly filled the doorway. "Odd," she remarked as Emilee slipped past and tried to control the unkind thoughts that had assaulted her for most of the day after Mercy had commandeered control of the kitchen and spent most of her time in the parsonage. Apparently while Mercy had been waiting she had rearranged the dishes and cookware stored on the shelves of a corner cupboard while a stack of dirty dishes lay unwashed.

"Odd?" Emilee replied as she took the dessert out of the pie safe. Just imagining Mercy snooping through the parsonage made Emilee's hand heavy as she sliced the knife through crusted fruit and cut the pie into wide slices.

"Olivia still hasn't arrived. I've been paying close attention to the front door, just in case—"

"I'm sure she'll be here," Emilee managed through a gritted smile.

"It would be understandable for her to stay home. It's still her mourning period, but considering how close you've been—"

"Yes. We're very close." She nipped Mercy's whine with words far gentler than Mercy deserved. Emilee would not add kindling to the woman's smoldering love for gossip by revealing how concerned Emilee had been as the day progressed and Olivia had not made an appearance. "I'll check on her later to make sure she's all right."

"Ezra and I will stop on our way home." Mercy sniffed, clucking disapproval as Emilee swiped the broad side of the knife with her finger and plopped a dollop of thick, heavy juice into her mouth.

Mercy mopped her brow with a lace-edged handkerchief and eased into the chair at the head of the table. "The donations are not as generous as in years past, but I finally got the pantry in order."

As well as my dishes and cookware.

Emilee stepped up to the sink, pumped fresh water to vent her outrage, and washed her sticky hands. "Thank you. You didn't need to bother yourself," she said with her back to Mercy. She turned away from the sink to reach for a towel and caught Mercy just after she had stolen a cherry from a slice of pie. She had the dripping fruit halfway to her mouth when her eyes met Emilee's. A crimson flush stained her cheeks the same color as the fruit, and her eyes widened.

Feeling more compassionate than vindictive, Emilee dropped her gaze and turned drying her hands into a long, elaborate ritual so that by the time she had finished, Mercy had recovered her dignity. Without another word, Emilee retrieved the pie and carried it outside.

She had taken only a few steps when she noticed the acrid smell of smoke and a black cloud billowing toward the sky just north of the parsonage. Simultaneously, the fire bell clanged and Quentin Baker tore around the corner of the parsonage. Chest heaving, he pointed northward. "Fire! Two cabins engulfed so far. A third near to follow."

Gaiety immediately sobered into hushed concern. As the

male guests scrambled to their feet and made hasty retreats to help extinguish the fire, the womenfolk made quick work of cleaning away the picnic and gathering up the children. While Emilee put the oldest girls in charge of watching the younger children, she searched in vain for Randall.

With all hands needed to help fight the fire, she rushed off with the other women as they hurried to join their husbands and sons. Dread weighed heavy in the pit of her stomach. The fact that the meetinghouse and new church lay to the south did little to ease her fears. The small cottage where Olivia lived alone, now that her husband had passed over and Emilee and Randall occupied the parsonage, lay at the north end of the village and concern for Randall added yet more haste to her steps.

The parade of women included Mercy, who still dogged Emilee, and as they hurried toward the town square, a haze of smoke greeted them. The smoke grew thicker, and the stench of burning wood grew stronger as they approached the bucket brigade of men. Shouts filled the heavy air, and flames leaping skyward mesmerized Emilee and added fuel to her fears.

Ordered chaos reigned. As the women replaced men passing buckets of water in a long line that led down the bluff to the river, she saw that many of the laborers had joined the long-term residents to fight a fire that, if left to burn, would engulf the workmen's tents below.

A gust of wind cleared the smoke for just long enough to confirm her worst fears: Olivia's cottage had been reduced to ashes. Her eyes already smarting, she gulped back tears and prayed fervently that Olivia had escaped unharmed before the fire consumed her home. Emilee left Olivia's fate in the hands of the Lord and worked silently, passing bucket after bucket until the muscles in her arms cramped, her fingers grew numb, and spasms wrenched her back with even the slightest movement.

As she worked, she searched frantically for any sign of Randall, who still carried scars on his shoulders from a fire that had consumed his lodging house while attending Yale. Would he be able to overcome his deathly fear of fire to help battle the blaze and minister to the wounded and displaced? She added yet another prayer for him to her litany for Olivia. Concentrating on the prayers prevented her mind from focusing on the heavy physical labor that taxed her strength.

Taking advantage of a brief lapse between buckets, she wiped her brow and noticed that Mercy was nowhere to be seen. When and how the woman managed to find a way to avoid any kind of work she considered beneath her station was far less important to Emilee that the fact that her faithful shadow had finally left her alone.

"Clear!"

Cheers answered the cry that the fire had been put out, and drowned out rumors that the fire had been accidentally set by a careless laborer who occupied the cabin next to Olivia's cottage. Emilee dropped her hold on a bucket and started racing toward the waterlogged remains of still-sizzling embers before it hit the ground. Her feet splashed through puddles of muddy water as she worked her way through the throng of exhausted workers and the worried spouses who searched for them.

She found Randall standing off to the side. Alone. His face was pale, and the glazed look in his eyes reflected the depth of his paralyzing fear. Unlike the other men, whose soggy clothes were covered with filth and ash, he remained nearly as impeccably dressed as he had been at the picnic.

She went to his side and urged him farther away from the crowd. "It's over now," she crooned. When he nodded, a tic twitched his fleshy cheek, and her heart trembled with sympathy. "The worst is over, but there's still work to be done. People have lost their homes. Perhaps you can arrange for some temporary housing for them for the night."

He gazed at her, his eyes moist. "You see me as a coward," he managed to croak.

She shook her head. "Your fear is real and your memories are still raw. Time and prayer will heal all," she murmured.

His Adam's apple bobbed up and down. "Time and prayer," he repeated as he brought her hand to his lips. "You are a blessing to me. Truly a blessing."

The sound of approaching footsteps prevented her reply, and as Emilee turned around, Olivia stretched out one of her arms and moved swiftly to pull her into an embrace.

Relief and gratitude for the Lord's mercy washed over Emilee, but she forced the widow to stand back from her for a thorough inspection. Although the hem of Olivia's gown was singed and her cheeks were smudged, she appeared to be shaken but unharmed. "Praise God you're safe," Emilee gushed.

"It's gone. All of it," the widow lamented, clutching the only possession she had managed to save: her family Bible. "My sweet little home. My clothes . . ." Tears spilled down her cheeks, creating silver paths through smudges on her cheeks. "And now that—"

"You have a home with us. For as long as you need one," Emilee blurted. Aghast that she had spoken without consulting with her husband, she turned to him. She dismissed a fleeting glimpse of reluctance as an aftershock to his ordeal rather than any meanspiritedness until she realized that his greatest concern would be the loss of privacy with the presence of another person living in the parsonage.

"Of course," he murmured. "For as long—"

"But you don't understand," Olivia cried and turned away from both of them to scan the crowd that still remained.

Emilee stiffened as Mercy and her husband approached, but Olivia seemed to ignore them. She grew more and more agitated until finally her face lit with a smile. "Here! Over here," she cried as she waved her free arm over her head.

Intrigued, Emilee tried to follow Olivia's line of vision, but with so many people milling about, it was hard to discern which one's attention Olivia was trying to gain. Was it Ansel Woerner or Jackson Ives? Both were longtime friends and neighbors who had settled in Surrey the same year as Benjamin and Olivia Burke. While both men acknowledged Olivia's cry with a weary wave, they did not veer from their path.

"Here!"

This time, at the sound of Olivia's cry, a man stepped through the crowd and raced toward her. Emilee closed her eyes and her mind against the impossible. Her heart lurched so hard she thought it might lodge permanently in her throat. Shaking from head to toe, she opened her eyes, blinked, and sank back against her husband.

Even as the image of the man blurred when he swooped Olivia into his arms and lifted her off her feet in a crushing embrace, Emilee knew without a doubt that the man standing just a few feet away was the very same stranger she had encountered in the cemetery earlier that day. She took a deep breath and grimaced as the cool twilit air irritated her raw throat. A glance at Randall revealed a quizzical look she had no intention of easing.

"I've been frantic trying to find you," the stranger murmured as he set Olivia back on her feet. His voice was hoarse, but still fearfully familiar.

Within one quick glance, Emilee knew he had been at the front of the efforts to battle the fire. Drenched trousers clung to the curves of his legs. Black soot coated his once-immaculate linen shirt, and the waistcoat draped over one of his arms was singed beyond repair. Even though his face was streaked black, she immediately recognized the startling gray eyes that suddenly locked with hers.

Recognition sparkled back at her, but before she could react, he had turned his attention back to the older woman who stood by his side. He bent his head down and listened intently as she whispered to him. When he lifted his head, he nodded to Randall and Emilee, silently acknowledging his mother's apparent explanation of who they were as she leaned against him.

Lips quivering, Olivia brushed away her tears, and her eyes filled with an odd combination of sadness and pride as his arm tightened around her slumped shoulders. "My Jared's come home," she managed before emotion choked the rest of her words.

Shock surpassed Emilee's worst nightmare, and she bit her lip, scolding herself for not realizing who this man was back at the cemetery. His resemblance to Reverend Burke was so uncanny she was astounded she had missed it earlier. Same build. Same facial bone structure. Same charm and charisma.

And then she knew, in a sudden flash of insight, that Jared had not been merely resting in that part of the cemetery by chance. He had stopped there deliberately to visit his father's grave.

Fear tempered her joy for Olivia, who had nearly given up hope that the son who had left Surrey years before Emilee had arrived would someday return home. Would he acknowledge their earlier meeting? Would her deliberate omission about their encounter open a rift between her and her husband? She took a step closer to Randall and slipped her hand into his when she realized that her invitation to Olivia to move into the parsonage now would have to include her son.

The mere thought sent Emilee's world spinning so fast it crashed into oblivion, while she waited for Jared to acknowledge their earlier meeting and seal her immediate fate by unwittingly revealing her as a liar to her husband.

THREE

Jared took one look at Emilee's stricken face and decided to let another secret slip in beside the one he had protected so long. He extended his hand to the pristine man standing next to her, took one look at the grime that stained his hand black, and dropped it. "Sorry." He chuckled. "I'm still a bit of a mess. Rather a dramatic homecoming, but it's good to meet you. Both of you," he added, testing the soil before venturing to plant seeds of discord between the couple who faced him.

Relief flickered briefly in her eyes, and her stiff shoulders slumped with apparent relief, which let him know he had gauged her expression correctly. It did not surprise him that she had obviously failed to mention their chance meeting at the cemetery to her husband. A quick glance at the minister, who was probably the only able-bodied man who escaped tonight without dirtying his hands, spoke volumes about the man. That he had apparently reduced his wife to tears earlier added another layer to the man's character that turned dislike into disdain.

"Jared? Is . . . is that truly you?"

He turned to the face behind the screeched words that prevented Randall from responding to Jared. Mercy Traymore and her husband charged and then stopped within close range. The years had been kind to her, but then she had been matronly even as the young woman he remembered. Ezra had grown nearly bald, but he carried himself with an authority that bespoke the place he now held in the community, judging by his role in organizing the efforts to contain the fire. "Mr. and Mrs. Traymore. It's good to see you again, even under unfortunate circumstances."

He was referring to the fire, but when Mercy swiped away

tears even before they formed, she must have thought he was referring to his father's death. "Such a good man. We all miss him," she offered, affirming Jared's judgment she had misconstrued his reference to the fire. "He suffered for so long. It's terribly sad you weren't able to be with him or your mother at the end."

Recognizing a barb, even one so guarded in sympathy, Jared bit back all but the barest of explanations. "Mother's letters arrived too late. I travel a great deal, and by the time they had reached me—"

"You're here with me now," his mother intervened as she looped her hand through his arm.

Eyes glittering, Mercy glanced from him to the young couple and back again as she pursed her lips. "It appears you've already met our new minister, Reverend Greene, and his wife, Emilee. She's Ellen's daughter. I'm sure you remember Ellen Clarke."

He searched his memory while he gazed at Emilee, who blanched momentarily before her cheeks flamed as though she had been struck. Ellen Clarke. Hazy memories rushed back in a confusing torrent. He tried to sort through them and juxtapose his vague recollections of her mother and trouble of some sort with the vision of goodness and loveliness who stood before him, but he was too exhausted at the moment to retrieve more than one word: scandal.

His mother moved swiftly to Emilee's side and slid her arm protectively around the young woman's waist. "Emilee is the daughter of my heart and an inspiration to all who truly know her."

His mother's affection for Emilee was obvious, and he regretted that the short time before the fire had broken out had been spent giving his mother a full accounting of his years abroad. For the second time that afternoon, he also wished he had read all of his mother's letters, but he vaguely recalled her mentioning an orphaned girl his parents had taken in after he had left for Europe. That this girl had been Ellen's daughter surprised him, but he also knew his mother had always mourned the baby girls she had buried before he had been born and cared not a whit for what others might have thought.

Nonplussed, Randall remained silent.

Ezra shook his head and cleared his throat. "Now that the fire's out, Reverend, we could use your help. We've got two dead laborers. The family in the cabin on the other side escaped with a few burns. Nothing real serious, but they're with Dr. Pounds, who's tending to them. They'll need a place to stay. Maybe I should go with you to see some of the other selectmen and convince them to open up the schoolhouse, since the winter session is still a few weeks away."

Randall's shoulders straightened, and his expression brightened. "Of course."

"You'll need a place to stay too," Mercy gushed to Olivia before the two men could take their leave. "Both of you," she added with a glance at Jared before directing a quizzical look to her husband. He nodded, and she smiled. "We insist you stay with us. Ezra and I have more than enough room in our new home."

No doubt the mansion he had seen earlier, Jared mused. "Your offer is very kind, but I can see to my mother's welfare," he responded firmly. "I'll see to rooms at the inn for a few days until we decide—"

"The inn's near overflowing with riffraff." Mercy huffed. "So are the boardinghouses. You won't find rooms anywhere now that the canal's under construction."

Thwarted, Jared looked to his mother, allowing her the dignity of accepting the Traymores' invitation, a courtesy his father would not have allowed her.

His mother's eyes flickered, and she hugged Emilee closer to her. "Randall and Emilee have already graciously invited me to share their home until I decide what to do. I'm sure they would have room for Jared, too."

"Seems a good solution," Ezra mumbled. "The parsonage was your home for many years, Olivia. I'm sure you'll feel more comfortable there, and Jared, too, since he grew up there."

Mercy's expression crumbled into a frown, but Emilee captured Jared's full attention. Eyes wide, bottom lip quivering, she moistened her lips, but deferred to her husband.

Randall nodded, although Jared thought he detected a modicum of reluctance that intrigued him. "Olivia's son is always welcome in our home. Now if you'll excuse me, I'd best go with Ezra now." He kissed his wife's forehead. "Don't wait up for me. I will probably be home very late," he whispered before abruptly engaging Ezra in conversation as they walked away.

Jared stood rooted to the spot while the women discussed plans to organize help for the displaced families. He had been spared from sharing a home with the village gossip, but the prospect of living in his childhood home and all the memories it contained was almost as unnerving as spending days under the same roof with a beguiling green-eyed creature and daughter of scandal who, through some miracle of miracles, had become the minister's wife.

He refused to consider the nights.

With Olivia now sleeping in the guest chamber across the hall from her own room, Emilee tiptoed down the rear steps that led to the kitchen without benefit of a candle. The sound of sloshing water outside overwhelmed the crickets chirping a protest to cooler autumn nights and leaves falling from rustling trees that swayed in a soft breeze and told her Jared was still bathing.

She averted her gaze from the window and cleared away the cups and dishes from the table. She and Olivia had both bathed soon after they had returned to the house, with Jared gallantly carrying buckets of heated water to fill the copper tub. While she and Olivia had shared a light snack and consumed an entire pot of chamomile tea, Jared had set more water to heat on the cookstove and carried the tub outside.

Not an overly considerate gesture, he had insisted. Just realistic. He was grimy and sweaty to the extreme, and his clothes carried so much dirt and stench that just tossing them aside in the house would make another mess to clean up.

The night air had grown chilly, but from the length of time he had been outside, he was not rushing through his bath.

Second bath, actually, since he had dirtied the first tub of water when barely half done, or so he had claimed when he called out to have his mother set another pot of water on the stove.

Emilee's hand trembled as she pumped water to wash the dishes. The curtains on the window had been tied back so that light from the oil lamp in the kitchen would spill out into the rear yard, giving Jared light enough to bathe. Fearful that she might catch a glimpse of him, she kept her eyes downcast as she quickly washed and rinsed the dishes. She might have been tempted to leave them till morning to avoid Jared entirely, but Randall insisted on an orderly home, and she did not want to provoke him, especially with guests in the house.

She took a fresh cloth from a drawer, dried the dishes, and had them back in the corner cupboard in a matter of minutes. Long minutes. Awkward minutes that kept her ears alert so she might make an escape before Jared finished and returned to the house. She put the cutlery back into the small drawer that ran underneath the center of the table and set the chairs back into place, then paused long enough to wipe the table again.

Her kitchen set to Randall's standards, she made her way to the second step on the staircase, but stopped abruptly. Earlier Jared had been settling his horse into the barn while she and Olivia had eaten. Certain he had worked up a hunger battling the fire, Emilee cocked her head and listened carefully. He was still bathing.

Torn between her own need to avoid him as much as possible and her duty to her guest, she hesitated only briefly before turning around and going back into the kitchen. Working as quickly as she could, she set out several thick slices of buttered bread and slabs of boiled beef she had made for the picnic, and a pitcher of fresh cider. From the pantry she secured a jar of corn relish and applesauce, but left them unopened in case they did not suit him. Acting on a hunch he might have the same sweet tooth as his father, she piled a plate with molasses cookies and set a place for one. She had just folded a napkin into place when she heard his footsteps approaching the house.

She scurried across the room and had just reached the safety of the staircase when the door opened and he stepped inside. Caught. She did an immediate pirouette, and her feet caught in her skirts as though tangled in a spider's sticky web. She braced her hand on the wall to steady herself. With one glimpse at him, her mouth went dry, her heart started to pound, and her fingers curled against the rough plaster wall.

He was dressed only in trousers as dark as his hair, and the ebony curls on his bare, muscled chest still glistened with droplets of water. Damp tendrils of wavy black hair framed a face shadowed by a full day's growth of stubble.

Mercy!

Her mind immediately brought Mercy Traymore's image to mind, and Emilee could have kicked herself twice for invoking that lament.

Luminous gray eyes captured her gaze and widened with surprise, and he quickly donned the shirt he carried in with him. "I'm sorry. I—I thought you'd be abed."

She dropped her gaze as a heated blush worked its way up her neck to her cheeks and the tips of her ears. "I wanted to tidy the kitchen and make something for you to eat. In case you're hungry."

"Starved," he admitted as he walked over to the table and grabbed a slice of bread.

She backed her way up the first step.

"Was Mother able to get to sleep?"

His question caught her halfway to the next step, and she pulled her foot back to keep her balance. "Yes. And I've put clean sheets and another set of towels for you in the room next to hers. If there's anything else you need . . ."

She backed up the second and third steps.

He paused with the slice of bread resting on his lower lip. "A little company while I eat. If . . . if you wouldn't mind. It's been a long and complex day, and I'd really like to ask you a few questions. Mother and I didn't have much of a chance to talk, about Surrey anyway, and I have the feeling I need to catch up on things that have been happening while I've been gone."

She certainly could not refuse his request, but at the moment she would rather spend time with Mercy than Jared, a horrifying thought in and of itself. Emilee was curious, however, and anxious enough to settle the issue of their first encounter while no one else was around to misinterpret or misunderstand their conversation. She also had a host of questions of her own. Beginning with why he had not told her he was Reverend Burke's son, given he had had the chance, and continuing through a series of questions about why he had really left home and never once, since Emilee had arrived, returned home to visit his parents.

Back down the steps she came.

She took a seat in the chair he pulled out for her, folded her hands on her lap, and stared at the tabletop. He settled down across from her and started to demolish the meal she had set out, with a gusto that applauded her cooking skills in a way mere words could never do.

He finally paused to take a long pull of cider, set the tankard down, and leaned back in his chair. Silence. The sound of their uneven breathing. More silence.

When she finally looked up, his expression was sober, even grim, and his eyes flickered as though he was trying to decide which question he might first pose.

Before he had a chance to say a word, she spoke up, intending to clear away the issue of their meeting at the cemetery lest he think she was the kind of woman who commonly misled her husband. "I should thank you. For . . . for not mentioning . . . for not telling . . ." She paused, finding it harder than she had imagined. What exactly did she want to say that would not reflect badly on either Randall or herself?

He cocked his head, but he did not make it any easier for her by attempting to complete her feeble attempt to vocalize or explain her gratitude. His gray eyes smoldered and reflected the light from the oil lamp in the middle of the table.

She took a deep breath and tried again. "I was upset this morning, and I wouldn't want my husband to think I had betrayed a confidence by weeping on another man's shoulder."

There. It was out. Clean, and to the point.

Her heartbeat slowed to a more normal pace.

"Does he bully you often?"

Her heart immediately pounded disbelief. "Randall doesn't bully me," she countered.

"He made you cry."

"He did not!"

It was a lie neither of them pursued.

"I'm sorry," he murmured as he rubbed his brow. "Maybe this was a bad idea."

She could not have agreed more, but she could not think of a courteous way to say so. She thought about simply getting up, excusing herself, and slipping up the stairs to her chamber, but when he ignored the rest of his meal and grabbed a handful of molasses cookies, she smiled. "Your father had a weakness for sweets too."

He put the cookies back. His eyes darkened to the color of rain-dampened slate, and his lips stretched into a taut frown. Instantly she regretted mentioning his father when only today, Jared had visited the cemetery for the first time. "I'm sorry. I'm not usually so thoughtless. I didn't mean to add greater burden to your grief."

He nodded. "Perhaps my questions should wait for another time. If you don't mind, I'd welcome some time alone."

His soft-spoken words did not ease the guilt she felt for upsetting him, and she left him sitting at the table without saying another word. She went to her chamber, where she, too, would be alone with only her prayers for company.

Jared waited until her footsteps faded before he cleared away the remnants of his meal. Prolonging the inevitable, he tidied the kitchen, brought in a stack of firewood for the morning, and carried the copper tub back inside before he extinguished the oil lamp.

Exhaustion finally kicked in, and he decided to use the back staircase rather than risk stumbling his way through the first floor in the dark. He reached the second floor, stopped at the door to his mother's room, listened hard, but he heard no sound. Satisfied she was resting comfortably, he took note of the light spilling out from beneath the door to the chamber across the hall. He pushed away visions of Emilee dressed in her night shift and waiting in bed for her husband to return.

Proceeding to the chamber she had prepared for him, he tried to keep his footsteps light. Had she known it was the same room he had claimed as a child? He opened the door, stepped inside, and eased it closed. His gaze scanned the moonlit room. Even in muted shadows, the room seemed to have changed little. A single bed flanked by two chests of drawers lined the wall to his left, and a pair of small braided rugs covered the floor on either side of the bed. After side-stepping his saddlebags, he removed his clothes, eased into bed, and wondered if somehow it still harbored the dreams of his youth.

Or his nightmares.

Sore muscles relaxed. His eyes shuttered closed. Just as he felt himself drifting into sleep, booted footsteps echoed a man's ascent up the front staircase. All senses alert, Jared listened as the footsteps continued and then stopped directly in front of his door. A pause. A door creaked open and shut. The sound was so close, he knew the door in question was directly opposite his room.

Incredulous, he turned his back to the door and stared out the window. "Bloody fool," he grumbled as he punched his pillow into a more comfortable cushion for his head. "He doesn't even share his wife's bed."

Every pore and muscle in his body cried out for sleep, but he tossed and turned for what seemed like hours. Muttering to himself, he untangled the sheets and crossed his arms behind his head. He stared at the ceiling.

I thought you might have your father's weakness . . .

Her words haunted him, tore through his defenses, and touched the nerve of the secret he held locked up inside of him. He broke out in a sweat that a breeze from the window turned into a chill.

If she only knew.

FOUR

Tragedy and sorrow were a normal part of life, and villagers in Surrey did not need a sermon at meeting to inspire charity and compassion. It was just midmorning, yet the large sewing room opposite Randall's study was already bursting. Emilee carried another armful of donations inside and plopped it onto the floor.

Olivia had cleared a small space on the narrow table where, side by side, she and Emilee used to cut patterns and alter clothing. A pitcher of cider and a small plate of salted pretzels were temptations she couldn't resist. Mouth watering, she wiped her hands on her apron and grinned at Olivia, who was perched on top of a mound of blankets within arm's reach of the snack.

"Time for a rest," she said, patting the small hill of bedclothes next to her.

Chuckling, Emilee offered no protest and took her appointed place. Selecting a small pretzel from the plate Olivia passed to her, she nibbled at the knots first and closed her eyes. She rolled the still-warm, heavy dough in her mouth and savored the sting of the rough salt on her tongue before taking a peek at Olivia. Never one to waste, she had been taking scraps of leftover dough to make these special treats for as long as Emilee could remember. Tasting the pretzel unleashed a good many of her memories growing up in the parsonage, and she realized, once again, how much she missed having Olivia's daily companionship and guidance. "Remember when Mrs. Traymore tried to find the recipe for your pretzels?"

Olivia laughed so hard she nearly choked down a bit of pretzel. "Caught Mercy red-handed. The poor woman couldn't stutter her way out of it, though she tried."

"She thinks you've given the recipe to me," Emilee remarked, with yesterday's memory of Mercy hibernating in the parsonage still fresh.

Careful to swallow first, Olivia laughed again. "It's driving the woman silly." Her expression sobered. "Keeping the recipe to myself is selfish. I admit it and confess it to God. I got that recipe from a young baker who was heading west and buried his sweet young wife on the way. It was all he had as an offering for the service at his wife's grave, and I'll be twice buried before I'll let Mercy have that recipe. She'd have George selling pretzels in the general store the next day. Turning a profit on a man's heartache just doesn't seem right."

"I wonder what she'd think if she found out I still haven't learned how to twist the dough properly. Not that I haven't tried."

"You've far more important things to do now," Olivia offered in support. "And if Mercy assumes you're making the treats to take to the children on your home visits, I'll be the last to tell her otherwise. Besides, it gives me something to do with my time."

Nodding her approval, Emilee licked the salt from her fingertips before she poured out two glasses of cider and passed one to Olivia. The older woman took a sip and held the glass on her lap with both hands. Her lips quivered. "I had a whole tin of pretzels all set to bring yesterday. The crunchier ones that keep longer, just in case the children . . ." Her voice dropped below a whisper, and her hands began to tremble.

Emilee covered the woman's work-worn hands with her own. "I wish there was something I could do or say—"

Olivia shook her head. "The Lord always tempers our sorrows with joy. Jared is here with me now, and he'll help me. I just wish we didn't have to crowd you. It's hard enough settling into married life without having full-time boarders in the way."

"This is your home. It always will be," Emilee countered. As much as she welcomed Olivia back, having Jared here would be difficult enough without Randall complaining about having two houseguests. He had confided as much earlier that morning before he had taken to his bed with a severe head-ache, and Emilee worried Olivia might have overheard their conversation in the study.

"Following in the footsteps of a man as beloved as my Benjamin hasn't been easy for Randall," Olivia murmured. "I know he's anxious for you to separate yourself from me. It's not a matter of pride or selfishness. It's the right thing to do. People won't fully accept him as long as I'm standing in the way reminding them of the beloved minister they've lost."

Her worst fears confirmed, Emilee swallowed hard. "Randall isn't as flexible—"

"He will be. Give him time. He's young and a vibrant speaker in the pulpit. He's also got twice the ministry from a year ago with so many moving into the area. Your work is doubled from mine, too. That's why I think we'd best keep my stay here short." She set both of their glasses back onto the table, stood up, and tugged Emilee to her feet. "Jared is down to the bank settling a few affairs. I don't even know . . . well, that's best left till I talk to Jared first. In the meantime, I think you and I should speak about how I can help you the most while I'm here."

"Before or after we organize all these?" Emilee asked as she looked around the room at the mounds of donations.

"After." Olivia chuckled, as resilient as ever. "And I have a hunch if I suggest I take over your housekeeping duties so you can help your husband tend to his flock, you won't argue with me for more than a minute."

"Maybe two," Emilee teased as she started sorting through the pile of bedclothes. Relinquishing her housekeeping duties to Olivia would do more than free Emilee to keep up her home visits and the rest of the obligations of a minister's wife. Full homecooked meals and a sparkling house would be sure to soften Randall's reservations about having long-term company and spare Emilee from his complaints, but she also welcomed the opportunity to keep a good distance from Jared.

She prayed away a frequent but sinful desire to have a simpler life, one that centered on her own home instead of others'. It was her faith in the Lord that had blessed away her past and given her a respectable life that had far exceeded any of her dreams. Dedicating herself to Him by ministering to others and opening her home to Olivia and her son seemed little to offer in return.

Even if that meant living in the same house, for a time, with the greatest temptation ever placed before her: Jared Burke.

Meeting old friends and neighbors along the way delayed Jared's short jaunt down Main Street. By the time he left the bank, one of several establishments spawned by the burst of economic activity that accompanied construction of the canal, he had filled in many of the gaps created by his seventeen-year absence.

When he added what he learned to the tidbits of information he remembered from when his parents traveled east to attend his graduation from Yale, his grandfather's funeral, and Jared's departure for Europe, he had many of the answers he had intended to get from his mother and, later last night, from Emilee. The rest of the answers he sought were in the leather case of letters he had stored under the bed in his room, and as soon as he had the opportunity, he would read each and every one of them, no matter how painful it might be.

He waited for a passing wagon before crossing the street and heading for the general store to look for Ezra, pausing long enough for the condolences for his father's passing and the fond accolades to his father's character to churn and twist in his mind. He clenched his fists as he walked. He had not expected his return to be easy, but preparing for what people would say was a far cry from actually living through the experience. Fortunately, people seemed to take his taut smile and grim expression as normal for a grieving man. By the time they might grow suspicious and think otherwise, he would have full control of his emotions and be able to mask them better.

At least that was his plan, and if he extended half the energy and force of will he had used to build his business enterprises to the point where he was wealthy enough to retire and live off the interest of his varied investments, he would succeed.

Not that he had often entertained the extent of his fortune. He had never been motivated by wealth for its intrinsic value; instead, he equated wealth with the freedom to live by his own code of honor and on his own set of values and responsibilities. His mother needed him now, and by the time the sun had set tonight, he would have set all the wheels into motion to use his wealth to guarantee her future as well as his own.

He entered the general store, mercifully empty except for the clerk who was standing on a ladder adding wares to the shelves behind the counter. Jared glanced around at the barrels of sugar, flour, and salted fish, tables filled with bolts of colorful cloth and sewing notions, and the array of farm and household implements displayed on the far wall. The familiar scents and sights evoked more memories as he approached the counter.

As his footsteps echoed on the wide-planked floor, the clerk twisted around on his perch. "Jared?" The man grinned and climbed down to extend his hand.

"George Traymore! You haven't changed a bit." Jared grinned his lie and shook the man's hand.

His old friend and schoolhouse compatriot grinned back. "Still charming your way through life, I see." He chuckled and ran his hand through thinning hair before patting the mound of flesh that curved his canvas apron. "Like father, like son, so they say." His eyes widened, and he dropped his hand. "Sorry. I didn't even stop to think. It's been six months since—"

"Not a problem," Jared assured him. "Folks have been caught a bit unawares all day. You always did rush to speak your mind, if memory serves me right. I seem to recall a certain tutor . . ."

"Mr. Stillwill," George prompted. "Didn't take kindly to my position on the first amendment to the Constitution."

" 'Free speech has its limits, Master Traymore,' " Jared mimicked as the episode cleared its way through a multitude of similar ones long stored in the past. "It was during the spring session." He furrowed his brow. "And a debate about whether or not the switch was conducive to inspiring proper behavior.''

George winced and tapped the seat of his trousers. "It was hardly a debate. More like a soliloquy. 'It's my will or no will, young man.' '' He shook his head. "I can't believe I have young 'uns that age now. Can't convince them I know every trick and stunt before they think them up, either.''

"I'd be glad to oblige. Tell a few tales—''

"Not on your life! A man has a right to a few secrets!''

Was it a right, a duty, or a curse? Unable to find the answer or discuss it with anyone, Jared was not sure. He cleared his throat. "I was looking for your father. Is he here?''

George shook his head. "Stops in once or twice a day to handle the post. Other than that, he leaves me in charge here and spends most of his time at his offices in the new house. Sadie and I live upstairs now.''

"Sadie Bell?''

"Been married ten years now. Three boys. Another due this spring,'' he said proudly. "Yourself?''

"No. No, I'm not married,'' Jared responded.

"Don't wait too long. Takes a young man to keep a firm hold on young 'uns today.''

He nodded, unwilling to admit even to himself that not having children was as much a necessity as it was a choice. "I guess I'd better be off to see your father.''

"Tell your mother if there's anything we can do . . .''

"I will.'' Jared turned away, took a few steps, and walked back to the counter. "Mother and I are staying at the parsonage until we can make other arrangements.''

"So I've heard.''

"Let me have a pencil. I'd like you to take a few things over there.'' Guided by experience which had taught him well, he made a list of supplies to offset the added expense of having two houseguests. He settled his mother's account and added funds for her use before he left to complete his day's mission, but only after securing a promise the order would be delivered within the next few hours.

Back out in the sunshine, it took a few minutes for his

vision to adjust before he managed his way to the Traymore mansion without incident. Mechanics working below the bluff added a cacophony of sounds to the more peaceful aura surrounding the farmhouses and homesteads that dotted the rolling hills in every direction.

"Progress," he remarked to himself and recalled his conversation with Emilee at the cemetery. Only the first of several they had shared, each had been marked by wariness and a crackle of physical magnetism which undermined his attempts to focus beyond the unusual shape of her eyes or the intriguing color of her hair. He had not intended to embarrass her at the cemetery or to act ungrateful last night, and he had escaped the parsonage early this morning before anyone else had risen, to avoid seeing her until he had a tighter grip on his self-control.

He turned up the walkway to the mansion, making a mental note of Mercy's feeble attempts to line the walkway with a garden of roses. With most already pruned back, they would need an extra layer of salt hay to survive the coming winter. Deadwood crowded many of the canes, and the bushes were planted so close together he did not need to inspect them closely to know they had fallen prey to any number of diseases that proper air circulation could have prevented.

After stopping long enough to remove a wayward shoot that snagged on the hem of his trousers, he climbed the single step to the front porch and tapped the clapper on the front door. A young servant girl, no more than fourteen, greeted him and let him inside. The smell of beeswax permeated the air, and he spied a servant in the parlor to his left polishing furniture obviously imported from dealers in the city. A crystal chandelier overhead centered a foyer flooded with sunlight that poured in through tall crown glass windows on either side of the front door and created an ornate shadow that danced on the plush Oriental carpet beneath his feet.

Ezra came out of a doorway to his left. "I've been expecting you, Jared," he said as he extended his hand and clapped him on the back. "I trust you and your mother are none the worse for your dreadful experience."

"We're fine. George said I'd find you here. I haven't seen Charles yet, but I suspect I will before too long."

At the mention of George's older brother, Ezra narrowed his eyes and stiffened his chin. "Charles moved west a number of years ago. Settled in Ohio, last we heard." His words were cold and he waved toward the doorway without further explanation.

Aware he had apparently broached an unwelcome subject, Jared preceded his host into an office any New York businessman would have envied. A massive mahogany desk anchored by twin floor-to-ceiling bookcases lined the far inside wall. Thick brown carpeting cushioned a grouping of chairs in front of a marble fireplace, a globe suspended in an elaborate case on wooden legs, a humidor, and a sideboard with decanters of liquor and a tray of glasses.

A prominent man's domain, and Jared was impressed, but not intimidated. He took a chair in front of the desk, declined an offer of liquid refreshment, and leaned back. "I understand you hold the mortgage on my mother's cottage," he began, choosing not to mince words.

Ezra opened a drawer, pulled out an account book, and opened it. He ran his finger down one page and stopped nearly at the bottom. "There's a balance—"

"See Garth Leigh at the bank. He has a draft waiting. Give the figures to him."

Ezra puffed out his chest. "There's no need to rush matters. Under the circumstances—"

"I'm here to assume full responsibility for my mother now that she's alone. I fully expected to handle her debts, and I'd appreciate it if you'd see Leigh before the end of the week."

A nod. A spark of interest, even respect. "What are your plans, if I can be bold enough to inquire?"

"That's precisely why I'm here. To solicit your help and your advice."

A smile.

After asking a number of questions and securing Ezra's promise of total confidence, Jared laid out tentative plans he had made on the voyage across the Atlantic and modified within the past twenty-four hours with mathematical precision. If everything went smoothly, he would be able to move his mother out of the parsonage before the first snow fell in November.

By the time Jared had finished, the top of Ezra's bald head was glistening with sweat that ran down onto his forehead. He pulled a thick handkerchief out of his waistcoat and mopped his brow. "I believe I can help you," he ventured. He drew a rough map of the area showing four available properties and handed it to Jared. "There are also a number of other investments and the like I might suggest when you have the time. Now that the canal is no longer a matter of wishful thinking, a man of means could certainly take advantage of an opportunity that only comes once, if you catch my meaning."

After he had the map in his pocket, Jared smiled, taking more than a small measure of satisfaction in his position as he concluded his visit and walked back to the parsonage. The minister's son had come home a far wealthier man than anyone might have imagined, especially Ezra Traymore. While Jared had no purpose beyond securing an existence for himself and his mother that might accommodate both their needs, he also wanted to serve notice that he took his responsibilities to heart, his long absence notwithstanding.

He walked around to the back of the parsonage and saw Emilee struggling with a sack of flour and a jug of honey she was attempting to carry into the house. She was the only element he had not anticipated in his future, and he realized his equation was now unbalanced.

"Hopelessly unbalanced," he muttered under his breath as he rushed forward past a stack of supplies to help her: "Living under the same roof with her is no smarter than inviting a bear to hibernate inside of a honey pot and expecting the honey to be there come spring."

FIVE

Emilee could feel the jug of honey sliding down her hip, and the heavy sack of flour on her other hip tilted her off balance. She squeezed her eyes shut and struggled to hold on to her wares. Chiding herself as she lost the battle, she knew the time she had tried to save would be probably spent cleaning up a very sticky mess.

In one startling moment, however, a strong force braced the sack steady and another pressed the jug against her hip. Her eyes flew open. "Jared!"

With one hand on the sack and a palm cradling the jug, he was so close she could see his chest rising and falling as he took a breath.

"Thought you might need an extra hand or two. Sure would be a waste of good honey if the jug slipped out of your grasp." He grinned and cocked his head. "Your choice. Should I take the flour or the honey?"

She giggled nervously and nodded to her left as she pitched her hip slightly forward and tried to right herself at the same time. "The flour. Please."

"Be still a minute," he ordered as he tried to keep his hold steady. "If we don't do this just right, we'll still be in more trouble."

No, trouble is how fast you make my heart beat.

"On the count of two," he suggested. "Ready? One. Two!"

In a synchronized but awkward motion, she let go of the flour and reached over to cup her left palm around the jug as he pulled the sack up and away from her.

His eyes dancing, his lips curled into a gentle smile of rebuke. "Do you make a habit of tackling more than you can handle? Maybe you'd better warn me now so I can be here to watch out for you.''

"I tend to do things in a bit of a rush," she admitted. Grateful he could not hear the hammering of her heart or see the tingles that rushed through her body, she took a step back to put a proper social distance between them. "Thank you for helping me. And for being so generous."

He glanced at the stack of supplies and frowned. "Where's George? Why didn't he carry all this inside for you?"

"He offered, but I didn't want to keep him away from the store for too long."

"And your husband?"

She felt her back stiffen. "He's not feeling well," she explained before starting back into the house. Jared fell in step beside her and followed her into the kitchen. "You can set the flour in the pantry, if you can find the room. Donation Day was yesterday," she said as she sat the sticky jug of honey next to the sink.

He walked past her, poked his head into the pantry, and groaned. "Looks like I underestimated your stores."

"All of it will be put to good use," she assured him as she swiped her finger at the trickle of honey oozing down the side of the jug and savored the taste of the sweet luxury before wiping the outside of the jug with a damp cloth. "Winter's coming, and the need will be great for many of the less fortunate."

He accepted her explanation without comment and disappeared into the small pantry. She could hear him rearranging things a bit, and he returned moments later empty-handed. "I'll see to the rest of the supplies, but maybe I'd better put everything just inside the pantry door so you can store the supplies where you can find them easily."

She smiled, wondering if Mercy might ever be as considerate. "Thank you. Again." A chorus of high-pitched giggles filtering in from the front of the parsonage prevented her from saying anything more.

Jared looked at her quizzically. "Mother?"

"She's in the parlor with Mrs. Shale, Mrs. Hopkins, and

Mrs. Woerner. The sisters stopped by to help your mother alter some of the donated clothing to replace what she lost in the fire. They sound like schoolgirls planning a prank, don't they?''

He chuckled. "I think they really were schoolgirls together years ago.''

"And good friends ever since," she added as she walked to the cookstove to stir the stew Olivia had prepared. "They're staying for dinner and will be glad to see you're back in time to join them. You've been the topic of conversation for most of their visit.''

She tasted a spoonful of stock. "The stew is ready. Once you've gotten the rest of the supplies inside, why don't you go see if they can break away from their work?''

He sniffed the air and nodded. "Smells awfully good. Shouldn't take too much convincing to get the ladies to the table.''

He made quick work of his task and went to the parlor while she put the stew into a large pewter bowl and set it down on the table. She had just finished making a tray with two platters for Randall and herself when her guests entered the kitchen.

Maryam Shale's frown deepened the scarred dimple in her cheek. "You're not joining us?''

"Randall isn't feeling well. I thought I'd take him a tray. Maybe I can convince him to eat a bit if I stay with him.''

Olivia ushered her friends to the table. "We'll add a prayer for him to our blessing, dear. Jared, sit at the head of the table, won't you?''

While her guests were preoccupied, Emilee took to the staircase and carried the tray directly to Randall's chamber. As she made her way down the hall, she noted with relief that the bevy of voices did not carry as far as the front chambers on the second floor. She rapped softly on his door before she opened it and slipped inside.

Randall was still asleep, stretched out on top of the bed-covers. She set the tray down on top of a chest of drawers. Walking softly, she went to his side and laid her hand on top of the now-warm cloth that lay across his forehead.

He stirred. "Emilee?"

"I'm here. Are you feeling better?"

He lifted the cloth away and handed it to her as he sat up and leaned back against the headboard. He closed his eyes briefly and waved toward the window. "The headache is less severe. The cold cloth helped a great deal, but the light . . ."

She pulled the window drapes closed and set the cloth alongside a bowl of water on the nightstand next to his bed. "You should try to eat something. I've brought a tray so we can eat together, if you like."

In a room now bathed in twilight, he took her hand and pressed it to his lips. "You're such a good wife. What would I ever do without you?"

A good wife, she mused, would not find another man so attractive or so unnerving. She moistened her lips to keep from sharing her guilty feelings with Randall because he would not forgive her weakness so easily. "Would you like to say the blessing before we eat?"

He folded his hands over hers. "Lord God Creator, You have blessed us both with deep faith and Your abiding love. Bless this food, that our bodies may be strengthened, and bless our hearts, that we may always be true to Your Word."

"Amen," she whispered and added a silent prayer of her own that Randall might be spared his headaches and that she might be kept safe from temptation so new, yet so achingly familiar to her deepest fears. Finding comfort in the touch of his hands, she took even breaths of air. With the exception of his occasional outbursts, he kept her safe—from gossip, from idleness, and from herself.

She turned and picked up the bed tray leaning against the wall and placed it over Randall's lap. After arranging his platter in front of him, she pulled a chair over to the bed and balanced her platter on her lap.

During the meal, she discussed Olivia's offer with him and her plans for the afternoon. After they finished eating and she cleared away the dishes, she convinced him to rest awhile longer. She placed a fresh damp cloth on his forehead before carrying away the tray.

Instead of returning the tray to the kitchen where her guests were still dining, she took it to her room, freshened her appearance, and grabbed her bonnet and reticule. She left a note for Olivia in her room and descended to the first floor by way of the front staircase. After a quick stop in Randall's study to secure a Bible, she left the house.

Emilee scribbled a number of items on one of the scraps of brown wrapping paper she kept in her reticule. She slipped the stub of a pencil away and handed the list to Nancy Walters. "If you leave now, I'm sure Mr. Burke will still be there. He'll help you carry everything back. Unless you'd rather wait for your husband to finish work."

A woman only a few years older than Emilee, Nancy stared at the list and closed her bandaged fingers around it. Her three small children, one with singed hair and a reddened face, huddled around her, each claiming a bit of her skirts with tiny fists. The Bible Emilee had brought lay on Nancy's lap. "We're not even members of your church." Her voice cracked, and she touched her blistered lips with the tips of her fingers.

"God doesn't read the membership rolls, and neither do we." Emilee glanced around the one-room schoolhouse, which had been opened hastily and converted into a temporary home for the displaced family.

Nancy stared at the list. "You've done so much already. Reverend Greene saw to everything last night and stayed with us till we were settled here. My . . . my husband set out early before work to see Mr. Traymore. There's a cabin, not much more than a lean-to, and if the rent's not too steep, we might be able to settle there in a few days. Till Robert can find something more permanent."

She rubbed the list with her thumb, and her eyes filled with longing. "Robert doesn't take well to charity."

"I understand," Emilee murmured, only too aware how quickly tragedy tested a man's pride. Or a woman's. "Once you're settled, maybe you can help us in return. Several of the women meet on Saturdays to sweep the meetinghouse and get it ready for meeting. With the weather turning cold soon, we'll be needing a stack of firewood for the stove whether we're in the meetinghouse or the new church.''

The woman's eyes brightened. ''He could chop wood, but . . . but would I be able to bring the children with me on Saturday?''

''I don't see why not. Sadie Traymore always brings her boys. Come spring, she'll even bring her new baby with her.''

With a wistful smile, Nancy slid her hand across her stomach. Emilee understood the silent gesture and wondered how the woman would find the strength to care for a family that apparently added a new child every two years. Randall's sermons might convince her husband to temper his lust and spare his wife. ''Would you like me to stay here with the children while you go up to the parsonage?''

Nancy shook her head. ''They don't want me out of their sight. Not since the fire. I think they'd like to see Mrs. Burke, too. She's been a good neighbor.'' She set the Bible onto a nearby school desk and lifted the youngest girl to her lap. Remarkably well-behaved, the children had been quiet during Emilee's visit. A touch of shock left over from the fire, perhaps.

Emilee rose from her seat and waited while Nancy put on her bonnet, no small feat considering she juggled the toddler on her hip and still managed to tie a limp bow beneath her chin. After they left the schoolhouse and bade one another goodbye, Emilee watched the two little ones tag alongside their mother for a moment and checked the clouds overhead for signs of rain. After deciding the good weather would probably hold, she headed to Dr. Pounds's office with the hope that Jared would not mind helping Nancy Burke. Mentally checking off her schedule for the afternoon, she hurried her steps to make sure she would be back before sundown.

Taking to his chamber was not an option. Not with the minister just across the hall. Luck would have the man recover from his headache, ready to engage Jared in conversation that would no doubt center on his father's righteousness. He could not use his father's former study without catching his mother's interest. Like it or not, the cemetery offered Jared privacy he could get nowhere else.

Delivering the supplies Emilee requested for the Walters family had given him an excuse to end his visit with his mother's friends. He had taken the leather case filled with his mother's letters with him. Now seated next to the marble angel, he glanced at the open leather case at his side and let out a deep sigh. He was hardly in the mood to read words that would add another halo for each of those virtues to his father's head. *Blessed man. Saint. Patient. Loving. Kind . . .*

If only half the accolades were true, his father would be bent double from carrying the weight of half the halos ever earned by the saints in heaven. If he were still alive. But he was not alive. He was dead and buried, and Jared stared at the marble angel next to him as though he needed concrete proof. Or had he come here in a macabre attempt to force his father to witness the legacy of guilt and shame he had left to his son?

Again, the accolades rained through his mind, swelling a river of bitter memories till a flood of antithetical responses created a new litany: Liar. Cheat. Hypocrite . . . He pounded his fist on the ground to silence the rest.

Jared had never confronted his father while he was alive; instead, he had hardened his heart against his father and turned against him. Retreat, not confrontation, was a self-protective mechanism he had fine-tuned over the years into a strategy that had served him well in business and personal affairs when confronted with an implacable competitor: Retreat long enough to study your opposition, develop a plan, and then attack from the rear.

He had acquired a great deal of prime property in Europe and hired enough experts away from competitors to know the strategy had worked well for him in the past. He would use it again now as he confronted his past, if only to forge a decent future here.

The letter case lay open at his side, but he had yet to unseal any of the letters yellowed with age and carefully arranged in chronological order, and the excuses he had used not to read them before now seemed petty and selfish. In his youth, he had been consumed with the adventure of beginning a new and exciting life. Once established as a merchant, he had spent every waking hour obsessed with turning his initial investment into a fortune. Traveling throughout Europe, he had not spent time in any one place long enough to receive much by post.

Following instructions that he now regretting giving, his partner had held the letters from his mother in New York City and only forwarded them in bunches once or twice a year when he knew where Jared would be for several months. On his long voyage home, he had thought it pointless to read the letters and had spent his time planning on how best to care for his mother and put the past behind him.

He raked his fingers through his hair. He had been selfish. He had been a coward, and he was as ashamed of himself now as he always had been of his father. His father, however, had gone to his grave never admitting to what he had done. In an attempt to prove himself the better man now, Jared would read every one of his mother's letters, word for painful word, and in the process he might find answers to the many questions his return home had prompted.

His hands shook when he broke the seal on the first letter. He unfolded the brittle paper and knew instantly he would not go through the letters quickly if the first was any indication of the rest.

Ever frugal, his mother first had written horizontally before turning the paper ninety degrees and writing horizontally again, crisscrossing the original lines with more sprawled, evenly spaced words.

He clenched his jaw and narrowed his gaze. It would take reading several crossed letters before his vision would adjust so he could read at a normal pace. He glanced at the date, the only entry set apart from the others: November 16, 1820.

His mind traveled back in time. He had just settled in New York City after graduating from Yale. Memories of that time in his life were still laced with bitterness, and he decided if he focused on Emilee instead, he might make his task easier.

In 1820, she would have been . . . He paused, calculating back-ward in time. According to his mother, Emilee was now twenty-two. In 1820, she would have been eight years old. Was she even in Surrey then? He thought hard, but he could not remember either his mother or his father mentioning Ellen Clarke or her daughter during their visit the month before the letter; nevertheless, it was a good place to begin to learn more about her.

A stiff gust of wind rustled the paper in his hands, and he used both hands to hold it still. Reading as quickly and as carefully as he could, he scanned the first letter, found his vision acclimated to the difficult script by the third, and bolted alert while reading the sixth. He was halfway down the first page when he stopped, marked his place with his finger, and checked the date: August 23, 1823. His gaze returned to the script:

We have buried Widow Jameson next to her devoted hus-band, but can find no place for her ward and niece, Em-ilee. I continue to pray for the child, whose short life has been touched by more scandal and tragedy than a soul might endure and know that the Lord awaits her with open arms if she would but accept Him as her Saviour. May He also touch the hearts of our neighbors so one of them might do their Christian duty and bid for the in-nocent child's care and provide a loving home for her.

His heart began to pound. There was no further reference to Emilee, but he was encouraged enough to ignore his weary eyes and continue reading another letter. He laid the last letter face down on top of the others that were piled in the lid of the case. The next letter, dated several weeks later, rambled with reports of harsh weather and the storm that held his father snowbound at the Weston farm while on circuit. He turned the page to help stem another wave of bitter memories. He saw Emilee's name again, blinked his eyes to clear his vision, and reread the passage more slowly.

Your father's faithful heart and goodness is an abiding
blessing to my life. We have opened our home to Emilee.
Sweet, gentle child. She trembles when anyone else is
here. Such has been her sorry experience with those who
proudly wear the mantle of their Christian faith yet whis-
per cruel and malicious gossip. None dare hurt the child
now under your father's protection and guidance. . . .

He read through a detailed glorification of his father's character and skimmed through mention of the few church members who supported his parents' decision. He had almost
decided to skip the final paragraph when a familiar name
caught his eye. "Charles Traymore," he whispered. He started
to read out loud when the first few lines became harder to
decipher. " 'Gone . . . west just this past . . . night. My heart
grieves for his mother for I know the pain that distance between a mother and son can bring.' "

His heart heavy with guilt, he swallowed hard before continuing to read aloud, although the following lines were
clearer. " 'He is a young man driven by anger and pride.
Though many years have passed, he has taken the existence
of this child in our home as a personal affront to his children,
blessed as they are with legitimate birth. As though this child
should bear the sins of her mother! *I* am her mother now. . . .' "

His voice trailed off, and his mind quickly connected memories he had as a ten-year-old child, Mercy Traymore's barbed
introduction to the minister's wife, his conversation with Ezra
earlier that day, and the letters he had just read. Heart pounding, he folded the letter and his mind closed against the idea
that Emilee was born a bastard child.

"I thought that was you I spied! I was just going home and
took a shortcut through the cemetery."

Startled, he looked up. Emilee approached him and stopped
only a few feet away. His cheeks heated with the knowledge
he now had of her and the curiosity that made him want answers to questions he had yet to pose, even in his mind.

"Reading old letters?"

He nodded, barely able to breathe as a knot tightened in his chest. Images of her as a young girl, apparently the pariah of the community, flashed before his mind's eye. His respect and admiration for her grew with every beat of his heart. So did envy and the idea he yet one day might find a way to live with the burdens of the secret he had carried back home, just as she had obviously transformed her life from one of shame to respectability.

"If you'd rather be alone . . ."

"No," he croaked. "No. I wouldn't."

She looked at the letter in his hand and smiled as she moved under the shade of the tree and sat down. "Are those your mother's letters?"

He tightened his hold on the letter in his hands.

"Your mother kept all of your letters, but they were probably lost in the fire. She used to tell me some of what you had written. What country you were in or what new variety of rose you had discovered. I thought you led a very exciting life, but a lonely one."

"At times," he admitted, noting the way her voice softened as though she were reliving the lonely days of her early years.

Her brows lifted when she saw the letters in the leather case. The unbroken seals were like flares that illuminated his crime. He could not think of any explanation to offer, other than the truth. Oddly, he did not feel threatened. Only awkward. "I saved all her letters, but . . ."

"You never read them."

"No. I never did." A long silence.

"You don't know very much about me, do you?" she asked.

He shook his head, relieved she had not broached the subject of why he had not read the letters before and chose to do so now. He was ready to admit to curiosity. Nothing more.

"A bit unfair of me, isn't it?"

"Unfair?"

She smiled again. "I spent twelve years with your parents before my marriage. I know everything that's happened to your mother. I helped care for your father toward the end of his days. And . . . and I know you through your letters to your mother. You must feel a bit . . . left out?''

''You're very special to Mother,'' he offered, wondering if he had the right or the courage to pose any of the questions that swirled through his mind and trembled within his soul. He looked deep into her eyes, now a dark, shimmering shade of green that reminded him of blades of grass kissed by morning dew. Her gaze held him spellbound as he searched beyond physical attraction to the depths of her spirit for the source of her contentment.

''Last night you said you had questions,'' she suggested quietly.

He nodded. ''I've been gone a long time. I'm not sure I have the right—''

''There's nothing to hide that hasn't already been discussed at great length by most of the villagers.''

He thought her expression was calm, even serene, until he saw the anguish in her eyes.

''I suppose the most curious question you have is how a whore's bastard child came to be your parents' ward before growing up to become the minister's wife.''

SIX

The thudding of her heartbeat pounded out all other sounds around her, but Emilee held her gaze steady and her head high. Although he had not seemed to recall her mother when Mercy had introduced her to him as Ellen Clarke's daughter, Emilee knew this moment would come. Half a lifetime spent staring down her mother's sin, however, did not mean it was easy or pleasant, and admitting her past to Jared took more courage than she had thought it would.

Fortunately, her public confession and conversion had given her some experience in openly admitting her past. Judging by the incredulous look in Jared's eyes, either she had spoken too bluntly or he had mistaken her attempt to conceal their first encounter from her husband as a tendency to lie. She hoped the former was more likely. "I'm sorry. Perhaps I've spoken too frankly."

"You do tend to rush right into matters," he said, obviously shaken, but quick to regain his wit. He fumbled with the letter in his hand and placed it on top of the others. "I feel rather ashamed of myself, actually."

"Most people here in Surrey have put this all behind them. Except for the newcomers."

His smile was thin. "That includes me, I suppose." He ran his hand across his brow. "You said most people."

She nodded. Except for—"

"The Traymores."

"Mr. Traymore and George have become more tolerant, but Mercy . . . to be fair, it hasn't been easy for her. She's lost her firstborn son. Do you know about Charles?"

His gray eyes filled with uncertainty. "Ezra said Charles was living somewhere out west. One of my mother's letters mentioned him, but she wasn't very explicit about why he seemed to resent your presence here. Did your mother . . . ? Was he . . . ?''

"No. He wasn't my father," she offered, to correct a misassumption that obviously distressed him. "My mother had been betrothed to Charles Traymore." She lowered her gaze. Before her decision to be fully honest wavered into cowardice, she blurted out the rest of her tale. "On the day they were to have been married, she disappeared. Aunt Phoebe, my mother's sister, later told me my mother had been slipping out in the middle of the night to meet her beau. Aunt Phoebe assumed my mother had been meeting Charles, but . . . but the note my mother had left on her pillow said she had been seeing someone else. Someone who could give her a more exciting life.''

"She never identified this man?"

Emilee shook her head. "There had been several young men touring the area on their vacation from one of the universities back east. Perhaps one of them made promises. . . .''

"Did he keep those promises?"

"Hardly. After he abandoned her, she spent her days as a tavern maid and her nights tending to her illegitimate child.'' Her voice hardened. "My mother sinned against God. She shamed her family. She broke Charles's heart and stole his pride.''

She paused to take a deep breath before she looked at Jared again. "A sordid tale, but it's the truth. I've learned to accept it," she added, to ease the apparent embarrassment that flushed his cheeks.

His gaze softened, and now that she had told him the worst of it, her heartbeat slipped back into a normal cadence. "I probably never would have known any of this if she had lived. I don't really recall very much of her at all. I was only six when she died. All I can remember is being very frightened, taking a long ride on a stagecoach, and then Aunt Phoebe taking me to her home.'' She closed her eyes and tried to block out the memory of her aunt's taunts and ugly accusations. "She and Uncle Nathan never had children of their own. He was killed felling a tree shortly after I'd arrived. 'God's pun-

ishment,' she said, for taking in her sister's bastard child.''
Her eyes filled with tears, and she paused to blink them back.
Jared reached out and laid his hand on top of hers. ''If she
didn't want you, why did she take you in?''

His touch was as gentle and warm as his voice. ''Guilt,''
she whispered. ''Aunt Phoebe couldn't bear the guilt she carried for keeping my mother's trysts a secret. I was to be her
penance.''

''That's ridiculous. Penance?'' he scoffed. ''How could caring for a child be penance?''

She slipped her hand away and loosened the tie on her bonnet, hoping she might find it easier to breathe. ''No one in the
village would speak to her. She was shunned and isolated from
her friends. She never forgave herself. She never forgave my
mother . . . and she never forgave me, even on the day she died
two years after I had come to live with her.''

''That's when you came to live with my parents.'' He
pointed to the pile of opened letters. ''Mother wrote how very
much she wanted to have you with her.''

For the first time, she brightened and joy subsumed all the
sorrow their conversation had brought back to life. ''Your
mother and father loved me from the minute they took me into
their home. I . . . I really don't remember specific words they
might have said or things they might have done. I just remember feeling . . . feeling very loved and wanted for the first time
in my life.''

''And you were. I just read one of her letters in which she
wrote that she felt she was your mother.''

''She's the only one I've truly known. I love her as dearly
as I loved your father.'' She turned her head to study the
monument over his grave. ''I miss him very much.''

When Jared did not offer a response, she turned back to
face him. ''I know how difficult it must be for you.''

His pale eyes darkened into fathomless pools of anguish so
profound she felt her heart tremble, but she never had an opportunity to say more. Thunder rumbled in the distance, and
she looked up at the sky to see the storm that had been threat-

ening all day. Thick black clouds were moving in from the west, and the wind began to gust.

Jared scrambled to his feet and grabbed a letter caught by the wind, while she held the other letters in place. He packed the letters he had read back into the case and latched it closed. "We'd better leave the rest of my questions for another time," he suggested.

She had the distinct impression the approaching storm had less to do with his decision than the turmoil that appeared to trouble his spirit.

The first pellets of rain dropped fast and hard. "How proper do you suppose it would be to race home?" he shouted over the din of thunder and the crackle of lightning that lit the sky a few miles away.

She tightened the bow beneath her chin and bunched her billowing skirts with her hand. "You have unfair advantage!"

He grinned and grabbed her other hand. "We'll make a run for it together."

She held on tight as they ran across the grass to the roadway. The wind at her back propelled her faster than she had thought possible, but she still found it breathtaking to keep up with him. The pellets of rain eased into finer raindrops, and the storm quickened into a downpour as they sped over slippery cinders on the roadbed. She nearly lost her balance twice, but each time he tightened his grip and held her fast with his own strength.

Fully drenched, her gown clung to her skin, but her bonnet kept her hair dry and the brim protected her face, and she could at least see where she was going. Jared, however, wore no hat. The rain plastered his hair against his head and pelted his face. He had no hands free to protect his eyes, which he kept half-closed.

"This way," she yelled and tugged him to the left.

"I can hardly see," he hollered and turned to wipe his brow against his shoulder as they ran.

"At last I have an advantage!"

He laughed.

She laughed back.

And by the time they had run through countless puddles on the deserted roadway to reach the front porch of the parsonage, she had a stitch in her side and her stomach muscles were sore from laughing.

They practically leaped up onto the porch. Jared leaned against the wall of the house and pulled her alongside him. "I won!" he declared, taking deep gulps of dry air.

She tugged his hand to protest. "It was a tie!" she croaked. Her throat was raw from breathing too hard and too fast.

His laughter at her demand to share victory was as spontaneous as it was infectious, and she gave up trying to stop any thought of resisting. The heavy rain shifted into a light drizzle, but she was laughing too hard to pay much attention. She had forgotten how good it felt to laugh until she was limp with exhaustion or to turn a storm into fun, like children can do if given half a chance.

When the front door opened, she turned her head and froze in place. Chills tingled her spine. Her heart dropped and sank into the puddles of water in her slippers, and every bubble of laughter burst into dread. "Randall," she murmured.

Her husband walked out onto the porch and crossed his arms over his chest Mercy Traymore stepped out two rapid heartbeats later. Her mouth dropped open, and her eyes flew open wider than Emilee thought humanly possible.

Although she was aware of her bedraggled state, she was puzzled by the extent of their disapproval. She looked from her husband to Mercy and back again before she realized why both of them looked at her as if she had horns growing out of her head.

She was still holding Jared's hand.

She eased herself away from the house and stood up straight as she slipped her hand away from him.

Jared recovered quickly, and his exhilaration quickly evaporated into concern for Emilee. He tightened his grip on the handle of the leather case. He dared not risk a full glance at the woman by his side, but from the corner of his eye he could see her trembling.

The unspoken but very clear accusations that hung in the

air pricked his pride. He also knew Emilee was vulnerable to even the slightest innuendo of impropriety. He wiped away a stream of water that trickled down his forehead into his eyes, to clear his vision and give him time to organize his thoughts. "Reverend Greene. Mrs. Traymore. Rather nasty storm. Unfortunately, Mrs. Greene and I were caught too far from home to avoid a solid drenching. You were fortunate to be indoors."

His attempt to shift attention away from himself and Emilee did not ease the tension or gain a response from either of the two people staring at them.

The minister's expression grew more stern as he draped his waistcoat around her shoulders. "Emilee? What were you thinking, running through the streets . . . ?"

She moistened lips already wet from the rain. "I was thinking of getting home as quickly as possible," she said softly. "I was taking the shortcut through the cemetery when I met Jared. We were talking when the storm hit, and we ran for home as fast as we could."

Her short account was as direct as it was honest, precisely the opposite of how she had reacted when she and Jared had met for the second time and she hid their previous meeting from her husband. Randall seemed more concerned than angry, but Mercy's expression condemned both Emilee and Jared, and curled lips twitched as though she had gossip just waiting to be spread.

Until his mother stepped into the open doorway. She took one look at both Jared and Emilee and chuckled. "You look . . . just awful! Both of you," she admonished.

"Awful indeed," Mercy sputtered. "When I decided to bring our donation for the victims of the fire here personally, I had no idea—"

"The Traymores have been more than generous," Olivia interjected.

Jared was quite sure she had not seen him holding hands with Emilee, but apparently she was quick to detect a situation far more serious than it was awkward.

"Mercy was kind enough to bring me several yards of new cloth from the general store so I can fashion a few new dresses for myself instead of having to alter the donated ones.''

"How very kind.'' Jared gritted his teeth, finding it hard to associate kindness with that woman. ''I intended to tell you I put funds into your account at the general store today when I ordered supplies.''

Mercy's gaze narrowed and focused on Emilee, but she directed her words to Jared. "Obviously, you had other matters far more pressing.''

"As a matter of fact, I did,'' he responded and decided to make Mercy swallow some of her own words. "I met with Ezra for several hours. He's got several properties in mind for us, so I reserved a wagon at the livery for tomorrow. We'll make a day of it, Mother.''

"Not if you catch cold and wind up in bed,'' his mother scolded and quickly took charge. ''Inside with you, but use the back door. We can talk this through after you've gotten into a set of dry clothes.''

She nodded to the others. ''Randall, why don't you take Emilee straight up the front staircase? Mercy, I'm sorry you have to be on your way, but do take my gratitude back to your husband. You've both been very supportive and kind.''

Hard-pressed to find a way to prolong her visit, judging by the way her forehead creased into deep folds of flesh, Mercy seemed ready to forfeit another verbal assault.

Or so Jared thought.

"I'll be anxious to hear your sermon at meeting tomorrow, Reverend.'' She sniffed, tilted her chin up, and strode away.

While his mother ushered Randall and Emilee back inside, Jared made his way around to the back door. Emilee had not exaggerated the depth of Mercy's bitterness. No matter how he might argue or even accept full blame for putting Emilee into a compromising situation, Mercy would not let go of her suspicions easily. Would Randall take Emilee at her word that nothing outrageously improper had happened?

Jared paused before opening the kitchen door. He deserved blame. Not Emilee. He had grabbed her hand and tugged her home. He had still held her hand long after they had reached the porch. He had . . .

He shook his head to get rid of the excess water that was running down his neck to trickle down his back, but he was far less effective in his attempt to shake away the image of Emilee's body so clearly outlined by her drenched gown, or the sound of her laughter and her playful words.

He twisted the doorknob and found it sticky with . . . "Honey," he grumbled, remembering his time with Emilee that morning. He wiped his hand on his wet trousers as he walked into the kitchen and looked around. The teakettle and a pot of water had been set on the stove to heat. Towels had been stacked on a chair, and his mother sat at the head of the table.

Curiosity mixed with concern etched her face. She pointed to a chair that had already been pulled out, obviously for him. "I'd like an explanation."

He carried the leather case with him and did as he was told, feeling more like a twelve-year-old than a grown man of thirty-four. The concerns that churned in his own mind and body, however, were very adult. He knew he was to blame for what had happened. He accepted it and prayed he had not caused too great a rift between the minister and the woman who had opened her past to Jared and given him more of herself in the process than he had any right to expect. Or to claim.

Emilee was kind and giving, understanding and compassionate, as well as beautiful. In the future, he would have to be very, very careful lest he awaken the sleeping demons in his soul. In the space of thirty-six hours, his past had unraveled and smashed hard into his future—a future which could not and would not include a green-eyed angel.

Retreat, he mused, reverting to form. *Fast and hard.*

He would not retreat, however, from telling his mother the truth about this afternoon's events, including the debacle on the porch. He looked at his mother, took a deep breath, and told her exactly what had happened, sparing only his innermost thoughts about Emilee. When he had finished, she gazed at him with the affection he had missed seeing for so long.

"You never read any of my letters?" Her voice was soft

and full of sadness. "How deep runs the river of your hurt," she whispered. "I've prayed so long and so hard that you might have healed and forgiven whatever . . . whatever drove you to harden your heart against your father." She held up her hand when he tried to speak. "He never told me what happened. Nor did I ask. But I never guessed your pain was so intense you couldn't bear to read my letters."

Guilt and shame tore at his spirit. He reached over and squeezed her hands. "It was never you," he whispered. His throat tightened as her words strangled any hope he had been able to hide his animosity toward his father. "Never you."

Tears welled in her eyes. "Even at the end, when his suffering was so severe, he spoke of you. How he loved you and missed you and prayed for you—even as he drew his last breath."

Jared swallowed hard and held a firm grip on his mother's hands. His conscience slammed the secret he had held deep in his heart and soul against the barrier of his will, but he braced against the assault and refused to surrender. He loved his mother too much to add to her anguish, now or ever. "Will you forgive me?"

She smiled through her tears and pressed his hands against her aged cheek. "Forgive you? I love you, child. Even if you look like . . ." She looked at him and started to chuckle as her emotions swung full sway in the opposite direction. "I'm reminded of the day you and George played hooky from school to go fishing. Poor Mr. . . . Mr. . . ."

"Stillwill," he supplied, relieved the mood had lightened. "We thought we had heard someone coming and fell into the river when we were scrambling to hide. Too late, though. He had spied us from the bluff."

"He brought you straight home to your father, who was working on a sermon about the loaves and the fishes. Remember?"

The memory of a good solid whipping still smarted, and Jared squirmed in his seat. "I deserved my punishment," he admitted before he raised one brow. "The old coot got away with our stash of fish, though."

His mother dropped his hands and brought her own hands to her cheeks. "He never said a word about that!"

"And neither did I." He laughed again. "He knew as well as I did that Father would have sent those fish straight to a needy family. I guess he considered the catch as his reward."

"And we never suspected a thing. He was so righteous and strong in his faith. Not that he could surpass your father. A finer man never lived."

His body went cold and rigid. When he heard the sound of footsteps overhead, he glanced up at the ceiling. "Will Emilee be all right?"

"Randall is a good man. He trusts Emilee, and I trust you at your word. At best, you put her in a delicate situation, and I should hope you'd be more careful in the future."

He did not dare consider the worst, particularly when Mercy came to mind. His lips tightened into a frown. Determined to see his plans into action before he had the opportunity to place Emilee under any other shadow of suspicion, he made arrangements with his mother to leave for a tour of the properties right after meeting.

Emilee snuggled under the covers and tried to explain away the shudders in her body as a consequence of her run through the storm instead of fear for what Randall would have to say about her behavior today. He had taken her directly to her chamber with instructions she get out of her dripping clothes and rest awhile in bed. Damp tendrils of hair at the nape of her neck were the only evidence now of her misguided adventure, and she fiddled with them while she waited for him to join her.

When he opened the door and entered her chamber, he wore a wan smile. "Feeling better?"

"Much," she assured him. He took a seat next to her on the bed, and the mattress dipped beneath his weight. She scooted farther away from him to accommodate the slant that tilted her sideways. "Randall, I want to explain—"

"Let me speak first," he admonished and silenced her attempts to offer an explanation for her behavior. He captured her gaze and held it. "Do you trust me, Emilee?"

"Of . . . of course I do, but—"

"And I trust you in return. You were very foolish today, but I have no doubts about your behavior today as anything more."

She gulped back tears. "I'm so sorry. So truly sorry. I never meant to do anything that would cast a shadow on your name."

"We are husband and wife," he said softly. His voice grew firmer as he spoke. "Without trust, our marriage would not be strong and resilient, but you must never again give anyone cause to gossip. I have an important calling, and you are a minister's wife. Everything you do will be scrutinized and judged far more closely and more harshly than you might deserve."

His veiled reference to her past hurt less than his confidence in her as a faithful and dutiful wife. She had failed him, the man who had put her before all others and given her the privilege of helping him in his ministry. Sharp talons of regret and guilt pierced her heart, and she vowed never to hurt him again.

"Let us pray together," he suggested.

He folded his hands over hers in a familiar gesture that she welcomed. She bowed her head and closed her eyes.

"Merciful Father," he began, "we ask You for Your blessing and Your indulgence. May You keep us safe from the world's temptations and keep us close to You. Keep our bodies pure and our actions above reproach, and with the power of Your infinite grace, heal those who suffer. Still the urge to gossip so that all who might claim You as their God will be inclined to goodwill and understanding."

"Amen," she whispered. Certain that she had been blessed already with the gift of this man as her husband, she wished that she might channel her attraction to Jared to the man by her side.

She felt the mattress shift again when Randall left her to study the sermon she had helped him write several days ago. No one, of course, knew that she advised him on topics and helped him select Bible passages to anchor his message.

She could not bear to see his confidence undermined any more than it already was simply by virtue of his assuming responsibility for a church whose members had almost adored Reverend Burke. She did not blame them. The former minister had established this church and ministered here for nearly forty years. He never had to worry that the members might become disappointed with his services and vote to hire another minister they preferred over him, like Randall did. She had no doubt that once Randall had established himself firmly in the hearts of the membership, he would be able to relax and fully assume his duties without her help.

As she drifted off to sleep, she reviewed the sermon they had planned for meeting tomorrow. Given what had transpired today, she surmised that Mercy would be thoroughly convinced Reverend Greene had spent all night writing the sermon just for Emilee.

SEVEN

The prayers had been said, the hymns had been sung, and the offerings had been given. As Reverend Greene concluded his sermon, Jared's attention was split between the black-robed man in the pulpit and Emilee, who was sitting two seats away next to Jared's mother.

The transformation of this rather meek and unassuming man into a vibrant, powerful speaker had been as amazing as his sermon had been cleverly inspired, a welcome diversion from memories that hit fast and furious the moment Jared had entered the meetinghouse.

The wide-planked floor, paneled walls, and crude wooden benches facing the pulpit were exactly as he remembered. The windows at the rear of the building, however, had been covered with wood to protect them as workmen constructed the new church directly behind the old structure.

He sat in the first bench, reserved for the minister's family and now, it seemed, for the former minister's family as well. With his back to the rest of the assembly of maybe a hundred attendees, he could worship with his expression virtually unobserved, except by the minister—a fact he had learned very quickly and painfully as a child.

While he had been curious about his reactions to being inside the meetinghouse again, he was more than intrigued by what he had been observing between Emilee and her husband. Jared continued to steal well-timed glances at her. At first he thought it odd that she was praying silently during the sermon, but he was convinced now she had been mouthing the very words her husband was preaching. Had she helped him to practice his deliverance?

If so, Jared's esteem for the minister dropped another notch. Correctly anticipating the minister's next pause, he quickly turned his full attention to Emilee. Her lips moved ever so subtly, and seconds later, her husband resumed his sermon. She was prompting him!

Jared was too disgusted to care what the minister said next, and whether Jared liked it or not, he had to admit that his father could deliver a sermon on a moment's notice and still preach as powerfully as he would have if he had spent days preparing.

His regard for the Reverend Mr. Greene dropped again.

At this rate, it would land at the gates of hell before another week had passed. He was even soured enough to entertain the idea that Emilee might have written the entire sermon, a thought he dismissed as ludicrous and beneath even his own concept of fairness as the minister reached the end of his message.

"And so I say to each and every one of you, amen. Amen, brothers and sisters! Go forth. Carry God's message in your hearts and put His words into deeds. Until we meet again."

The applause from the worshipers startled Jared, who found this experience at meeting very odd. Had his father or the man who had taken his place instituted this practice? Jared clapped his hands together once or twice to avoid drawing attention to himself, and he had to suppress a grin thinking Mercy might be doing the same thing.

By the time he filed with his mother and Emilee to the front door, Reverend Greene had greeted the rest of the congregation. A few gathered in small groups in front of the meetinghouse to chat while most had quickly dispersed back to their homes.

"Would you like to take a peek at the new church?"

His mother's question caught him off guard. He was anxious to start on their way to view the prospective properties, but he was not going to add more disappointments to the long list he had already caused her. He quickly agreed to a short tour, which Randall obligingly consented to conduct. Avoiding more than a cursory glimpse of Emilee to assure himself she and her husband had resolved yesterday's difficulties, Jared escorted his mother around the side of the meetinghouse behind the minister and his wife.

Straight ahead and fully framed and painted, the white clapboard church was impressive in size. Two stories high, it dwarfed the tiny log meetinghouse. Four tall columns rose from ground level to the roof and drew attention to a bell tower still devoid of its bell. The boarded windows had yet to be filled with glass.

Randall produced a set of keys and unlocked a pair of wide doors opening into a vestibule that led to a sanctuary twice the size of the meetinghouse. Once they had all stepped inside, Randall took charge. "There will be pews and benches," he began as he waved his arms to indicate where they would be placed. "The pulpit, of course, will be on the left, separated from the pews by a low railing." His face glowed with pride, but his gestures and his tone of voice were far more reserved than only minutes ago when he had been preaching.

With Emilee by his side, Randall droned on about the bell that would be installed as soon as it arrived. Jared's mother leaned close. "The pulpit will be real marble," she whispered. "Your father worked hard, even when he was too ill to preach anymore, to raise the contributions that made this church possible. It was his dream . . . and now . . ." She shook her head slowly from side to side. "Life must go on," she said sadly.

"Indeed," he responded, torn by how difficult it was to watch and listen to his mother grieve and at the same time keep a lid on his own emotions, at least where his father was concerned.

". . . and I'm certain the church elders would be very pleased to have you attend."

Jared looked up and realized Randall obviously had extended an invitation of some kind, but Jared had been preoccupied with his mother and his own thoughts, and he did not know just exactly what Randall had in mind. "I beg your pardon?"

"This coming Wednesday at eight o'clock," he repeated.

Emilee apparently noticed the quizzical expression on Jared's face. "The church elders are meeting to discuss final plans for the opening of the church."

"I think you should go," his mother urged.

Attending a meeting with church elders appealed to him as much as watching mud dry into dirt. He smiled his acceptance anyway, already resenting every minute he would waste at the meeting and wondering if it was too great a sin to pray Randall might develop a headache late Wednesday afternoon so the meeting might have to be canceled.

"Perhaps we should be on our way," he suggested before Randall could extend another invitation, in which case Jared would definitely say that prayer, sin or no sin.

"Would you mind terribly if Randall and Emilee joined us?"

He snapped his head to the side and stared at his mother. She managed to look remarkably innocent despite the twinkle in her eye which spelled trouble if he denied her request. He looked at Emilee and Randall, who seemed genuinely embarrassed that Olivia had asked for them to go along without speaking to Jared privately first.

"Maybe we should stay home. Randall has had a busy week," Emilee suggested, giving Jared an easy way to decline his mother's request.

"Nonsense," his mother countered. "A ride in the countryside would do you both a world of good. Don't forget what Dr. Pounds ordered for Randall's headaches: plenty of fresh air and rest. It's the best relief for stress and might just help. Nothing else seems to."

Now thoroughly mired in his mother's subtle form of treachery, Jared acquiesced. "I'll see if the livery can give us a wagon with a double seat."

"We'll have a wonderful time together," she crooned, as though savoring an important victory. "We'll go back to the parsonage and pack a picnic while you fetch the wagon home." Arm in arm, she ushered Emilee and Randall back outside, and Jared followed them. Instead of waiting while the minister relocked the doors, he headed directly to the livery. With every step he took, he promised himself he would have a very long talk with his mother—if he ever had the chance to speak with her alone.

By the time he returned to the parsonage with a double-seated wagon, Jared had decided that having the added company today was not all bad. Granted, he would not be able to talk as frankly with his mother as he might have had they been alone; on the other hand, it could not hurt matters to let Randall see for himself that Jared intended to distance himself from the village—and the minister's wife.

He parked the wagon by the kitchen door. The two women immediately carried out two baskets of food for the picnic, and he helped to store them securely under the second seat while Randall watched the preparations. Jared left them momentarily to get rid of his formal dress and change into a comfortable pair of trousers, a flannel shirt, and a vest, where he had stored the map Ezra had given him, a pencil, and a small notebook. He grabbed a pair of gloves and headed back to the wagon.

He had taken less than half a dozen steps outside the kitchen before he braced to a halt. He stared at the wagon and shook his head. His mother and Emilee were seated together, directly behind Randall, which precluded any opportunity Jared might have had to speak to his mother easily while they rode. He really would have to have a nice long chat with that mother of his!

"Is something wrong, dear?"

"Nothing to worry about, Mother," he muttered as he walked to the driver's seat and climbed aboard. He clicked the reins and drove the wagon past the barn and back to the roadway.

The first property lay north of the village near the border of the town line. The most direct route was down Main Street and past the charred remains of his mother's cottage, but he had no other choice if he intended to inspect each of the four properties today. He hoped she would not find the route too painful, which was only one of the reasons he had wanted her to sit up front with him. He knew Emilee well enough, however, to know that she would be quick to comfort his mother if she became upset.

He proceeded down Main Street past the general store, which was closed for the Sabbath, and the town square, where a fair number of people had gathered to enjoy the warm weather before winter's bite kept them all indoors. Not surprisingly, the Traymores were nowhere to be seen. While the women chatted behind him, Randall identified many of the people who were milling about the village center whom Jared did not know.

They had only reached the center of the village when Jared realized they had attracted a fair amount of attention. Glances turned into long looks before people smiled and waved, and it suddenly occurred to him that his mother was far more astute than she was overly social.

By the time the dust from the wagon wheels settled back into the roadway, there would be few who had not seen or heard about Randall and Jared riding out of town side by side, obviously engaged in friendly conversation, and any gossip that Mercy had spread would be thoroughly undermined. After the sermon Randall had preached today, no one would take him for a fool. And only a fool would ride down Main Street sitting next to the man reported to be uncommonly interested in the minister's wife.

Jared had no doubt Randall's presence on the front seat next to him instead of the back seat next to Emilee had been rather deliberately and cleverly orchestrated by his mother.

Retreat, study your opposition, and attack from behind.

A brilliant strategy, and one perhaps he had learned without realizing it from his mother. With that humbling thought, he leaned back in his seat and decided he'd best be prepared . . . just in case she had other surprises in store for him today.

Much to his mother's dismay, Jared found the first property totally unsuitable. The second, even farther north, had possibilities, and he had taken copious notes before leaving. After a brief stop to rest the horses and have a picnic, he had headed southwest in a wide arc that curved back eventually to Surrey.

After crossing a small creek marked as Martin's Creek on the map, he turned down a narrow dirt roadway that wound through dense trees, up and over small hills. He slowed the wagon at a break in the treeline on the crest of a hill and saw the property below and to his right. His heart began to race, but he said nothing until he had reached the property itself. He parked the wagon and they all disembarked to have a closer look.

Nestled below the leeward side of a low mountain, nearly twenty acres of cleared but overgrown land stretched before him. From the map he carried, he knew Beaver Pond lay at the northern end of the property and the forest that framed the fields held another forty acres.

He knew then he did not have to bother looking any further and quickly dismissed traveling on to the last property; besides, the sun hung low enough in the sky that there was little chance they could proceed to the last property and still get home by nightfall.

"Quite impressive," Randall commented, clearly more interested in this property than any of the others located closer to the village.

Emilee nodded, but she kept her thoughts to herself. His mother fidgeted with the lacing on her shawl. "It's terribly far from the village," she ventured.

"Not so," Jared countered as he walked toward several long-abandoned outbuildings. "The village is about an hour away. Maybe more in bad weather." He continued walking toward the site where a cabin had once stood. All that remained was a crumbling pile of blackened rocks that had once been part of the chimney or hearth. He picked up one of the smaller rocks and held it in his hand as he inspected the site, while the others held back and remained close to the wagon.

"Looks like they just rolled up the cabin and moved it," he noted calmly, although he was not at all pleased to think he would have to extend his stay at the parsonage until he could have some sort of dwelling erected.

He rejoined the others. "Did you know the Petersons?"

Randall shook his head. "I can't say I recall the name. They

weren't members of the church, unless that was before I came
here.''

"No, I don't think I knew them." His mother furrowed her
brow, deep in thought, and eventually shook her head. "No.
I'm sure we didn't know them at all. I didn't usually come
out this far from the village on home visits, and I'm quite sure
your father never mentioned them, either. Do you remember
anything about them, Emilee?"

"No."

She offered nothing more—not surprising, since she had
been very polite but withdrawn most of the day. Except when
she was with his mother in the wagon. She had not seemed at
a loss for words then, although the noise from the wagon prevented Jared from catching most of their conversation.

Randall pointed to the overgrown fields that stretched before
them. "Looks like good land. Do you intend to farm?"

"Yes, in a manner of speaking. I do," Jared responded,
already laying out the land as he had envisioned in his mind.

"A man could homestead here and raise everything he
would need for himself and his family. Grain is always a good
crop. Dairying might offer even more potential. There's good
grazing available on the land as it is. If you have a mind to
profit, that is," Randall suggested.

Jared smiled. "Roses."

Three surprised faces stared back at him as if he had told
them he was going to grow rocks.

"Roses," he repeated. "I'm going to establish a nursery
here and grow roses." He paused to enjoy the rush of excitement that was building so fast his heart began to race. Only
now, when he had actually seen the property, did he admit to
himself that he was ready for this change in his life and the
challenge it represented.

"I discussed the details with my partner in New York City
before I continued to Surrey. With the Chenango Canal already under construction, it's only a matter of time before this
area is connected to the Erie Canal and the markets back east.
I'll use those years to plant stock and experiment with hybrids.

"Businesswise, it makes sense," he argued when he saw

the skeptical look on his mother's face, but noted how Randall seemed to stiffen at the mention of the canal. "We can reduce costs by consolidating some of our European nurseries and eliminating the rest. I'll need to go to Europe occasionally, but most of the time I'll be here. With you," he added as he walked over to his mother. "What do you think of my plans?"

She hesitated briefly and moistened her lips. "It would be wonderful to have you nearby."

He was speechless. It had never occurred to him that his mother might have thought he was only home for an extended visit, but since they had had little if any time alone, he should not have been surprised. In the past, he had not given her any hope he might return for a visit, let alone settle down permanently.

Before he could try to explain himself, she laid her hand on his arm. "I don't want you to feel pressured . . . or obligated . . ."

He cocked his head and scratched his chin with his finger. "Obligated. Hmmm . . . yes, I suppose I am. I wonder if I can demand some kind of compensation."

He caught Randall's shocked look out of the corner of his eye, but he could not see Emilee's reaction. He was most interested, however, in his mother, and he gazed down at her. "Let's see," he began. "It would seem to me we could draw up an agreement. Twice a week, you'll be obligated to bake half a dozen soft pretzels, with honey and cinnamon, of course. Once a month, a tin of the crunchy variety."

His mother finally began to smile, and he knew he had been right to use his favorite childhood treats as part of his agreement—treats that would evoke happier times they had shared together. "As for me," he whispered, "I shall be obligated to protect you, provide for your welfare, and continue to love you. Now then, have we an agreement, or do you want to amend the contract?"

Gently weeping, she stepped into his waiting arms and hugged him. He held her close, knowing that whatever his demons, he would fight them with every bit of courage he possessed to keep her happy.

She sniffled and looked up at him. "How will you do all this work alone?"

He squeezed her playfully. "I won't be alone. You'll be here with me after I've had a home built for us. That's part of the deal."

She stiffened immediately and took a step back from him. She squared her small shoulders and tightened her shawl. "I'm afraid I've . . . I've made other arrangements."

Stunned, he glanced over to Randall and Emilee, but they looked just as bewildered as he. "Arrangements?" he croaked.

She nodded. "Arrangements. We're only an hour from home, and I'll tell you all about them after we're there and my teeth settle back into place after rattling around for the better part of the day."

He could not argue and insist she explain herself without being totally insensitive, and he might even be able to figure out what she had in mind during the hour's ride back to the village, especially if he drove more slowly to assure her comfort.

EIGHT

If only Olivia had not fallen asleep halfway home!

The older woman's head rested against Emilee's shoulder, and she slipped her arm around Olivia's shoulders to keep her from falling off the narrow seat. Without companionship or conversation, Emilee had tried to pass the time surveying the countryside shimmering with the first colors of autumn and contemplating what arrangements Olivia had made for her future, obviously without consulting either Jared or Emilee.

Gaining nothing more than a kink in her neck, she had little choice now but to look straight ahead at the backs of the two men in the front seat—her husband and her temptation.

With an inward groan, Emilee wished she could sprout wings and fly the rest of the way to the parsonage—or far beyond to a world free from struggle. Not that she had any angelic pretensions or visions of being welcomed at the gates of eternity if she found her way there. The thoughts and feelings about Jared that coursed through her mind and body were more than wicked. They were sinful, and if she was any kind of angel at all, she was a fallen angel. Like her mother.

Had she come this far in her faith only to discover that faith alone could not change the legacy of her birth?

Comparing the two men was virtually impossible to avoid, since they sat mere inches in front of her. The physical difference between the two men was obvious. Even seated, Jared was a full head taller than Randall, whose loose, dark-colored waistcoat concealed a body softened by the nature of his life's work. As Jared handled the reins and flexed his arms and shoulders, his flannel shirt grew taut against tight muscles and broad shoulders.

She was almost tempted to reach out and feel the hard flesh beneath the soft fabric. The thought of what it would be like to be held in his arms and to feel his strength was like a rock of wantonness tossed into the calm, smooth waters of her good life. Tingles, delicious and warm, rippled across her skin. Her heart began to race, and a rock of wickedness sank to the depths of her soul and shook the foundation of her existence.

When the wagon rounded a curve, she had to brace her feet against the floorboards and hold tight to her companion, praying at the same time she might be able to rein in her physical weakness for this man as well. Even if she did, she would still face the challenge of comparing the character and nature of the two men.

Jared was outgoing, even playful at times, yet he could be sensitive and kind. He had a vibrant force around him, one that suggested he lived life fully, on his own terms, and on his own merits. Randall was restrained in both manners and speech. His confidence in his abilities as a minister had not grown after replacing Reverend Burke; instead, he had leaned on Emilee even more. Had she encouraged his dependence on her? Had she viewed his dependence as strength instead of weakness because she had allowed the sin of pride to stain her soul?

She did not have the answers to her questions, but it was clear to her that she was weak—in faith as well as spirit. It was her weakness alone that allowed Jared to slip past all her defenses and give her a glimpse of a relationship between a man and a woman based on physical attraction as well as mutual strengths and dependence. Trembles replaced the ripples of delight and turned into deep shudders that shook her spine.

Body, mind, and soul. Jared threatened each and every particle of her being.

She stiffened her spine until her muscles were taut, and strengthened her resolve to resist him. Distance would help, and she prayed he would be able to purchase the property and settle there soon. It would take at least a few weeks to raise even a simple cabin. Would she be able to find a way to suggest a tent like some of the laborers working on the canal used for temporary shelter? If so, Jared could be out of the parsonage in less than a week.

With the wagon traveling more slowly than earlier in the day, she could easily eavesdrop on Jared's and Randall's occasional bursts of conversation and perhaps include herself, if only to get an opportunity to offer her suggestion.

"Is Mother still asleep?"

His question startled her, and she instinctively tightened her hold. "Quite. I should think she'll rest most of the way home. She's accustomed to an afternoon nap," she offered, to dispel any worries he might have that he had overtaxed his mother.

His shoulders tensed, but he kept his gaze on the roadway ahead. "Between my homecoming, the fire, and Sunday meeting, she hasn't had much chance to rest in the afternoons. I should have postponed our outing until later in the week."

The regret in his words was as deep as his voice, but she did not want him to delay his preparations to leave. "I'll see that she rests."

Randall half-turned in his seat to look at her. "You should rest, too. You're looking a bit strained by the outing as well."

Or by a man as tempting as Jared?

If her cheeks flamed as red as they felt hot, she was sure Randall would think her fevered. She lowered her head to tilt the bonnet and shadow more of her face. "I'm fine. Just a bit lonely without someone to talk to now."

Jared's chuckles flexed the muscles in his back, and he tossed her a quick, playful glance. "We could always talk about the sermon today."

Dread pooled in the pit of her stomach and slowly drained to her toes. He knew! She saw it disguised in his playful words and the twinkle in his eye. Left speechless, she sighed with relief when Randall intervened.

"It's one of my favorites," he drawled as he turned back around to sit fully facing the front. He straightened his shoulders and sat more erect in his seat. "I've polished it through the years, but the parable itself is ageless and usually needed as an important lesson from time to time," he explained and continued to review the sermon in detail.

She shrank in her seat and thought again about needing a pair of wings to escape. Randall had no clue Jared had already figured out that she, not her husband, had written the sermon. She had no idea how Jared had done it, but he had. She closed her eyes briefly and wondered if the parable she had chosen for Randall's sermon today had been divinely inspired, not for Mercy, but for herself.

"... and the Miracle at Cana was so much more than a literal account of water being turned into wine," Randall explained. "Our Savior meant to show us His power to defeat the Prince of Darkness and his most able allies and transform them into virtues. Greed becomes generosity, lies turn into truths, and malicious gossip is transformed into words of love and praise."

And lust becomes true, selfless love?

She bit her lower lip as she shoved that disgraceful, thoroughly wanton, outrageous, and irrational thought out of her mind. Instead, she tried to think of a way to salvage Randall's image as well as her own. Her derelict guardian angel, roused back to attention, must have inspired the idea that popped into her head. "Randall studied at Yale," she offered, hoping to impress Jared by mentioning a college famous as a theological training ground for future ministers and persuade him Randall was capable of writing the sermon himself.

Jared turned his head toward Randall. "Class of 1820. You were a few years behind me, I gather. Was it '24 or '25?"

"I graduated in '28." Randall responded so abruptly she thought he might be trying to stonewall any further discussion. She cringed. How had she forgotten Jared had also attended Yale? Was mere mention of the school enough to trigger memories Randall still tried to forget? Or was the fire that consumed Olivia's cottage still too recent a reminder of the day he had almost lost his life? She felt guilty for dredging up this part of his life, yet she could not go back and choose another way to divert the conversation away from the sermon itself.

Seemingly unaware of the tension that held Randall rigid in his seat, Jared regaled them with a few college tales of his own, chuckling from time to time, and she found herself wishing Randall had had experiences at school that made him as happy, upon reflection, as Jared apparently had been.

Randall seemed to slump lower and lower in his seat as Jared tried, unsuccessfully, to compare names of instructors or his partner's younger brother, who would have been at Yale at the same time as Randall. It was obvious that Jared had made a good many friends at school. He also had had the benefit of his grandfather's name and wealth, according to what Olivia had told Emilee about Jared while she was growing up.

Randall would not be happy with her for defending him or for speaking up about his past, but she did not want Jared to linger on this sensitive topic any longer. Thoroughly disgusted with herself for bringing up the subject in the first place, she intended to bring it to an end.

She cleared her throat and took a deep breath. "Randall worked through school. As most of the church members know, he was an orphan. The Eastern Bible Society sponsored him and paid his tuition, but he still had to work to secure lodging and even food. We're all very proud of his sacrifices and his calling to help others."

Randall stiffened in his seat. "I'm sure Jared doesn't need to hear about that."

"On the contrary," Jared argued, but paused long enough to guide the wagon around a fallen limb in the roadway. "I was duly intrigued this morning at meeting. From what Emilee tells me now, I should be doubly so. It's a rare man who can remake his life so completely."

"Only the Heavenly Father can so inspire a man," her husband whispered, so softly she could barely hear him. "He holds us all in the palm of His hand. He loves us and teaches us, if only we would all be willing to accept His love and follow His word."

Randall turned partway in his seat to face Jared. "I'm surprised you didn't follow your father and take up a ministry. He was the most powerful preacher I've ever been privileged to hear. It must have been a rather unique experience to have him as your minister as well as your father."

No quick wit. No chuckles. Only long silence, and a tensing of Jared's body before he responded. "It was . . . unique," he murmured before clicking the reins and urging the horses into a trot.

Any further attempts at conversation were now impossible. Disappointed she had been unable to introduce a conversation about Jared's property and how soon he might be leaving the parsonage, Emilee forced herself to be content for the time being.

After they arrived home Olivia had promised to talk to them about her future living arrangements, a topic that would almost certainly include a discussion about Jared's plans. Once Emilee knew when he was leaving for good, she could rest more easily. A few extra prayers would not hurt her cause, since she no doubt would need heavenly help to turn her growing attraction to Jared into nothing more than friendship—a much more powerful miracle to expect than turning water into wine.

She welcomed the sight of the Ives farm that bordered the rear of the parsonage with a sigh of relief.

Olivia stirred and sat up while blinking herself awake. "Oh, dear, I must have nodded off for a few minutes," she murmured.

Giggling, Emilee patted Olivia's hand. "More than a few. We're almost home."

"And none too soon," Olivia grumbled loudly as she jostled in her seat, clearly disappointed that the wagon traveled too quickly and too noisily for a decent conversation to exist or for comfort to be considered.

By the time Jared had driven the wagon into the rear yard, even Emilee was forced to admit to a sore bottom. Randall disembarked a bit slowly, but helped both women to reach solid ground. With a curt nod, Jared left to return the wagon to the livery, and Randall and the two women approached the parsonage.

As soon as Randall opened the kitchen door, Emilee saw a note that had been slipped beneath the door during their absence. She scooped it up and handed it to her husband once they were all inside the kitchen.

Already looking peaked, Randall whitened to the color of sun-bleached muslin.

Concerned, Emilee touched his arm. "What's wrong?"

"Anna Leary. She's taken a turn for the worse. Dr. Pounds thinks it wise for me to see her as soon as possible."

Urgency and sadness replaced the inner turmoil inspired by the day's outing. "You don't look well," she noted with increasing worry.

He held his hand to his brow and closed his eyes for only a moment. "Another headache."

"Do you think you can go without resting first?"

"I don't have a choice," he responded wearily. "She may not last the night. Dr. Pounds has arranged for Maryam Shale to watch during the day. Will you be able to be watcher at night like you usually do?"

Olivia removed her bonnet and shawl. "You'll be too exhausted after today, Emilee. Why don't you see if her sister can go in your place? Rozilla wouldn't mind. I'm sure she wouldn't."

Emilee shook her head. "I promised Anna that when this happened, I'd be there for her. I'll just need to change and gather a few things. I won't be long. Will you wait for me, Randall?"

He sighed. "Of course, but hurry. Dr. Pounds left the note hours ago."

Without another word, Emilee slipped up the back staircase to her chamber, changed into an old, comfortable gown, and put her Bible into the small carrying case she kept beneath her bed, ready for the always unexpected news that one of the villagers was taking the last few steps Home.

Unlike most of the old women for whom Emilee had kept watch, Anna Leary was a young woman with a devoted husband and three small children. Consumption, however, spared neither young nor old, and Emilee fought the tears that welled in her eyes as she made her way back down the staircase.

The Leary farm was less than a mile's walk, but in the time it would take to get there, Emilee would have to find the right words to help Anna say her final good-bye to her husband and her babies.

With more than a little worry for her husband, Emilee was grateful he would be able to keep his deathbed visit short. After a promise from Olivia that she would see to Randall's comfort when he returned home, Emilee left with him on one of her most difficult tasks as the minister's wife: to help a woman die at peace.

Feeling very selfish for wishing for her own miracles today, she prayed for only one miracle tonight—one that might transform a family's grief and confusion into acceptance.

She would worry about her own troubles tomorrow.

NINE

After returning the rented wagon to the livery, Jared headed toward home. Main Street was deserted—not surprising, since it was growing dusk. His stomach growled. Supper hour. Even more reason why he found himself walking home alone with puzzling questions that needed answers, most of which he was sure he would not like.

Reluctant to go back to the parsonage before he could sort through the confusions of the day, he stopped at the town square and cut across the grass to take a seat on one of the benches that flanked a bronze statue of George Washington.

Remnants of the annual village celebration of Independence Day, tattered red, white, and blue ribbons on a wreath of dried, withered flowers, decayed at the base of the statue. He closed his eyes for a moment, and childhood memories flooded his mind with parades of war veterans, long-winded speeches, music, and fireworks. All centered here with the Father of the Nation overseeing the gay festivities.

He studied the statue that towered over him. "How many secrets did you take to your grave?" he murmured. He shook his head. First the marble angel. Now a bronze statue. He must be addled to be having conversations with monuments, and even more addled if he expected any answers. Not that he had indulged to any degree in fermented cider today, or any other form of alcohol.

Only Emilee—an intoxicant far more tempting and dangerous.

He leaned back against the bench rest, let out a deep sigh, and tried to figure out precisely why he found her so irresistibly appealing. She was uncommonly lovely, with her mahogany hair and lush green eyes, but he had known a fair number of beautiful women, even bedded them from time to time. She was bright and quick, which set her apart from most of the women he had encountered. She was kind and understanding, but he would expect a minister's wife to be a godly woman.

He managed a smile as he recalled several of his conquests. Fortunately, *godly* did not fit those women, or they would never have invited him to their beds knowing full well their time with him would be short-lived. No promises. Nothing permanent. He would not make promises he could not, in all good conscience, expect to keep. Truth be told, he had yet to find a woman who captured and held his interest long enough to want to try.

He sat up straighter. Maybe he had found the key to discovering Emilee's lure for him. A unique combination of virtue, sensuality, and intelligence, she was the first woman he had ever met whom he would consider worth the risk of a permanent union, and precisely the kind of woman he had avoided successfully—until now.

He reached down to the ground, grabbed a few blades of grass, and chewed thoughtfully. The woman was definitely off-limits. She was *married*! That alone would be incentive enough to back away, yet he knew he would not pursue his interest in her for a much more compelling reason, even if that cast him as a thorough cad.

He could not risk finding out, beyond any doubt at all, that he was truly his father's son.

The very real possibility soured the taste in his mouth, and he tossed the blades of grass away. He had to get away from her. Now. Before he let his attraction for her deepen and grow strong enough to strangle his better judgment, destroy his own moral sensibilities, and prove his blood had been tainted at birth by the sins of his father.

He glanced up Main Street and stared at the green-shuttered parsonage where his mother waited for him. He could not simply leave Surrey like he had left other towns and villages when he found himself growing interested in a woman. He had responsibility now for his mother, and he had hoped to make a home for both of them on the land he had inspected today. The property was close enough for his mother to return to the village occasionally to visit her friends, yet far enough to keep him limited to nothing more than a chance meeting with Emilee.

It was not a perfect solution to stifle his interest in Emilee, but it was one he could tolerate for his mother's sake. At least that had been his intention until his mother unexpectedly knocked a hole in his plans big enough to sink a schooner.

"Arrangements," he muttered as he got to his feet and headed directly for the parsonage. He was more than mildly curious about her plans now that he had sorted through the reasons for his attraction to Emilee. The more he considered what his mother might have in mind, the faster he walked. And the quicker he covered the distance home, the more determined he became that there was only one "arrangement" he would persuade his mother to make. She would have to live with him in the home he intended to erect on his property, where he could see that all her needs were met and avoid Emilee completely.

He stepped up to the porch and opened the front door. Following the tempting aromas coming from the rear of the house, he bypassed the staircase and walked down the hall to the kitchen. If he had any kind of luck, he would find his mother alone, but there was as much chance of that happening as creating a rose that bloomed all winter, a fancy that had long captured his imagination.

The minute he spied the two places set at the table and saw his mother at the cookstove, his heart began to race. He visualized the biggest rose blooming on a trellis covered with snow he could imagine and began to chuckle with his own foolishness.

His mother turned around abruptly. "Jared! I didn't hear you come in."

He snatched a pickle off a plate on the table and glanced around. "We're alone for supper?" When she nodded, he detected a sadness in her eyes that had consumed her tiredness. "Is everything all right? Has Randall gotten another headache?"

"No, I wish that was all it was. It's Anna Leary. She's taken a turn for the worse, and Dr. Pounds left a note for Randall and Emilee. She'll be watching with Anna."

He furrowed his brow and tried to place the name. "Leary. Is she William Leary's wife?"

His mother carried a bowl of soup to the table for each of them. "William moved back to Connecticut. Anna is married to his younger brother, Paul. He bought the old homestead from William. Now . . . he's got three young children he'll have to raise on his own. Sad. So very sad."

He held out his mother's chair and waited for her to take her seat before he joined her at the table. "You said Emilee was staying at the Learys'. What about Randall?" he asked, wondering why his mother had not set three places.

"He's upstairs in his chamber. Poor Dr. Pounds has just about given up any hope of curing Randall's headaches. They seem to be more frequent and more intense than they used to be. He's even written to a specialist back east for advice. I hope it will come soon."

"Indeed," Jared agreed. He was too preoccupied with his mother and even Emilee at the moment to give the minister much thought for now. Jared had a nagging dislike for the man, and after the way he had fidgeted through their conversation and gotten caught in a number of outright lies, not the least of which involved today's sermon, Jared did not trust him, either.

He set a steaming bowl of soup aside till it cooled. His feelings toward Randall were complicated and snarled in Jared's attraction for Emilee. He could not afford to waste any time trying to unravel his thoughts when he had yet to get an explanation for his mother's surprise announcement earlier today. He buttered a thick slice of wheat bread and rested his forearms on the table. "I'd like to hear more about these arrangements you've made," he said quietly.

His mother finished sipping a spoonful of soup before she answered. "When Maryam and Roz visited yesterday, they invited me to come live with them. We talked about it at great length before I accepted. I won't settle in, of course, until

you're able to move. It wouldn't be proper for you to stay at
the parsonage without me here, too. So . . . there you have it!"
she said, glancing at him as though she had just made a formal
announcement at the governor's mansion.

He cocked his head. "That's it? I don't have any say in the
matter? Don't you care what I think?"

"Seems to me I could ask the same questions of you," she
countered. "Especially since you proceeded without saying
one word to me about your plans." Her gaze softened, and
she put down her spoon and rested her hands on her lap. She
furrowed brows sprinkled with silver, and the wrinkles in her
cheeks deepened. "Of course I care," she added in a softer
voice. Her eyes glistened. "I love you. Having you come
home is an answer to my prayers, but you have your own life
to live. I know that."

"My life," he argued, "is with you now."

She shook her head. "You're accustomed to living on your
own. You've traveled and seen much of the world—"

"And now I've come home. I want to be here with you."

"And I want you here. But you need to understand something, too. My life did not stand still while you were gone. I
raised Emilee. I helped your father, and I took care of him
just like other members of the church. It sounds selfish even
to my own ears, but . . . but I'd like to spend the few years I
have left however I choose."

Heavy with hurt and guilt, Jared's heart lurched in his chest.
"I didn't mean I expected you to be my housekeeper or my
caretaker," he whispered. "I have funds to hire help—"

"I know what you meant, and I love you all the more for
what you were trying to do for me. I suppose I'm not making
myself very clear."

He sighed and ran his hand across his brow. "I don't suppose I am, either."

Smiling, she reached across the table to hold his hand.
"Let's agree we each have our own lives to live. You'll have
your nursery to keep you occupied. I'll have my friends here
in the village. But most of all, we have one another close by.

For visits," she emphasized as her eyes began to twinkle before she went back to eating her soup.

"Visits," he repeated, and in his mind's eye he saw a winter rose wilted in the snow. "No winter rose, either," he whispered, knowing a winter rose always would be a figment of his imagination, just like his plans to care for his mother on the property he had shown her today.

"Winter roses?" she asked as she moved his bowl of soup closer to him.

Caught in his own foolishness, he coughed. "Just an odd expression."

"Odd indeed, but it's rather a lovely notion, isn't it?"

She continued to eat and apparently dismissed the thought, but Jared found his appetite had suddenly disappeared. His homecoming, it seemed, had become far more complicated than he had ever expected.

Accustomed to living a self-ordered life where he made all the decisions, he was quite unprepared to find himself now in very different circumstances. His new situation was odd, but tenable. For one thing, he needed to learn to consult with his mother before he made any plans that concerned her welfare, which meant he needed to have another long talk with her about the account he had set up for her at the bank and the general store.

Even stranger, he found himself feeling alone and wanting someone with whom he could talk, other than his mother. Someone to listen. To care. To love.

Emilee.

He excused himself from the table and decided to take a long ride to clear his mind from thoughts of her. One quick glance out the window told him it was fully dark outside now, which made it too dangerous to ride as fast and as long as he had in mind. He went straight to his chamber, lit a candle, packed a few things into one of his travel bags, and got ready to turn in for a full night's rest.

His plan for tomorrow was now set in his mind. He would get up early, see Traymore at his home to arrange for the purchase of the property, and then ride until he was winded and he had cleared away every image of her from his brain. "End of problem," he vowed as he yanked the covers back and slid into bed before blowing out the candle.

He closed his eyes and forced his tense muscles to relax while he made a mental reminder for himself to leave a note for his mother telling her where he was going, and he felt rather proud of himself for remembering he was not living alone—at least temporarily.

Although abed, he stayed alert, waiting for the sound of Emilee's footsteps in the hallway and the creak of her chamber door opening and closing that would reassure him Emilee had come home, ready to take to her bed. Alone. She would be exhausted, mentally, physically, and emotionally, with no one to hold her or comfort her after a sad and distressing vigil at a woman's deathbed, since her husband obviously preferred the privacy of his own bedchamber.

"The man's not a bloody fool. He's a selfish bastard," Jared grumbled as he rolled over to face the door so he could hear her better when she arrived. He listened to the sound of his own heartbeat, as convinced he would never have permitted a woman like Emilee to sleep alone tonight or any other night as he was certain he could never discover or create a rose that bloomed in winter.

TEN

A s a watcher, Emilee had observed life's greatest lesson in the power of faith often enough to recognize a definite pattern.

The fear of death always filled a household with a distinctive tension, even panic, that tested a family's faith when a loved one hovered between this world and the next. When death was most imminent, however, a quiet peace descended to ease the heartache, hush the sobs, and turn fear into gentle acceptance. Only then would the soul be ready to depart and the family be prepared to mourn and then heal.

In the hours just before dawn on Tuesday, she felt the change. It had happened very slowly, as though a flock of angels had descended very quietly from every corner of heaven to assemble here together. Some already had been here to prepare Paul and his children for the loss of their beloved wife and mother. Others had just arrived to escort Anna Home, while others would remain to comfort the grieving family.

Exhausted by her long watch, she sat on the floor by the hearth in the parlor with a quilt wrapped around her shoulders. The ticking of the mantel clock echoed in the stillness and matched the steady cadence of Emilee's heartbeat as she prayed the end for Anna would be as kind as her suffering had been cruel. Still clinging to life, Anna had defied the doctor's predictions, and Emilee had stayed for fear she would not be there for Anna at the very end as promised.

The three children were all asleep. Just after midnight, Paul had come to Anna's room asking for some time alone with his wife. Emilee sat here now waiting to be needed.

When she heard the opening of a door and heavy footsteps on the staircase, she slipped off the quilt, folded it, and placed it on the seat of a chair. By the time Paul reached the parlor, she had freshened her appearance as best she could.

Looking haggard and much older than his twenty-nine years, Paul stood in the doorway. "It's . . . it's time," he murmured.

She saw the resignation in his eyes and the relief that his wife's suffering was near the end. "Are you sure you don't want to stay with her?"

"We've said our final goodbye. Anna wants me to stay with the children . . . in case they wake up. She . . . she doesn't want them to be afraid." He turned and looked back up the staircase. "Please. I don't want her to be alone now. Just . . . just come to the children's room. After. I mean . . . when . . ."

"I'll come for you," she assured him and followed him back up the staircase. He paused and waited for her to go into the chamber he had shared with his wife for over eight years, before continuing to the next room where the children slept.

Emilee softly closed the door and went directly to the bed where Anna lay propped by a mound of pillows. Half a dozen candles placed about lit the room and chased away the shadows of night and cast a glow to her sleeping face, pale and shrunken from the ravages of her illness. Emilee noticed an indentation on a pillow next to Anna, and wrinkled bedclothes, and knew Paul must have been laying beside his wife for the last time. Emilee's eyes welled with tears as she turned to pull a chair closer to the bed.

"No. Come. Sit here. Close to me."

Anna's words were soft enough to have been whispered by an angel, and Emilee turned back to face the bed wondering if she had really heard them. When Anna lifted her hand only inches from the mattress, Emilee went to her side and took her hand as she sat down on the edge of the mattress. "I'm here," she murmured, and noticed how cold Anna's hand felt. "Would you like me to read to you from the Bible again?"

Anna's eyes flickered open, and her cracked lips formed a tiny smile even as she shook her head ever so slightly. "Did . . . did you ever wonder, all the times you kept watch, what . . . heaven really must be like?"

She nodded.

"It's not like Reverend Burke said. Angels and trumpets and . . . and white pearly gates."

Her heart began to race. Had Anna seen a glimpse of heaven like others Emilee had watched? Was Anna so close to leaving her loved ones behind? Or had she only been dreaming?

Anna trembled and closed her eyes, apparently too weak to keep them open. Was she envisioning heaven at this very instant? Emilee held tight to Anna's hand and closed her own eyes for only a moment. "Tell me," she urged. "What is heaven really like?"

"Valleys. Endless valleys. Lush and green, filled with little children." A deep sigh. A broad smile. "We are all children again in heaven, happy and free and innocent. Imagine," Anna whispered, her voice growing softer and sounding younger.

Emilee trembled at the vision of heaven Anna described. Was it possible that the passage from the Bible where Jesus asked for all the children to come unto Him was so literally true that after death we became children again? Or had Anna's vision of heaven been inspired by her concern about leaving her own children behind?

"They want me to come and play with them." Anna's brow furrowed, and she caught her lower lip with her teeth for a moment and frowned. "I . . . I can't. I have to stay here," she cried. Becoming more and more agitated, she tossed her head from side to side and gripped Emilee's hand even harder. "I mustn't go. Not yet. My babies."

Her distress set off a series of body-wracking coughs, and Emilee propped Anna's head up and held her till they subsided. After laying her head back on the pillows, Emilee used a moist cloth to bathe the sheen of perspiration from the woman's face and the blood from her lips. Whether the woman had become delirious or had truly seen heaven itself, she still clung to the ties that kept her bound to earth and prolonged her own suffering.

Emilee glanced around the room. Acting from past experience, she blew out all the candles save the one on the chest of drawers on the far side of the room. She took her place beside Anna on the bed, now cast in gentle shadows. She appeared to be sleeping, but only moments later she opened her eyes and tugged on Emilee's hand. "Is Paul with the babies? I want him to be with the babies."

Emilee nodded. "He's with them now."

Anna closed her eyes and slept again, even as silent tears trickled down her cheeks. Her breathing slowed and become more ragged, and her hand grew colder still. Finally she stirred, and her face grew peaceful. She opened her eyes and captured Emilee's gaze. "I want to be with the children."

With a heart heavy with sorrow, Emilee cupped Anna's cheek. "I know you do, but Paul—"

"They're such . . . such beautiful little ones," she whispered as her gaze grew distant. "They . . . they still want me to play with them."

Choking back tears, Emilee realized Anna was referring to the children in heaven and had to find her voice before she could respond. "You may go with them now," she murmured and gave up her battle to hold back tears when Anna's face lit with a beatific smile.

"I won't stay long. Just a little while," she managed before she took her last breath and slipped away . . . to play with God's precious children.

"Until we meet again, dear friend." Emilee bowed her head and prayed for the soul of her sister-in-faith. As a sweet peace consumed the sorrow in her spirit, she wiped the tears from her cheeks. Anna's passing had been blessedly gentle after months of cruel suffering, although her vision of eternity was unlike anything Emilee had ever encountered as a watcher.

Thinking of heaven as a world filled with happy children, instead of angels or loved ones who had patiently waited for their relatives to follow them, brought a smile to her heart, and she wondered if one day she would be reunited with her mother. An unlikely possibility, since heaven had no place for harlots or whores, but no thought Emilee ever had about her mother was rational or logical when her defenses were down.

She busied herself about the room getting everything necessary to prepare Anna's body before waking Paul. Sheer will functioned to give her strength after less than four hours' sleep and very little to eat in the past two days. Randall had gotten up from his own sickbed to make one brief visit yesterday. She could not remember if it had been in the morning or afternoon because the hours had blurred together, leaving her a bit disoriented and confused.

She was certain, however, that once she had gotten some rest, she could again push any thoughts about her mother back behind a very old but sturdy curtain in her mind, and until then she would be busy enough to keep her limited memories of her mother at bay.

At dawn, she gently washed Anna's body before slipping on a fresh gown. After changing the bedclothes, she brushed Anna's long brown hair and let damp tendrils curl against the pillow. Now satisfied all was done, she left Anna just long enough to go and wake Paul and tell him he was now left alone with no one by his side to share the burden of raising three children, to keep his home, or to warm his bed on long winter nights.

She paused at the door to the chamber where he had gone to stay with his children. Would Randall mourn her passing if she were to die? Would he show the same courage as Paul had demonstrated throughout these last difficult days? There seemed to be a different bond between Anna and Paul than the one that bound Emilee and her husband. Was it because the other couple had children? Was it because before Anna's illness, they had shared a very physical relationship, too?

Her cheeks blushed with shame for even considering something so private, but Anna had often spoken about the joy she had found in the marriage bed, boasting she and Paul had never slept apart until this last bout with her illness. Did a strong bond of physical intimacy make a marriage stronger than she had been led to believe?

Emilee had nothing in her limited experience to know for sure. She had never spent a full night with her husband on the rare occasions he did visit her bed. After he had sated his lust, he always prayed for greater strength, and returned to his chamber.

If her reaction to Jared was any indication, she had the feeling he would never tolerate private chambers for himself and his wife, and he would not resist physical intimacy. He would tempt his wife to bed and keep her there blissfully pleasured night after night.

She rapped at the chamber door and opened it slowly, hoping the sight of Paul's face would help to chase away her very improper thoughts about Jared. The hectic activities of the next few hours should keep her mind focused on the tasks at hand instead of sinful fantasies, now that she would no longer be alone with her thoughts.

Fortunately, the dawn itself blurred into midmorning before she had finished and Maryam Shale had arrived to take Emilee's place. Preferring to let Paul stay with his children, Emilee turned down his offer to escort her home. With her emotions nearly numb and her body weakened by fatigue and hunger, she headed for home to get some rest. Later that afternoon, Randall would revisit the family to offer consolation and make arrangements with Paul for his wife's funeral service tomorrow.

To save time and energy, she decided to take a shortcut over harvested, barren fields and past a small copse of trees lining a shallow brook to reach the border of the Ives farm. From there she could cut through to the rear of the parsonage.

The sun was bright and clear, the air brisk and warm for late September. Despite being shorter, the shortcut was much more vigorous than walking along the roadway, and she was to the point of collapse by the time she reached the shaded brook. She sank down to her knees. Cushioned by a bed of moss, she scooped a handful of chilly water and drank greedily before she dipped the hem of her apron into the brook and bathed her face.

Feeling refreshed enough not to sleepwalk the rest of the way home, she was about to get up when she saw something small and furry lying close to the opposite bank, with its tiny head resting on a pillow of mud. Curious, she stepped on a series of small stones to cross to the other side and nearly lost her balance when she got close enough to see it was a small black kitten.

She let out a tiny cry and reached down to pull the limp body completely out of the water, but knew immediately she was too late to save the poor creature. Drowning unwanted kittens was common enough, but she could never bring herself to do such a thing. The brook was far too shallow for anyone to have tossed a full litter here and expect them all to drown. More than likely, if there had been a litter, it had been tossed farther upstream where the brook twisted sharply to the north, creating a pool of deeper water.

Unable to bear the thought that the rest of the kittens might be lying along the brook with their little bodies nothing more than food for scavengers, she searched along the bank looking for more kittens. She found a second kitten caught in the curved crescent of jagged rocks, scooped up the body, and put it into the lap of her apron. Holding her apron by the hem to fashion a makeshift carryall, she renewed her depressing search. Several hundred yards away, she found two drowned kittens snagged on a pile of twigs and added them to her burden.

By now her slippers were soaked though, water seeped from her apron, and the hem of her gown was dripping wet, but she continued to search for the burlap sack in which the litter probably had been tossed away. When she had found it, she would know to stop searching any further.

She reached the twist in the brook and immediately spied an old grain sack floating on the surface of the pool.

Heartened there would be no more drowned kittens, she turned to head back when she heard an odd sound that gave her pause. She looked around the edge of the pool and listened. Nothing caught her eye or ear. She took several more steps and heard the sound again. She untied her apron and left the bundle of dead kittens behind to follow the sound that suggested, even on a day as sad as this one had been, the world still held the promise of life and hope.

*   *   *

Jared escorted his mother to the Leary farm with a promise to himself to keep some sort of wagon readily available for her use. She was too old to be walking long distances like this, not that he felt any younger than her sixty-six years at the moment.

After a fitful sleep Sunday night, he left as planned, fully convinced he had somehow fallen asleep and missed hearing Emilee's return. After arranging for the purchase of the property with Traymore and a short delay at the bank and the general store, he had ridden out to his property and had spent the entire day astride until he had inspected every square inch of the sixty-odd acres. Returning home well after dark Monday night, he had been more than surprised to learn Emilee was still at the Leary farm, while her husband had left his sickroom only long enough to make a brief visit to Anna.

Another fitful night only compounded the aches and pains his physical outing had produced and had proved the folly of his attempt to get Emilee out of his system as easily as he had thought he could.

He held his mother's arm now as they approached the two-story frame dwelling. A black bow hung limply on the front door, and he tightened his grip. "It's over now," he said quietly as relief for both Anna and Emilee eased his concern for each of them.

His mother slowed her steps and stopped just shy of the door. "I'm surprised Emilee has stayed this long. She must be exhausted. Why don't you wait here and let me send her out so you can make sure she gets back home safely?" she suggested, disappearing inside before he could answer.

He waited outside and tried to prepare himself to spend time alone with Emilee. Moments later, his mother came back out, shaking her head. Worry creased her brow and troubled her gaze. "Emilee left an hour ago. She should have been home before we even left, or at the very least we should have met her along the way. It's not like her to wander off without telling someone where she's going."

The cemetery.

He knew exactly where she might have gone, but he could

not tell his mother without revealing how he knew where to find Emilee. "I'll have a look around," he offered. "She couldn't be too far off."

His mother brightened. "Try the shortcut between here and home. Emilee's prone to use them."

"Show me where you mean," he asked and listened carefully as his mother pointed across acres of harvested fields and a blur of trees in the distance. He was certain Emilee should have arrived home long before he had left if she had used the shortcut. She was more likely to be at the cemetery, and he assured his mother he would find Emilee and see her home.

Rather than trudge through the fields in formal dress, he walked back to the parsonage along the same route that had brought him here and quickly changed before he saddled his horse. The thought of riding again made his sore muscles tense in protest, but he had no other choice if he wanted to find her quickly.

He rode straight to the cemetery. No Emilee. Not at the marble statue or anywhere else on the grounds. He recalled both of their conversations here and suddenly remembered the second time they had met at the marble angel. Hadn't she said something about taking a shortcut home?

Spurring his horse around, he headed back to the Leary farm, cursing himself for not listening to his mother. He rode past the farmhouse and through the fields at a gallop. Dust swirled in the air and coated his lips, and with every beat of the mare's hooves on the dry earth, he grew more and more worried about Emilee.

He reined to a halt when he reached the shade beneath the copse of trees and scanned the moss-covered area and the width of the brook in either direction for as far as he could see. No Emilee. His heart began to pound in his chest. His throat went dry. And his mind conjured up all sorts of dreadful images that tightened a band of fear around his chest.

When his mount tried to edge closer to the brook, he gave her free rein. She started to satisfy her thirst, and he dismounted to quench his own and took a handkerchief out of his pocket to wipe the dirt from his face. He stood up, put his foot into the stirrup, and froze the instant he saw her.

"Jared! Come see what I've found!"

Face beaming, Emilee walked toward him carrying something dripping wet and heavy in her apron and cuddling something else in her arm. Mud clung to the hem of her skirts, and the folds were snagged and pricked as though she had stumbled through a briar patch.

He chuckled as he took his foot out of the stirrup and led his horse across to the other side to meet her.

"Looks like trouble," he remarked.

She scowled at him and laid her bundled apron onto the ground next to his feet. "It's not trouble at all. It's a kitten." She lifted her elbow and tilted her shoulder so he could see the small gray ball of fur nestled in the crook of her arm, which was covered with scratches.

Every time he thought he had figured out this woman, she surprised him. She should have been practically dead on her feet; instead, she was cavorting through the woods fairly glowing with energy and ecstatic she had found a mangy kitten. When he looked closer, however, he could see she was overtired and operating on sheer nervous energy.

"Her name is Rose. Isn't she sweet? The others all drowned, poor things, but this little one got free and wound up tangled in a brier bush covered with roses."

He lifted the kitten out of her arm and cradled it in the palm of his hand as he brushed its head with one of his fingers until it purred. "Looks almost brand-new, doesn't she? None the worse for her bad time, though."

"Most men don't like cats."

He shrugged his shoulders to dismiss the surprise in her voice. "Most men don't go traipsing halfway around the world to search for the perfect rose, and most women," he added, "don't usually wander off and let other folks worry about them. Mother was concerned for you," was the best he could offer without revealing how worried he had been.

"Oh, I'm . . . I'm sorry. I was so tired I just thought to rest awhile at the brook. Then I . . ."

When she paused to cover a yawn, he lifted the kitten by

the scruff of the neck, put her back into Emilee's arms, and held back a chuckle. Forcing himself to look stern, he led Emilee by the shoulders to his horse and lifted her up and into the saddle so she sat sideways. She felt sturdier than she looked, but just as soft and feminine as he knew she would.

Eyes wide, she gripped the saddle horn with her one free hand and opened her mouth as if to protest. "No argument," he warned. "You're going straight home to bed."

"But the other kittens!" She glanced toward the brook and her throat tightened. "There's another one over there."

He glanced at the sodden lump in her apron that still lay on the ground. "I'll come back later and bury them if you'd like me to."

She nodded and stifled another yawn. "Excuse me," she murmured. "Don't you want me to tell you how I found the kitten?"

He grinned and stared at her bedraggled gown. "That I can guess. Just hold on and I'll walk you back home. Find something to keep you thinking so you don't fall asleep and tumble off the saddle." He led the horse away from the brook and skirted the edge of the Ives farm. He deliberately kept their pace slow and easy.

"Oo . . . oops!"

He managed to catch her before she slipped completely off the saddle, but his rescue was none too graceful. His hands were wrapped around her narrow waist, and her skirts billowed in his face. "Maybe you'd better walk since I don't have a sidesaddle. Confounded skirts," he grumbled as he lifted her back to the ground and tried to put aside a second brief glimpse of her ankles. He could even feel his cheeks flush, an odd and totally new experience.

She giggled and swayed on her feet, giddy with exhaustion. He took her by the arm, walked beside her to keep her from stumbling over her own two feet, and trailed the horse behind them. "Now think about something," he ordered as her head began to loll against his shoulder.

She straightened up immediately. "I'm too tired to think."

"Well, you don't have much choice. Either you think hard

enough to keep from falling asleep on your feet or I'll have to carry you home."

She looked up and giggled at him. "Just like Rose?"

Was the woman addled? If he did not know her better, he would swear the woman was flirting with him. Giggling? Flirting? Was this the real Emilee, or had he found her identical twin?

"Not exactly like Rose," he muttered, knowing full well he would carry Emilee home exactly the same way. He could almost feel her breasts pressing against his chest, and her soft, round buttocks curving against his forearm. Her head would rest against his shoulder, and if he had his druthers, he'd yank off that bonnet and set her hair free. Was it long enough to fall the length of his arm, or would it reach just far enough to brush against his neck?

"Think of a new name for that critter of yours," he gritted, more to distract his own thoughts than to hurt her feelings. "Rose doesn't fit."

"But it does," she argued. "I found her caught on the thorns of a brier rose, which is too long a name for such a tiny little thing. So I shortened it to Rose."

"Still doesn't fit," he argued, but he had to stifle a laugh. As long as he kept her arguing, he could keep her on her feet and get her home.

"I don't see why," she whined.

He stopped and put one of his hands on top of the kitten as if he was going to lift it up and show her its underside. "Would you like me to show you why *he* wouldn't like it?"

He had seen women blush before, but he had never seen cheeks redden so fast or a scarlet flush that spread from her neck to the tip of her ears. For a married woman, she was rather prudish at times. At others . . . He shook his head and took her arm again to start them home, with Emilee embarrassed into total silence.

If he had any sense at all, he would march her straight to her husband's chamber and force the man to take care of his wife. Jared could pack up his things and ride straight to the livery to get a wagon. With any kind of luck at all, he could pick up the supplies he had ordered earlier from the general store and be far away on his own property before supper.

The image of the winter rose flashed in his mind's eye to remind him of his own foolishness and ill-fated luck. He had not been able to convince his mother to make her home with him, and he had not been able to keep Emilee's image out of his mind for more than a few moments. He even had the sore muscles to prove how hard he had tried yesterday.

If he gave in to his greater urges and desires, he would take her home and put her to bed properly himself. He would lay beside her, hold her, and cherish her, even as she slept. Fortunately, the thought of her husband in the adjoining chamber was enough to dampen those dangerous thoughts.

Finally past the grove of sugar maples, he led her around the barn and into the house. When Emilee stopped to remove her bonnet and read a note left on the kitchen table, he read it over her shoulder. Randall had gone to see Dr. Pounds, which meant Jared and Emilee were totally alone in the house.

His heartbeat stammered as he followed her up the back staircase with his hand pressed against the small of her back to keep her on her feet, since she used both arms to cradle the kitchen. "Now who's the bloody fool?" he whispered, trying to convince himself that when they reached the second floor he would do the right thing—for both of them.

ELEVEN

Emilee tripped over the last step and pitched headlong into the upstairs hallway. Before she hit the floor, strong hands grabbed her waist from behind and knocked the air out of her lungs, which captured her cry of distress before it reached her lips. Heart pounding, she kept her arms tight around her precious find as Jared swooped her off her feet and straight into his arms.

The blood rushed back down from her head, and she caught her breath—only to lose it again when she realized the very compromising situation she found herself in as a result of her own clumsiness and his gallantry.

Randall had been very calm and understanding when he had seen Jared holding her hand on the porch, but seeing his wife in Jared's embrace just beyond her chamber door would be too much to expect him to tolerate, much less forgive.

Especially if Randall saw how her forehead rested in the hollow just below Jared's chin and her face lay against his chest just under his shoulder. She could feel his heart beating against her cheek and see the cleft in his chin, which was only inches from her lips.

Physical desire oozed through her veins as thick and sweet as honey. She moistened her lips with the tip of her tongue. Even Reverend Burke had underestimated the seductive, conscience-paralyzing power of wickedness, and in the space of a single heartbeat, voices from the past reminded her she was not a hairbreadth better than her mother.

Nearly languid from exhaustion and the aftereffects of her near fall, she squirmed in Jared's arms. ''I'm fine now, thank you. Will you put me down?''

Her request sounded weaker than she had hoped, and he simply tightened his arms as he took the final few steps to her chamber door. "Just making sure you both get safely to you chamber." He had no sooner made his promise than he kept it.

Her feet had scarcely hit the floor when she backed up against it and held the kitten in front of her as if that sleeping gray ball of fur would protect her from Jared—or from herself. Smoldering gray eyes gazed down at her, sending tingles down her spine to the tips of her toes, and her heart skipped a beat. She swallowed hard. She was not sure what to say or do, but she had to do something to divert the very real physical energy that flowed between them before she shamed them both.

"Moses," she blurted as she stroked the kitten behind the ears.

A long, deep sigh. A flash of hesitation. A smile. "Moses?" he asked, his voice thick with emotions dueling in his eyes and turning them the color of churning water in a stony brook.

She lowered her gaze, suddenly realizing the kitten's fur almost mirrored the precise color of Jared's eyes. "She . . . he wasn't exactly c-cast into the river in a reed basket, b-but . . ."

"He's a survivor. It's a good name." He began to chuckle. "At least it fits him better than Rose."

She laughed with him, and their laughter seemed to relieve the physical tension between them. She even began to hope she could survive the next few weeks with Jared as a guest, leaving her virtue and her faith shattered only into shards large enough she had some chance of piecing back together.

Her deep religious faith, her determination to rise above the ugly scandal surrounding her birth, and her commitment to her marriage would be the glue she would use to restore her spirit and soul to their former state. Beginning here. Beginning now. Before it was too late.

"Please accept my thanks for seeing me home and tell your mother I'm sorry to have caused her any worry," she said, pleased her voice sounded proper and prim again.

"I will." He paused and cleared his throat before he took a single step toward her. "Emilee, sweet Emilee . . ."

She did the first thing she could think to stop him and plopped Moses into one of Jared's outstretched hands. "I'm so tired, I'm afraid I'll be fast asleep and won't hear him when he's ready to eat. Poor thing. He's so thin. The last I looked, there was milk in the icebox and a bit of ham, in case he'll take solid food. He's a bit grimy. You might give him a bath, too," she suggested, rambling off her words as fast as a kite caught in an upward draft of wind.

Or as fast as her heart was beating?

Before he could decline or protest, she turned around and opened her chamber door to slip inside. The minute the door was fully closed, she leaned back against it and closed her eyes. Once her heart settled down from a wild thumping to a normal rhythm, she listened for the sound of his footsteps as he walked away.

No sound at all beyond her own breathing.

She turned her body and put her ear to the solid wood door. Still nothing more.

Her heart began to beat faster again, and she spread her palms flat against the door. With each shallow breath of air she took, the length of her body pressed against the door, reminding her of the hard planes and solid strength of Jared's body. Her chin began to quiver. Her eyes filled with tears. Her will began to weaken. "Please go," she whispered, certain now that the road to damnation, offering every sensual pleasure her sinful body demanded, led only as far as the other side of the door and into Jared's arms.

With a new respect for the power of physical attraction, she also had a glimmer of understanding for her mother and her scandalous behavior. Perhaps she had been more weak than wicked, an interesting twist in Emilee's perceptions of her mother's nature—and one that made her tremble even harder.

Footsteps.

He was walking away, finally, and she heaved a huge sigh of relief. She was safe from him for now. The real test, however, would be how safe she would be for the next few weeks from herself.

Jared swore out loud, used one hand to grab the kitten by the back of the neck to hold it still while he picked up a towel with the other hand. In one clumsy, painful motion, he lifted the hissing little pincushion out of the sink and onto the counter. Without bothering to be very gentle, he buried Moses in the towel.

Scratched from elbow to elbow, Jared glowered at the red welts that stung like holy heaven. "Careful," he spat as the kitten twisted inside the towel. "You might suffocate yet. Not that I'd mind, you little beast."

He loosened the ends of the towel and kicked himself almost literally for even thinking he should give Moses a bath. Jared knew better, but where Emilee was concerned, his better judgment melted like butter on a hot griddle.

Sharp teeth nipped his fingertips, and he pulled his hand away. "Keep that up and I'll heat a griddle for you, too," he snapped. Blood trickled from his index finger and stained his shirt, which was already dripping wet. He had slipped in water puddled on the floor twice while trying to bathe an animal that felt more like a pile of thorned rose stems, and tried not to slip again.

He kept the towel over the kitten and rubbed it dry, convinced Emilee had probably chosen a better name for the kitten after all. "It would serve you right to keep the name," he grumbled, finding it hard to believe he was actually taking pleasure in having a male cat spend the rest of his days answering to "Rose."

Jared snorted. "Vengeance is mine, sayeth the wounded. Let's take a look at you, Rose." He pulled his hand away and let the kitten wriggle its own way free.

The kitten emerged back end first, its crooked tail swishing from side to side, before the rest of it. No longer matted, downy fur stretched over a rail-thin body. With a final yank, Rose pulled his head free, and Jared was finally able to survey any improvement a bath might have made.

Floppy ears, probably permanently creased from his ordeal. Big round eyes still half blue, but turning gold. Ivory whiskers. A patch of white fur under his chin. Cute, in a pathetic way.

"Ornery little tyke, aren't you?" Jared crooned. Crooned? Was that *his* voice that had risen almost to a falsetto? He cleared his throat. "Definitely not," he said aloud, pleased to hear the normal timbre of his own voice again.

When the kitten started to meow, Jared carried him to the kitchen table, towel and all, and sat him down in front of a china saucer full of milk. After one hesitant sniff, Rose lapped up all the milk, cleaned his whiskers, and meowed again.

"Try this," Jared urged as he pushed a teacup filled with tiny bits of ham closer to the animal. Another hesitant sniff, and moments later the ham had been nearly devoured. Before the kitten finished and prowled around the tabletop, Jared went back to the icebox to get more milk and ham. He heard a crash and whipped around.

One very unholy mess greeted him. Honey dripped onto the smashed remnants of a ceramic vase, and the honey jar lay precariously close to the edge of the table. "Ornery, *clumsy* critter," he growled and pounced across the distance between the icebox and the table—reaching the kitten only seconds after he had buried his nose in the butter tub.

"Rose!" Jared grabbed the kitten by all four paws and pulled him away. He righted the honey jar, took a seat at the table, and sat the kitten in the palm of his hand, which rested against his chest. Blissfully occupied grooming himself to get at the last smears of butter, Rose appeared to pose no immediate threat, and Jared sat back to survey the extent of the damage done to the kitchen.

"You've sure managed to make a mess of my life in short order," he complained, "but no more than I have." Absently stroking the kitten's back, Jared looked up at the ceiling. He had not heard any movement from Emilee's chamber overhead for a while, and he assumed she had finally gone to her bed.

Maybe she had put the scene upstairs behind her, but he would never forget standing in front of her chamber, poised to step over the portal that would have led to his ultimate downfall—and hers as well. Holding her in his arms had been a mistake. He knew it then, and he knew it now. It would have been much easier to simply deposit her at her chamber door and leave, but once he had cradled her close enough to inhale the sweet scent of her, he had been consumed with emotions and desire more intense than he had ever known.

His physical desire was undeniable, and he doubted he had ever wanted a woman as badly as he wanted Emilee, yet he wanted more than just pleasuring her body as well as his own. He wanted her spirit and her soul. He wanted to hold her and protect her when she was afraid, to see joy sparkling in her eyes, to hear her purr with contentment after they had made love, to taste her tears and kiss them away. He wanted . . .

"I don't have the right to a blessed thing. Not even one sweet kiss," he whispered to the kitten, who had curled into a ball and gone to sleep.

But he would have kissed her—and more—if he had not heard her whisper plaintively, "Please go." Her words echoed in his mind and every beat of his heart told him he had acted worse than a selfish bastard, which was exactly what he had called Randall.

Instead of comforting Emilee, Jared had caused her anguish. He had frightened her, tempted her, and made her tremble. Thoroughly ashamed of himself, he rested his neck against the back of the chair, tilted his head back, and closed his eyes. Regret slashed deep across his heart, sliced it open, and in that moment he realized why the pain was so intense.

He loved her.

Beyond reason. Beyond all of his best intentions. Beyond all that was moral and right. And only because he loved her had he been able to walk away from her chamber door.

His aching heart pounded weakly in his chest, sending agony throughout his body and to the depths of his selfish spirit. He *hurt,* body and soul, yet he cherished every spasm of pain, every regret, and every ounce of sorrow as a measure of himself as a man who was truly his father's son after all: He had fallen in love with a married woman.

Yet even as he had proved himself to be his father's son, he had been able to do something—once—that his father had failed to do: He had walked away from the woman he loved rather than shame either one of them.

It had taken Emilee's plea to touch deep within his heart and inspire him to be moral and strong, but he vowed to protect the scar across his heart even though it had yet to form as a reminder of his shame. He sighed, and within the depths of his anguish, he found new self-knowledge. He had spent more than half of his lifetime running away from love because he had been afraid he would only measure up to the pitiful example his father had given to him.

Now, after traveling thousands of miles and ending up right back where he had started, one special woman—the minister's wife—had taught him something that had eluded him all these years. He did not have to run. He only had to stand tall and face his demons down.

True love, he had learned too late, meant making choices, and only by finding love would Jared have ever faced the true challenge of his life: To choose to love unselfishly. To choose to love completely. To choose to love with a lifetime commitment of faithfulness.

Since he had fallen in love with Emilee, he had only one choice to make and only one difficult path to follow that would lead to self-respect: He would have to deny himself the joy of loving Emilee as his wife and keep the love he had for her pure and untainted. If he could do that, he would know, beyond a heartbeat of doubt, that he was more than his father's son. He was his mother's son, too, and he was a man of honor.

No small task, but he would begin by finding a way to apologize to Emilee and reassure her he would never again step beyond the bounds of decency and morality. And then he would be ready to face the challenge well, one day at a time.

One day. One lifetime. One goal.

And one very scarred and broken heart.

TWELVE

The dream was so vivid, yet so frightening, it startled Emilee into wakefulness. The man with dark wavy hair and pale gray eyes, who had followed her into her dream, had seduced her with such tenderness and affection her body still tingled in the most intimate of places and her lips ached with longing for one more tantalizing kiss.

Little relieved that her dream had been interrupted before she had committed the ultimate betrayal of her marriage vows, her heart still fluttered and her soul trembled. She glanced frantically toward the inside bolt on her door and let out a heavy sigh.

The bolt was still in place, the only concrete proof she had only been dreaming. She had not committed adultery, but a bolted door had not been enough to protect her from her own sinful desires and the weakness that linked her now and forever with her mother.

She looked down and saw the bedclothes twisted into disarray, a visual reminder her soul was in the same sorry state, not to mention her nightdress, which was shockingly bunched at her waist. She hauled herself up, leaned back against the headboard, and tugged at the hem of her nightdress until it was back down to her ankles.

Too afraid to close her eyes and risk falling asleep only to dream her way right back into Jared's arms, she got out of bed. Even though she had only gotten an hour's rest at most, she straightened the bedclothes, folded the yellow-trimmed quilt, and laid it across the foot of the bed.

Still exhausted from her two-day watch, she removed her nightdress and donned a fresh gown. She stood in front of the mirror to brush her hair, tangled into knots as though she actually had been making love. Randall's brisk, impersonal visits to her bed had left her feeling used as a vessel for his lust, but Jared . . . She blinked her eyes to erase the vision of mutual pleasure and satisfaction from his touch that left her trembling even now.

Her hands shook so hard she could not fashion a braid or even a simple knot. She settled for tying a white ribbon at the nape of her neck to keep her hair in place, only to find her thoughts straying back to her dream about Jared and the way he had fondled her hair and let it slip through his fingers with a look of total wonder in his eyes.

If she only had some sort of moral ribbon to control her wayward emotions as easily as she could tie back her hair.

Tears welled in her eyes, and her throat tightened as she fought to keep the tears from escaping. Shame, sharp and swift, pierced her heart. She reached out and gripped the hairbrush until her knuckles ached. She felt as though she had been set adrift in a sea of wickedness where the unrelenting winds of her past blew her straight into a sinful future with no hope the storm would end soon.

The echo of the front door to the parsonage as it closed hard slammed her out of her reverie and into the reality of the present. "Randall," she whispered as she set down the brush. She had not even given her husband a single one of her thoughts and guilt added another layer of blush to her cheeks. He was the moral anchor in the righteous life she tried to lead, and she needed him now.

She had not seen him for more than a few minutes a day when he had come to the Leary farm, which might account for her lapse in faith and virtue. Vowing not to be separated from him again any more than absolutely necessary for the sake of her very soul, she prayed she had heard her husband enter the parsonage and not Jared, since he tended to use the kitchen door.

She rushed from her room, through the hall, and down the front staircase to find her husband and tell him Anna had passed away. She heard a sound coming from the parlor, but just as she approached the doorway, Randall walked into the hall. Relief quickly turned into surprise, and she took one step back.

With one hand cradling Moses' head against his chest and the other on the kitten's bottom, Randall looked over at her. "Emilee! You're finally home." His face grew solemn. "Has the end finally come?"

She nodded and swallowed a lump in her throat. "Just before dawn. Mrs. Burke and Mrs. Shale are with Paul and the children now. He's . . . he's expecting you later this afternoon." She studied her husband's pale face and noted the tension that creased his brows. "Are you well enough to go?"

"I suppose I can try after I've had a rest. The sun is so bright . . ." He closed his eyes briefly while he sighed. When Moses scratched at the waistcoat lapel, Randall reached around and lifted the kitten's paws away. "I caught him trying to scale the curtains," he explained as he positioned the kitten against his shoulder and stroked the fur on his back. "Does he have a name?"

"M-Moses," she stammered, surprised Randall apparently had taken to the kitten without any of the objections she had anticipated. "I—I found him today by the brook just beyond the Ives farm. The rest of the litter had drowned. He won't be any trouble."

"I am more concerned about his name. Moses is . . . well, it's almost irreverent. A cat's name shouldn't come from the Bible."

His gaze grew distant, and his smile suggested he was reliving happy memories even though he never liked to talk about his past. Considering how difficult it had been for him to lose his parents as a young child and spend the rest of his childhood in an orphanage, she tried not to ask him about his life before he had come to Surrey.

"I don't remember much about my parents before they died," he said softly, "but I do know my mother loved cats. One had white paws. She called him Boots. Another one, Sugarloaf, was pure white and very sweet. Do you see what I mean? Moses just won't do at all." His smile dimpled his puffy cheeks. "Would you mind if I named him?"

"N-no. Not at all," she responded, too amazed he wanted to keep the kitten to argue or even wonder what he would say if she told him she had originally called the kitten Rose. "I asked Jared to get the kitten something to eat while I rested, and I was just coming downstairs to see how he was doing,"

Randall nodded toward the kitchen. "Let's see if he's ready for more to eat. He certainly has some catching up to do."

Quite pleased the kitten apparently helped Randall to take his mind off his headache, at least for a time, she followed him to the kitchen. When he braced to a halt just inside the doorway, she stepped around him and covered her mouth to keep a squeal of surprise from escaping her lips.

Jared had fallen asleep in a chair at the table, but it took her only a quick glance at the disaster in the kitchen to guess it had been made before he had fallen asleep. If Randall had entertained any doubts about keeping the kitten, he would be convinced of them now. Her heart lurched into a full galloping rhythm.

Tidy to the brink of being obsessively fastidious, he was likely to bellow any moment, and she braced for his outburst by closing her eyes and cringing.

The sound of laughter filled her ears. Deep, belly-rolling laughter. Her eyes snapped open, and she stared at Randall. He was laughing so hard tears ran down his cheeks.

Jared bolted awake and tipped the chair over as he leaped to his feet. He blinked several times before gazing at Randall and Emilee and stiffened his shoulders. "Sorry for the mess. Rose gave me a bit of a fight," he mumbled as he set his chair upright again.

"Rose?" Randall sniffed. "The kitten's a male, my good man."

Emilee flinched, expecting Jared to lay blame for the mistaken name on her shoulders, but he remained silent. He did not, however, attempt to conceal the wicked twinkle in his eyes, which he directed straight at her.

"I'll clean up the mess," she offered. Anxious to escape his gaze, she busied herself first at the sink. After she dumped the tub of stale bathwater, she knelt down to mop up the floor with a cloth. She stole an occasional glance at the two men, who had each taken a seat at the table.

Jared sat stiff and erect, but Randall practically lounged in his chair with the kitten still placed possessively against his shoulder, yet another odd departure from Randall's usual formal behavior. "I've got a name for him," her husband announced before taking a swipe of butter and letting the kitten lick it off his fingers. "Troubles."

She gulped back her reaction and tried to smile. The kitten had certainly been trouble from the instant she had tried to untangle him from the brier rosebush and only escalated from there. She had been too bashful to check the kitten's gender and had misnamed him. She had shamelessly flirted with Jared while carrying the kitten home, and she had hidden behind the kitten to force Jared to leave her in front of her chamber door before either of them could fall into total disgrace. "I think it's rather fitting," she agreed, although she knew Randall would be appalled if he knew precisely why.

Jared snorted and held out his badly scratched arms. "He's trouble, all right, but he's thornier than any rosebush I've ever encountered. Rose might be a better name for him after all."

Randall laughed again, and the smile on his face made him look so much younger than the frown he usually wore. "Then it's only by majority consent, but Troubles it is. Come on, Troubles. Let's see if we can't find something in the barn you can use for a bed. Emilee, are there still baskets hanging from the rafters?"

Too speechless to utter a word, she nodded and watched with total amazement as Randall carried Troubles outside with him. To think Randall would allow her to keep a kitten was surprising, but to adopt it away from her and allow the kitten to live indoors was mind-numbing.

To keep herself too occupied for Jared to start a conversation, she finished mopping up the last puddle of water and exchanged her dirty cloth for a clean one. After dampening it with water, she tentatively approached the table under Jared's steady gaze.

"Looks like you get to keep Rose in the house," Jared drawled.

She dropped her gaze and tried not to make any comment about the name he insisted on using for the kitten. "Randall is a kind man," she managed. She made quick work of cleaning up the spilled honey and wiped the honey jar, too. This was the second time she had cleaned up spilled honey with Jared watching her, and she gathered the ceramic shards and put them next to the sink to be buried in the trash pit later to try to get away from the sweet reminder of the soul-shattering temptation he had become.

The only thing left was the tub of butter. She looked at the gray hairs floating atop the creamy yellow butter. "The butter's a total loss."

Jared shrugged his shoulders. "You might try setting it aside and letting him have a spoonful every once in a while. It's good for his coat."

"I suppose." She hesitated and glanced at the outside kitchen door, wishing Randall would come back soon.

In the next breath, Jared stood up and turned her to face him. "I need to apologize for what almost happened today. For what did happen," he said softly. "I'm truly sorry, and I promise it will never—"

The kitchen door swung open, and Randall interrupted the rest of what Jared had meant to say. Troubles was resting comfortably in the middle of a wicker basket. "He'll outgrow it in a few weeks, but for now—" Randall stopped abruptly. His easy demeanor disappeared when he looked directly at Jared and Emilee, who were standing face-to-face and much too close to be considered anything more than improper, particularly after what had happened last week on the porch.

Jared stepped away immediately. "I was just apologizing to Emilee. I forgot about the other kittens who were drowned," he explained as he walked toward Randall. "I promised to bury them, but this little fella just wore me out." He put his hand on top of Troubles's head and gave his ears a playful rub.

Randall's gaze narrowed. "There's a section in the barn with tools. You'll find a shovel there."

"Then I guess I'll head out now."

Jared started for the door. "Don't forget the kitten by the brook, too," Emilee reminded him before he could leave.

He gazed at her over his shoulder. "I won't forget. I take my promises to heart. As I tried to explain a moment ago, I always keep my word."

He left immediately, and the awkwardness that had invaded the kitchen seemed to disappear as well. When Randall asked her to find an old piece of cloth to line the basket while he took the kitten upstairs to his chamber, she went straight to the sewing room and sorted through some of the leftover donations. She quickly found an old remnant of faded pink flannel that had probably been left from making a cradle sheet.

She trembled as she carried the cloth upstairs. In his own decisive way, Jared had made it clear he had been wrong and promised not to let anything happen between them in the future. Satisfied in her own mind she had nothing further to fear from him, she mounted the stairs slowly. With each step, she counted her blessings and vowed never again to betray the man who waited for her upstairs—in thought or deed.

Or in her dreams.

She found Randall resting in bed. He had not bothered to turn down the bedclothes first, and Troubles had curled up next to him. While she folded the flannel and tucked it to fit the basket at the foot of the bed, she suddenly remembered where Randall had been earlier. "Did Dr. Pounds have any news from New York?"

Randall's forehead creased when he frowned. "The specialist in New York City wants me to come there for an examination."

Emilee's heart started to race. She could not bear to be left here alone with Jared still living in the house, although Olivia had told her about the arrangements she had made during a visit to the Learys' and had promised to stay at the parsonage until Jared was able to settle on his new property. Neither could she let her own weakness keep Randall at home and prevent him from getting the medical help he needed. "When would you go?"

"I'm not."

His gaze was as stern as his voice, and in the depths of his dark eyes she saw fear—raw and powerful. Although he professed a stronger faith than hers, he was not a saint. He was as frail in his faith as she was in her own, and he needed her as much as she needed him.

"I trust Dr. Pounds," he said quietly, "and the good Lord even more. The specialist already confirmed what Dr. Pounds thought might be the problem, and I can't be wasting time traveling to New York City."

"But if it would help—"

He admonished her into silence with a look that reminded her never to contradict him, especially in matters concerning his health. "I'm needed here, Emilee, and I intend to stay here. In the meantime, Dr. Pounds can still oversee my care and try some of the specialist's recommendations. Would that ease your mind?"

She laid her hand in his. "I want you well. What does the specialist recommend for your headaches?"

Randall took a deep breath. "Eye drops as a first resort. He tends to think the headaches are caused by some sort of progressive eye disease, which is why I seem to be growing more sensitive to light and the headaches are growing more severe. Dr. Pounds had the drops prepared according to the specialist's prescription. I'm to try them for a week or two. With God's help, the drops will cure the disease."

"And if they don't?" She bowed her head, trying to imaging how Randall would be able to continue an active ministry without a permanent cure for his debilitating headaches.

"My dear Emilee," he murmured. "The road to salvation is never an easy one, but the Lord never makes the cross of true faith we carry too heavy to bear. Perhaps if you prayed more often, you wouldn't be so quick to forget."

He patted the space beside him on the bed. "Come. Lay with me and tell me about Anna."

Emilee had never been in Randall's bed before. Although

she was almost certain he meant only to talk, she hesitated. Surely he would not want to . . . to become intimate in the full light of day when he was not feeling well.

He shook his head as though she had accused him of some awful sin. "I just want to talk."

She walked around the bed, moved Troubles to the foot, and laid down next to her husband. He reached out to take her hand, but edged away from her so their bodies did not touch. She told him about Anna, and while they discussed the funeral service which Randall would schedule when he visited Paul later in the afternoon, Troubles climbed onto Randall's chest and laid there purring contentedly. Fully prone, Emilee found her eyes drooping, and she did not argue when her husband suggested they take a short nap together. She promptly fell asleep before she could wonder longer than a heartbeat about the day's peculiar twists that left her lying in bed with one man and praying she would not dream about another.

Jared returned to the parsonage, stored the shovel back in the barn, and went directly up the back stairs to his chamber. He walked past Emilee's door and deliberately kept his eyes on the floorboards. He quietly entered his own chamber, secured the leather case filled with his mother's letters, and turned around to leave.

He rocked back on his heels. Directly across the hall, Randall's chamber door was ajar, and Jared could see into the room. He immediately averted his gaze, although he could not control the rapid beat of his heart or the band of regret that tightened around his chest.

One glance into the room had engraved a painful vision on his mind. Laying side by side, Emilee and her husband had fallen asleep together. They were practically far enough apart to put another person in the bed between them, instead of a small kitten which had stretched, turned his head to stare at Jared, and sat back on his haunches to groom his paws.

In the space of a single heartbeat, Jared had captured every detail of her lovely countenance, the soft swell of her bosom, and the narrow waist he had circled with his hands only hours ago. The dark circles under her eyes made her complexion look even paler and her musky pink lips parted in her sleep. When he saw her hand beneath Randall's, Jared swallowed a lump in his throat and turned away.

It hurt too much to see the woman he loved beside another man in bed, but Jared added the painful image to the other he had already stored away. As he walked down the back staircase and headed out to the cemetery to read his mother's letters, he grudgingly admitted his esteem for Randall had gone up a notch for a change. Jared was not entirely convinced his shame had more to do with it than Randall's rather decent treatment of the kitten earlier.

Shame, however, had nothing to do with Jared's growing suspicion that Randall Greene had a great deal hidden behind the righteous facade he had created for himself as the village minister. Was Jared just overly suspicious because he coveted the minister's wife? Had he been so jaded by his father's hypocritical life he suspected all ministers were above-average sinners who hid their private sins behind their public ministry? Or had the vision of Randall asleep next to Emilee hurt so badly Jared had let jealousy cloud his mind with unfair judgment?

He was not sure what had fueled his growing uneasiness about the minister, but Jared knew for certain he would never be completely happy or content for the rest of his life—without Emilee.

Heart-wrenching pain and soul-searing anguish would be his constant companions now, replacing the fear and bitterness which had made their home in his heart for so long.

Although he could not have the woman he loved by his side, he would always act honorably. He would love her and watch over her—from a distance—for the rest of his life. And if the day ever came that she needed him in the weeks or months or years ahead, he would be there for her.

Always.

He would keep his love for her in his thoughts and deep in his heart beneath the deep scar which had already formed, and close to his dreams of the winter rose which would always elude him, too.

THIRTEEN

A moist wind blew across the cemetery, and the sun struggled in vain to peek through low clouds as the last mourners filtered away from the freshly filled grave. The sound of canal workers in the distance was a stark reminder that life continued uninterrupted for many on this sad day, and within the hour the mourners would be back at their normal tasks. For Paul and his little children, today and all the days that followed would be very different now that Anna had been laid to rest.

For Emilee, the day was marked by conflicting emotions, and not all of them were sparked by Anna's funeral. She tried to find joy knowing Anna was no longer is such pain, but sorrow ran deep for the loved ones she had left behind. Emilee also suffered true remorse for her fall from grace yesterday and renewed her determination to be a good and deserving wife for her husband.

Having bade Paul and his children farewell, she held Randall's arm as they walked with Olivia and Jared to visit Reverend Burke's resting place. She kept her gaze averted from the stand of trees where she and Jared had spent time together, to avoid stirring up memories best forgotten, along with yesterday's events, and tried to refocus her life.

As they approached the marble angel, Jared led Olivia ahead and helped her place a small cross fashioned from wildflowers at the base of the statue. "Do you like the monument?" Olivia asked as she brushed away several dried leaves that had caught on one of the angel's wings. "When the sun is very bright, the shadow from the angel's hands actually reaches over your sisters' graves."

Jared focused his gaze on the two small markers and smiled.

"I like that," he murmured, but offered no comment on the monument itself.

She sighed. "Your father would, too. He loved those sweet little girls. And he loved you, too, Emilee."

A warm glow filled Emilee's heart. "I always knew he loved me. Always."

Olivia bent down to reposition the flowered cross, which had toppled over. Steady for only a few seconds, it slid to the side again. "Let me help," Jared insisted and bent the cross slightly in the middle so it curved inward and rested more securely against the base.

His mother smiled with approval. "Thank you, dear. You're so very helpful. Just like your father in so many ways. It's no wonder you've chosen to make raising roses your life's work. Your father loved flowers, too," she said softly as she looked up at him. "He was so proud of my gardens. He used to tease me about talking to my flowers. Remember?"

Jared's smile looked forced, but Olivia did not seem to notice. "I remember."

"He always insisted on fresh flowers for meeting, except in winter, of course." She glanced at Emilee and caught her gaze. "You tried to make paper flowers for him one year. I think you were only thirteen."

Emilee chuckled. "I knew they were pitiful, but he pretended they were absolutely exquisite and displayed them in the meetinghouse."

Sighing again, Olivia shook her head. "He was always so kind and so caring, so worried about making other people happy. I do miss him so."

Jared seemed almost aloof, and Emilee could tell by the stiff set of his shoulders and his taut lips he was not at ease discussing his father. Was grief still too new and raw? Did Jared find Emilee and Randall's presence today an intrusion, or did he feel uncomfortable being with them after what had happened yesterday?

She took a step closer to Randall. "Perhaps we're intruding. It might be best if we leave Mrs. Burke and Jared alone here for a while," she suggested, trying to keep her voice low and soft.

Before Randall could answer, Olivia frowned at her. "You're not intruding at all." She pointed to the epitaph and urged her son to study it. "The words are lovely, aren't they? Randall helped me to decide what to put as your father's inscription. In fact," she added, "he helped me a great deal after your father died, even though he was very busy with church matters."

Jared nodded once, but a wounded look haunted his eyes. "Then I'm indebted to you, Reverend Greene. The epitaph is quite fitting. I'm certain Father would be pleased."

"I tried to keep it simple," his mother explained. "He was a humble man, despite his many talents. He sought worldly honors for the Lord, not for himself. He blessed us all with his gifts, and he was a living example of a righteous man we all should follow."

As Olivia spoke, Emilee watched Jared closely. He clenched one of his fists, and his eyes hardened into slate. Obviously he found his mother's words difficult, but Emilee did not know him well enough to know how to help him accept his father's death. As much as she would like to offer to help, she had to distance herself from him if she had any hope of ending her attraction for him.

When Olivia suggested it was time to leave, Emilee was as relieved as Jared appeared to be. Chilled by the damp air, she was anxious to get back to the parsonage, and she was also worried about Randall. Although he claimed the eye drops had already offered some improvement, he looked unusually pale.

"Let's go this way," Olivia suggested and led them several rows down to a double grave with a flat bronze marker. "I thought I'd try to get you up to date a bit while we're here, Jared. You remember Mr. and Mrs. Alloway, don't you? They passed on just days apart several years ago."

Jared's eyes widened. "You're . . . you're taking me on a tour of the cemetery to meet—"

"And why not? It seems a logical way to let you know who isn't still alive so you don't ask about them in the village."

She glanced past her son to Randall. "I'm not being blasphemous or . . . or disrespectful of the dead, am I?"

Randall's lips quivered a bit before he answered. "I wouldn't think so. It is a bit . . . unusual," he answered as he loosened the collar of his shirt.

Emilee stifled a grin. Many of the older folks seemed much more at ease at the cemetery than the younger generation, probably because there were so many more of their friends and loved ones here as they aged. Or maybe the elderly just liked to think that visitors would stop to visit them long after they had passed to the other side. It did seem a bit odd to her, but rather harmless.

As though sensing he had hurt his mother's feelings, Jared immediately acquiesced. "If you insist, I don't suppose there's any harm to visiting a few." He paused to check his pocket watch. "I have several errands, but I suppose I can delay them for a short while."

"And don't forget your meeting tonight with the church elders," she admonished—for the fourth time that day alone, that Emilee had overheard.

This time his smile was genuine. "At eight o'clock. Now let's get this tour started."

Olivia pursed her lips. "It's not a tour. It's a . . . a . . ."

"Tour." He chuckled and held out his arm to guide her.

"You may as well come along, Randall. You'll learn a lot, too, and we can't leave Emilee alone," she suggested, giving them no choice but to accompany her.

For the next twenty minutes, Olivia led them through and around the cemetery, reminiscing about deceased friends and neighbors, many of them part of the small community of believers who had been founding members of the church. Jared seemed to express real interest at times, but Randall appeared to be uncommonly preoccupied.

Olivia stopped at a single grave with a small granite cross as a marker. "This is the last one. For today."

Emilee was so grateful she could have cried. Her slippers were soaked clear through from walking over wet grass, and her toes were nearly numb. She pulled her black cape tighter around her shoulders to keep the cool air from chilling her straight through as she read the marker quickly:

VIOLET WESTON
BELOVED WIFE OF WILLIAM HOWARD
MAY 25, 1780–JUNE 22, 1833

"You remember Mrs. Weston, don't you, Randall? Her funeral service was one of the first you conducted by yourself. I'm not sure if you'd remember Violet, Jared. She was a lovely woman. Childless, so you wouldn't have gone to school with any of her children. She didn't come to meeting very often. Her husband never approved. He did let her enter the church fair once. I don't remember if it was her apple pie or her corn relish, but she won the blue ribbon. Never set foot in the village again after that."

"Mother, it's time for me to go."

"Let me finish," she admonished, continuing before Jared could object again. "Her husband used to come to the village for supplies, but spent most of his time in the tavern. Your father took William home often enough after he'd had a day or two to sober up. He moved away after she died, and I can't help but wonder—"

"It's time to go," Jared announced abruptly and turned both women away from the marker.

His voice was so cold Emilee almost flinched. Olivia's long-winded account of Violet Weston's life was actually a bit shorter than any of the others, and Jared had been very tolerant to this point. His patience, however, had obviously been stretched to the breaking point, and even Randall seemed restless.

Dismissing their odd behavior as nothing more than the likelihood both men were as cold as she had become, she was also relieved when Olivia gave in rather gracefully and chatted on the way back to the parsonage about the tour she would take them on next time.

While Emilee walked home beside her husband, she was already planning for the rest of the day. She would start with a change of slippers, a good, hot cup of mulled cider, and several of Olivia's crunchy pretzel treats, and, she hoped, finishing up with a quiet evening in her chamber spent working on the sampler she was making for Olivia's new home while Randall attended the meeting with Jared.

The moment Jared stepped into Ezra Traymore's spacious office with Reverend Greene, he knew the meeting of the church elders had obviously started well before eight o'clock.

In addition to Traymore, six other men sat around a long table, which had not been in front of the fireplace during Jared's previous visits. Stacks of papers lay in disarray in the center of the table as though they had already been read and discussed. The heavy aroma of cigar smoke veiled the room with a light haze, and the fire was burning low.

Usually as punctual as he was organized, Jared chafed at being late. "I'd been told to come at eight," he apologized as Traymore rose to greet Jared and the minister.

The grandfather clock in the hall began to chime the eighth hour, and Traymore chuckled. "Right on time. We appreciate your coming. Reverend, why don't you take your regular seat? Jared, I think you know some of the elders, but let me introduce you to the others."

He escorted Jared around the table as Randall took a seat at the head. Walking to his left, Jared shook hands with the banker, Garth Leigh, Ansel Woerner, and Caleb Rogers. On the other side of the table, he was introduced to lawyer Thomas Barnett, innkeeper Richard Fenton, and Sheriff Robert Dennis.

By the time Jared had taken his seat at the end of the table opposite Randall, Jared had an uneasy feeling deep in the pit of his stomach. In part, his mother had reminded him of this meeting so many times today he had begun to worry about her state of mind, especially after the bizarre tour she had led them on. Now that he had observed that the meeting had begun well before his arrival, he suspected his presence here fed an ulterior motive beyond welcoming home the son of their former minister.

Did they intend to offer him a position on the Board of Elders as a token of respect for his father? Stiffening his resolve to refuse any more association with the church than absolutely necessary for reasons he would never be able to discuss with anyone, he did not let down his guard when the conversation started on a business level.

"As you may not all know," Traymore began, "Jared is settling back in Surrey permanently. We just closed the transfer of the old Peterson farm to him this Monday past."

"Good land," Rogers commented as he adjusted his spectacles, which had slipped to the end of his nose. "You figure to get a crop in? Might not be too late for winter wheat."

"I've ordered stock and expect to be finished by early November," Jared responded. Only a select few knew his plans for a nursery, and he expected to raise more than a few eyebrows when word finally spread that he was raising roses.

Woerner cocked his head to the side. "Stock? Guess you're doing some dairying, then. Waste of good farmland," he muttered. "Too far out of the village to haul milk every day once the canal's open."

Jared chuckled. "Definitely no cows. No apples, either. I couldn't begin to compete with you. How many varieties do you have now?"

"Just three." Ansel's eyes began to twinkle. "Some of them on a single tree. Tried a fourth, but couldn't get the trees to cooperate," he teased, setting off chuckles around the table.

When all eyes focused back on Jared, he took a deep breath. Rather than depend on gossip, he preferred to set the record straight himself. "I've spent the better part of the past ten years in Europe on business. Now that my mother is alone, I've decided to settle back here and have turned over most of my European responsibilities to someone who will remain there in my place. My partner in New York City will continue to operate the business end while I establish an experimental nursery here."

When he paused, most of the men leaned forward. All except for Randall, who already knew most of Jared's plans.

"A nursery? Sounds like you're planning to raise young

'uns!'' Woerner exclaimed. "Best get yourself a wife first, or the good reverend here will be preaching at you something fierce, not to mention what the womenfolk would do to you."

No wife and no children had ever been in Jared's future, but he was unprepared for the sharp pain of regret that sliced through his heart and nicked the love for Emilee he had stored there. "Roses," he said, but kept his secret quest for a winter rose private. "They're as temperamental as a woman and as delicate as little children," he joked. "I'll expect they'll keep me busy enough that I won't have time for courting, let alone marriage," he added to forestall any matchmaking attempts before they started.

There was something about a man choosing to remain single that most people saw as a challenge. Women automatically assumed he could not survive without a wife. Most men seemed to operate on the assumption that since they were chained to one woman by the bonds of holy matrimony, they had another link in the chain all ready for him.

He looked around the table at the faces of all the elders. With the exception of Randall, whose views on matrimony were no doubt Bible-based, every single one of them had a look in his eyes that told Jared he was right. He could almost hear their chains rattling beneath the table and wondered if, had the chain that bound his father to his mother been literal instead of moral, he might have been faithful to her.

Randall leaned forward and folded his hands on the table. "Emilee and I accompanied Jared and his mother when he inspected the property. Jared, I may be speaking out of turn, but I know how anxious you are to get situated."

Without giving Jared any chance to stop him, Randall continued. "There's no cabin on the property, and it will take weeks for Jared to get one built. As a result, he may not be able to plant, at least not to any great degree. As a community of faith, we've helped members to raise barns or harvest crops when necessary. Gentlemen, I'd like to see us work together to build a cabin for Jared. It may not be precisely what he has in mind for a permanent structure, but I'm sure—"

"Consider it built."

"Glad to help."

"Just let us know when."

A chorus of affirmations echoed in the room. Genuinely touched, Jared could do no more than shake his head. "I never intended to come here tonight to—"

"It's settled. No argument," Woerner warned. "My bones are telling me we've got clear weather for the next few days, so Saturday we'll help you build that cabin. Jared, you see Marcus Kline at the sawmill and order what you need. If you need credit, see Garth here at the bank. I'll vouch for you. Ezra, spread the word when folks come for the post and get that boy of yours to put a sign up at the general store. I'll get Hester and those sisters of hers to get the women organized. We'll be working up a real appetite."

Jared could scarcely believe how anxious the men were to help him and how quickly Ansel had organized their efforts. "I can't let you all—"

"Can and will, son. Maybe you've been gone so long you've forgotten our ways. We're all friends and neighbors here. When one of us needs a helping hand, we're ready. Don't worry," he warned again as he poked his finger at Jared. "You'll get to return the favor so many times you'll work hard enough to have built ten cabins on that property to yours."

Jared ran his hand across his brow and tried not to feel guilty for being so jaded in his suspicions about the purpose for the meeting. For the first time that night, he allowed himself to lower his guard. His tense muscles relaxed, and he leaned back in his chair. "I don't suppose there's anything I can say to tell you how much this will mean to me. Thank you. And I'll be ready whenever you need me to help someone else."

"Of course you will," Ansel agreed. "And now, Ezra, before it gets so late my sweet darlin' wife thinks I've been kidnapped, let's get to the real purpose for having Jared out on a chilly night so I can get home."

Every muscle in Jared's body immediately tensed again, and his guard slammed back to full alert. His heart began to pound, and his mind raced with amazement at how easily he had been outmaneuvered. How was he going to refuse the board anything after accepting their offer to help him?

Traymore reached over to the stack of papers in the middle of the table and sorted through them. He selected one and rolled it closed before he handed it to Jared, who held his breath and waited for Traymore to explain exactly why Jared had been invited to the meeting.

FOURTEEN

As head of the board, Traymore stood up and addressed Jared formally. "Through the Board of Elders, the members of the church have chosen to honor your father for his dedication and devotion to our small community of faith. We can think of no better way to express our appreciation or to keep his memory alive for all those who come after us than by dedicating our new church in his name. Now that you're back among us, we'd like you to approve the plaque which will hang in the church vestibule before we have it made."

Shock. Like a ragged bolt of lightning, pure shock surged through Jared's body, ripped open his heart, and struck the secret he had buried there. His hand tightened around the roll of paper, and he clenched his jaw to keep from choking. It was hard to listen to his mother or her friends extol his father's virtues, but in time, he hoped memories of his father would fade away. To have a church dedicated to his father was tantamount to hypocrisy nearly as great as his father's.

He forced himself to remain calm and keep a decent expression on his face. How on God's big earth could he get these men to change their minds without telling them the real reasons he objected? He had few qualms about destroying their false impression of his father and none about shattering his father's name. There was only one reason to give him pause: his mother.

Now he knew she had reminded him repeatedly about the meeting because she had known about the board's intentions tonight and wanted him to be sure to attend and be surprised. The surprise, however, had boomeranged. He had left home because he had not had the courage to tell her about his father's infidelities when he was alive. As a widow, all she had left in her remaining years were her happy memories. If he spoke up now and she learned the truth, those memories would turn into bitterness that would crush her heart and soul.

As hard as it might be, Jared had to put his mother's welfare first, which was precisely why he had returned to Surrey in the first place. Privately, he had scoffed at the ostentatious marble angel over his father's grave, but he had hidden his disdain from his mother. But a whole church dedicated to his father with a plaque at the front door? How could he see that plaque displayed without eventually becoming so bitter he destroyed himself?

He looked around the table. Everyone, even Randall, expected him to embrace the plan, but how could he change their minds without telling them the truth? His only chance lay in using his father's reputation and their perceptions of him against them. If he failed, he would have to stall for time to find another way to destroy it.

He cleared his throat and tried not to choke on his words. "Gentlemen, I'm more than overwhelmed," he began, which was closer to the truth than any of them possibly knew.

Woerner grinned at him. "Speechless is more to the point. We thought you'd be surprised."

"Thoroughly," Jared said quietly as he garnered the courage to lie effectively. "I'm not sure what to say. My father was a remarkable man, but he never sought worldly honors for himself. Only the Lord." As best he could, Jared parroted the words his mother had used earlier at the cemetery to justify his father's epitaph. "I worry what he would think about having the church dedicated to him. At the very least, I think he'd be . . . well . . . embarrassed," he offered, thinking more along the likes of ashamed or mortified, now that his father was burning in hell and knew how deeply he had wronged his family and his community.

Randall fidgeted in his chair. "I didn't know your father as long as most of the others here, but I did work closely by his side. He set a tremendous example for me to follow. For all of us. And it's more than fitting to have the new church dedicated to his memory. It's his due."

"Besides," Rogers chimed in, "he's not here to argue with

us. That man could outtalk and outdebate Daniel Webster!"

All the men chuckled, and Jared quickly tried a different tact. "I'd like to discuss this with Mother first. She—"

"No!"

Traymore's word was sharp enough to slice through marble. His cheeks flushed pink. "Sorry," he mumbled. "Actually, Jared, we'd like to surprise her. It's been hard to keep it a secret from her, but I think we've managed so far."

Jared frowned. He had hoped to get his mother to help him, but now that was a useless thought unless the elders were wrong about having kept this a secret from her. "I hate to disappoint you, but she must have reminded me to come to this meeting twenty times. Obviously she must have found out about the dedication and wanted to make sure I attended."

"I believe that's partially my fault," Randall interjected. All heads turned toward the opposite end of the table. "She did know it was important for you to be here tonight, but only because I discussed the cabin-raising with her. She has no idea about the church dedication."

Traymore narrowed his gaze. "Are you sure she doesn't know?"

Randall looked offended. "I'm quite positive."

With a collective sigh of relief around the table, all heads turned toward Traymore again, and he puffed out his chest. "Then I think we should proceed as we planned. Jared, once you've taken a look at the plaque, we're ready to have it made in plenty of time before the church officially opens. Garth, you've been checking on the progress of the construction. Can we still plan on mid-December?"

When Garth nodded, Traymore smiled. "Then we'll leave this with you, Jared. Feel free to make any suggestions you think would make the plaque more meaningful, and don't worry about the date. Once we're certain there won't be any delay in the church construction, we'll insert the date."

Jared had no intention of reading the proposed plaque in front of the board and he had no suggestions ready now, short of tossing the plaque straight to hell and letting the fires of damnation destroy it while his father watched. He was more than unhappy with apparent defeat now, and he settled for stalling, all the while thinking he might be able to turn his mother's ignorance of the planned dedication to his own advantage. "If you don't mind, I'd like a few weeks."

"You can have two, if you need them. Any more than that, we'd have to delay the dedication. We need to allow two months for Eldridge Cleary to make a model and cast the actual plaque."

"No more than two weeks," Jared promised.

"Then we can adjourn," Traymore announced. "Ansel, you have to run off home, but I hope the rest of you can join me in a small celebration. Why don't we move to the parlor for a proper toast now that we have Jared's support? Begging your pardon, of course, Reverend."

Jared wanted to have a celebration as much as he wanted to eat a barrel of thorns, but Randall looked anxious. His eyes glittered and a tic disturbed his right cheek. Within seconds, however, Randall shuttered his gaze and appeared solemn. "Temperance is a virtue, but I believe the good Lord would forgive a small celebration. I'll trust Him to keep a good watch," he said in the same tone of voice he had used when preaching last Sunday. After a few polite words, he excused himself and left with Ansel.

Jared followed the other men to the parlor, hoping to learn enough about some of the men he had met tonight to find their weaknesses and develop an effective plan to thwart their intentions. He carried his secret with stoic determination, but the burden was getting heavier with each day he spent in Surrey. He had no one to help him carry the burden. No one who could just listen or offer advice. No one at all—particularly the one woman he had no right to ask for even a smile of affection.

Forcing thoughts of Emilee aside, he strengthened his resolve to carry the burden alone. He was just as determined there would be no plaque hanging in the new church to honor his father. Jared had two weeks to achieve his goal . . . and a lifetime cursed with bitterness if he failed.

*   *   *

The light of a full harvest moon guided Emilee's steps as she walked down Main Street. She cut across the town square, nodded to Washington's statue, which kept perpetual vigil over the village, and hurried toward home. Warm summer nights had bowed to autumn's chill, which she knew was only a prelude to the blustery winter cold that would arrive within a few months.

Headed into a stiff wind, she pulled her hooded cape tight at her throat and waist. She passed the darkened Traymore mansion, but knew the meeting had concluded hours ago. Randall would be home by now. So would Jared. They both would be asleep by now, and she was disappointed to have to wait until morning to learn how Jared had reacted when he learned the new church would be dedicated to his father. She would have to be very discreet and make sure Olivia did not overhear a word so the dedication would be a complete surprise to her.

Anxious to take to her bed, she would have to slip upstairs very quietly so as not to awaken the others. Olivia had already gone to bed when Robert Walters had arrived at the parsonage asking for Emilee to come talk to his wife, Nancy, who had miscarried only a few days after Emilee had visited her in their temporary home in the schoolhouse. After leaving a note for Randall in his chamber so he would not worry about her, she had gone with Robert to the far end of the village, where he had resettled his family in what Nancy had described earlier as a lean-to and turned out to be little more.

Emilee had sat with Nancy while the woman tried to sort through her grief about losing the child she had carried in her womb. She had done little more than listen, offer encouragement, and hold Nancy's hand. By the time she had left, Nancy seemed more at peace with what had happened. She never would have been able to open her heart and speak so freely with Randall, which is why Emilee's role as the minister's wife was so important.

Shivering now from her long walk, she tried to hold on to that thought instead of lamenting the very relaxing night she had planned working on Olivia's sampler. Shivering now from her long walk and longing to be tucked into her warm bed, she hitched up her skirts and expended her last ounce of energy to run the rest of the way home. Randall would be appalled if he saw her running through the streets like a child, not to mention what some of the village matrons might say, but they were not even awake and she was cold!

She did not stop when the hood of her cape fell back and her hair pulled free from the ribbon at the nape of her neck to catch on the wind. When she finally burst into the kitchen, her cheeks were stinging and the tips of her ears were numb.

Chest heaving as she tried to catch her breath, she smelled the distinct aroma of coffee. At nearly midnight? Curious, she made her way through the darkened kitchen and approached Randall's study. Enough light trickled from beneath the closed door to guide her, and she rapped softly as she opened the door. "Randall? What are you—" She swallowed the last of her words and froze. "Jared," she whispered, surprised to find him in her husband's study.

He was seated behind Randall's desk, and Jared's hands held opposite ends of a large square of paper. The lamp behind him cast shadows on the angular planes of his face and highlighted his dark hair. "I didn't mean to disturb you," he mumbled as he quickly rolled up the paper and stood. He took one glance at her and frowned. "Obviously I didn't wake you."

She clutched the opening of her cape. "No. I was just coming in when I saw the light coming from the study. Actually, I smelled the coffee first." She glanced at the pot of coffee sitting on a tray by the desk. Next to a cup and saucer, Troubles had curled into a ball and fallen asleep with his head barely touching another saucer half-full of coffee.

Emilee stared at the kitten to avoid looking into Jared's eyes and tried to still the hammering of her heart. He was halfway across the room, but his very presence unleashed a host of physical reactions that left her trembling. "I'm sorry. I didn't mean to interrupt you. I thought Randall was using the study," she mumbled weakly as she backed out of the room.

He studied her face, hesitated, and waved his hand over the pot. "You're even shaking with cold. Would you like a cup of coffee? It's a fresh pot. The second I've made so far to-night," he said as he rubbed his brow with the back of his hand.

She backed up another step. "I shouldn't."

"You shouldn't be out in the middle of the night alone, either, but obviously you were. At least leave a note so I'll know to wait and make sure—"

"I left a note for Randall in his chamber."

He immediately tensed and rolled the paper between both hands. "I apologize. I . . . it's been a long night. Forgive me." He sighed and started to turn away from the desk. "I should be going to my chamber now anyway, but please stay and warm yourself before you go to bed."

"No. Stay," she blurted before she could stop herself. He obviously had not been pleased by the board's announcement tonight, and she was curious to know why. She could not risk talking to him tomorrow, since it would be very difficult to make sure Olivia did not overhear their conversation. Alert, however, to the danger she faced by being alone with him now, she made sure the door was left open before she took a seat in a chair to the right of the desk.

While Jared went to the kitchen for another cup, she removed her cape, smoothed her hair back, discovered the ribbon had blown away, and settled for bunching her hair and positioning it behind her. Satisfied in her appearance now, she was stroking the sleeping kitten when he returned.

He poured a cup of coffee and handed it to her. "Would you like milk or sugar?"

"No," she answered, too afraid she would brush his hand when he passed them to her. She sipped the steaming brew and concentrated on the bitter taste to avoid thinking about how easily Jared's touch invited a physical response from her body.

He sat down behind the desk and poured another cup for himself, adding generous lumps of sugar scraped from the loaf he insisted was not a luxury, but a necessity of life. He stirred the sugar to melt it, and the sound of the spoon clicking against china echoed in the room. Troubles woke up, stretched, and sniffed at his saucer. Jared added a splash of hot coffee and a good portion of milk to the kitten's saucer. When he sprinkled sugar on top, Troubles immediately started to lap up the brew.

She chuckled. "Kittens don't normally drink coffee."

Jared laughed with her. "He liked it well enough to drink mine, so I thought I'd give him his own. Speaking of normal," he said as he cocked his head, "do you ever get a normal night's sleep?"

Her smile faded. "I'm afraid this is normal." What was not normal was how fast her heart was beating and how quickly she had swept aside her vow to keep her distance from him.

He leaned back in his chair and sipped his coffee. Grimacing, he added another spoonful, tasted it again, and smiled before he looked at her. "You're not afraid to be out alone so late?"

I'm only afraid of how you make me feel.

She dropped her gaze and toyed with the cup she held on her lap. "No."

"You should be." His voice was an odd combination of gentleness and sternness. When she glanced up at him, he captured her gaze and held it. "The village is growing every day with laborers and new families, not to mention transients and vultures looking for a quick kill."

"I suppose you're right," she admitted, although she had yet to meet someone who had not been polite and courteous. Still, she had never encountered someone at night.

"Next time, at least let someone walk you home."

Her pulse began to race. "How do you know someone didn't?" she asked defensively. Had he been watching her out the window?

He chuckled. "You came in through the back door. If someone walked you home, you would have come through the front and gone directly upstairs without seeing the light under the door."

"I smelled the coffee," she countered.

"From the kitchen."

Satisfied he had not been watching her rather childish race back to the parsonage, her pulse dropped back to normal.

"Oh," was all she managed to say. In the awkward silence that filled the room, she could hear the sound of her own breathing, and his, as she sipped her coffee. "Did your meeting with the church elders go well?"

He put his cup down and picked up the rolled paper to stand it on end. From her new vantage point, she could see his face clearly, and his eyes churned with worry.

"Not well?" she asked.

He sighed. "Well enough." His gaze softened when he retold the conversation that ended with the plans to build his cabin on Saturday.

Randall had not mentioned this idea to her, but she was not surprised the church members would offer to help. Hanging from an emotional pendulum that swung from relief to disappointment Jared would be leaving, she was pleased Jared appeared genuinely excited at the prospect of settling on his property so soon. Apparently the source of the concern that creased his brow and troubled his gaze was the proposed dedication of the church to his father, but she did not want to broach the subject unless Jared invited her opinion.

"Are those the plans you've drawn up for your cabin?" she asked, hoping to continue their conversation long enough for him to feel comfortable discussing his objections to the dedication. She set down her cup on the edge of the desk.

He shrugged his shoulders. "I'm set to do that tomorrow when I meet with Marcus Kline at the mill." His gaze grew distant for a moment, and her heart began to pound. "You knew about the church dedication," he murmured.

"Yes."

"This is a copy of the proposed plaque," he said as he tapped the edge of the rolled paper on the desk which immediately caught Troubles's attention. Swatting at the paper with both paws, the kitten batted it away from Jared and played with it like he would a mouse. She reached over to steady the tray. Jared rescued the paper before it landed in Troubles's saucer, but his hand tipped the saucer over. The kitten immediately changed interest and started to lap up the spilled coffee.

"Is it the wording you don't like?" Emilee asked, to resume the conversation.

Jared stared at the paper. "I haven't read it yet." He laid down the paper, put his elbow to the desk, and leaned against his hand to rub his eyes. "It's late," he murmured. "I can't even seem to think clearly."

She swallowed the lump in her throat. If it was not the plaque, then it was the dedication itself that troubled him. She had suspected for some time that Jared's long absence from home was more than just a son leaving to make his own mark on the world. Given Reverend Burke's reputation, it would have been hard for any son to live up to his father's name. She sensed now she had been right to think Jared and his father had somehow become estranged. Now that his father was dead, there would never be any reconciliation. Was it grief, hopelessness, and regret that troubled Jared? "Sometimes it helps to pray on a matter that troubles you," she offered.

He snorted as he raised his head. "Prayer won't help."

Surprised by the bitterness in his voice, she persisted. "There are times when prayers don't solve our problems easily, but prayer itself can offer a different perspective—one that leads to either a solution or acceptance of something we can't change."

He cocked his head and challenged her with his gaze. "It doesn't always work that way. Granted, not every problem has a quick or easy solution, but acceptance isn't always an option, either. It's a damn heavy burden that hurts like hell, if you'll pardon my language."

She flinched, not from his use of profanity, but from his despair. "Either you learn to accept the burden as a blessing or it will destroy you," she whispered, refusing to drop her gaze.

He clenched the paper in his fist and stood up. "Maybe it already has," he murmured before he walked out of the study.

She listened to the sound of his footsteps as he walked down the hall and up the front staircase. Whatever his burden, it heavied his steps as much as it troubled his heart, but he carried his burden alone.

Whatever her fears about her feelings for Jared, she thought only about helping him. Reverend Burke and his wife had given Emilee a home when no one else would take her in. They had loved her and guided her to a life of faith and acceptance by the very people who had judged her according to her mother's sin. In addition to living a moral life to make them proud of her, the very least she could do in return was help their son.

She set her cape aside, gathered up the china, and carried the tray back into the kitchen. It would be no easy task to help Jared. He was independent, strong-willed, and self-contained. She had had several private conversations with him, however, enough to know there were several cracks in the wall he had built around himself. Through one crack, he allowed his love for his mother to flow through. Through another, interest in his life's pursuit gave him joy. She suspected there were a few more openings, and if she tried, she might be able to slip through and get close enough to reach deep within his heart where he stored past hurts and help to ease them.

She knew the way well. She would need time and patience, but she would follow the very same path the Burkes had taken to help her. She would listen without judgment. She would care more about him than herself. There was but one challenge that frightened her more than anything. She had to find a way to help him and slip back through the cracks in his defenses without leaving her heart behind next to his.

FIFTEEN

At dawn on Saturday, Jared had arrived at his property well before any of the others. Working from a set of plans, he had carefully staked out the perimeter of a compact, L-shaped cabin several hundred yards north of the old outbuildings and the former cabin location. Every window in the front of the cabin would have a view of the land that would someday be filled with endless rows of breathtaking color, and westerly winds would fill every room with delicate rose fragrances from spring to late autumn. Protected on either side by trees, the cabin backed up to a wide stream where he had already spotted several varieties of wild roses.

By eight o'clock in the morning, volunteers started to arrive, some with their whole families, driving wagons filled with tools; others had driven oxen and plows to tackle the fields. Through Ezra, one of the canal contractors had sent half a dozen laborers assigned to the cabin-raising today instead of their normal duties.

Jared knew many of the families, which turned the cabin-raising into a grand reunion made easier since he had finally finished reading his mother's letters. Greeting old friends and townspeople who lived beyond the boundaries of the village itself, was a far better way to fill in the gaps left missing from his time away than touring the cemetery with his mother. There was but one drawback the two methods had in common: stories.

Like Jared's mother, nearly every man, woman, and child had felt compelled to share a personal experience they had had with his father, who was either the kindest, most compassionate, most loving, or most religious of all men, depending on the tale. Both awed and disgusted by their regard for his father, he had kept such a tight smile on his face he thought his cheeks would crack.

His father, the Reverend Mr. Benjamin Burke, not only had betrayed his wife and nearly destroyed his son, he had deceived an entire congregation. The upcoming church dedication suddenly became far more than hypocritical. It would be a travesty, and Jared reinforced his determination to prevent it.

How he would stop the dedication now presented a greater challenge. These were good people, honest, hardworking, and trusting. Exposing his father as an adulterer who used the Word to convince his son to remain silent would send shock waves throughout the membership and the village.

To find escape and work off some of his frustrations, Jared perched himself on the roof of his cabin nailing down shingles on the front side, while George tackled the back. A similar team of men was at the opposite end of the roof. With a bird's-eye view of the virtual army that had invaded his property, Jared blocked the noonday glare of the sun with his hand to his brow to glance at the work in the fields. The front ten acres of land had been covered with compost and cow manure and were now being plowed under. He shook his head in amazement and nailed down another shingle.

A cacophony of noises filled the air. Directly below and inside the cabin, Ansel and Garth were supervising several of the laborers who were setting the floorboards into place. Ezra stood watch over the supplies, carefully checking them off a list as they were used, while teams of three men each set glass windows into the log walls. Nearby, the women were preparing a noon meal, and the breeze carried the sweet aromas of roasting meats and the sound of laughing children at play while they collected more wood for the open fires.

George leaned back on his haunches and wiped the sweat pouring from his forehead into his eyes. He grinned at Jared. "This full community effort is sure paying off. You might even get to sleep here tonight. I'd think about staying on with you, but Sadie is waiting for me. She was disappointed to be stuck minding the store."

Jared took one more hit on a nail head and paused to take a rest with George. "You and I will both be back tonight. Maybe I can settle in permanently in a night or two. The cabin itself will be done today, but the stove won't be in place by nightfall."

George laughed. "It's being set up as we speak. A couple of big, brawny Irishmen just carried it inside."

"Already? What about the floorboards?"

"All done except the sleeping room. Good thing you had the bed delivered," George teased. "There are enough single women here today to keep it filled for nearly a week." He winked at Jared. "What the good reverend don't know won't hurt him any."

"No, but it just might ruffle a few concerned fathers," Jared joked. "I never was one to favor facing a loaded shotgun. Guess we'd best get back to work before we look like laggards."

He quickly scanned the area around the house looking for the one woman he would ever want in his bed. Emilee had spent most of the morning with the other women while her husband had stayed home to prepare his sermon for tomorrow's meeting. Randall had arrived only a short time ago.

He pulled out a half dozen nails from the pouch around his waist, clamped them between his teeth, and nailed them into the shingles one at a time. Wet nails would rust quicker and hold tighter. Maybe if he had had a rusty nail last night to hold his tongue, he would have gotten a decent night's rest instead of worrying about his conversation with Emilee.

She had slipped through his defenses so easily, he had nearly told her why he objected to the dedication. Fortunately for him, he had realized his mistake and rushed out of the study to the relative safety of his own chamber. He needed time alone to patch the hole in his heart which had allowed her to get far too close to his yearning for her and just as close to his secret.

He looked up and saw her now sitting with Nancy Walters and several other women, including his mother, under the shade of a tree. Each woman was sewing something pink. He nailed down another row of nails and pointed the women out to George. "What are they doing?"

George chuckled. "Making curtains or bedclothes, I'd reckon."

Jared scowled and hammered in another nail. "Curtains? *Pink* curtains?"

"You can't stop them from nesting, as my grandmother used to say. Every woman likes a cozy little nest. Just like birds, only a whole sight prettier."

Jared slammed the hammer on his thumb and yelped.

"Nervous, old friend?"

His thumb throbbed as hard as his heart pounded. His scowl deepened, and the set of his jaw tightened.

George looked at him and burst out laughing. "It's better not to fight it. Just relax. Your mother will be there to protect you and make sure not a one of those lonely single women sets her cap for you without your mother's approval."

"My mother," Jared gritted as he attempted to aim the hammer without slamming it into his thumb again, "won't be here. She's moving in with the widowed twins, remember?"

"That gives you triple protection. You may need it, from the looks of some of those women, especially Julia Prack and her mother. How'd you get so lucky?"

Jared glared at him and immediately dismissed using the same ploy he had used earlier with his mother when she had tried to convince him it was time to look for a wife. His thumb hurt too much for him to be anything but blunt. "I'm not interested in getting married. Not now. Not tomorrow. Not ever. Maybe I should have you put up a sign in the store."

"Give it up, man. Get yourself hitched like the rest of us. The womenfolk won't give you any peace till you do," George responded with a shrug of his shoulders and went back to work.

As far as Jared was concerned, there was only one woman he wanted to marry. Unfortunately, she was already married to someone else. He turned and looked around until he saw Randall by the dwindling stack of supplies. He was talking with Ezra. Dressed formally with his Geneva lace collar white enough to reflect sunlight, Randall obviously did not intend to do any manual labor today. Big surprise.

Jared pounded at the nails with a vengeance. Even if he admitted he disliked the man because he coveted the man's wife, Jared could not shake away a number of annoying inconsistencies in the Reverend Mr. Randall Greene. Despite fairly rigid training at Yale, he depended on his wife to write one sermon that Jared knew of and to prompt him while preaching—at least once—although Jared suspected it had not been the first time.

Even more to the point, the man had not been able to recall a single tutor Jared had mentioned the day they had inspected the property. Had the man even attended Yale? Jared had his doubts. Were they valid?

"Jealousy breeds contempt," he grumbled as he finished another line of shingles and faced the truth. His father would have checked and double-checked the man's credentials before inviting him to preach at meeting and recommending him to the Board of Elders as his replacement.

Finding himself faced with a stalemate just as frustrating as the proposed church dedication, Jared could resolve this one quickly. With a short letter to his partner, Will Cooper, in New York City, Jared could have the minister's credentials and background verified. If he was not mistaken, Will's brother had followed him to Yale and would have been there around same time as Randall.

It would be easy enough for Will to check with his brother discreetly as a matter of curiosity rather than anything else. If Jared was wrong about Randall, he could dismiss his suspicions and accept the fact they had no basis in fact and indeed had been prompted by Jared's very real wish the man did not even exist.

"Enough!" George laid down his hammer and sniffed the air. "Smells ready to me." He looked over to his left and smiled. "Tables are full of food. Ready to eat?"

Jared nodded. "You take the ladder first. I'll follow you down." He waited until George was on the ground before starting down the ladder steps, but his mind was still preoccupied with Randall. By investigating the minister, Jared very well might trip and fall straight down to hell's gateway, but he would know for sure if the minister in the pulpit now actually deserved to be there. If Jared was wrong about the man who had taken his father's place, no one would ever have to know. If he was even close to being right . . .

He reached solid ground and stepped away from the ladder convinced he had become totally obsessed with anything remotely connected to his father. Or to Emilee. He followed George around the cabin to wash up at the stream and dismissed his thoughts about investigating Randall as nothing more than a waste of time more wisely spent opposing the church dedication.

Laden with food, three makeshift tables lined up end to end had been set up under the trees on the north side of the cabin. Emilee took a place at the end next to several other women along one side, while the men and children formed a line at the opposite end. They would file along the table, and the women would fill their plates with food. At the head of the table standing next to Jared, Randall stretched his arms out in front of him, palms up, and raised his face to the heavens. On cue, boisterous conversations ceased, and after a nudge or two, even the children grew quiet.

"Heavenly Father," he prayed. "Thou art merciful and just, giving all who come to Thee love and protection. We thank You today for Thy presence among us and for the gift of Christian fellowship which has opened our hearts and brought us together to help one of Your own. We thank You for the bright sunshine which warms us as we work. We thank You for the earth's bounty which will strengthen our bodies for our earthly lives and for the Word which will help purify our souls to make us worthy of eternal salvation. In Jesus' name, we pray. Amen."

"Amen," she whispered, joining her voice with a chorus of others which rose from the assembled crowd.

Beaming, Randall scanned the faces of the volunteers. "Jared would like to say a word or two before we eat."

A collective groan accompanied a few good-natured shouts and taunts. "Keep it short, Burke. Food's a-waitin'."

"Take too long and we'll never get the cabin finished!"

"If you're half as long-winded as your father, the food will be frozen before we get to it."

Laughing, Jared held up his hand. "Only a few remarks. On my word."

While the crowd settled into some semblance of quiet, Emilee looked at Jared. With Mercy on her immediate left, followed by Olivia, Mrs. Prack, her daughter Julia, and Hester Woerner, Emilee was close enough to see Jared's face clearly, but far enough away to avoid any speculation she was studying him instead of her husband.

Gratitude and joy had replaced the bitterness she had heard in his voice last night. A full and genuine smile lit his features, but she still detected a haunting look in his eyes. At least he looked more rested, in spite of his toil today. She would have given anything to be able to further their conversation of Wednesday night, but there were too many ears and eyes around today to risk a private conversation.

Not that she really should try. With his shirtsleeves rolled to his elbows and his tight work jeans, he was the image of sheer masculine strength. Added to his dark, appealing looks, he exuded a near-fatal dose of pure physical temptation that left her breathless.

"Ladies and gentlemen. My friends," he began. "I want to thank you all for coming and helping me."

"Amen!" George shouted from his place first in line. "Now let's eat!"

Jared hurled an exaggerated scowl at him. "I wasn't finished."

"Yes, you were. You thanked us like you should. And you're welcome." He spun around to face the rest of the men in the line. "So that's that, folks. Right? Just say 'you're welcome' to the nice man so we can eat."

When they shouted, "You're welcome," George turned around, grinned at Jared, and started the line moving along the table.

Shaking his head, Jared bent down to listen to something Randall was saying and nodded. Too far away to hear their conversation, Emily was quickly engaged in ladling out bubbly beans baked in molasses on the volunteers' plates already overflowing with slabs of roasted pork and beef, a variety of cold relishes women had donated from their pantries, and potatoes baked in the coals of the open fires. She stopped occasionally to swat away recalcitrant bees who invited themselves to the feast, and chatted with many of her friends.

By the time Randall and Jared approached at the end of the line, she had sticky fingers and streaks of molasses up to her wrists, not to mention a few wayward beans sticking to the cuffs of her sleeves, and the boards around the bean pot were puddled with sticky spills that attracted more of the pesky insects.

She stole a quick glance up at Randall to see if she had time to clean up a bit and noticed she was a sad sight indeed compared to the other women, who were as neat as when they had started. Olivia was putting several slices of beef on his plate, and it was too late for Emilee to do more than shake the beans from her cuffs by the time Randall stood in front of her.

He held out his plate, took one look at the mess she had made of the table and herself, and leaned toward her. "Can't you find a cloth at least to wipe your face?"

Recoiling from his harsh whisper, she reached up to her face with her free hand and felt a sticky streak of molasses on her cheek. Hands trembling, she sat aside her ladle and used the hem of her apron to wipe at her cheek. "I'm—I'm sorry. I've been battling a pesky bees," she murmured. A heated flush stole up her neck and made her cheeks burn as she quickly ladled beans onto his plate.

Before he could say anything more, Jared held out his plate. "The beans smell good and look even better. Hope they taste as good as they look."

She blinked back a tear and dropped her gaze, only to find herself studying the scratches he had gotten on his arms from battling Troubles, but had nearly healed. Mercy spoke up before Emilee had a chance to find her voice. "Judith made them for today," she said, her voice low enough to keep Judith or her mother from overhearing. "Wonderful cook and neat as they come, just like her mother. Born well and raised well," she pronounced, apparently following the advice in Randall's sermon to turn her gift for hurtful gossip into praise.

Emilee flinched, amazed at how skillfully Mercy had managed to do both and had chosen very specific words of praise for Judith that subtly highlighted Emilee's faults. She stole a glance at Jared while she ladled beans onto his plate.

He looked straight at Mercy and grinned. "I'll be sure to keep that in mind if I run into a man looking for a wife. I'm afraid my heart already belongs to Rose," he quipped, nudging his plate for Emilee to add another ladle of beans.

Mercy furrowed her brow and cocked her head to the side. "Rose? Do we have anyone named Rose hereabouts, Olivia?"

He turned his head slightly to wink at Emilee without anyone else seeing him, she hoped, and realized no one else but Randall knew the name Jared used for Troubles.

"Don't pay him any mind," Olivia warned as she cast her son a warning glance which prompted Emilee to stifle the giggle about to burst from her lips. "He's trying to tell you he's married to his work raising roses. He did the very same thing to me just this morning. I told him he'd regret spending all his time planting and growing roses without making room in his life for a family."

Mercy's face turned as red as the silk flower pinned to the collar of her dress. She huffed and tilted up her chin. "It's not natural for a man to be alone," she mumbled, casting a glance at Emilee that cut through any notion she might have had that Randall's sermon had truly touched the woman's heart or eased her wicked suspicions about Emilee and Jared.

"And it's not polite to tease your elders," his mother added firmly.

"And for that, I'm truly sorry, ladies," he said quickly. "Especially since you've all worked so hard today on my behalf. It just seems as though everyone I talked to today has been almighty worried about my personal affairs."

Randall watched the exchange without commenting, but Emilee could tell from the set of his jaw he was not pleased by the frivolous banter which involved his wife even to a subtle degree.

"Eventually you'll change your mind," Mercy announced. "You'll need a good and faithful wife by your side and children to carry on your name. The Good Book tells us all to 'go forth and multiply.' Isn't that right, Reverend Greene?"

Randall paled and clutched his plate to his chest. "I'm certain that particular passage refers not to marriage and procreation, but rather to spreading the Gospel and increasing the fold of true believers in Christ. You do raise an interesting interpretation, however. Perhaps I can have your permission to pursue it further with prayer and focus on the subject in one of my sermons."

"Sounds like a good idea to me," Jared commented and raised his plate to point at an empty shady spot nearby. "Why don't you ladies fix something for yourselves to eat while Reverend Greene and I wait for you over there?"

Mercy seemed placated enough by Randall's compliment to agree. While she and Olivia started to the head of the table for plates and the men left with their platters full, Emilee excused herself to freshen her appearance. Jared's kindness and sense of humor had softened her husband's reprimand, but she did not want to embarrass Randall any more than she already had.

Leaving the crowd of volunteers occupied with their meals, she walked around the cabin and down to the wide stream that flowed behind it. The air felt cooler here, and she sat down on a patch of moss near the bank. She closed her eyes. Soft breezes caressed her face and the sound of the gentle current gradually soothed away the rest of her hurt and disappointment in her husband.

Randall was stuck on formality and propriety most of the time, and she often fell short of his high expectations. With Olivia leaving within the next few days, Emilee would once again have to strike a balance between her many duties as the minister's wife and keeping an impeccable house for her husband. She had a feeling Randall's headaches, in part, might be caused by her inadequacies, which only added another layer of guilt to her already heavy burden.

She laid her right hand on top of her left to say a quick prayer that she might be a better wife. Seconds later, she felt a series of sharp stings on her hands and cried out. Her eyes snapped open, and she batted away a trio of bees caught between her hands as they feasted on her as well as the sweet, sticky residue she had not yet washed off.

She cried out again as yet another bee stung her left palm. Close to panic, she leaned forward and plunged both of her hands into the cold stream. The pain from the multiple stings filled her eyes with tears that cascaded down her cheeks. Taking big gulps of air, she trailed her hands through the water, praying the cold would help to lessen the pain.

"Emilee?"

Her heart leaped into her throat, and she choked back a cry when she turned her head and saw Jared standing at the corner of the cabin. "I'm—I'm almost finished. I'll join everyone in just a . . . just a minute."

He studied her for a moment and started walking toward her. "Is anything wrong?"

Battling the throbbing pain, she could not find her voice.

"Randall was worried about you."

His voice was louder as he drew closer, and she tried to wipe her cheeks against her shoulders before he could see she was crying. "I'm fine," she insisted.

He reached the stream bank and stooped down beside her. Shoulders slumped, she pulled her hands from the water. Two angry red welts puffed the back of her right hand alongside the faint scratches left from her attempts to free the kitten from the brier rose, and she quickly turned her hand palm up.

He grabbed her hand and turned it over. "You have to get the stingers out," he said as he propped her hand on his knee.

After he deftly removed both stingers, she offered him her other hand and turned the palm up. "I think there might be one here, too."

He held her palm up close to inspect it and shook his head.

"That one's already out. What happened?" he asked as he scooped up some mud and packed it on both of her hands.

She sniffed. "I guess I was woolgathering and wasn't paying any attention."

"It'll hurt like tarnation for a few hours, but by tomorrow you'll only be good and sore. Just hold still for a few more minutes and let the mud packs do their work." His voice was low and soothing, and his gaze was tender. So very, very tender. Her heart felt like it had lodged in her throat. Her lips tingled and ached. She trembled. "Jared," she whispered, frightened more by the sensations that were crashing through her body than by the prospect that someone might see them alone together. "I can't be here with you. I have to get—"

"Shhh. Just rest here another minute or two, then we'll wash off the mud and I'll take you back."

She struggled to get to her feet, but it was very awkward without the use of her hands. "I can't stay here with you," she argued as the pain numbed the back of her hand and her thoughts cleared. "People will talk. Randall—"

Jared put his hands around her waist and lifted her to her feet. "I'm just trying to help you. No one can fault either one of us for that," he countered as his hands lingered a bit on her waist to keep her steady.

"Emilee? Jared?"

Mercy's voice preceded her, and Emilee groaned. She heard the woman's footsteps and the swish of her skirts. "If anyone will find fault, she will," Emilee whispered as Jared quickly stepped away from her.

"Not again," he muttered under his breath. "The woman has the most annoying habits." He turned his head to the side and grinned. "She's like a swarm of bees at a picnic."

Emilee chuckled in spite of herself and held out her mud-covered hands as Mercy approached them. "Would you be so kind as to help me wash off the mud packs? Jared can go and tell Randall I've been stung."

Mercy braced to a halt and stared at Emilee's hands. "You're a mess! What did you say? You've been . . . what?"

"Stung," Jared repeated as he walked past her. "Bees. Be

careful. They seem to be swarming a lot back here by the stream.''

Mercy took a few tentative steps backward. "I'll go get Olivia. She'll know exactly what to do," she offered, then turned around and raced away, with her skirts revealing her ankles.

Emilee sighed and sank back down on the moss. At least Mercy would not be able to start any gossip about either Emilee or Jared this time, since Emilee at least had minor injuries to prove them both innocent. This time.

For both their sakes, there could not be another. If Emilee had any hope of helping Jared, she would have to find a way for them to be alone to talk. It was her only plan, but unless she was very careful, the injuries she sustained in the process could be fatal—to her marriage, to her reputation, and to her very soul.

SIXTEEN

Like a brand-new bow on an old bonnet, the sun slipped close to the brim of the earth, and ribbons of amber and shocking pink streaked the sky by the time the cabin was finished—inside and out. Almost all of the volunteers had left for home, but their generosity and kindness still whispered across the land and throughout the modest structure they had built together.

Jared guided his mother, the widowed twins Maryam and Roz, and their sister, Hester, on a final walk-through while Ansel waited outside to drive all the women back to the village. They crowded together in the sleeping chamber, which now held a double-sized bed covered by a quilt donated after the fire. The trunks he'd had shipped home from Europe, and which had arrived only days ago, lined the opposite wall. "Let's keep the tour moving," he teased as he ushered them all through a door which led to the rear of the main room in the cabin.

Directly ahead, a small cooking and eating area, complete with a small cupboard, a cookstove, and a table with benches, opened into a sitting room completely devoid of heavy furniture. For now, he had a single rocking chair placed by the front window. Another trunk, containing his books and copious notes made during his decade in Europe, served as a table for a kerosene lamp, and a potbellied stove along the outer wall would provide heat.

His mother and her friends chatted together as they walked through the room. She left the group to fuss with the gingham curtains on the window. "They do add a homey touch. Do you like them, Jared?"

"Love them," he muttered. "Did they have to be pink?"

The sisters all giggled, but his mother frowned. "Your father loved pink."

"Only for your gowns," Maryam reminded her friend.

"Or your nightdresses," Roz added.

His mother blushed. "That was when I was much younger."

"Ansel has been waiting a good while. Don't you think it's time to go?" Jared prompted, finding it awkward to watch his mother and her friends act like schoolgirls.

His mother sighed. "I suppose you're right. Are you sure you won't come back to the parsonage for tonight? You still have an empty cupboard and no wood cut for the stove. What will you do for food in the morning before you ride back to the village to take me to meeting?"

He groaned and patted his stomach. "I ate enough this afternoon to keep me content for a week."

"You'll be hungry in an hour," she argued.

"Then I'll just have to suffer through the leftovers from the picnic Julia packed for me. I think if you open the cupboard, you'll find enough food to tide me over till I get my supplies."

"Julia did?" She nudged Roz with her elbow and grinned. "What a thoughtful young woman."

Maryam pouted. "She's not nearly as sweet as Melody Hughes or Emilee. I wonder how the poor girl is feeling."

His mother clucked and frowned. "I'm sure Randall is tending to her. He seemed very concerned and attentive."

"For a change," Maryam snorted. She looked directly at Jared, her eyes twinkling with devilment. "What exactly did you two do to Mercy? She came running back from the stream faster than she ever ran races at the Fourth of July celebrations when she was a girl."

Hester giggled. "Didn't even take care to keep her ankles decently covered."

Jared put his hand over his heart and feigned a shocked look. "We didn't do anything. Emilee just asked Mercy to help her wash off the mud packs, and I—"

His mother cut him off with a scowl. "You scared her half to death. Swarming bees! Jared, you really shouldn't tease

Mercy. The way she told the story to Julia and her mother, there was a whole hive ready to attack Mercy next.''

"Sure would be a bigger feast than they found on Emilee. Lots more meat. Too bad a few couldn't sting her gossiping lips.''

"Maryam!'' his mother exclaimed. "What an unkind thing to say.''

"You're right. And it probably was not Jared's doing at all. More than likely, Mercy didn't want to get her hands dirty helping Emilee. Now that Ezra's built her that fine mansion, she fashions herself a lady of refinement.''

Jared started to chuckle, and he began to understand why his mother had decided to live with her friends. None of them ever would spend a single moment being lonely or bored. They would bicker and banter, reminisce and gossip together, and through it all they would have one another as friends.

The front door opened, and Ansel stepped inside. "I got tired of waiting outside,'' he grumbled. Reed-thin, with joints gnarled by age and cracked, weathered skin, he looked very much like a skinny old tree trunk. "Were you ladies planning to leave now, or did you want to ride home in the dark?''

Hester nodded to her husband. "I think we're ready now. We were just talking—''

"Keep talking, then. I want to talk to Jared for a short bit. I had an idea while I was waiting. Give us ten minutes and we'll meet you by the wagon.''

Curious, Jared followed Ansel outside and around the wagon. They walked together, passing the old outbuildings before reaching the edge of the plowed and fertilized fields. Ansel took a good heavy whiff of air. "Nothing smells as good as freshly turned earth,'' he said nostalgically.

Resisting the urge to follow suit, Jared chuckled. "How long will the smell of manure be . . . well, overpowering?''

Ansel twisted his lips and narrowed his gaze. "Maybe a week. A good soaking rain will help. It's coming, too. I'd bet my aching bones on it. In the meantime, I have something I'd like to discuss with you.''

Immediately suspecting some sort of chicanery or advice, Jared nodded for the older man to continue.

Ansel let out a deep sigh. "I'm getting older, son. With Michael and Philip gone, there's no one to take over my orchards. I've got maybe five good working years left before I sell out and get a smaller place with just enough of an orchard to keep me amused."

Jared swallowed hard. He vaguely remembered Ansel's two sons, but he would never forget the double funeral in which a grieving community had buried the two men who had given their lives for the cause in the War of 1812.

"The land's prime for growing apples, and I've made a good life for myself and Hester," he continued. "It's situated damn close to the canal, which should open up within a couple of years now. I'll get more than a fair price for the land, but I don't expect the orchards will stay. Some factory or such will yield better profits."

"You're probably right," Jared murmured. He had already met with Ezra about investing in land bordering the canal before prices soared any higher, and he knew many farmers would be selling their farms. He had not expected Ansel to be one of them, and it seemed odd to think the apple trees grafted with three varieties of apples, which had become a local landmark along the roadway, would one day disappear.

"Progress hurts some folks more than others," Ansel noted. "I've spent my whole life experimenting and perfecting my trees." He stopped to clear his throat. "Now, here's where I get to make a proposal. Think it over and don't you hesitate for more than a minute or two to turn it down flat if you don't like it."

"That's a promise."

Ansel pointed to the stands of trees on either side of the cabin. "I'd like to think my trees will be here a good long while after I'm gone, just like those trees over there. So . . . I was just thinking about that when I was sitting outside waiting for the ladies. You've got a lot of land here, and I expect it'll be a number of years before you use more than half of it for your nursery. If you don't object, over the next few years, I'd like to transplant some of my best saplings, build you a fine orchard, teach you what I've learned over the past forty years.''

He turned and looked up at Jared. ''Hester keeps warning me about a selfish streak, and I guess she's right. I'm not trying to take your father's place, mind you, but if I'm going to be honest, I'd sure like to think of you as my son. Maybe you even could keep my trees alive for a bit. I sorta favor the idea of keeping my memory alive.''

Emotion choked the breath out of Jared's lungs. His heart pumped so fast and so hard he could hear it pounding in his ears. Standing before him was a man Jared had always admired as a rather humorous eccentric, but he saw him now as the epitome of the kind of man he had always wanted his father to be. Jared had hidden the shattered bonds between himself and his father from everyone except his mother, and Ansel's offer reached deep inside his spirit to give him something far more precious than an orchard. He offered Jared a legacy of decency that might someday blossom and bear the fruit of his own redemption. ''I'd be honored,'' he managed and watched in awe as relief and joy washed a good ten years off of Ansel's age.

Ansel straightened his bent back and stood a bit taller, and his handshake was as firm as Jared's. ''I won't be in the way, at least most of the time. Have you got any plans for Monday?''

Jared cocked his head. ''If I'm not mistaken, I'm going to be starting an orchard and planting trees.''

He was rewarded with a grin. ''Not just any trees, no sir. They're the best trees in the whole state of New York. Let's head back now and get those women in the wagon,'' he suggested. ''The sun's dipping pretty fast.''

As they walked back together, Ansel started describing exactly which varieties needed to be transplanted first and how he would carefully select each sapling, and Jared could only wonder at the amazing transformation of his life in the span of a few weeks.

His good fortune, however, was as deceiving as a beautiful

rose which hid its thorns behind lush foliage and exacted a costly price for those who dared try to pick the fragrant blossom. Once a loner, he was now surrounded with friends and neighbors, and he had been reunited with his mother. Opening his heart to accept their regard and his mother's love only quickened his guilt for concealing the truth about his father. Still torn by the need to stop the church dedication, he had agreed to attend the elders' meeting Wednesday evening and had accepted an invitation from Ezra to consider joining the Surrey Canal Association, which met next on Thursday night.

Still, there was no greater hurt than having learned to love one very special, but unattainable woman. Like the blossom of a rose, his love for Emilee was very dangerous and nearly impossible to share with her without inflicting pain. With a future both promising and grim, he faced the years ahead realistically, with no small measure of disappointment, and one very small hope he would someday look back and see his life had turned out very differently from what he anticipated now.

Blessed with a few hours alone, Emilee sat by the window in her chamber to catch the waning daylight, with her sewing basket at her feet and the sampler for Olivia on her lap. Her good intentions to complete the sampler tonight, however, quickly dissipated into wishful thinking.

The angry red welts on her hands, which had paled to white lumps, had become more annoying and sore than painful, but after attempting only a few stitches, her hands began to throb. Disappointed, she folded the sampler into a square, set it aside on the windowsill, and poked the needle back into a pincushion.

Rested after a brief nap, which Randall had insisted upon after he had brought her home, she decided to tackle a less demanding project. She did not have to look far for something to do. She reached into the sewing basket and lifted out a tangled ball of sewing threads dyed every color found in nature. She probably should not have started the sampler without sorting through the threads and separating the colors, but as usual, she had simply plunged ahead. Now that she had nothing else to do, she decided to make amends and backtrack while Troubles was sleeping in the next chamber with Randall, who had gone to bed early to be rested for meeting tomorrow.

She placed both feet flat on the floor, made a table of her lap, and placed the multicolored ball in the valley between her legs. Working slowly, she managed well enough, and within half an hour, intervals of different-colored threads draped over the flat arms on her wooden chair and decorated her lap. When she encountered a knot, she simply snipped it with her scissors, salvaged what she could, and saved the waste to serve as stuffing for a future pincushion.

Less than halfway done, she paused to rest her hands, feeling very much like she was perched in the middle of an artist's palette. Hues of purple and blue hung on the left side of the chair, brown and black threads lay opposite white, yellow, and beige ones on her lap, and colors ranging from soft pink through deep red striped the right arm of the chair.

She sighed, wishing it was as easy to sort through her tangled thoughts and feelings as it was to separate the sewing threads. Oddly, she found by using a little imagination she actually could see the colors of her life spread around her. In the dark shades to her left, she saw the difficult and painful years of her early childhood; to her right, the brighter hues symbolized her life after coming to live with the Burkes, her conversion, and her acceptance by the community.

If she stitched a sampler representing her life, she would need to use threads of every color, and she quickly rethought her idea for Olivia. Emilee closed her eyes, let her imagination run through her feelings for Olivia, and immediately envisioned a far different design than the one she had already stenciled. Instead of using a verse from Genesis stitched in dark colors, she would cross-stitch the image of the meeting house below a joyful Psalm using lots of pastels.

Intrigued by her sudden burst of creativity and insight, she opened her eyes, took a pencil and a small slip of paper out of her sewing basket, and wrote down several ideas for Psalms and soft colors that should accent each one. When her hands started to protest, she set the paper and pencil aside.

Rather impressed with herself, she sat back and contemplated the two men who occupied most of her thoughts lately: her husband and her temptation. What colors did each man inspire in her thoughts and imagination?

She thought about her husband and pictured him in her mind, immediately fingering the black and brown threads because he was so somber and serious. An inflexible and formal man, he saw life as duty and responsibility, but had little time for joy or fun, a sure reflection of a man whose early life as an orphan had colored his inner qualities and his perspective on life. She gazed longingly at the brighter colors to her right, and her mind instantly created Jared's image. Strong but vulnerable, intense yet witty and charming, he was a vibrant man. His complex personality fascinated her as much as his dark, rugged features. He demanded hues of nearly every color, which would also represent his struggle with his own humanity.

With a sigh that came from deep inside of her spirit, she put her imagination to rest, picked up the tangled ball of thread, and resumed her task. Tomorrow, Jared would return briefly for the rest of his belongings, and Olivia would move in with the widowed twins. Emilee and Randall would resume their normal, day-to-day lives, and she could not help but wonder what the future held—for all of them.

Only the good Lord knew His plans for their lives, and she would turn all her worries over to Him at meeting tomorrow. For tonight, she would simply concentrate on doing all she could with one very stubborn, tangled mess of sewing thread and try not to think about a very tall man with dark wavy hair, pale gray eyes, and a smile that could light up a woman's troubled soul.

SEVENTEEN

Jared woke up late on Wednesday morning, pulled the curtains aside, glanced out the window to confirm his suspicions, and groaned. As much as he appreciated a soaking rain to help dissipate the manure's odor and to water the ten saplings he and Ansel had transplanted on Monday, he did not relish an hour's ride into the village later today to have supper with his mother and attend the elders' meeting scheduled for its normal hour of seven o'clock.

Relegated to indoor work for the entire day, and possibly several more if he judged the storm correctly as a northeaster, he rolled out of bed. After setting a fresh pot of coffee to heat on the cookstove, he ambled back to his chamber to dress. After a mad dash to one of the old outbuildings that still served well enough as a barn, he fed and watered his horse. He was drenched by the time he got back, and the welcome smell of coffee filled the cabin. He changed, poured a mug to the rim with hot coffee, and added extra sugar to make up for having no milk.

He drank cautiously as he carried the mug to the sitting room and set the beverage down on the trunk, careful to avoid the stack of wooden planks and tools he had stored inside last night, anticipating the rain. He lit the kerosene lamp, tugged the curtains aside to add a little daylight, and added wood to the stove to cut the damp chill.

Within a few hours, he had a single shelf containing his notes and books running above a crude bench along the longest outer wall that would serve double duty. At the far end, near the front window, the bench would serve as a desk; the opposite end near the potbellied stove would be his workbench, where he now temporarily stored his diagrams for the nursery.

He checked the weather again. The rain remained steady and thick. Low cloud cover convinced him he would have the rare privilege of riding in the rain again tomorrow night for the Canal Association meeting. His mother's invitation to stay overnight occasionally in a spare chamber in the twins' home suddenly sounded appealing, and he decided to pack a small travel bag just in case he needed to accept her offer later tonight.

He pulled a sitting bench from the kitchen to his desk and sat down to unroll the plans for the proposed plaque even though he had every word memorized. The words and phrases had been running through his head every day since he had read them for the first time and echoed in his dreams at night, but he was no closer to putting a stop to the church dedication than a week ago when he had first learned of the idea at the elders' meeting. With a heavy sigh, he stared at the precise lettering:

THIS HOUSE OF WORSHIP
IS DEDICATED TO
THE REVEREND MR. BENJAMIN BURKE
1760–1834
FOUNDING MINISTER OF THE
FIRST CHURCH OF SURREY

THAT ALL WHO ENTER HERE TO WORSHIP
MAY REMEMBER A HUMBLE MAN ALWAYS
FAITHFUL TO HIS CALLING, HIS FAMILY,
AND THE WORD.

DEDICATED ON THIS _____ DAY OF _____
IN THE YEAR OF OUR LORD 1834

"FOR WE LIVE BY FAITH, NOT BY SIGHT."
I CORINTHIANS 5:7

Bile soured his mouth, but short of inserting a date after the Final Judgment, he had no idea how to stop the dedication without destroying his mother and shaking the faith of the entire community. Pressured with only a week left before he had to give the Board of Elders his final approval, he had never felt greater disdain or deeper resentment for his father.

His mind traveled back in time, and he relived the worst day of his life, but he was just as unsuccessful now in his attempt to alter the events of that fateful day as he had been countless times in the past. Guilt, ugly and pervasive, deepened his legacy of shame. His breathing quickened and grew ragged. With a snarl of frustration, he rolled the paper tight and shoved it onto the bookshelf, but it was not as easy to erase his memories.

With his every thought embroiled, he paced around the cabin like a hungry panther chained just out of reach of a victim of prey. Afraid he could not affect the future any more effectively than he could change the past, he stormed to his chamber and packed a small travel bag. After securing the inside of the cabin, he donned an oilcloth poncho and a wide-brimmed hat before he braved the elements and headed to the barn to saddle his horse.

With any luck, an hour's ride in the pouring rain would soak clear through his body and douse the seething embers of guilt and shame in his soul, allowing him to think rationally and bring an end to an odyssey that was as long and painful as it was lonely.

For the first half hour, Emilee tried not to envision the worst, but as the minutes continued to drag on, she admitted defeat. She got up from her seat and paced back and forth across the parlor. Wringing her hands until they ached, her heartbeat shifted from a mild thumping to wild pounding. She paced faster, and her rustling skirts fairly crackled.

Not a sound drifted down from the upstairs chamber, and her mind raced with a number of scenarios soon to develop. None of them were good. In the space of a few days, her life had been upended and swirled out of control as if she had been shoved headlong into a raging river. Totally helpless, she was at the mercy of a strong current that pulled her under and left her gasping for air and frantically searching for a lifeline.

A door creaked. Muffled footsteps walked down the hallway overhead.

She ran to the foot of the front staircase, caught her breath, and held it as she waited for him to appear in sight, just as she had done for the past three days. She did not know how much longer she could win the battle against the fear of the unknown. Maybe now. Maybe this time she would have some sort of answer from the man who held her fate and her husband's life in his hands.

Dr. Pounds started down the staircase, and she frantically searched his face as he descended. Fear tapped an erratic dance through her body. Her mouth went dry, and she prayed she could bear the news about Randall with dignity and courage.

As soon as Dr. Pounds reached her, he put his arm around her shoulders and led her back into the parlor. "Sit. Before I have another patient to worry about," he ordered, but his voice was weary.

Overwrought, she sat down on an upholstered settee, but perched nervously on the edge of the seat. She folded her hands together on her lap to keep them from trembling and tried to calm down enough to prepare herself to hear the worst.

Shortly after Jared and his mother had moved out on Sunday, Randall had gotten a headache more severe than any he had ever had before. Suffering with intense, blinding pain and blurred vision, he had vomited several times before allowing her to summon Dr. Pounds. Now, three days later, Randall remained bedridden, unable to take solid nourishment, to tolerate the slightest sound, or to bear more than the barest of light.

Dr. Pounds sat down beside her and covered her hands to squeeze them briefly. "He's not resting very comfortably, but I wanted to talk to you before I gave him any laudanum."

She swallowed a lump of fear. "What about his vision?"

"The blurring has cleared for now, but his headache remains quite severe."

Tears welled in her eyes and spilled down her cheeks. "I thought the eyedrops were working."

He shook his head. "So did I. Apparently Randall knew they did little to help him, but he didn't tell either of us. He was relying on prayer, but . . ."

"Isn't there something you can do?" she argued.

He sighed, and his eyes filled with regret. "I'm almost at a total loss. He should have gone to New York City to consult with the specialist in person months ago, but Randall adamantly refused to go and still won't consider it. Can't you talk to him and convince him he's got no other choice?"

She wiped the tears from her cheeks. "I've tried, but he only gets angry and starts to rant. . . . I was afraid I was only making him worse." She turned to face him and gripped his hand. "Please. There must be something you can try. Anything you do has to be better than just watching him suffer day after day."

His eyes glistened and filled with sympathy. "I'm a country doctor, Emilee. I deliver babies, set bones, and stitch folks up from time to time, and this is well beyond me. I've done everything the specialist recommended—"

"Please," she whispered.

He squeezed her hand, stood up, and began to walk back and forth with his hands behind his back. Deep in thought for several moments, he stopped abruptly. "There was a case I read about. I don't know the particulars, and I'm not even sure—"

"What is it?" she prompted, her heart now more hopeful than afraid.

"I read an account in one of the New York papers about a stage actress. I forget her name. Her husband was her manager and agent. They've since resettled in France, I believe." He paused and his gaze grew distant for several seconds before he shook his head and continued. "As I recall, her husband suffered from severe headaches, and they originally traveled to Europe seeking medical help after failing here. He was cured, eventually, but it took several months of complete rest in bed."

Hope briefly dipped into despair and sprung back again. "Is that all that was done? Just complete rest in bed?"

"Not at all," Dr. Pounds explained. "He had to have his room altered. No light at all, either natural or artificial, and he needed quiet. I believe he could tolerate some hushed conversation, but nothing more, and certainly no visitors under any circumstances."

"But he was cured? He recovered fully?"

The doctor nodded. "It's unconventional, to say the least, and I'm not even sure their conditions are the same. If I'm wrong, or Randall's condition is rooted in a different cause . . ."

"We have to try," she urged. "If it doesn't work, then maybe Randall will see he has no other choice than to go to the city to consult the specialist. Will you help me to tell him what needs to be done?" she asked, knowing there was a great deal more at stake than just using a very long and questionable course of treatment to restore Randall's health.

If he agreed to the treatment, he would have to notify the church membership through the Board of Elders. Since he served at their will, they could decide to replace him temporarily or even permanently. His ministry was his life, and she was his helpmate, but she could not perform his duties. Although he could always seek an appointment with another church, it would be difficult given his precarious health and his insecurity about his abilities. She pleaded with Dr. Pounds with a gaze filled with tears.

He held his hand on her elbow and helped her to her feet. "If you'll come back upstairs with me, I'll tell him about the treatment, but only on the condition I can try once more to convince him to go to the specialist. If he still refuses, I need to explain there's no guarantee this treatment will work."

"It has to work," she whispered, "especially if we have everyone praying for him. It has to work because it simply must." Without his health fully restored, Randall could have no ministry or any other means to support himself. He was too proud to permit her to work and support them both, however poorly, and he would never permit them to accept charity.

"It has to work," she repeated as Dr. Pounds led her upstairs to Randall's chamber, already planning the changes she would have to make to his chamber to put the treatment into effect and the alterations in her daily routine that would allow her to nurse him back to health. Randall had forbidden her or Dr. Pounds to tell anyone about his worsened condition, but now she had no choice but to disobey him. She needed help, and whether Randall approved or not, she was going to ask for it.

The twin widows shared a comfortable two-story frame home off Main Street within sight of the town square. In dour spirits, Jared had arrived soaked to the skin, changed and stored his travel bag in the guest chamber, and toured the spacious home and the two rooms his mother now occupied before taking supper with the three women. On edge anticipating the elders' meeting, he tolerated the afternoon chatter, which invariably or inevitably concerned his father, with bristled patience.

More cautious than concerned about the subject of the private conversation his mother had requested, he now took a seat in one of two cushioned chairs set before a marble fireplace in a room far more elegantly decorated than his cabin or even the parsonage.

Embossed white linen paper covered the high-ceilinged walls, and a thick wool carpet in a deep shade of forest green accented the golden upholstered chairs. A portrait of Maryam at sixteen hung over the mantel, and a pair of crystal lamps lit the room with a cheery glow.

Seated beside him, his mother looked rested and content as she gazed for a moment into the fire he had lit earlier to chase away the dampness. "I'm very proud of you," she murmured.

He chuckled. "So you've told me a dozen times today."

She laughed with him. "I can't help it. I love you, and I'm very proud of you. That's not to say I won't tell you when I think you're wrong," she admonished.

His heart began to pound. "Do you have something specific in mind, or is this just a general warning?"

"Something specific."

"I'm listening."

She smiled at him. "Good, because I only intend to say this once."

He managed a weak grin. "That's a relief."

"I want you to close my account at the bank."

He was almost too shocked to breathe. "Close your account? Why?"

"I don't need all that money," she argued. "It's almost embarrassing. Besides, you'll need that money for your nursery."

"I have more than I need," he countered and leaned close to whisper in her ear. "I'm rich, Mother. Very, very rich. Remember?"

She blushed and pushed him away. "So you've told me. More than once."

He chuckled. "Family trait. I inherited it from my mother, who absolutely refuses to let me share my good fortune with her. She won't let me build her a home of her own in the village, and now she won't let me keep a few funds in the bank for her to spend as foolishly or as outrageously as her heart desires. Tell me, what should I do with this woman? I'd give her anything."

Her smile turned devious. "Anything?"

"Name it," he challenged, hoping for once she would let him spoil her and shoving aside the absurd notion she deliberately had led him down this path of conversation.

She took a deep breath and stared into the fire. "Would you mind very much if I made a few suggestions for the plaque honoring your father?"

He bolted to his feet and literally choked. "The . . . the what?"

"The plaque," she repeated. "I know the board asked for your approval and any suggestions you might have. I thought we could discuss it together before you give them your final answer."

He dropped back into the chair and tossed his head back to stare at the ceiling. The fact that his mother knew about the church dedication and the plaque, despite the board's assumption otherwise, thoroughly complicated his intention to scuttle the whole idea.

"You said anything," she reminded him as she got up, walked across the room, and returned with a glass of water for him. "Now drink this down and try to get your wits back so we can talk."

He drank the water in a single gulp. "Just how do you know about the dedication and the plaque?"

She patted his shoulder and sat down next to him again. "I just know," she murmured as she gazed at him. "Just like I know every agenda, the every detail of their discussions, and all their decisions before they're ever announced."

He searched her eyes and knew he had little chance of stopping the dedication now. His heart slid down through his body so fast he was afraid he would find it thumping in his shoe.

"Don't worry, dear," she purred. "I'll act very, very surprised at the dedication. It's going to be lovely. I can't imagine being any prouder of your father than I am right now, but I will be on dedication day."

He could barely breathe, let alone think of what to say. "Maybe talking about the plaque isn't such a bad idea after all," he muttered to himself, knowing he would never be able to find a way to convince her not to support the dedication as easily as she had managed to drop an avalanche on the prevailing notion the dedication would be a total and complete surprise.

Better yet, he decided, he should exchange some of his old perceptions of his mother for new ones—either that or run the risk that she would outmaneuver him time and time again. How his father had managed to hoodwink this woman into believing he was a faithful husband was beyond imagination, but if Jared had any hope of convincing her the dedication was a bad idea, he would have to become more his father's son than his mother's, at least temporarily.

The very notion shook his soul.

Eighteen

With the same grit and determination Emilee had used to change her life from one of scandal to one of respectability, she vowed to turn failure into success.

Dr. Pounds had failed to convince Randall to see the specialist in the city, and Randall had begged her to help him remain in Surrey near his flock. With no other choice, she set to work to see that his treatment began immediately. With Dr. Pounds's help, she covered the two windows in her husband's chamber with heavy blankets, and the doctor took his leave after promising to stop daily about suppertime to check on Randall's progress.

While Randall dozed, she gathered a stack of fresh cloths to use as cold compresses Randall claimed helped to lessen the pain, and a supply of candles she would use instead of oil lamps to keep the light in his chamber as dim as possible, yet safe enough for her to move about.

She stored the items across the hall in the room Jared had occupied, and while she worked, she decided to sleep there as well. The doors to the two chambers were directly opposite one another, and she would be able to hear him better here if he should call out for her in the middle of the night than in her own chamber down the hall.

After stopping to check on her husband and make sure he was still asleep, she changed into a burgundy gown with a touch of lace at the collar and fixed her hair into a severe knot at the nape of her neck. She gathered up her hooded green cloak, put it on the seat of the oak settle by the front door, and climbed the front staircase to return to Randall's darkened chamber with a pitcher of fresh water, which she sat on the bed table.

Satisfied she had done everything to initiate Randall's treatment, she sat down in the high-backed cushioned chair Dr. Pounds had carried up from the parlor and positioned next to Randall's bed. She laid her head back and let the steady, gentle rhythm of the raindrops dancing on the roof overhead soothe her taut nerves. Gradually her tense muscles relaxed, and she had to fight to keep from drifting off to sleep.

"Emilee?"

She bolted upright and leaned forward to grip his outstretched hand, barely visible in the deeply shadowed room. "I'm here. Are you in pain?" she whispered, wishing she could see his face clearly to know for sure if he answered her honestly.

"No . . . no worse than before." When his hand began to tremble, she laid it back down on the bed. "Oh, Emilee," he murmured. His voice cracked, and he sounded as if his heart was breaking. "I'm . . . I'm so confused and so afraid. I don't understand why . . ." His words choked off. Had he begun to cry? She was not quite sure what was happening until the bed began to shake and the room echoed with his sobs.

Randall had never been a strong man. He had been unsure of himself, even self-deprecating at times, particularly where his abilities as a minister were concerned. With the exception of his occasional volatile outbursts, which she now attributed to the stress and severity of his illness, he had been a mild-spoken, very private man whose religious faith was the one constant in his entire existence.

No longer whole in either body or spirit, he was a broken man, and she was more frightened than she had been in her entire experience as his wife. She had helped to nurse men who were desperately ill. She had watched men die, but she had never heard a man cry like this before.

Silent tears trickled down her face, but she could not afford to be self-indulgent or weak. She had to be strong now—for both Randall and herself. She waited until his sobs subsided before she wiped his face with a cool cloth. "Hush," she murmured. "It's going to be all right. Please don't cry anymore. Have faith and trust in the Lord."

When his breathing grew more regular, he sighed. "You

don't understand. . . . All my prayers . . . my work . . . It's so unfair. The burden is too great for me to bear.''

She struggled to recall a passage from the Bible to help him. "Remember Psalm Fifty-five? 'Cast thy burden upon the Lord, and He shall sustain thee.' Please don't despair. He will help you, and I will be here for you, too," she promised and began to say a prayer out loud to soothe him.

He wept softly, but he did not join his voice to her prayer. He clung to her hand as she continued to pray, and when his hand went limp and his breathing more even, she realized he had fallen asleep.

Badly shaken, she stayed with him awhile and added a silent prayer he would remain asleep at least for a few hours. After adding yet another prayer for the success of his treatment, she tiptoed from the chamber and went downstairs.

More convinced than ever she had to proceed with the plan she had discussed with Dr. Pounds, she donned her cloak, pulled her hood tight around her head, and slipped out the front door. Gusts of wind blew at her cloak, and she stepped off the porch into a driving rain. She had only two stops to make, and she did not have far to go. As each hurried step carried her through the stormy night, she prayed with all her heart her husband would one day forgive her for what she now had to do.

By comparison, the drama of this elders' meeting fell far short of the last one. The same members of the board, with the exception of Reverend Greene, sat around the table in Traymore's office in what appeared to Jared to be assigned seats. His discussion with his mother still echoed in his mind. He was determined to avoid any discussion about the plaque, since he still had one week left before his decision was due, and he remained alert to forestall any attempt to turn the topic in his direction.

Following several recaps concerning the progress of construction on the new church and the announcement that the bell for the steeple tower would arrive before the end of October, Jared agreed to have his suggestions for the plaque, if any, by the following week as promised.

"That brings us to the final item," Traymore announced. "We have few options to consider for the old meetinghouse now that it appears certain the new church will be ready for services by mid-December. Frankly, gentlemen, I don't think we have any choice. Garth, have you been able to estimate the cost of moving the meetinghouse to the town square?"

An average-looking man with very pale blond hair, Garth Leigh had the shrewd eyes of a man born to be a banker. "I only have one bid, but it seems reasonable."

Heads nodded as he detailed the bid, and Traymore quickly took an official vote that ended up to be unanimous and binding, pending a courtesy discussion with the minister. While Traymore drew up a hasty document for Jared to present to the council, the men chatted among themselves.

Jared checked his pocket watch and allowed for perhaps ten more minutes before he could leave without seeming rude. He caught the sound of voices that seemed to be engaged in agitated conversation in the foyer just outside the office door. Moments later, the door burst open and Mercy stood in the doorway. With her eyes frantic and her face drawn, she looked like a sentry about to deliver the news the enemy had broken through the final line of defense and had launched a fatal siege.

"I tried to stop . . . I'm absolutely appalled," she spewed as blotches of red anger stained her cheeks. Chest heaving, she put her hands on her hips. "Ezra, you simply must excuse yourself and handle this . . . this . . ."

Even sputtered into silence, Mercy had the complete attention of everyone in the room, and Ezra abruptly rose from his seat and started toward his wife. "Calm down, Mercy. Can't you handle whatever it is until I finish? The meeting is still in progress."

Before Mercy could answer, the dark figure of a woman slipped inside the doorway and stepped in front of Mercy so quickly, she had little time to react. "No, I'm afraid she can't," the woman said firmly.

He recognized her voice even before she removed her

hooded green cloak to reveal her face and form, but he caught his breath the moment their eyes met. Emilee was paler and thinner than she had been only last Saturday. Faint circles under her eyes added a haunted look to her fragile features, but her eyes were bright and determined.

"You can't address the board. It's outrageous," Mercy spat. "You're not a member. Women aren't permitted—"

"I'm here to speak on my husband's behalf," Emilee said, shifting her gaze from Jared and speaking directly to the elders, while ignoring Mercy completely. With shoulders straight and head held high, Emilee kept her gaze steady.

Like the other men in the room, Jared was totally speechless. Unlike the others, however, he was absolutely enthralled by the stunningly assertive woman who defied convention in the very house the village gossip claimed as her domain. He quickly glanced at the other men and realized he was wrong. They were as mesmerized as he was. After several long, tense moments, he did not hesitate any longer. He got up and walked to the other end of the table and pulled out the chair her husband usually occupied.

She cast him a grateful look and handed her sodden cloak to Mercy, who accepted it by holding it with her fingertips as though the garment had been contaminated and abruptly stormed back out of the room and kicked the door closed behind her.

Emilee walked past Ezra and took her seat. His heart pounding, Jared returned to his chair and Traymore did the same, although Jared remained on the edge of his seat and waited for her to begin to explain her purpose for invading the male bastion of power within the church. With a drama set to begin that far exceeded his earlier expectations or assumptions, he had little doubt this meeting would be far more memorable than the last.

NINETEEN

Oddly calm now that she sat at the end of the table in the eye of yet another storm, Emilee gripped the sturdy arms of her chair. With her personal life battered by emotional upheaval and her gown and slippers drenched by the rainstorm, she moistened her lips and looked straight ahead into Jared's eyes.

He captured her gaze and held it, silently reaching out to her to offer support as well as encouragement. Like a beacon of light from shore, he held her course steady in a sea churning with possible scandal and disgrace, and her heart began to tremble.

Shivering from the cold and the fear of failure, she tensed her back and squared her shoulders before she addressed Ezra Traymore as the head of the Board of Elders. "With your indulgence," she began in a clear voice that did not tremble, "I would like to address the board on a matter of utmost urgency."

"Let her speak," Ansel interjected and gave Traymore a stare that invited no objection.

Traymore nodded reluctantly, and she took a deep breath. "My husband is gravely ill. Although we pray for a full recovery, he will need an extended period of time to regain his health before he can resume his duties." She paused, allowing several questions concerning the nature of his illness and the treatment which she assured them had already begun. As the questioning became more intense, she put a stop to it. "Dr. Pounds has agreed to appear before the board to answer your questions more specifically. He'll be arriving soon, and I'm sure he can ease your concerns better than I can.

"There are, however, a number of requests I should like to make. First and most important, Randall and I ask for your prayers and those of the entire community. Next," she continued, without allowing anyone to offer a comment, "I recommend you contact Reverend Shelton in Glendale. He retired several years ago, but I believe he would consider presiding over Sunday meeting while Randall remains ill. Mrs. Burke has known him for many years, and she has kindly agreed to approach him on your behalf if you should approve."

Murmurs buzzed around the table, but she ignored them, determined to plead the rest of her case uninterrupted before she took her leave and allowed the elders to consider her requests. She had already breached social custom by appearing before the board, which was traditionally limited to male members only, and she had no desire to overstep her welcome any more than absolutely necessary.

"Finally, I would like to reassure you all that while I will not be available as I have been in the past, members of the Ladies Benevolent Association will carry on my duties so that I can devote my full attention to my husband's care." Without waiting for someone to ask her to leave now that she had spoken her piece, she rose from her seat and motioned the men to remain seated. "As you consider my requests, I only ask all of you to remember how hard Randall has worked on your behalf for the past three years."

Her voice started to crack, and she blinked back tears as she cleared her throat. "Should the treatment fail, you will be faced with the necessary task of hiring a new minister, but until we know for sure whether the treatment will be successful or not, I would ask for your patience and your loyalty, as well as—"

A knock on the door interrupted her and caught everyone's attention. When Dr. Pounds entered the room, she sighed with relief and walked over to him without a backward glance at the elders.

"Have they agreed?" he whispered.

She shook her head. "I've only had time to present my requests. I'm sure they have questions for you. I—I need to get back to Randall," she murmured and quickly left the room, shutting the door behind her.

She glanced about the foyer, but Mercy had disappeared, along with Emilee's cloak. Stubborn enough to want to deny Mercy another opportunity to berate her, Emilee let herself out the front door and walked home in the driving, relentless rain. She did not have the energy to run, and it was senseless to expect running all the way back to the parsonage would save her from being drenched to the bone. She already was.

She walked calmly and directly toward home as the rain that pelted her face diluted the salty stream of tears pouring down her face. She had disobeyed her husband's express orders to keep his illness private, and she had defied convention by addressing the Board of Elders, thoroughly alienating Mercy Traymore in the process.

No doubt by this time tomorrow the entire village would be humming with gossip and rumors which either would work to her favor or destroy her. Although Mercy could be as persuasive as she was vindictive, Emilee counted on the church members to support her and to nudge the elders to accept her requests should the men be reluctant. She knew each man on the board well enough to assume how he might vote, but it was always difficult to predict how the board would vote as a collective body. No woman had ever appeared before the board, not even Mrs. Burke, who was beloved by all, and the elders could fear setting a precedent by granting her requests and giving other women the idea they, too, could appear before the board and expect their requests to be honored.

With her husband's future and her entire life dangling on the whims of six male elders, she trudged down Main Street, mindless of the puddles or the gusts of wind that tore at her skirts. She had kept a brave face to the world. She had remained faithfully optimistic to Randall, but inside she was quaking. Being isolated in the parsonage for the next several months, she would be totally alone, with no one to share her fears or her hopes, just as she had been when she had arrived in Surrey as a frightened six-year-old girl.

With her life completing a full circle, she prayed for courage and faith, wondering if her entire life was destined to be marked by one lonely struggle after another.

*   *   *

After the doctor left, a heated discussion had ensued. The board now considered Ansel's compromise recommendation to postpone taking any action on Emilee's requests for two weeks. At that time, Dr. Pounds would present an update on the minister's condition and a more definite prognosis of his chance for a full recovery. While it was fairly common knowledge the minister suffered from frequent headaches, everyone, including Jared, had been surprised to learn the apparent seriousness of the minister's affliction.

Jared had paid some attention to the bickering and complaining, but most of his thoughts were focused on Emilee and her direct but eloquent and thoughtful appeal. Stunningly composed and hauntingly strong, she had revealed yet another facet of her personality that enhanced his perceptions of her as a remarkable woman and deepened his concern for her welfare.

Unable to leave the meeting to escort her home without adding yet another layer of impropriety to her reputation, he had remained at the meeting. He could not love her openly for all the world to see, but as the son of the former minister, he could offer support for her requests. He was surprised to hear a limited number of elders freely express their disapproval of the minister, and he suspected his mother's support for Randall had helped to keep most of his detractors at bay.

"We'll need to vote on the postponement," Traymore announced in a raised voice that ended a quarrel between Garth Leigh and Ansel Woerner. "All in favor, raise your right hand."

As a guest, Jared had no vote, and he studied the men around the table to assess where they stood on the issue. Four hands shot into the air, and he focused on the two men who objected: Traymore and Leigh.

"By a majority, the matter is postponed for two weeks." Clearly disgruntled, Traymore adjourned the meeting, but made no offer to serve refreshments. He had been defeated in his efforts to have the board put the minister on a leave of absence and initiate a search for a permanent replacement, and he did not hide his disappointment.

Jared did not particularly like Traymore, but had underestimated the influence of the man's wife, who still harbored resentment for Emilee and no doubt passed on that dislike to the man she had married. Leigh, however, was another matter altogether. A bit stodgy, he was usually very conservative but fair. During the discussion about the minister, however, Leigh had been outspoken and adamant in his opposition.

Deliberately choosing to leave at the same time as the banker, while the others huddled around the table to continue belaboring Emilee's requests, Jared stepped outside right behind Leigh. The rain had stopped, at least for the moment. "Looks like we got lucky," he remarked.

Leigh grumbled to himself as he adjusted his hat. "Miserable, lousy weather. Chills a man clear through to his bones day after day. Traymore's the lucky one. He gets to stay indoors and will have a maid serve him a warm toddy before we're even halfway home."

"I hear the tavern serves a tasty toddy. Since we have a break in the weather, I think I'll stop in on the way home. I'd welcome the company if you'd care to come along," Jared suggested, hoping to have time alone with Leigh to explore his objections to the minister further.

"Not a bad idea at all," Leigh remarked and accompanied Jared to the village tavern. Crowded with hard-drinking, fun-loving Irishmen who labored on the canal, the Bent Thistle was less than ideal for the kind of probing conversation Jared had in mind, but he had not been to the tavern since his return and could not change his mind now even if he wanted to.

Leigh, however, seemed quite at home and shoved his way through the crowd of men to secure a small table in the rear, where he held one of two seats for Jared, who found the whole atmosphere disheartening. Laborers arm-wrestled at various tables around the room, invoking sporadic but boisterous roars. Several men to their right were engaged in a darting tournament, and serving maids hustled to supply drinks and avoid pinches at the same time.

A few drinks later, Leigh offered another toast. "To progress, which spawns prosperity," he shouted above the din with a silly grin on his flushed face.

"Prosperity," Jared murmured, realizing Leigh was, not surprisingly, one of the most ardent supporters of the canal. As the president of the bank, Leigh saw only the economic advantages of linking Surrey through a tributary canal system to the Erie Canal and the eastern markets. As a relative newcomer to Surrey three or four years ago, he had no inkling how the construction of the canal had changed the flavor of life in Surrey, but Jared did, and he was fully convinced progress had its drawbacks as well as its advantages.

When the final two opponents in the darting tournament took their places, the din settled to a more bearable level as most men stopped what they had been doing to witness the outcome. His ears still ringing, Jared welcomed the respite. "Prosperity has its price," he moaned, shaking his head.

"Now you sound like Reverend Greene," Leigh muttered as he drained his tankard. "With all due respect to most of the other members of the board, they're making a big mistake. They had a golden opportunity to get rid of the minister, and they let it pass them by. I tried to tell them. Even Traymore had the gumption to vote no, but . . ."

He let his voice drift off, but Jared wanted to know more. "I take it Reverend Greene hasn't been very supportive of the canal."

Leigh snorted. "He's a fossil. Oh, he preaches the Word as good as the best of them, but he's like Finney and the rest of the revivalists. They're all threatened by change. Reverend Greene has been hell-bent on opposing the canal, and he used the pulpit to try to frighten the villagers."

Without being here several years ago to witness the apparent controversy over the canal, Jared was at a distinct disadvantage. "Frighten them? How?" Jared prompted, needing some answers now rather than later.

Leigh leaned forward and lowered his voice. "He used the women. Won them over to his side with all the new gibberish about putting women on some moral pedestal and making them the safeguards of every man's soul. They parroted his warnings about the evils of the city floating straight to our doorstep.'' He chortled. ''To hear him, you'd think he was as familiar with evil as he is with the Word.''

''Maybe he is,'' Jared mumbled under his breath. The possibility shot through Jared's mind and exploded with enough force to shatter any reservations he had about sending a letter to his partner to verify Randall's background.

Guided by his own self-interest, Leigh probably had an exaggerated view of Randall, an assessment Leigh himself confirmed when he changed the topic to his plans for the bank and the loans he would make to help villagers improve their lives and increase their profits as the canal neared completion.

When it came to the Reverend Mr. Randall Greene, however, Jared had his own self-interests at stake. His love for Emilee aside, he already carried a heavy burden for keeping his father's secret and allowing his mother and the church members to believe his father had been a man who deserved their admiration and respect. If there was the remotest chance Randall had something in his past to discredit him as a man of the cloth, Jared had no choice but to uncover the truth, yet another burden he had to carry alone.

He had to admit it was entirely likely Randall deserved the Geneva lace bands he wore as a minister, in which case Jared could dismiss his suspicions and rest easy. If not, Jared felt obligated to see the minister removed from the pulpit, provided the board did not decide to replace him in the meantime.

Emilee. His heart lurched in his chest, and his body went rigid. For her sake, he prayed Randall was thoroughly legitimate. If an inquiry revealed otherwise, more than the man's ministry would end. Jared would destroy her reputation and her role as the minister's wife as well.

Could he put his sense of obligation above the welfare of the woman he loved with all his heart? Would she forgive him, whether he was proven right or wrong? He had no right to expect he would be able to talk to her and share his concerns without turning her against him forever. His love for her had been doomed from the start, but he could never hurt her. Never.

When Leigh bade him good night with a good-natured rib about Jared being too addled to hold much of a conversation, he did not argue the point and admit he had been consumed by his thoughts of Emilee rather than alcohol. He waited for Garth to leave before heading out himself.

Greeted by another cloudburst outside, he hunched his shoulders and lowered the brim of his hat. Lured by longing and awash with confusion, he walked headlong into the stormy night. His gait was slow, his steps uncertain as he wandered through mud and rain under the cover of darkness. Without any hope he might find solace or answers to the questions that plagued his soul, he roamed aimlessly through the streets of the village.

He had traipsed halfway across Europe and had spent half of his lifetime running away from the past, but he had never felt as alone or as lonely as he did tonight. He shut down his thoughts, simply taking one step at a time, walking anywhere and everywhere in the wind and the rain until he was numb enough not to worry or care where he might yet end this day because he could not be where his heart and his soul yearned to be: with Emilee.

TWENTY

Bone-tired and soul-weary, Emilee crawled under the covers on the bed in Jared's old chamber, laid her head down, and closed her eyes. With the very first breath she drew, she inhaled his musky scent, which still clung to the pillow cushioning her cheek. Her heart began to race. Her body tingled. And with every quick breath she drew, she envisioned his long, muscular body resting on the mattress beneath her, wrapped in the same bedclothes that covered her now.

Groaning out loud, she realized, too late, she had been so consumed by her husband's illness since Sunday afternoon, she had neglected to clean the guest chambers or change the bedclothes after Olivia and Jared each had moved out. She clutched the edge of the bedsheets, unable to deny her body ached for him now as strongly and sinfully as ever before, and her heart and her spirit yearned to claim the comfort and security she would also find in his arms.

Her feelings for him were as complex and perplexing as the man himself, and she curled deeper under the covers, wrapped her arms around the pillow, and snuggled closer to him—if only in her vivid imagination.

There was no sound to distract her thoughts. The storm outside had finally taken a rest, and the heavy rain had abated to a drizzly mist. Randall had awakened shortly after her return from the elders' meeting, but he had eventually asked for a dose of laudanum, which would keep him asleep for hours yet. Even Troubles had given up the day's adventures and lay dozing atop the bedclothes at the foot of Randall's bed.

All alone with her thoughts and feelings for Jared in the dark hours just before midnight, she lay very still. She listened to the sound of her own breathing and felt the rapid beat of her heart as his scent surrounded her and brought his face and form to her mind's eye. Mesmerized by the powerful force of his presence, she could scarcely breathe as a most amazing thought tiptoed from the depths of her heart to the forefront of her mind: She had fallen in love with Jared Burke.

Not suddenly or violently, like a hurricane that battered the earth and destroyed nature's beauty, but slowly like a gentle mist that changed to drizzle and then rain that fell to water the flowers which in turn would fill the world with incredible hues and delicate fragrances. Her love for Jared had been planted in the seeds of physical attraction and blossomed from the tender bud of affection into love that colored her moments with him with joy and filled them with the scent of happiness.

It had happened so gradually, she had been unable to prevent it. Her conscience rebelled, but her lonely heart trembled with joy. She loved him in so many ways she found it impossible to believe she had not realized it until now. She loved the way the cleft in his chin deepened when he smiled, the way his body moved when he walked, and the way his eyes deepened in color whenever he looked at her. His quick wit made her laugh, and when she was with him, the world was a happy place made for love and laughter. She could talk to him and share her deepest fears or doubts and know he would understand because he had them, too.

Earlier tonight at the elders' meeting, when she had gazed deep into Jared's eyes, she had seen something far more compelling than lust glistening in those pale gray depths. She had seen encouragement, even before he had known why she had interrupted the meeting. She had seen understanding and support.

Her love for him was wrong. It was ill-fated, but it was also strong enough to override her values and her conscience to tempt her to deny them both. If she did, she would only bring shame to the greatest joy to ever gift her life.

With a heavy heart, she wrapped her love for him with her dreams and tucked it deep inside her heart, where it would be kept unblemished by guilt or shame and as fresh and new at the end of her life as it was at this very moment.

Tears of regret welled in her eyes, and she twisted the slim gold band on her finger. Randall was her husband, not Jared, and she sadly admitted to herself her marriage had been a mistake—one she would have to live with for the rest of her life.

She had married Randall for all the wrong reasons. Tears rolled down her cheeks and dampened her pillow. So afraid she would follow the same path as her mother and let love lead her astray, Emilee had taken a road that had ultimately led to the same end: heartache.

She had married for position instead of love. As the minister's wife, she had an important and very visible place in the community, one that proved to all those who had taunted her as a child that they had been wrong. This bastard child, daughter of a whore, had transcended the scandal of her birth and become the most righteous of all women: the minister's wife. Dedicated to serving the very people who had once shunned her, Emilee had, in the end, committed a sin as potentially scandalous as her mother's: She had fallen in love with another man.

She had only one path open to her now to keep scandal at bay and to prove herself, for all time, better than her mother: She had to keep her vows and her commitment to the life she had so poorly chosen. The price for her mistake, losing any chance for happiness with Jared, would be the greatest sorrow in her life, but she had no one but herself to blame.

She got out of bed, put a robe over her nightdress, and slid slippers onto her feet, too distraught to remain in this bed where her thoughts were only of Jared. Working quickly, she changed the bedclothes and carried them downstairs to the kitchen to be laundered the first full day of sunshine. She cinched the tie at her waist tighter and lit the kerosene lamp on the kitchen table. She put a pot of sweet cider on the cookstove, but did not plan to be downstairs long enough to warrant stoking the fire in the hearth.

While she waited for the cider to heat and her thoughts about Jared simmered in the back of her mind, she tried to concentrate on her husband and whether or not the elders would give him the time he needed to recuperate. She paced around the kitchen, and her slippered steps echoed in the room.

She replayed the elders' meeting over and over in her mind to figure out the consequences of her surprise appearance. Had she made a mistake by leaving so abruptly? She had already scandalized herself by appearing before the board, and it hardly seemed likely she could have made it any worse by staying to defend her requests. Instead of asking one of the elders to present her concerns like other women did when they felt they had an issue for the board to consider, had she been inspired to speak herself because of her deep concern for Randall or because she needed to protect her own position in the community as the minister's wife?

The answer to her questions whispered the selfish truth, which left her trembling anew and restarted the echo of Mercy's angry words when she had attempted to dissuade Emilee from her mission. For the first time in her entire marriage, she saw that Randall's complaints about her were right. More often than not, she either rushed ahead to solve a problem without carefully thinking about the consequences or she failed to see a task through to its finish.

Burning with shame and flushed with guilt, she walked over to the window to crack it open and get some fresh air. She approached her reflection in the window and realized she had also forgotten to repair and rehang the curtain after Troubles had torn it down just before Randall had taken ill. The curtain was still folded on a chair waiting to be repaired. She shook her head, almost grateful Randall was confined upstairs and could not fault her again for her haphazard housekeeping skills.

Standing directly in front of the window, she put her hands on the top of the lower window frame to slide it up. Her body now blocked most of the light from the lamp, and she could see almost clearly through to the rear yard.

She saw something oddly out of place halfway between the house and the barn, but it was so misty, she could not tell for sure what it might be. When she pressed her forehead against the cold glass, she squinted her eyes to see better and immediately covered her mouth to catch a loud gasp.

A tall man stood outside in the shadows just beyond the light that filtered outside from the window, and he was staring directly at her. Cold fear trickled down her spine and held her frozen in place. Her pulse immediately pounded so hard she could barely think straight. With her mind and body paralyzed, she watched as he took several steps to stand within the light, and her hand slid down from her mouth to her heart.

"Jared?" she whispered, but the relief that flooded her body was short-lived. She stepped back from the window. A thousand questions washed her mind with confusion. Why was he here? What awful news carried him here in the middle of the night? Her heart thudded beneath her hand. The meeting. Had she pushed the Board of Elders too far? Or had something happened to Olivia?

Emilee trembled as she made her way to the door. The moment she opened it, cold, misty air greeted her and turned her trembles of worry to hard shivers. She pulled her wrapper tight and held on to the doorknob. "Jared? Is something wrong?"

He turned toward her, and his face registered surprise as well as embarrassment. He removed his hat and walked toward her. "I'm sorry. I didn't mean to frighten you. I didn't think you'd be awake, but when I saw the light in the window—"

"How long have you been standing outside?" she blurted.

He shrugged his shoulders beneath the oilcloth poncho he was wearing and twisted the brim of his hat. "Not long."

"Only long enough to get drenched." She tightened her hold on the doorknob. Judging by his appearance, he had been standing outside for hours, which only reinforced her fears the news he carried was important. "Is it your mother? Has she taken ill?"

He stopped several feet away from her, and his eyes widened. "Mother? No, she's fine."

Relieved, Emilee knew he must have come to tell her about the meeting. "Come inside," she urged, shivering uncontrollably as the mist swirled beneath her nightclothes and chilled her legs. "I have cider heating on the cookstove."

"I shouldn't have come," he murmured. "It's late, and it wouldn't be proper."

She had to clench her jaw to keep her teeth from chattering. "Proper or late, you're soaked to the skin. I'm freezing out here, and by the time you finish telling me about the elders' decision, I'll be drenched, too. At least come inside and tell me what happened. If you don't, I won't get a minute's sleep for worrying."

When he hesitated, she cocked her head. "You did come to tell me about the meeting, didn't you?"

"The meeting? Uh . . . yes, I did."

"Then come inside, or I'll have Dr. Pounds send you the bill when he has to treat me for pneumonia!" she teased.

He chuckled and the tension seemed to drain from his face. "If you're trying to prick my conscience, you're doing a convincing job." He cocked his head, took a deep whiff of air, and frowned. "Did you say you were heating cider?"

Puzzled by his frown, she sniffed the air. "It's boiling over!" she gasped, bolted back into the kitchen, and left the door ajar behind her in her haste to get to the cookstove. The air reeked with the smell of burned cider, which had bubbled over to trickle onto the floor, and brown puddles of burned cider crusted the top of the cookstove.

She grabbed the handle of the pot, yelped, and pulled her hand away. Pain sliced across her fingertips, and tears welled in her eyes. Biting back the pain, she used her other hand to grab a padded mitt and slid the pot to the other side of the cookstove.

"Is everything all right?"

Jared's voice startled her, and she twirled around, cupping her burned hand in front of her, to see him standing in the open doorway. "The cider's ruined and my cookstove is a disaster," she moaned, already dreading the drudgery of cleaning up the mess.

His eyes narrowed, and he walked toward her. "How badly did you burn your hand?"

She pursed her lips and held out her hand. "It's not so bad. It just stings a little," she responded, reminded that her bee stings had scarcely healed before she had injured her hand again.

He looked at her fingers and shook his head. "You're lucky. If you soak your hand in some cold water, you might not even get blisters."

Blisters were the very last of her worries at the moment. He was standing far too close and his scent made her too mindful of the moments she had slept in his bed. Her heart continued to race even after she turned around and walked over to the sink and pumped cold water on her hand. While the water eased the throbbing in her fingertips, it did little to dampen the sinfully warm feelings that flowed through her body when he was so near. She wrapped a cold wet cloth over her hand and tried to focus on the true purpose for Jared's late night visit.

"If you don't mind, I'll stoke the fire a bit to get warm," he suggested. He removed his rain-slicked poncho and put it close to the hearth along with his hat.

"No, I don't mind at all," she responded, although a blazing fire could not warm away the physical response to him that left her shivering anew. "I can heat more cider."

He chuckled as he stacked several logs in the fireplace. "Not in that pot. Would you mind if we had coffee instead?"

Before she could answer, he stood up, glanced at her, and immediately dropped his gaze. "I'll put a pot of coffee on while you . . . you might want to change into something . . . warmer."

Puzzled by his sudden awkwardness, she was more distressed to think she had not been able to hide her body's reaction to him. Fortunately, he had assumed she was merely chilled from standing outside, and she slipped upstairs to change while he made coffee.

The moment she stepped into her chamber, lit the oil lamp, and caught a glimpse of herself in the mirror, her distress turned to horror. The mist had dampened her white wrapper and the nightdress underneath, and misted her hair, which hung shamelessly down her back. With the tie cinched around her waist, her breasts and hips were provocatively outlined.

Shame flushed her cheeks, and using only one hand, she awkwardly changed into the darkest, baggiest gown she could find in her wardrobe. She smoothed her hair and retied the ribbon at the nape of her neck. Before returning to the kitchen, she went to Randall's chamber. He was still asleep, and Troubles had moved from the foot of the bed to curl on top of Randall's chest.

Tiptoeing back to her chamber, she doused the oil lamp and went down the staircase to the kitchen. Speechless, she glanced around the room. The cookstove gleamed. Both the floor and the crusty pot had been washed, and the curtain had been rehung on the window.

Jared sat at the table, which he had set with two mugs of steaming coffee, a small pitcher of fresh milk, a generous plate of sugar lumps, spoons, and an empty saucer. "You've been busy," she murmured as she took a seat directly across from him.

He nodded. "You look . . . warmer," he commented before he looked away and glanced around the room. "I was hoping Rose might be around. I've missed the ornery critter."

Emilee glanced at the empty saucer again and smiled. "Troubles," she began, using the kitten's proper name, "is upstairs asleep with Randall. He's grown quite attached to the kitten." She felt more than awkward having her husband upstairs while she sat in the kitchen with Jared. She felt tense, and she sat stiffly in her chair.

She left her injured hand on her lap and wrapped her other hand around the mug of coffee. Her gaze met Jared's, and she studied his haggard features. Worry creased his forehead. Confusion and pain shimmered in his eyes. She bowed her head and braced herself to hear the worst. Obviously the news he brought was bad, and she knew she must have overstepped her bounds by appearing at the meeting. Randall would be more furious with her for disobeying him in such a scandalous manner and devastated to learn the board had not been willing to give him time to recover from his illness. If he did.

With a sinking heart, she realized she had let him down tonight. Her guilt was swift and painful, but drove deeper

when she admitted she had done far worse than played false
with his trust in her. She had betrayed her vows to be faithful
to him. She had not committed adultery in the flesh, but she
had committed a sin just as grievous: She had given her heart
to another man.

She trembled as her life crashed into jagged pieces that
pierced her heart and sliced at her blackened soul. When she
raised her head, she looked at Jared. She had no tears of shame
or prayer to offer for forgiveness. Only determination to put
the pieces of her life back together. Cracked and weakened as
it might be, she owed Randall her full and total loyalty. Beginning here. Beginning now. ''Tell me what the elders decided,'' she said softly, wondering if she could fall out of love
with Jared in much less time than it had taken to realize she
had fallen in love with him.

TWENTY-ONE

J ared gazed deep into Emilee's eyes, so haunted by worry and fear they had turned a husky shade of green that reminded him of the color of the foliage on his roses after a heavy night of rain. Although she was under the false impression he had come to give her the details of the board's decision on her requests, the least he could do after frightening her and invading her privacy so late at night would be to answer her question and allay her fears.

"They've held off making a final decision for now. In fact," he said to reassure her, "they've postponed taking any action to give the treatment time to have some effect, however minimal that might be. They've asked Dr. Pounds to give them another report in two weeks, and then they'll decide what to do."

Relief washed over her face, although he detected a hint of dismay in the way her eyes clouded and the very corner of her lips trembled.

"A postponement isn't a rejection," he offered, hoping to soften her disappointment. He was reluctant to tell her how divided the board had been or how difficult it had been to reach a compromise, for fear he might fuel her worry. "They just asked for a little time. No one knew how serious Randall's headaches turned out to be. The elders were just taken by surprise."

"By Randall's illness or my appearance?" she asked, in a tone that made it clear she was aware she may not have helped her husband's situation by breaking tradition and appearing in person on his behalf—at least in the minds of several elders.

He chuckled softly. "Frankly, I think it was a little of both."

Her hands shook as she tried to take another sip of coffee.

"Randall doesn't know I went to the board. He doesn't want anyone to know how ill he is, but he won't be in any condition to conduct Sunday meetings for a good while. I trusted Dr. Pounds not to disclose anything, but rumors were bound to circulate. Gossip can be as unfair as it is inevitable, and I just wanted the elders to know the truth and to make plans to keep the congregation well-served until Randall can return to the pulpit."

"You could have asked Ansel Woerner to bring your concerns to the elders. He's very fond of you."

"I know," she whispered. "But—"

"But you don't like to ask anyone to help," he interjected, recognizing his own sense of isolation as well as a streak of independence in the tone of her voice.

Her cheeks flushed a delightful shade of pink. "I tend to act rashly at times."

"I was thinking more on the lines of courageous."

"Or foolish," she amended, self-consciously toying with her spoon.

"Or maybe a little of both."

She laughed with him, and her smile captivated him. Held hostage by the longing in his heart to spend the rest of his days with her by his side, he had no illusions. She was married to the minister, for better or for worse, and Jared's love for her was doomed to remain as unrequited as it was ill-fated, regardless of the board's decision.

Jared tucked the memory of her smile into his heart to savor it along with other flashes of her image for the long, lonely years ahead. "I wouldn't worry overmuch. In a couple of weeks they'll have had time to mull everything over, and by then Randall may be well on his way back to health."

She laid down her spoon and sighed. "Will you be going to the meeting the night they decide what to do about granting Randall a temporary leave of absence?"

He stiffened. "No. I'm not attending any after next week's board meeting when I return the plans for the plaque."

His words were clipped and cold, even to his own ears. He stared into the mug of coffee at his own reflection for several long heartbeats as an awkward silence replaced the easy conversation between them. He had no right to ask her to share the burden of his secret, but he was no closer to finding a solution to his dilemma now than he had been a week ago. He knew in his heart he would only find answers here with her. Would his own position be any different if his father's shame had been made public years ago? If he had never come home, would he ever have found the peace and contentment she had claimed for herself?

He raised his gaze and looked at her again. "Have you ever wondered what it would have been like for you if you hadn't come back to Surrey after your mother died?"

She shrugged her shoulders. "I didn't really have any choice. Aunt Phoebe was the only family I had left."

"What about after she died? What if my parents hadn't taken you into their home?"

"But they did. I don't see what difference—"

"It would have made all the difference," he pressed. "You probably would have been indentured out to another town where no one knew about your mother. You could have grown up without scandal shadowing your life."

"Someone would have found out. Even if they hadn't, I would have carried the shame. Here," she said, pointing to her heart, "I still do."

She dropped her gaze and her voice softened. "Very few people understand how hard it is to wake up each day to face the past and know it's here in the present, waiting to trip each word you speak or every step you take, making the future seem so uncertain."

He swallowed hard, recognizing the mirror image of the pain and loneliness that had etched his life and amazed at how well she had kept it hidden behind a facade of contentment and purpose. The guilt and shame that had festered in his heart and soul tightened in his chest and made it hard to draw a deep breath. "I do," he murmured.

Her eyes widened, and she reached across the table to cover his hand with her own. "You've seemed so troubled since you've come home. Do you want to talk about it?"

He nodded, squeezed her hand, and held on tight as he gazed into her eyes. "I didn't really come here tonight to tell you about the meeting. Ezra is coming first thing in the morning as the board's representative to speak to you. After I left the meeting, I went to the tavern for a while, then I just wandered around, walking the streets . . ." His throat constricted, and his mouth went dry.

"In the rain," she prompted with a smile.

"I hardly even noticed," he admitted, finding it hard to believe he had been so encompassed in his thoughts he never felt the water seeping into his boots or felt his trousers dripping. He shivered, grateful for the fire that had warmed the room and had begun to dry his clothing. "The next thing I knew, I was standing outside the parsonage, trying to make some sense out of life. I never expected you'd get up in the middle of the night. When you lit the lamp in the kitchen and looked out the window . . . I'm sorry, I really didn't mean to frighten you."

"You didn't," she protested, and when he raised his brow, she chuckled. "Well, just for a minute, but then you helped to ease my worries by telling me about the meeting." She paused and moistened her lips. "Won't you let me return the favor now? Something is troubling you. At first I thought you might feel guilty for not being here for your father's last days or to help your mother, but I've long sensed it's also something more . . . more painful you need to reconcile. Whatever the rift between you and your father, I'm sure he had forgiven it many times over before he died. He was a good man, Jared. He loved you."

Flinching, he tried to focus on the strength and reassurance she offered him instead of grief or anger. Her insight, however flawed, touched him deeply and lanced the guilt and shame that had been festering in his soul. "I shouldn't burden you," he began, "but there's no one else who might understand without judging—"

"Just tell me," she whispered.

He took a deep breath and with one swift slice of the blade of truth to free his secret, he spoke as bluntly to her about his father as she had the day she had talked about her mother at the cemetery. "You're right. I do feel guilty for not being here to support my mother, but I have no regrets about not seeing my father. He was a hypocrite, a liar, and an adulterous bastard."

"Jared!" she blurted and pulled her hand back to cover her mouth. Pale and still, she looked as though her entire body had gone numb and his words had paralyzed every thought in her mind except disbelief. Very gradually, while his own heartbeat pounded in his chest, a faint blush colored her cheeks and she shook her head. "That's so far beyond outrageous, it's ludicrous. It can't be true, Jared. It can't be. Someone lied to you, poisoned you against your father—"

"No one lied to me. What I'm saying is true, and I know it's true because I saw my father making love to another woman. Don't you understand? I saw him with my own eyes."

He let go of her hand, stood up, and walked over to the hearth. He braced each of his hands on the mantel and stared into the fire, but its warmth did not touch the chills that shuddered through his frame. Painful images of the most awful day in his life danced in the flames to haunt him, and he recounted that day to exorcise it once and for all. "I was twelve years old. My father still rode circuit back then, and he was away. Most of my friends were busy with chores, and I was bored. I'd gone with my father once to take Weston home after one of his drunken binges, and he'd invited me to go fishing in the big old pond on his farm anytime I wanted. He had poles stored in the barn and told me to help myself, so I went fishing."

He closed his eyes, but the images he had seen dancing in the fire had been burned into his memory, as vivid as that day so long ago. "I found my father with Violet Weston rutting on a blanket in a secluded spot near the pond. I just stood there with my mouth open and my eyes bulging out of my head. When he finally looked up and saw me, I ran away. He didn't even bother to come after me, but later that night, after he'd arrived home, he gave me a long-winded sermon about honoring my father and keeping his little secret. And I did.

God help me, I did, even when I knew he continued his affair with William Weston's wife.''

He opened his eyes and turned around to face her. The fire warmed his back, but his soul had turned to ice. Emilee looked at him with tears in her eyes. "What an awful thing to do to a child," she murmured. "He had no right to implicate you in his sin. None."

"Right or not, that's exactly what he did," he argued. "I couldn't even look at my mother without wanting to blurt out what he had done to her. I used to watch him in the pulpit at meeting and want to scream the truth so the whole world would know him for what he was: an adulterer who twisted the Word to suit himself."

"But you didn't," she whispered.

"No. I just left Surrey for good as soon as I could. Fortunately, my grandfather offered to send me to school. I took my father's vile little secret with me and carried it wherever I traveled. It never got any easier, but when I learned he had died, I thought . . ." He paused to clear his throat. "I thought I could come home, make amends to my mother for being away from her for so long, and put it all to rest."

She sighed, wringing her hands on her lap. "And then you learned about the church dedication."

He nodded. "It's been hard enough listening to everyone talk about my father as though he were a saint, but he no more deserves the honor of having the church dedicated to him than Satan does." He ran his hand over his brow. "I should have confronted him then, but I just didn't know how, so I acted the coward and left. Now this."

He shook his head. "It's wrong to honor a man who betrayed his vows to my mother and misrepresented himself to his congregation, but I don't know how to stop it. If I reveal him as the lying, sneaking adulterer he really was, I'll destroy my mother and shatter the faith of every villager who ever stepped into the meetinghouse to hear my father preach. If I keep quiet," he added softly, "I'll destroy whatever sense of honor I have left, and in the end, I'll be just as hypocritical as he was."

With her world reeling and spinning out of control, Emilee gripped the edge of the table. Reverend Burke was the only father she had really known, and Olivia was as dear to her as life itself. It was hard to believe that the man who had been so good and kind and loving had committed such an awful sin against the woman who carried his name and the very faith he proclaimed from the pulpit at meeting. It was harder still to see the man she loved with all her heart taking blame for his father's sin. There was no easy solution to the dilemma he faced, and she had no easy answer to suggest.

She could not, however, let him continue to carry his guilt any longer. "You were young," she argued. "You were torn between your mother and your father, Jared. No child should have to choose between either of his parents. That's not fair."

"Life isn't always fair," he countered bitterly.

"You did what you could do. The fourth commandment orders us to honor both our parents, not one, and you spared your mother great hurt by keeping silent. What purpose would it serve to tell your mother the truth now? Your father is gone, and so is Violet Weston. The shame belongs to them, not to you or your mother."

He sighed and ran his hand across his brow. "Even if what you're saying is true, you're still suggesting I have to approve the plaque, allow the dedication to take place, and just forget what my father did?"

"No. You'll never forget what your father did," she explained. "No more than I can forget what my mother did. But you can learn to forgive him. You can't undo the past, but you can live with it by changing your perceptions of it."

His expression hardened. "It's real difficult to perceive adultery and fornication as anything other than wrong."

Her heart was racing and her words poured out in a rush. "Let go of your guilt and open your heart to forgive him and fill it with happier, sweeter memories of him. You're not his judge. You're only his son."

"You sound as if I can just snap my fingers, forgive him, and go on with my life. It's not that easy, as you well know.

You've never forgiven your mother or filled your heart with good memories of her.''

Emilee felt the blood drain from her face. "It's not the same thing at all. My mother didn't give me anything but scandal and shame. Your father gave you—''

"It is the same," he argued. "How can you give me advice and expect me to follow it when you won't even take it yourself?''

Finding it hard to deny his logic, she still persisted. "I've never heard a single good thing about my mother, but you've admitted yourself people constantly remind you what good your father's done. I didn't mean to imply it would be easy, but it's not just the right thing to do. It's the only thing you can do. You must," she murmured.

She stood up and walked around the table. Heart pounding, she approached him, and when he opened his arms to her, she stepped into his embrace to console him. His arms wrapped around her shoulders, and he held her so tight she could feel his heart pounding furiously against her cheek. Her hands pressed against the hard muscles in his back, and his breath fanned her face.

His breathing was ragged, and he moved his hands up and down along her spine, urging the full length of her body to mold against him. She clung to him, savoring the joy of offering him her support and her understanding. She was not sure when comfort turned into physical pleasure and need, but she recognized the danger signals. Her body began to tingle, her lips began to ache for his kiss, and she was scarcely able to breathe.

She stiffened and eased awkwardly from his embrace.

"Emilee?" he whispered, his voice hoarse with passionate emotion.

She kept her gaze down and stood very still. "Please go," she pleaded, praying he would leave her before she disgraced herself any further. Too afraid to breathe, she held her breath as he hesitated, then turned to gather his outer garments, and walked away. She let out her breath when the door finally closed behind him, ever thankful he had more courage and more strength to resist temptation than she did.

Feeling more shame than remorse, she tidied up the kitchen and climbed the staircase to seek her bed. Maybe Jared had been right to wonder what would have happened to her if she had never returned to her mother's birthplace. Even better, perhaps, for the state of her own soul, it might have been better if she had never been born.

TWENTY-TWO

Once a fool, but not twice.

With that thought echoing in his mind, Jared carried a post into the general store. George stopped working on a ledger book behind the counter as soon as Jared approached him and handed over the letter.

"You look a bit peaked this morning," George joked. "Heard you and Leigh spent a few hours at the tavern last night after the elders' meeting. Good thing you didn't get hustled into the dart tournament. The fix was in. Always is."

Jared chuckled. Apparently he looked as bad as he felt, yet his mood was anything but humorous. Any advantage he had gained by talking with Emilee had been lost the moment he held her in his arms. Too consumed with self-disgust to allow himself to savor the relief of finally unburdening his secret, he had spent the sleepless hours till dawn composing a letter he should have sent weeks ago. "How long will it take to get this to New York City?"

George pulled out his pocket watch and smiled. "There's still an hour yet till the stage arrives. My father is late doing the morning post, but he'll be here before the stage, which means your letter will go right out and should be there in four days. Maybe less. Depends on how quick they get it onto the packet in Utica."

"Good enough. Put the charge on my account."

George studied the name and address Jared had scrawled on the front of the letter. "Will Cooper. He's your partner, isn't he?"

Jared clenched his jaw. Life in a small town had definite drawbacks when it came to privacy—an irony, since his father had seemed to find enough of it. "That's right. I'm still trying to get everything organized. You haven't heard anything about the stock I ordered from New York, have you?''

"Nope. Rain held it up for sure, but the bad weather is clearing. Shouldn't be much longer. I'll send word as soon as it arrives. You heading back home today?''

"Tomorrow morning. I'm staying with my mother till then,'' Jared answered. Distracted by a display of trinket boxes set up at the other end of the counter, he wandered down to inspect it closer. He picked up a silver trinket box inlaid with ivory and a single silver rose on the lid. While an idea began to focus, he cursed himself again for being a complete cad last night with Emilee. Although he could offer no excuse for his loss of self-control, he could at least give her something as a peace offering, along with his promise not to step beyond propriety again.

"Just unpacked them yesterday,'' George remarked as he followed Jared down the length of the counter. "Imported all the way from France. Have you got a special young lady in mind?''

Scowling, Jared had a mind to tell him the 'special young lady' was the minister's wife, just to see him shocked into silence. "Just looking,'' he offered, grateful he at least had control of his better judgment.

"Julia Prack and her mother were just in yesterday. Even in all that bad weather, Julia still manages to look as fresh as one of those roses you're planning to grow. By the way, my mother wondered if you'd take a look at her rose garden before winter sets in and give her some advice. She hasn't had much luck getting them to bloom.''

Jared set the trinket box to the side and selected two more with identical designs. "Wrap these up for me, will you?''

"Three trinket boxes? You sure changed your mind in a hurry about doing some courting. Just be careful. Women can talk up a storm that blows through the village faster than a hurricane. If one of those women you're planning to court finds out you gave another woman the very same trinket box . . . Are you sure you want all three? I've got some—''

"I'm sure,'' Jared insisted, refusing to dispel any of

George's misconceptions. "Tell your mother I'll stop by next week."

George shrugged his shoulders. "Don't say I didn't warn you," he muttered as he slid each of the trinkets into velvet sacks and wrapped them together in brown paper. As he tied the package closed with twine, he frowned. "Too bad about the reverend. Heard he might have to leave the pulpit permanently."

Stiffening his spine, Jared narrowed his gaze. Traymore's father, apparently, had already been hard at work spreading news about Randall's illness, focusing on the worst of all possible outcomes. "Not at all. He's undergoing some treatment that will take time. I'm sure he'll recover." He took his package, put it under his arm, bade George goodbye, and went directly back to his mother's new home.

He had promised to show her the plans for the plaque this afternoon and to discuss strategy for the town council meeting next Tuesday. After supper, he would attend the Canal Association meeting, get a good night's rest, and head for his cabin in the morning. He had not decided when and how he might deliver his gift to Emilee, but he would worry about that later. Right now, he had a full day and night ahead of him.

He had not had a moment's peace to ponder Emilee's suggestion to replace his bitter memories of his father with good ones or to make a final decision about approving the plaque and allowing the church dedication to take place. By this time tomorrow, he would be plowing acres of ground, and as he worked his body into exhaustion, he would think about taking her advice.

In the meantime, he could find some measure of satisfaction in knowing he was doing everything he could to avoid making the same mistake with Emilee he had made with his mother. He would protect Emilee with the truth by either confirming his suspicions about the minister or putting them to rest. He owed her that much—and more. If he ignored his suspicions and something happened later to discredit the minister, Jared would never forgive himself for having had the chance to warn

Emilee before it was too late. It was a small step toward his own redemption, but it was a beginning.

Prayer did not help. Neither did housecleaning, which Emilee attacked with a vengeance as soon as the sun had peaked over the horizon, but the Traymores' arrival just after breakfast was just what she needed to put Jared's late-night visit out of her mind. He had warned her Ezra would be stopping early today, and she should have known Mercy would tag along, especially after their confrontation last night. The woman gathered up little tidbits of information for her gossip mill like some women collected poems for their daybooks, and she would not miss an opportunity to get inside the parsonage to observe how Emilee would handle the news of the postponement.

Ezra and Mercy sat side by side on the settee while Emilee sat on a kitchen chair she had carried to the parlor to replace the upholstered chair now in Randall's sickroom. She glanced out into the hall and looked at her cape hanging on the oak settle by the front door and a plate of cookies, Mercy's usual sick-call offering, on the settle seat. She could easily have done without either of them if it meant being spared Mercy's company.

Mercy's good wishes for Randall's speedy recovery were as disinguous as they were condescending, but Ezra, to his credit, had been brief and conciliatory. When he finally finished explaining the board's position, Emilee smiled, easily hiding her disappointment only because she had been forewarned. "I appreciate the board's position, and I'm very hopeful Dr. Pounds will have good news to report about my husband's treatment. I must admit I was very distraught yesterday and hope you can express my apologies to the elders for disrupting their meeting. Under any other circumstances—"

"You should be more circumspect in the future," Mercy admonished. "I'm rather surprised your husband condoned such brazenness."

Emilee caught her lower lip with her teeth to keep from issuing a retort, which would only land her in more trouble, until she took a few deep breaths to calm down and try to separate Randall from her rash behavior. "Randall is very ill. I didn't trouble him by discussing it with him beforehand. His ministry is very important . . . to both of us. I was concerned for him and worried about the needs of the congregation as well."

Ezra fidgeted in his seat. "If there's nothing more, perhaps we should be going. I have to sort the morning post."

His wife glowered at him. "We can't leave without paying our respects to Reverend Greene."

"Randall is too ill to receive visitors," Emilee said firmly, convinced the very last thing Randall needed was a visit from the Traymores.

"We're here officially," Mercy countered. "Ezra is here to represent the board, and I'm the chairwoman of the home visiting committee for the Ladies' Benevolent Association."

"Dr. Pounds did say no visitors," Ezra said to support Emilee.

Mercy huffed. "The minister isn't contagious. He has a headache! I'm sure he'd appreciate seeing how concerned we are."

"I'll tell him you were here," Emilee offered, "but Dr. Pounds was quite emphatic that Randall not have any visitors, official or unofficial. As soon as he's permitted company, I'll be sure to let you know." She stood up and glanced toward the front staircase in the foyer. "I really should be getting back to see if he needs anything. May I show you to the door?"

Mercy opened her mouth as if she were about to argue, then closed it, apparently changing her mind. She pursed her lips and scowled at her husband as Emilee escorted them both to the door. Once they were safely outside, Emilee latched the door, took the plate of cookies to the kitchen, and made up a tray for Randall in case he felt able to take some nourishment when he awoke.

She climbed the rear staircase with the tray in one hand and her skirts in the other. Treading carefully to avoid falling, she remembered the day she had tripped over the last step and

Jared had caught her to keep her from falling. Her heart began to race. It was the first time he had held her in his arms, but regrettably, not the last, and memories of their embrace in the early hours of this morning only proved how weak and vulnerable she remained, despite her very best efforts to control her feelings or her body's response to him.

She reached the top of the staircase, paused to get a firmer grip on the tray, and stepped into the hallway without mishap. She walked past her old chamber, stopped, and looked inside. Sparkling and well-ordered after a thorough cleaning this morning, the room seemed to represent her life before unforeseen events left her world thoroughly disheveled with disillusionment and uncertainty.

Her husband lay desperately ill with his ministry hanging by a thread to a radical treatment, her regard for Reverend Burke had been tested with his humanity revealed as flawed, and the foundation of her marriage teetered on a precipice that could only lead to ruin. Unfortunately, there was only so much she could do to control the future. While she could devote her entire energies to nursing her husband back to health, only the Lord could see him healed.

It would take every ounce of her strength and faith to rediscover contentment in her marriage now that she had fallen in love with Jared, but she hoped she had helped him to reach a decision about the church dedication that would give him peace of mind.

Her advice to him to replace bitter memories with sweet ones rang false to her ears once again. Jared had been right to charge her with failing to follow her own advice, in part because she could not even recall her mother's face, let alone any memories from the first six years of her life. Any she might have recalled had been tainted by Aunt Phoebe's warped, destructive bitterness. If Emilee had any hope of reconstructing the shambles of her life, she had to follow her own advice and reconcile her bitter memories of her struggle to overcome the scandal and shame with forgiveness for the woman who had been her mother.

As Emilee closed the door to her old chamber, she opened

a shutter in the window of her heart. With a vow to take her own advice to search for sweet memories of her mother, she entered her husband's darkened chamber determined to put the past to rest—if only to safeguard her future.

With Randall finally resting after a long and difficult day, Emilee was exhausted. Olivia's arrival an hour and a half ago had interrupted Emilee's plans to seek her own bed and catch up on the hours of sleep she had missed the night before. Since Jared had stayed another night to attend the Canal Association meeting, Olivia had decided to visit Emilee later than usual and had asked Jared to stop by the parsonage after the meeting to escort her home.

The prospect of seeing Jared again so soon alarmed Emilee, but Olivia's warm companionship, along with a tin of freshly baked soft pretzels, soon lifted her spirits. Grappling with her disillusionment about Reverend Burke was hard. Hiding what she knew from Olivia was even more difficult, and she almost wished Jared had never told her the truth. The soft-spoken, gentle woman who sat beside her had battled nearly an entire community on Emilee's behalf, and she could not repay her by destroying her memories of the man she had loved with all her heart. Despite her best efforts to hide her weariness, Emilee yawned.

Olivia frowned at her. "You're tired, and I've overstayed my visit. I didn't think the meeting would go on so long. I expected Jared would be here by now."

Tired enough to sleep for a week, Emilee hoped the meeting might last till sunrise, to put off seeing Jared again. She sighed, still apprehensive about the consequences of her surprise appeal to the board. "Maybe I should have asked you to speak to the elders for me instead of doing it myself."

"You did well and good on your own," Olivia countered. "You shook them up a bit, but they deserved it. We women help to raise the funds to support the church, yet we have no voice on the board. They'll recover soon enough."

"Unless Mercy keeps reminding everyone that I barged into the meeting and broke tradition."

Olivia huffed. "Mercy Traymore is a busybody and a fool who wastes my patience. You just seem to draw out the worst in her, not that it's any fault of yours, mind you. It's been twenty-odd years since your mother left Charles at the alter. You'd think Mercy would let it rest."

Emilee let out a deep sigh. "It's not easy for her. Maybe if Charles hadn't gone away—"

"Well, he did. He would have left sooner or later. He wanted to be a farmer, not a shopkeeper, but he never could stand up to his father—or his mother, for that matter. Making an issue of your conversion was the perfect excuse he needed to leave, and it was far easier to save face and blame you than to admit to the entire village Charles simply did not want to be in business with his father. Mercy would make a pact with the devil himself to save face." She paused, her cheeks turning rosy. "Listen to me. I'm as bad as Mercy, gossiping like an old fool."

With the door to her past still open, Emilee ventured to step inside before it closed. "Do you think my mother would have been happy with Charles?"

Olivia tensed. After a long, awkward silence, she sighed. "In all these many years, you've never once asked about your mother."

"No," Emilee whispered. "I'd like to know more," she admitted, remembering only too well the hurtful things Aunt Phoebe had said, which had convinced Emilee asking questions only invited more pain. Inspired by Jared's challenge, she risked all and waited for Olivia to answer her.

"Well, let's see if I can answer your question. It's been so long, but I think perhaps she might have been happy with Charles," Olivia murmured. "Your mother was very young. Her father—your grandfather—raised his two girls alone, and they were his pride and joy. Once Charles bid for your mother's hand, she didn't have much choice. Even then, Ezra had considerable standing in the community. Your grandfather agreed to the match, but I often wonder . . ."

When her voice trailed off, Emilee tensed. "What did you wonder?" she prompted as her heart began to race.

"Oh, nothing much. To tell the honest truth, I was never really sure Ellen wanted the match as much as your grandfather did. On the day of the wedding, when we all found out she had run away, I knew I had been right. I felt terribly guilty for not reaching out to her, but they lived so far from the village and I had my responsibilities to my children and my duties with the church. . . . Obviously she was a terribly confused young woman and very vulnerable, if nothing else, which explains why she ran off with one of the young men who had been touring the area."

Emilee's racing heartbeat slowed to a dull thud that echoed her disappointment. While Olivia's recounting of her mother's reasons for running away was far more understanding that Aunt Phoebe's, Emilee had heard nothing to soften her memories of her mother. If anything, she identified with her mother's confusion and vulnerability. She could not, however, fathom being coerced into a marriage or condone what her mother had done. "If she was so unhappy with the betrothal, why didn't she simply break it?" she asked, struggling to find something good in her mother's flawed character.

"I don't think we'll ever know her reasons," Olivia admitted. "I do know one thing for certain. She loved you with all her heart. She could have abandoned you, just as she had been abandoned by your father, but she didn't. She kept you and loved you till the day she died. Whatever her faults or her sins, Emilee, your mother was devoted to you."

Devotion.

Emilee had barely formed the word in her mind when a sharp rap at the front door ended her thoughts of the past and jolted her back to the present.

"That's Jared now," Olivia said as she got to her feet. "I'll take this tin to the pantry for you and finish up drying the dishes so you can go right to bed."

While Olivia carried the tin to the kitchen, Emilee went to the front door and opened it. Even though she'd had had several hours to prepare herself to see Jared again, her heart still began to race the moment she saw him. Standing stiff and formal just within the light pouring out from the foyer, he was as handsome as ever. The black cravat at his throat was only a hint lighter than his hair, and the dark gray waistcoat he wore only made his eyes seem paler and more luminous. Hat in hand, he nodded toward the inside of the parsonage. "Is Mother ready to leave?"

"She's in the kitchen," Emilee murmured. "Come inside. She won't be more than a few minutes." She stepped aside, but he made no move to accept her invitation.

His gaze grew troubled. "Since we have a few minutes alone, I'd like to ask you to forgive me. I had no right to burden you with my troubles, and I had even less to bring your mother or your attempts to handle your memories of her into the conversation." He squared his shoulders. "For that I'm truly sorry, but even more . . . I betrayed your friendship and your trust. After you were kind enough to listen, I had no right—"

"There's nothing to forgive," she whispered. "You were upset. So was I."

He took a small package from his pocket and pressed it into her hands. "I've wanted to give you something for opening up your home to me and my mother until we could get settled. And now . . . it seems too little to make up for how I behaved last night. I'm leaving in the morning, and I won't be bothering you again."

She closed her eyes. His touch was warm, his words a plaintive plea. And his very tempting presence challenged her vow to harden her heart against him. When she opened her eyes, she averted her gaze to keep from looking at him directly. "I can't accept a gift from you. It wouldn't be proper."

"Please. It isn't much. I only wish I could fill it with happy memories about your mother for you. Maybe you can try."

She clutched the package in her hands as he stepped away from her. "I have a lot of soul-searching to do," he said quietly. "I'm not sure if I can take your advice, but I'm going to try. I only hope you might try, too. Maybe it will help knowing you're not alone."

Tears blurred her vision. "Jared, I . . . I—"

"There you are!" Olivia cried. "I've near worn out my

welcome," she complained as she came into the foyer and stopped to lift her cloak from the hook on the oak settle.

Emilee hid her package in the folds of her skirt when Olivia hugged her goodbye and stepped outside to join her son. "I'll stop by tomorrow afternoon. Maybe you can go outside and get some fresh air while I stay here in case Randall needs anything. Now go on to bed, and be sure to latch the door behind you," she urged, turning at once to her son. "As for you," she teased, poking him in the arm, "we need to talk about keeping your mother waiting."

Emilee waited until they had left the porch before closing the door and dousing the lamps in the foyer and the parlor. She carried Jared's gift upstairs with her to check on Randall before changing into her nightclothes. She climbed into bed in the moonlit chamber, and her fingers trembled as she opened the package.

When she slid the gift from its pale green velvet sack, she held the trinket box up to a shaft of moonlight and caught her breath. The intricate silver design in the small square box glistened as brightly as the tears that filled her eyes. An exquisite silver rose resting in a bed of inlaid ivory on the lid captivated her, and she lifted the lid to see a velvet lining identical in color to the sack that now lay on her lap.

She had never received a gift as beautiful as the one she held in her hands, and she clutched it to her heart and held it as dear as his efforts to take the blame for their improper embrace last night. Choking down tears, she slipped out of bed and went to her old chamber, still clutching her gift. She rifled through her sewing basket, found a remnant of black linen, and snipped off a piece no bigger than her small finger. Using her sewing chalk, she printed one word on the small scrap of linen, etching each letter carefully. When she was finished, she lifted the lid to the silver trinket box and laid the slip of cloth inside so she could see the word she had printed: *devotion.*

It was only the first, but with Jared's encouragement and her own determination, she hoped to fill the trinket box with good memories of her mother. With each good memory, Emilee would give up one of the bitter ones she had stored in her heart. Maybe someday, when the memory box was full, she would have no bad memories left, but the space left in her heart only meant that the love she had for Jared would have more room to grow.

TWENTY-THREE

For Jared, soul-searching meant monotonous, backbreaking, manual labor for four straight days of isolation on his property. With his body numbed and his mind freed by the rhythm of his work, he focused on the issues that had made his return home nothing shy of hell on earth.

A confident man of commerce accustomed to cutting his own wide, successful swath through competitors, he had been paralyzed in his personal life by adolescent fears compounded by very adult problems he could not run away from for the rest of his life. Not anymore. He could not relive the past few weeks of his life back in Surrey, but he would be damned if he was going to spend another minute as anything less than a man in control of his own fate and destiny.

He paused in the middle of his work on Tuesday morning to wipe his brow and drink thirstily from a jug of fresh water drawn from the well he had dug before his stock had arrived on Saturday. From his vantage point along the orchard, he could see the acres of rosebushes he had planted already, anxious for next spring and summer when hundreds of roses would be in full blossom and his life would be far better than it had been only a few short days ago.

He picked up the pruning hook and tackled his last project with a vengeance. For several hundred yards, brier roses had strangled most of the underbrush near the edge of the woods that bordered the orchard. Wild and left undisturbed for years, the bushes were a tangled mass of thorned streamers covered with dead blossoms that threatened to overrun the young saplings planted nearby.

He continued to prune the thorned limbs carefully and methodically, seeing the thicket as a living, natural symbol of his life which had been tangled and snarled by fear as well as anger and disappointment. With his arms and face pricked by unruly branches covered with thorns, he hacked and trimmed each section until it had been reduced to nothing more than foot-high stems. Come spring, he would tame and control the new shoots and be rewarded with a natural border that would blossom fragrantly—to his liking.

He would not, however, wait until spring to reshape his life. He had already lost precious weeks, if not years, and he would not waste any more time wallowing in the past and allowing it to overshadow his relationship with his mother or to dampen the friendships he had renewed.

Neither could he take credit for finding his way to self-respect and self-direction. He owed that to one very remarkable woman with hair the color of burnished copper, eyes so verdant green they took his breath away, and a spirit so giving she had claimed more than his heart. She owned his very soul. He heard her voice in the whisper of the wind and saw her smile in the sunlight that flashed through his window at dawn.

Emilee was as winsome as the fairest star in a sky filled with dreams and as elusive as the winter rose that had captured his imagination. He loved her. He wanted her. And he would wait a lifetime to have her by his side—if only for one day.

Chest heaving, he clipped the last thorned streamer and tossed the pruning hook to the ground. When he stooped to drag the cut branches aside, he caught a glimpse out of the corner of his eye of a man he quickly recognized. "Ansel! I didn't expect to see you till tomorrow night."

As he approached, the older man surveyed Jared and his work and grinned. "Looks like you've lost a few battles in this war. Briers sure are nasty work, but judging by that pile of branches, I'd say you won this one."

Chuckling, Jared removed his gloves and dropped them to the ground to shake hands. "It's cost me a good shirt and half a pound of flesh, but it's worth it. What brings you out here today?"

Ansel shrugged his bony shoulders. "The Ladies' Benevolent Association is meeting at the house today. Need I say more? I sure hope you can convince the town council tonight to accept the ladies' proposal for the meetinghouse.''

"I intend to do just that.''

"And you'll have my undying gratitude,'' Ansel promised. "I thought maybe I might go over some plans with you for the orchard, but I guess that might have to wait for another day. I did bring some dinner, though. Hester's convinced you're living on bread and water.''

"Sounds better than stacking these briers. I'm ready to call it quits for the day anyway. Why don't we go inside and talk while we eat?''

Ansel chuckled. "You read my hopes exactly, boy.''

The two men chatted as they walked back to the cabin, and continued nonstop over dinner. When Jared cleared the dishes away from the table, Ansel laid out his sketch for the orchard. He pointed to the alternating rows of the two varieties of saplings already planted and outlined the process of grafting several varieties together on the same tree.

Intrigued by the process and the possibility he might apply a similar concept to the roses he intended to grow, Jared thought again of someday cultivating a winter rose. "Do you think grafting might work on roses, too?''

Ansel's eyes narrowed for a moment as he skewed his face, pondering the question. "I never thought much about trying it on anything else.''

"But can it be done?''

"You could try,'' Ansel admitted. "Why don't you make some sketches of what you have in mind? I'll take a look at them at home, and we can talk about them next time I stop by.''

"When's the next ladies' meeting?'' Jared joked and held up his hands in mock surrender when Ansel glared at him. "I couldn't resist. I'll work on the plans after I get back on Thursday.''

"I take it you're staying over with your mother till the elders' meeting tomorrow night?''

Jared smiled. "One last time. Then I'm back at work here. I'll still ride in for Sunday meeting and spend the day with my mother once the minister is back in form.''

Frowning, Ansel shook his head. "From all accounts, he's not doing so well. Some of the ladies are pretty upset, and poor Emilee can't seem to get more than a few hours' rest at a time. Your mother is even talking about moving back into the parsonage for a spell to help Emilee. I sure hope Dr. Pounds knows what he's doing." He stood up and nodded toward the door. "In any event, I'd best be going home and let you freshen up and pack."

Lost in thought and worried about Emilee, Jared barely acknowledged Ansel's departure with more than a hasty expression of thanks and a promise to remember to bring his mother's tins with him so she could refill them. After a quick, bone-chilling dip in the stream, he dressed for the meeting and packed his travel bag. With less than an hour to spare, he had one last task to complete before he left.

He sat down at his desk, took out several sheaths of paper, and started to write the most important letter of his life. Words poured out faster than he could write them neatly, but he wrote furiously, from his heart to his fingertips, until he had drained every last bit of anger and hurt from his soul. Exhausted physically and emotionally, he folded his letter and put it into his waistcoat pocket, secured the cabin, and headed back to the village at sundown with a canvas sack latched to his saddle-bags.

He had just enough time to stop at his mother's and still make the meeting on time. Afterward, he would deliver the letter which would seal his fate and secure his future.

The parsonage had become a cocoon. Isolated deep inside and confined mostly to the second floor, Emilee dangled from a slender emotional thread surrounded by darkness. She measured every move, modulated every word to a whisper to accommodate Randall's illness, and turned away well-meaning visitors, including Olivia. During her first and last visit, Emilee had taken a brief walk, only to return to find Randall had awakened and grown highly agitated to learn Emilee was not there.

She had not left him again, nor did she venture far from the chamber across the hall when she did seek her own bed, except to prepare something for them to eat or to allow Dr. Pounds to make his daily call. Disoriented, with no sense of the normal cycle of day and night or the passage of time, she walked a tightrope, constantly trying to balance her behavior with her husband's ever-increasing needs.

No longer bedridden or mired in self-pity or denial, he simmered with anger like a teakettle on a slow-burning stove and spent his days sitting with Troubles on his lap in the chair she had moved away from the bed. Tense and afraid, Emilee prayed with him and for him, but his mood had turned ugly and resentful as he railed against the illness which threatened his ministry, and the God who had punished him for sins long since committed.

Relieved to escape his particularly surly attitude late Tuesday afternoon when he sent her to the kitchen to remake a cup of tea he claimed had been brewed too strong for his liking, she carried a new cup of tea back to his chamber with bated breath. She had had enough experience with his occasional bouts of temper to be very leery, and she approached him cautiously after her eyesight had adjusted to total darkness again.

"Set it down on the table," he ordered. "No doubt you've made it too hot to drink without scalding my mouth."

She did as she was told, offering no retort to prevent lighting the fuse that would lead to a volatile outburst of temper.

"Sit down."

She sat on a small chair she had moved from her old chamber and placed in front of her husband within easy arm's reach in case he should be in too much pain to speak and needed to reach out and take her hand to get her attention. "Would you like me to read to you again?"

She heard a heavy, agitated sigh and a light thud as Troubles landed on the floor, and then listened as the kitten padded out of the room.

"Not now. I want you to get Ezra Traymore and bring him here."

"But Dr. Pounds said—"

"I don't care what he said! I'm the patient, and I know what I need," he growled.

"I only—"

"Listen to me," he argued. "The elders have to be told about my illness, and I don't want Dr. Pounds or anyone else to tell them how uncertain the treatment is. My ministry is at stake, and I want to convince him the treatment will be long but effective, so the elders will give me the time I need to recover, and I don't need you to argue with me. Just do as you're told."

Cringing at his harsh, cold words, her heart began to race. She could lie to him, if only to wait for a time when he was less angry and more conciliatory, but she did not know what to tell him other than the truth, since Ezra would most certainly inform her husband about her appearance before the board of elders. She moistened her lips, braced herself by gripping the side of her seat with her hands, and tried to broach the subject obliquely. "The Board of Elders will be patient," she whispered, hoping her low voice would remind Randall to speak more softly to avoid triggering another headache. "Perhaps if you wait a few days until you're stronger . . ."

She heard him hiss as he bent forward in his chair. "I want to see him. Today. Now."

The lump in her throat was the only thing that kept her heart inside her body. "I've already spoken to the elders on your behalf, along with Dr. Pounds. They won't be making any decision—"

"You . . . you what?"

To a background of gurgling anger, tight, powerful hands wrapped around her neck and strangled the rest of her words. Choking for air, she yanked at his arms and frantically twisted her body to escape from his grasp. As her chair rocked from side to side, his grip tightened. Pain exploded in her throat, her head pounded, and brightly colored lights crackled in a chaotic dance in front of her eyes. She was unable to breathe or think. She could only react, although she was growing weaker by the second.

When her chair suddenly toppled to the side, breaking his

hold, she managed a precious gulp of air before her face struck the side of a chest of drawers. Stunned by pain that exploded across the lower part of her face, she crumpled to the floor. Gasping for breath, she curled into a ball and cradled her face against the arm pinned beneath her.

"Emilee!"

Above the thudding of her heart, she heard him cry out for her. Every muscle in her body trembled, but she scrambled away from him on her hands and knees as she heard him get to his feet.

"Emilee! My God! Sweet, merciful Lord, forgive me. Emilee! Please let me help you," he groaned before he collapsed back into his chair.

Plunged into her worst nightmare, she backed farther away until she was next to the bed. Clinging to the footboard for support, she pulled herself up to her feet, only to sway in a wave of dizziness. She tasted the bitter brine of blood mixed with tears and cupped her chin with her hand. Her lips throbbed with pain when she tried to speak and her hands were warm and sticky with blood that trickled from her mouth. She could not see even the dark shadows in the room with her vision blurred by tears, and she did not bother to try to speak.

"Emilee. The pain. My head. Please help me, Emilee!"

His voice was hoarse with pain, and she could hear him thrashing about in his chair. He cried out once more and fell silent and completely still. Fear battled and won over her compassion, and she hesitated for only a heartbeat before she turned and walked out of the room as fast as her shaking legs could carry her. With Jared's name on her lips, she fainted the moment she stepped into the hall.

Twilight, husky with the sweet scent of autumn, provided privacy. With the village resting quietly after a day filled with the noise of labor and daily commerce, nature supplied a peaceful backdrop to his isolated setting. Courage guided Jared's steps as he approached his father's grave with a small canvas sack in his hand.

He knelt down, paused to close his eyes, and listened to the sound of his own heartbeat and the echo of Emilee's advice. "Replace the bitter with the sweet," he murmured. He opened his eyes and used a small garden shovel stored in the canvas sack to dig a deep hole at the base of the marble statue. His hand trembled as he removed the letter from his pocket and clutched it in front of him. In the letter, he had written all the things he should have said to his father, but never had the courage to speak. Jared had penned every angry thought and every bitter disappointment with brutal honesty, and he reviewed them all in his mind now before he consigned them to the past once and for all. He placed the letter into the hole in the ground and covered it with dirt before taking a very small rosebush out of the sack and planting it directly on top of his letter. Using the garden shovel, he filled in the gaps around the roots and tamped down the soil until it was once again firmly packed.

He put the shovel away, straightened his back, and still kneeling, bowed his head. "I hated you, Father," he whispered. His throat tightened, and his heart began to pound. "But I loved you, too."

He remained on his knees while he offered a prayer for his father's soul. When he finished, he stood up, feeling calmer and more peaceful than he had expected—at least in this lifetime. Satisfied with his odd but soul-enriching ritual, he left the cemetery feeling stronger with every step he took. Whatever challenges lay ahead, he was ready now to face them, embrace them, and conquer them, one challenge at a time, one day at a time. With God's help and a free conscience, he was prepared to face only one obstacle that seemed as insurmountable as it was ironic, given his initial reaction to finding himself attracted to a married woman. He was anxious to win the heart and the hand of Emilee Greene—the woman he loved.

Oddly energized by his visit to the cemetery, he proceeded directly to the parsonage to deliver a note to Emilee from his mother, who had grown increasingly worried about her adopted daughter. He also wanted to speak to Emilee about his decision on the church dedication and his reconciliation with his past.

He approached the parsonage, curious about the blaze of light pouring from nearly every room on the first floor. When Dr. Pounds answered Jared's knock on the front door, curiosity turned to alarm.

Looking drawn and worried, the doctor ushered Jared inside. "Thank God. I was hoping someone would come by." He spoke quickly and explained the situation he had found when he had arrived less than an hour ago. "There's little more I can do tonight. She's resting comfortably after her fall, but Randall is far worse and he'll need care until she's recovered."

Jared nodded grimly and clenched his fists at his sides. "I'll stay here. If you'll stop at my mother's on your way home, ask her to bring my travel bag and pack a few things of her own. We'll stay until . . . for as long as we're needed."

The doctor hesitated. "I really shouldn't leave her now, but Randall is sedated—"

"I'll be with her," Jared whispered, his voice firm despite the quaking of his heart. The dreaded thought Emilee had suffered a mishap greater than marrying the wrong man grew into a very real possibility when he recalled how upset she had been after an argument with her husband the very first day Jared had met her at the cemetery. As soon as Dr. Pounds took his leave, Jared removed his waistcoat and hat and hung them on the oak settle. He walked up the front staircase and went directly to the chamber he had occupied before moving out to his cabin.

Ignoring the door to Randall's chamber, he softened his steps and walked to the bed where Emilee rested after allegedly falling down the steps. Bathed in flickering candlelight, she lay very still facing the wall. Her eyes were closed, and she was breathing evenly.

He knelt down at the side of her bed and tears filled his eyes the moment he saw the large bruise on the side of her face and the jagged row of stitches in her bottom lip. He reached out, took her hand, and pressed it to his lips. When his gaze rested on the angry, hand-print bruises wrapped around her neck, he trembled with rage. "My sweet, darling Emilee," he groaned. "What has he done to you?"

TWENTY-FOUR

Powerful arms and shoulders, comforting and protective. A familiar scent, distinctive and masculine. A heartbeat, steady and strong. A man, forbidden yet beloved: Jared.

His presence invaded Emilee's senses and slipped past all her defenses to answer the plaintive call of her heart. He surrounded her as never before and brought calm to her shattered world and broken spirit. Gentle motion lulled her into full consciousness, and her heart began to race. Jolts of throbbing pain overwhelmed the smell and taste of blood in her mouth and crusted on her swollen lips, slamming her from a dream-like state into the full aftermath of her nightmare.

Disoriented, she opened her eyes and realized someone was carrying her down the brightly lit hall. She gripped the fabric beneath her fingertips and struggled to lift her head. Instead of words of protest, she heard a garbled whimper escape from her lips.

"Shhh. I'm only taking you back to your old chamber."

Jared? Her mind was still dulled by medication, but she knew his voice beyond all others. She tilted her head back and recognized the cleft in his chin and the wisps of curly dark hair at the nape of his neck. Sinking against his chest, she did not question what was happening or why.

Jared was here. He held her in his arms, and she could think of no safer place to be—or more dangerous. Right or wrong held no sway over her conscience. She had neither the strength nor the will to care about pretenses or morality. He was simply here. She wanted him to be here. And she wanted him to stay.

He entered her softly lit chamber and carried her to her bed. When he attempted to lay her down, she stiffened and dug her fingers into his shoulder.

"I won't leave you," he whispered.

Trembling, she clung harder and burrowed against him. "H-hold me," she moaned and winced when her mouth tugged at the stitches Dr. Pounds had used to close the split in her bottom lip.

"You need your rest," he argued.

Tears stung her eyes. "Y-you. I . . . n-need . . . y-you."

He paused and twisted his body away from the bed. "There's no chair here," he murmured as though talking to himself. "Oh, damn the bloody chair! Just hold on. Let's see if I can do this with one hand." He cradled her against him and stacked the pillows against the headboard. When he sat down, he held her with both arms as he swung his legs up onto the mattress and turned his body so he could lean his back against the pillowed headboard to lay her beside him.

His chest cushioned the side of her face, and his arm curled around her shoulders. Listening to the sound of his steady heartbeat comforted her and reassured her. She sighed and closed her eyes when he clasped his hand over hers and held it against his hip.

"Are you all right now?"

She nodded, turned her hand, and laced her fingers with his, unable to stop the flow of tears that dampened his shirt. He stroked her head and lifted her hair away from her face, using his thumb to slowly massage her temple.

"Just rest for now. Don't try to talk. Dr. Pounds went to get my mother, and we'll both stay until you're well. Shhh. Hush. It's all over now. I'm here with you, and I won't let anything happen to you."

Soothed by his gentle touch and his soft words, she relaxed against him. Far too many questions coursed through her mind, but she had no desire to voice them or ponder the answers he might give her. For now, all she needed was the security of Jared's embrace. Her heartbeat slowed and her breathing became even again. Even the pain in her throat and face ebbed to bearable.

"Do you think you can sleep? Would you like some water?"

She shook her head very slowly and deliberately.

He squeezed her hand. "I don't want you to disturb those stitches, which means I get to do all the talking." He let out a deep sigh. "Maybe that's not a bad idea since I have an awful lot I need to say." He lifted her hand to his lips and pressed a kiss to the tips of each of her fingers. "You were right about everything," he said quietly.

She listened carefully as he told her about all the work he had done to his property, and when Jared described trimming back the brier rose, she thought back to the day she had found the kitten. When he shared with her the ritual he had used to make peace with his father and the secret that had been a burden for so many years, her heart swelled in her chest.

Jared was truly a singular, most sensitive man. While some might find the ritual at his father's grave a bit strange, she could only marvel at the depth of his insight and his remarkable determination to create a new life for himself free from the past. Without words, she could only use her body to express how proud she was of him, and she hugged him.

"I couldn't have done it without your advice," he admitted and hugged her back.

She longed to share how she had begun to create a memory chest out of the silver trinket box he had given to her and promised herself to remember to tell him as soon as she could talk easily and without pain. To a certain extent, she envied him. Her mother was buried in a potter's field in Boston, and there was no marker on her grave where Emilee might visit even if she could find it.

"The elders' meeting when I have to return the plans for the plaque is later tonight. I have an idea about that, too," he began, pulling her away from her thoughts.

As he detailed his intentions, she was surprised to learn both that Olivia knew about the church dedication and the nature of Jared's alternative proposal.

"So . . . what do you think?" he asked. "Squeeze once for yes, twice for no."

She squeezed hard. Once.

He chuckled. "I thought you'd like it. I only hope the elders will."

She squeezed him hard once again, but when she tried to lift her head away from him, he used his hand to keep her snuggled against his chest.

"Now that I have your full and undivided attention as well as your approval, there's something else I want to say. No. Just stay still and listen," he admonished when she tried to shift her position to be able to look at him. "We don't have much time before Dr. Pounds and my mother get here. Lord knows I'll have one devil of a time explaining why I'm here in bed with you if they get here before I finish, but I doubt I'll get a chance to be alone with you like this again once they do."

His body tensed beneath her, and his heartbeat fluttered against her cheek. His chest rose and fell with each deep breath he took, and she grew more and more curious as she waited for him to explain what was so important it could not wait.

"The last time we spoke, I told you I wouldn't bother you again." He paused, and she could feel and hear his heart begin to race. "I had no right to make that promise because I can't keep it. I love you, Emilee. Beyond what's right or holy, I love you with all that I am and all that I hope to be. I know this isn't precisely the time or the place . . ." He cupped the side of her head and toyed with her hair. "Sweet woman, I love you. Truly. I need you, and I want you by my side for every day I live and breathe on this earth."

His whispered declaration, hoarse with emotion, joined with the echo of the very words and sentiment she had stored deep in her heart. Instead of seconds, heartbeats measured time, and when her heart skipped into an erratic pattern, time itself changed in nature and existed only in their hearts. Caught in an aura of magic and mystery only love could inspire, she held very still and claimed this one precious moment as her heart's desire.

The rest of her life would be measured in ordinary seconds and minutes and hours, but this moment was created only for them. None of the hurts of the past existed. There was no future. Only the mystifying present, where she was not the minister's wife, but merely a woman who loved the man who held her in his arms with her whole heart and soul.

Trembling, she took his hand and placed it over her heart. Waiting. Yearning. Hoping he could feel with his hand how fast her heart was beating with the words she could not say and had no right to feel, except in this one blessed moment. "Truly," she whispered, praying with that one single word she could make him understand she loved him, too. She turned her face to look up at him and saw the miracle of love shining bright and true in the depths of his eyes. She caressed his beloved face with her gaze and wrapped her heart with his love. For now. Forever. Whatever the future might hold, she would know that once upon a dream, she had loved and been loved in return.

One dream. One very special and unique woman. One precious moment. Her heart beat beneath his fingertips, and Jared studied her features. They were battered and bruised, but he saw only the beauty of her spirit and the gentle light of love shimmering in her eyes. For one incredibly long heartbeat, he nearly forgot to breathe. He could not think. He could only feel the love that haunted her features. "Truly," he whispered, overwhelmed by the power of the emotions that warmed him and touched the very core of his soul.

Her ever-so-slight smile was a bit crooked, but it was the most beautiful smile he had ever seen, while also the most pathetically sad as tears began to cascade down her cheeks. The lump pounding in his throat could only be his heart, and he knew, just as she did, there were tremendous obstacles that blocked the road that would lead to their happiness together.

Unable to speak, he cradled her against his chest. After pressing a kiss to the tip of her nose, he rocked her gently until her tears subsided and her even breathing assured him she finally had fallen asleep in the crook of his arms.

With his mind awash with wonder and his very soul filled with joy, he closed his eyes to savor the miracle of their love. With every beat of his heart, he vowed to use the next few days as she recovered to protect her and keep her safe, but he was not willing to wait and watch the woman he loved be destroyed by the man in the chamber on the other side of the wall behind his back. Jared would fight to love her and keep her by his side no matter the price.

The front door to the parsonage opened and closed, and he stiffened. When hushed voices and footsteps on the staircase echoed in the hallway, he eased from the bed so as not to disturb Emilee from her sleep. He cushioned her head with a pillow and tucked the covers up around her shoulders. Bending down, he pressed a kiss to her temple and brought her hand to his heart. "Truly," he whispered. "On my honor, we will be together one day, my love."

He laid her hand beneath the covers, turned, and walked out into the hall. The secret of their love lay in his heart as a fragile, treasured gift, one he would protect with pride and carry with honor until the day he could proclaim it to the world—a day that might come sooner than he had ever dared to dream.

Body tense, Jared maintained his vigil in total darkness, unaware how close dawn might be. Seated on the blood-splattered chair at the foot of the sickbed, he was calm and determined. His mother had finally taken to her bed, and Dr. Pounds had long since left, but Jared had one last task before he acquiesced to total exhaustion.

He had won a grueling debate with the doctor, who had agreed to appear with Jared before the Board of Elders later that night. His mother, bless her heart, had not hesitated to move back into the parsonage and prepared herself for an indeterminate stay. Although she had not been convinced Emilee's injuries were purely accidental, she had not seen the hand-print bruises on her adopted daughter's throat. Once she did, Jared was certain his mother would agree Emilee had been attacked brutally by her husband. It would take much more, however, to convince either his mother or the doctor that Randall's violence was inborn rather than a temporary complication of his illness.

Jared knew better. That first day at the cemetery, he had seen Emilee reduced to tears after an argument with her husband. Jared had seen her humiliated the day of the cabin-raising. Now he had seen very real and compelling evidence her husband had escalated the pattern of verbal abuse into physical, and Jared had no intention of standing idly by and letting her be hurt again.

On his life, never again.

His love for Emilee, however, gave him the courage to turn fury into the cold, hard steel of determination. His self-control was implacable. When he heard the covers on the bed begin to rustle, his senses scrambled to full alert. His heart maintained a steady, even rhythm, and he held absolutely still.

"Emilee?"

Randall's croaking cry echoed in the room, and Jared clenched his fists as the mattress squeaked and the headboard creaked beneath Randall's weight.

"Emilee!"

The man's cry was stronger and carried higher. He must have sat up.

"Emilee!"

"She's not here," Jared gritted. Blanketed in total darkness, he could see nothing, but he could imagine the look of shock and confusion on the minister's face. Heavy breathing several feet in front of Jared laced the silence between them, and he let the tension build until the bed began to squeak again. "Don't get out of bed. Don't even move," he warned. "I only intend to stay here long enough to speak my piece." He heard a sharp intake of breath. Then more silence and rapid but heavy breathing.

"B-Burke?"

Jared grinned sardonically. "Very good. You're alert enough to listen to me very carefully. What I have to say won't take long."

"What's going on? What are you doing here? Where's my wife?"

Unmoved by the frantic tone in Randall's flurry of questions, Jared kept both feet planted on the floor and his spine stiff. "I'm here because Dr. Pounds asked me to be here, and Emilee is resting after the ordeal you put her through. Fortunately, she managed to escape before you strangled the life out of her.''

"I can't be held responsible for Emilee's accident. It was the medication or the treatment—''

"*I* hold you accountable," Jared argued, duly noting how Randall used his illness to excuse his behavior without bothering to reassert his earlier claims to Dr. Pounds that Emilee's injuries were caused directly by a clumsy fall and indirectly by Randall's fumbling attempts in the darkness to catch her.

Images of Emilee's battered face flashed through his mind, and he had no sympathy for the man who had inflicted her injuries. "There's been a modification in your treatment, and I'm going to explain it to you only once. Mother and I have moved back into the parsonage. She'll be taking over your care while Emilee recovers from her 'accident,' but I'll accompany my mother each time she enters your room. Dr. Pounds, of course, will continue to monitor your health on a daily basis, and there's a lock on the outside of your door to make sure you remain in your chamber to continue your treatment. If and when Emilee decides to speak to you, I'll escort her here and remain here until she's ready to leave. If you understand what I've said so far, just say yes. Nothing more.''

"Y-yes, but I want to—''

"As for your ministry," Jared continued, overriding Randall's attempted interruption, "Dr. Pounds and I will address the Board of Elders later tonight, where I'll present your letter of resignation.''

"Never!" Randall hissed. "You arrogant, miserable snake. How dare you invade a man's sickroom and insist on anything?''

"By all that's right, I dare," Jared snarled. "As far as you're concerned, that's all that matters.''

"All that matters? Hardly," Randall snapped. "I'm ill, but I'm not a fool. I've seen the way you look at my wife. You covet her. That's why you're really here. Your motives are sinful, not altruistic as you so nobly claim. Have you no fear of God? Have you no shame?''

"Shame?" Jared spat "There's only one man in this room

who should carry any shame. You stand in the pulpit every Sunday to preach the Word, yet you abuse your own wife?''

''My wife is no more your concern than my health. I'll speak to Dr. Pounds personally and make arrangements for someone to assist in my care as well as Emilee's until she can resume her responsibilities. At that time, I'll expect you and your mother to leave my home and tend to more important matters, such as the state of your soul.''

''Like hell,'' Jared snarled. The man was as arrogant as he was stubborn. ''You're in no position to make demands. Not one. Not about your treatment and not about your ministry.''

''I have more right than you do. How can you even presume to have the audacity to insist I resign? What right do you have to judge me?''

''I'm not going to waste my time arguing with you. I've set down my terms, and they're final. Be grateful they're not as harsh as I'd like them to be.''

Randall sighed. ''Then I'm afraid you leave me no other choice but to convince you otherwise.''

Jared's spine began to tingle and his pulse quickened.

''I'd hoped you'd be more reasonable. Apparently you're too consumed by your own wickedness, and you force me to respond in kind.'' He paused for only a moment. ''Do the names Agnes Hampton or Sarah Bridgeboro sound familiar? No, perhaps not, but you should recognize the name Violet Weston,'' he added tersely. ''She had a most interesting deathbed confession.''

Disbelief and shock shattered the shell of Jared's composure. Pure rage melted the glacier of his determination to protect Emilee and his mother, and he lunged forward to get to his feet.

''Sit down,'' Randall ordered.

Breathing hard, Jared sat on the edge of his seat.

''Now you're going to listen to me,'' Randall warned. ''I concede that I need time to recuperate, so I'll allow some of the conditions you've outlined. But resign?'' He snorted. ''That's absurd. I'll sign a letter you'll draft requesting a three-month temporary leave of absence after which I'll resume all of my duties—including my husbandly rights to the woman who carries *my* name. Not yours. If you dare to tell anyone Emilee's injuries were not purely accidental, I'll use the pulpit to reveal all of your father's dirty little sins."

Heart pounding, Jared forced himself to stay very still because if he moved as much as a single muscle, he would end up strangling the life out of Randall Greene without a bit of regret. "My father's dead," he spat.

"But you're still here. So is your mother."

"Leave my mother out of this!"

"My. My. How noble and very protective you are. Your father felt the same way. You're actually cast from the same mold in several ways, aren't you? The Burkes seem to have a lusty appetite for married women. Well, you'll crack, just like he did when he tried to persuade me I wasn't quite good enough to be his permanent replacement."

"Blackmail." Jared's word hung between them like a cannonball in midair, ready to fall the moment gravity asserted dominance over matter.

"Not blackmail. God's will, which shall always prevail," Randall countered. "This ministry was given to me by the hand of God. Only He can take it away. If I fail to recover completely, then so be it, but you will not interfere in God's plan without suffering the consequences. You alone will be responsible for your mother's heartbreak. Even if you do want to carry that burden, I wonder how you'll feel when I reveal your lust for my wife and your attempts to steal her affections. Will you shame Emilee as well as your mother and yourself?"

Jared gnashed his teeth together and swallowed the bile that stung his throat. He tensed each muscle in his body and forced his breathing to remain normal. Groping for time to turn apparent failure into victory, he had no choice at all. He stood up and spoke in a loud, clear voice. "You seem to have the upper hand after all, *Reverend*. But hear me well. If you breathe one word about my father or slander Emilee's name, I'll build my own gallows in advance before I kill you."

Without waiting for Randall to reply, Jared walked quickly

and deliberately from the room. Once outside, he locked the chamber door. Bristling at the sound of muted laughter that came from within the room, he entered his own chamber and stared out the window.

Dawn had broken, casting the world into a bright new day, but he saw only the darkness of his own future, where love and honor had no place but in his dreams. Unless he could volley a counterattack and pitch the cannonball, single-handedly, squarely back at the minister and destroy him. Jared had been outmaneuvered in this skirmish, but the minister's victory would be short-lived and doomed to failure as long as Jared had the strength to draw a single breath.

TWENTY-FIVE

While Olivia and Jared attended meeting with Reverend Shelton conducting the services, Emilee slipped out of bed and dressed quickly before she ventured a careful study of her appearance in the mirror over her dresser. In the strong light pouring through the window in her chamber, the bruises on her face and throat were garish hues of yellow and purple that gave her features a ghoulish, haunted look. At least her mouth was no longer hideously swollen, and the puckered stitches in her bottom lip were more annoying than painful. Although Dr. Pounds had promised to remove the stitches in a day or two, she was half-tempted to snip them herself.

Instead, she turned away from the mirrored dresser and gathered up her sewing basket to keep her hands occupied on the new sampler she had designed for Olivia. Nearly claustrophobic after five days' confinement in her chamber, Emilee went downstairs and settled herself at the kitchen table. She spread out the different-colored threads, but her mind was not on her task and her heart remained troubled.

The events preceding her "accidental fall" were still fuzzy, but she could no longer defend her husband's violence, at least in her own mind. To Jared and Olivia, she remained steadfast in her contention that the injuries were purely accidental, despite his insistence otherwise, if only to grant Randall one concession: While he was still battling his illness, she had pushed him over the edge by presenting his case to the Board of Elders. She remained in fear of him, however, and had not argued against the arrangements Jared had made for Randall's care. Neither did she begrudge how hastily the board had acted on Randall's letter granting him a three-month leave of absence.

As she selected gentle shades of blue and green for the

sampler's border, all of her thoughts were on Jared. Although he remained devoted, he had never again mentioned their mutual declaration of love. Olivia rarely left them alone together for more than a few minutes. Even then, there was only time for a gentle touch or a look of yearning that bespoke his affection for Emilee. As she recovered, she became more aware of the futility of their love for one another. As much as she longed to share his life and love, she could not overlook the one impossible barrier that stood between them: She was married to Randall.

For better or worse, she had taken vows to love, honor, and obey her husband. She had failed miserably on all three counts. She had fallen hopelessly in love with another man and dishonored herself and her husband in the process. She had disobeyed him, deliberately violating his wishes to keep the extent of his illness private, and his volatile reaction when he had learned what she had done was as much her fault as it was his.

Leaving Randall for another man would be as scandalous as it was wrong. As a divorced woman, she could never show her face in the village again, and Randall would be subjected to gossip and innuendo that could destroy him. Her shame also would be extended to Olivia, whose valiant opposition to the entire community as Emilee's protector would be proven wrong.

Most importantly, Jared would suffer as well. His homecoming had been a difficult ordeal, yet he had triumphed over personal pain and disappointment. He had reestablished himself in Surrey where he would be near his mother and continue his life's avocation on a property he loved. Emilee could not ask him to sacrifice his good name for loving her.

Her duty was clear. Her mind was set, but her heart was heavy with grief. She might never be able to fulfill all of her marriage vows save one: "Till death do us part."

There were many years ahead. Her future was full of uncertainty, especially if Randall did not fully recover. She would, however, live each day with honor that would be nourished by the joy of finding true love, having the courage to deny her heart's desire for the sake of others, and clinging to the promise of redemption in which one day she and Jared might spend eternity together.

Confident that her position was morally right, she turned away from her thoughts. She finished selecting her threads and laid the sampler flat on the table. She no sooner had reached inside the sewing basket to get her scissors and needles than Troubles leaped up onto the table. He romped through the threads and bumped the sampler to the floor before she could grab him.

"No!" she cried as she lifted him from the table and settled him on her lap. Bright yellow threads clung to his crooked tail, and red threads twined among his whiskers. Meowing, he nuzzled against her and batted at the end of the tie around her waist.

She giggled and scratched him behind the ears, but when she glanced at the table she saw that her threads had been tangled together like a field of wildflowers battered by a wind storm, she groaned. "You certainly deserve your name. Do you know how much work you've made for me? And just how did you get downstairs? I thought you were still with Randall," she remarked as she removed the yellow and red threads and laid them on the table.

"I'm afraid that's my fault."

Her head snapped up and her heart began to pound. "Jared! I—I thought you went to meeting with your mother."

His smile turned to a frown. "I won't leave you here alone. Not even for a few hours. Actually, I slept in later than usual." He walked over to her, lifted the kitten, and cradled it in his arms as he played with its still-floppy ears. "This young fella was meowing to be let out, so I obliged him. I didn't think he'd get in trouble so quickly."

Although Troubles spent most of his time with Randall, she had not visited her husband since her fall. She did not want to visit him until her stitches were removed and her bruises had faded. Even though Randall's chamber was always dark, light did filter in from the hallway whenever anyone entered, and she did not want Randall to be alarmed by her appearance.

Jared stood so close to her chair she could scarcely breathe. "Maybe he should go outside," she suggested. "At least until I gather up this disaster."

Chuckling, Jared bent down, picked up the sampler from the floor, and handed it to her after he took a few moments to study the design. "You're stitching a sampler of the meetinghouse?"

Her fingers brushed against his hand as she took back her sampler, and ever so familiar tingles raced up her arm. "It's a surprise for your mother," she explained and stored the sampler in her sewing basket while Jared put the kitten outside.

When Jared sat down next to her at the table, he grabbed a handful of threads and started to sort them by color. They worked together in awkward silence, and she kept her gaze averted to keep herself safe from the longing she knew she would find sparkling in the depths of his eyes.

He laid his hand on top of hers and caressed the back of her hand. "Emilee," he murmured. "We haven't had a chance to be alone since the night you were hurt."

She swallowed hard and tried to keep her heart from racing. She could feel his gaze on her face and slowly lifted her eyes as she turned to face him.

Too soon, her heart whispered, trembling to keep his love for just a little while longer.

Now. Before it's too late, her conscience insisted.

Joined hand in hand with the man she loved with all her heart, she blinked back her tears and held her jaw tight to keep her chin from quivering.

His eyes misted until they were pale gray pools of moonlight and promises. "I love you," he whispered. "Truly."

She closed her eyes for a brief moment and took several deep breaths before she met his gaze again. "As I truly love you."

He leaned toward her and cupped the side of her face with his hand. When he dipped his head to kiss her, she held very still and brushed her nagging conscience aside for one last time. One very last time, she vowed. Her lips ached with forbidden longing, and she closed her eyes, if only to heighten the sensation of the gift of his kiss—a kiss that would have to last a lifetime.

His breath was warm. His touch was tender and ever so light as he touched his lips to hers. Gently and lovingly, like a hummingbird might hover above a fragile flower, he kissed her with restraint and barely touched the stitches in her lip, but in that one kiss, she felt the full power of his affection and the redeeming power of love which erased all shame from their pasts and the present.

Love. Passion. Splendor. All those emotions and more swirled through her body and carried her straight to love's greatest pleasures with one very sweet kiss—a kiss that lasted no longer than a heartbeat, yet tempted her more than the shower of kisses he rained on her eyes and forehead.

"I love you," he murmured and his breathing grew heavy. "Be with me. Always."

She opened her eyes and traced the line of his jaw with her fingers. "We can't share anything like this again. Ever. There can never be more for us. Forgive me," she pleaded.

His eyes darkened with confusion and hurt. "I love you, and I'll find a way for us to marry and be together. Divorce may be difficult, but it's not impossible."

She shook her head. Her hand trembled as she pressed her fingertips against his lips. "Listen. Please just listen."

He nodded, but his body grew rigid.

"I could not love you the way I want to without honor. For better or worse, I'm married, Jared. I took vows before God, and I must trust He will protect me and watch over me. As much as I love you, I won't break my marriage vows or dissolve a union blessed by God. If I did, I'd lose more than my self-respect. I'd lose my soul. And I would lose you," she added in a whisper.

"You could lose your life! Your husband hurt you badly, Emilee, and next time—"

"No. When Randall has recovered, he won't harm me."

Jared's eyes widened into twin pools of black horror. "You can't believe that! He attacked you once. He'll do it again."

"He has a temper, but he's not evil," she protested. "When

he's well, things will be different, but . . . but even if they aren't, I can't simply leave him to marry you. Can't you see what would happen? Sooner or later, in the stillness of the night, you would lay beside me and wonder if I would keep my vows to you.''

He lifted her hand away from his face and held it tightly. ''I would never doubt you. Never.''

''Maybe not,'' she admitted, ''but no one here in the village would ever forget the scandal of a divorce. Your name will be linked forever to the minister's wife who abandoned her sick husband and made all their presumptions about her being shamed at birth ring true.''

''We don't have to live here. I've already got Robert Walters taking over for me at the nursery while I stay here. We can make our home anywhere or everywhere, as long as we're together.''

Her heart swelled, but her resolve never wavered, even as he battled each and every one of her reasons why their love would have to remain unfulfilled. ''The shame would be here,'' she said quietly. She pointed to her heart, choosing the one argument he would recognize as painfully as she did. ''Even if you never doubt my love, you'll eventually resent the price we'd each have to pay. Ultimately, the shame would destroy us. And our love.'' Her throat burned with the effort it took to keep tears from filling her eyes. She kept her hand over her heart. ''With honor, you will always be here. Always.''

He covered her hand with his own and entwined their fingers for one long heartbeat after another. ''For now. For always. With honor.'' His voice was ragged, and his gaze was troubled. ''Your love is the greatest gift of my life. I will cherish it as I treasure you, and I won't give you up without a fight. I'll find a way or make one for you to be by my side as my wife with honor, but until I do, I'll respect your wishes, if only to prove how much I love you and believe in the love we share with one another. I only ask you to make me one promise.''

''If I can.''

"Promise you'll let me stay here with my mother to protect you and keep you safe until I'm convinced Randall is completely recovered."

"That wouldn't be fair," she argued. "It may take months. You have your nursery—"

"And I've already told you I made with arrangements for that. Since the fire, Robert and Nancy Walters and their children have needed a permanent place to live instead of that lean-to. Working twelve hours a day, six days a week on the canal doesn't leave Robert much time to build a cabin. Winter will set in long before he's finished. They can live in my cabin while I'm here. Besides, Ansel is helping out by keeping an eye on the orchard for me. Say yes."

"What about—"

"Say yes, or I'll be forced to do something drastic," he teased, but his attempt at humor failed to veil his determination to stay whether she agreed with him or not. He glanced at the mess of threads on the table, and his eyes began to sparkle. "Better yet, say yes and I'll help you to untangle the disaster Troubles made."

She chuckled. "Yes. On one condition."

He raised one brow. "Condition? Such as . . ."

"Such as you do the dark colors and I'll do the pastels."

"You drive a hard bargain, but I accept," he grumbled and chose one lump of threads to begin his work.

Jared had evaded prolonging the argument with his customary good humor, but she knew him well enough to know that beneath his humor lay deep disappointment and equally deep determination to find a way for them to be together. As she joined him and tackled separating the sewing threads, she was far less sure if she could spend the next few months with him without weakening in her resolve to remain committed to her marriage to Randall.

Monday morning, Jared closed the door to the study and sat down at the desk. He still had not recovered from his talk with Emilee yesterday, which had cost him a full night of sleep as he struggled against each one of her arguments. He saw her face and heard her voice every time he closed his eyes, and he was more determined than ever to find a way for them to be together to claim the love they shared. With honor.

He admired her courage and her character as much as he loved her, but he was absolutely opposed to trusting this most precious woman to the likes of Randall Greene. Any man of the cloth who would resort to blackmail not once, but twice, to keep his ministry was either deranged or so unscrupulous he had to have something sordid in his background—something Jared planned to uncover and use against the minister.

Holding steady a letter from his partner, he broke the seal and skimmed the contents, hoping that the key to Randall's past might be there. He paused halfway through the scrawled message when he found Randall's name and read more slowly. He shook his head in disgust. Will's younger brother, David, had not been at Yale until Randall's last year, and the physical description David provided for Randall Greene fit him well enough, although he had evidently added considerable weight since his college days.

As Jared read further, he could find no fault with David's assessment of Randall as a quiet, overly shy student who did rather poorly academically or the confirmation that his attendance at Yale had been sponsored by a Bible society.

Jared's heart pounded with disappointment. So far, nothing seemed amiss. He had been a fool to think it would be easy to discredit Randall, and the process of having him declared deranged was fraught with difficulty as well as scandal. He rubbed his hand across his brow, his confidence badly fractured.

He went back to his letter to finish the last paragraph. He read it once. Then again, and pounded his fist on the desk. The words leaped off of the page and embedded themselves in Jared's mind.

Apparently, Greene hated cats. I have no idea how this came to be known, but if you remember our days together at Yale, you know how those things go. Unaware that Greene was also allergic to cats, some of his tormentors

*stole into his room at a local boardinghouse, tied Greene
to his bed, and left three cats in the room with him. By
morning, Greene was nearly dead, and he missed a good
month of the semester just recovering. At least that's how
David recalls the incident, but he was not at all certain
the victim of the prank actually had been Greene. It could
have been someone else, but mentioning Greene seemed
to trigger David's recollection of the event. It's entirely
possible Greene was one of the tormentors responsible
for staging the prank.*

"Cats? The man's allergic to cats?" Jared stared at the letter
in his hand. "Not *this* Randall Greene," he muttered as his
mind raced with all sorts of intriguing possibilities, some of
which threatened to dampen his excitement.

If David was mistaken about the victim's identity and
Greene was guilty of mischief as a prankster, it was a stretch
to link a prank-gone-bad with intentional violence. If David
was not mistaken and Greene indeed had been the victim, Jared was left with a double-edged sword. Either Greene had
outgrown his allergy to cats, which would explain his attach-
ment to Troubles, or the man who called himself Randall
Greene was an impostor, the odds of which seemed thinner
than the paper Jared held in his hand.

He had a number of options to consider now that it was
clear Randall's background needed further scrutiny. He paced
around the study, reviewing each one. He immediately ruled
out going east himself because he would not leave Emilee or
his mother alone. He could hire an investigator to check on
Randall's background, but that would waste weeks of time just
allowing for the posts to travel back and forth from New York
City. He could talk to Emilee, or even Randall, for that matter,
but Jared's information was not reliable enough to risk upsetting Emilee or tipping his hand with Randall before all the
facts were known.

Jared folded the letter and tucked it into his pocket. Left
with only the option of conducting an investigation through
his partner, Jared could save time by riding to Glendale and

using the telegraph. He would have to word his message very carefully to prevent the telegraph operator from understanding Jared's true intentions, to prevent gossip yet still convey an accurate message to his partner.

Feeling empowered for the first time since he had reached a stalemate with the minister, Jared sat down at the desk again. It took several attempts and half an hour to draft the telegraph message and another half an hour to write a fuller explanation in a follow-up letter he would send by regular post.

After changing into riding clothes, he made sure Randall was secure in his chamber and told Emilee and his mother there was business to tend to in Glendale which would keep Jared away for most of the afternoon. After securing a promise from each of them to stay out of Randall's chamber until Jared returned, he left immediately.

By riding hard, he would be back by sundown. He might even get a good night's rest knowing he had done all he could to undermine Randall's plan to remain in the pulpit by learning the truth about the man who called himself the Reverend Mr. Randall Greene—a truth which would either free Emilee or sentence her to a lifetime shackled to a man she did not love.

Concentrating on the former and refusing to consider the latter, he was glad he had also presented his partner with a request that may have been premature, but very necessary should Jared prevail in his quest to claim Emilee as his wife.

As he rode beyond the confines of the village, he urged his mount into a full gallop. While he had tried to counter all of Emilee's reasons for staying in her marriage, he could not argue against her sense of honor and commitment to keep her marriage vows. If, by some stroke of genius or luck, he could prove those vows invalid, he would free Emilee from her sacred promise.

Given that as a possibility, however remote, he intended to be prepared to handle each and every single argument she had used against him. The most damaging, of course, was the prospect of scandal, whether warranted or not. Given her background, Emilee was an easy target for gossipmongers, and he refused to allow her name or her reputation to be sullied.

The faster he rode, the quicker his mind worked through his options. The more he planned, the greater he became convinced his instincts about Randall Greene were right on target. Each time the horse's hooves pounded the ground, only one question echoed in his heart: How would he live without her if he failed?

"I still think we should wait," Olivia argued in a whisper. "Jared can't be much longer."

Standing next to Olivia outside of Randall's chamber, Emilee griped a supper tray with both hands. "It's very late, and Randall must be hungry. He won't even suspect Jared isn't with me," she countered with hushed words. She did not relish seeing Randall so soon, but she hid her reticence and knew the darkness would hide the extent of her injuries if she stayed in the shadows when her husband lit the small candle on his tray to give him enough light to eat by. "We'll stay just long enough to deliver his meal and see if there's anything else he needs. Where does Jared usually stand when you're inside the room?"

"Just inside the door, but—"

"Then that's where you'll stand. Please. Just unlock the door."

Seconds later, the bolt slid free. With her heart thumping, Emilee stepped into the dark chamber.

"I thought you'd forgotten all about me," Randall whined.

From the direction of his voice, she knew he was sitting in his usual chair, which was straight ahead of her. Her skirts rustled as she walked, and she detected the sound of Olivia's skirts rustling behind her. She offered a quick prayer Randall would not notice. As she neared the chair, she could hear him breathing. He was closer than she had thought, and she stubbed her toes on his feet. Bracing to a clumsy halt, she held on to the tray, but the dishes rattled ominously.

"Well, this is indeed an honor. A visit from my wife and Mrs. Burke. Be careful you don't fall and spill the tray, Emilee. I wouldn't want you to hurt yourself again, especially since you still seem to be having trouble accommodating the dreary conditions I'm forced to endure.''

She felt a strong pressure on the other side of the tray and relaxed her grip to let him take it from her. The aroma of fresh vegetable soup filled the air, but she could only taste her fear. She was standing almost at the precise spot where her ordeal had occurred.

Her mind knitted together the bits and pieces of her recollections of that night to bring the picture of her nightmare into full focus. Chills shuddered up her spine, and she stepped back out of harm's way. ''Is there anything else you need?''

''Just your company for a bit,'' he said quietly. ''Mrs. Burke, would you mind stepping out into the hall? I'd like a private moment with my wife.''

Olivia's reply was swift and confident. ''I can't do that. Jared wouldn't—''

''Your son obviously isn't here. You must know how hard it's been for me to sit here alone, hour after hour, worrying about Emilee. Surely you wouldn't begrudge either of us a moment of time alone together.''

For her own protection, Emilee took another step back, but she did not intend to let Randall intimidate her. ''It's only for a few minutes. Please. Leave the door open and wait for me in your chamber.''

She sighed in relief when Olivia did not argue and waited until no footsteps echoed in the hall to seize the initiative. ''I can't stay long. I'm still recovering,'' she said as firmly as she could without overly disturbing the stitches in her lip.

He sighed softly. ''I'm sorry about your fall, Emilee.''

Disappointed he did not take responsibility for her fall or the injuries to her neck, she clenched her hands into fists. She had to make it clear she would not tolerate being abused again or let him put all the blame on her shoulders. She would keep her marriage vows to him and accept the loss of Jared's love, but not at the price of her own dignity. ''I wouldn't have fallen if you hadn't lost your temper and attacked me. In the future, I'll be more careful to abide by your wishes and live up to your expectations, but you can never strike me again, or . . . or . . .''

"Or what?'' he prompted. "Will you forsake me as well as your marriage vows when I need you the most?'' Choked with emotion, his voice was almost plaintive. "My illness and my treatment are burdens we must bear together. I can't do it alone, not unless I know you'll be there for me when I'm well. I agreed to have someone else take over my care to keep you safe from the demons of darkness who have inflicted this illness on me because I'm spreading God's Word and doing His work.''

Her eyes misted with tears. "I will not forsake you, and I'll honor my vows to be a faithful and dutiful wife,'' she whispered. When her head started to pound and her lips began to ache, she rubbed her forehead. "I'm . . . I'm not feeling strong enough right now—''

"Then you must go and rest,'' he murmured. "I've missed our praying together. Will you come to see me again?''

She took a deep breath and backed toward the door. "I'll come again,'' she said. When she reached the outer hall, she closed the door, and she did not hesitate to bolt it closed. With only a few steps, she would be in Olivia's chamber and be able to reassure her all was well, but the course Emilee had reset for her life's journey stretched beyond the horizon of her heart into ordinary time that would be as lonely as it would be long.

TWENTY-SIX

The telegram that arrived the second week in November from the New York City investigator was as short as it was frustrating. Sequestered in the study, Jared read the message for a fifth time that day alone, crumpled the paper into a ball, and tossed it into the fire burning low in the hearth.

He walked back to the desk and poured a fresh mug of coffee. After he added an extra lump of sugar to his usual overindulgence, he carried the mug of near-liquid sugar back with him. He stared into the flames and studied the curled ashes of the news he had waited nearly a month to receive. With the background filled by the distant murmur of voices coming from the front parlor where Emilee and his mother were busy chatting with the widowed twins and their sister, he used this reprieve to ponder the message without fear of interruption while he waited for the stage to arrive with that day's afternoon postings.

Not that he really expected to decipher the cryptic message in the next few hours. He was no closer to understanding the telegram now than he had been a week ago when it had first arrived. He took several deep sips of coffee, set his mug on the mantel, and hoped the fire could warm the cold frustration that chilled his body and spirit. Amazingly, the words on the short missive danced in front of his eyes to torture his soul:

Documentation en route. STOP. Case on hold. STOP.
Advise status after review. STOP. Signed: A. Dumars

"Documentation," he grumbled. "En route to where? China?" He clenched and unclenched his left fist. He did not want the case to be "on hold." He wanted the case resolved, he hoped to his own advantage, and no post had arrived as promised. He understood the need for discretion in the telegram, but he never expected to have to wait so long for the promised documentation. With every passing day, he grew more restless, his mother urged him to return to his property, Randall grew stronger, and Emilee became more distant.

Not a particularly patient man, except when it came to working with his roses, Jared found it increasingly harder to hide his disappointment when he returned empty-handed from the general store twice each day when he went to check for his post. Randall had recovered sufficiently to have the blankets covering the drapes on his windows removed, although he still required quiet and solitude for the most part. Within the past week, he had begun to spend an hour or two in the parlor to receive visitors each night, where he fawned over Emilee and delivered pontificating sermons on God's healing power.

Jared's control over his anger and resentment was ready to snap. Night after night, he had lain in bed imagining all sorts of scenarios that would be the end result of his furtive investigation, but he had only been left with a pounding headache that made him wonder if Randall hadn't successfully prayed for his malady to be given to Jared.

The toll of the church bell diverted his attention. He strode to the window and pulled the heavy curtain aside. He could only see the top spiral of the church steeple and the bell tower in the distance, but the arrival of an early winter was evident in the thin blanket of snow that continued to fall and cover the landscape. The scaffolding which had been in place while the bell had been installed yesterday had already been removed. Since meeting would not be held until tomorrow, he could only assume the workers were testing the bell again.

He dropped the curtain back into place and retrieved his mug of coffee from the mantel. The afternoon stage would not arrive for another two hours or so. Rather than pace them away, he decided to spend his time more constructively. He opened a side drawer on the desk and pulled out the plans for the nursery and Ansel's grafting sketches to study them again. It probably would be a gross waste of his time to ponder the possibility of actually producing a hybrid rose that would bloom in winter, but he could think of nothing better to block out his driving curiosity about the overdue documentation on Randall's background.

Gradually engrossed in his work, he had only been working for an hour when there was a rap at the study door just before it creaked open. He looked up and Emilee greeted him with a tentative smile. She held on to the doorknob with one hand and cradled Troubles in her other arm. "Would you mind some company? Randall's bathing and Troubles is living up to his name. I'd rather not let him into the parlor. Once I do, I'll never keep him out, and—"

"I'll keep an eye on him," Jared offered, but he only had eyes for the woman he yearned for with every breath he took. She looked as lovely today as the first day he had seen her at the cemetery. With her bruises long since healed, the scar on her lower lip was no more than a dimple that made her smile even more distinctive and alluring, and the flesh just above the ivory lace collar on her pale rose gown was as supple and unflawed. Her complexion was pale and unblemished. She wore her hair simply, tied at the nape of her neck with a ribbon so her lustrous auburn tresses fell in a thick mass to the middle of her back and now swung over her arm and hung to the tip of her elbow. Only her dark green, haunted eyes gave him a glimpse of the same sorrow that grieved his own spirit.

She stepped farther into the room, closed the door behind her, and let the kitten leap to the floor. When Troubles stretched, walked over to the fireplace, and curled up into a ball in front of the fire, she sighed and shook her head. "I wonder why he wouldn't do that for Randall."

With the memory of bathing the kitten still fresh in his mind, Jared laughed. "He was probably afraid he was next in line for a bath."

A hint of a smile curved the corner of her mouth but, when she glanced at the desk, turned down into a frown. "I'm sorry. I've interrupted you."

He leaned back in his chair. He kept his gaze on her, but

he could not keep his heart from beating faster. "I'm glad you did. We don't often have time alone."

She dropped her gaze and put her hand into a deep pocket in her apron. "I—I've wanted to show you something, but there never seemed to be a moment when someone else wasn't around. Now that Randall's nearly recovered, you'll be leaving soon, and I may not get another chance."

She lifted her hand from the pocket and held up the silver trinket box he had given to her before fate had brought him back to the parsonage. "When you gave this to me, you asked me to replace all my bitter thoughts about my mother with happy ones. I wanted you to know that I have." She walked toward him and placed his gift on top of his papers on the desk. "Open it. Look at what's inside," she urged.

Intrigued, he lifted the lid and saw assorted scraps of fabric, neatly trimmed and inscribed with lettering. He spread the fabric strips on top of his diagrams to be able to decipher the words, and a lump in his throat nearly made it impossible to breathe: *Devotion. Laughter. Songs.*

"I only have three so far," she explained, "but I hope to get more to fill my memory chest. After talking to your mother and several of her friends, I have a different image of my mother now that gives me joy instead of pain. Despite her circumstances, I know she was devoted to me for the short time we were together, and I've learned she had a beautiful voice. She even sang in the choir at meeting, and . . . and she had a way of laughing that was contagious."

She paused, and her voice softened to a whisper. "They're good thoughts, Jared, and I wouldn't have them if it weren't for you. You gave me the courage to ask about her, and I won't ever be able to thank you enough."

Overwhelmed, he carefully replaced each scrap. When he closed the lid, he ran his finger over the embossed silver rose. "The longer I know you, the more you amaze me," he murmured. When he lifted his gaze, he found her smiling through tears. "I haven't given up hope for us. There's still time."

She shook her head. "Reverend Shelton will conduct his last service tomorrow, and the meetinghouse will be moved this week. The next meeting will be in the new church. By then, Randall will be able to take to the pulpit again, and I'll . . . I'll be by his side. It's my duty and it's . . . it's God's will," she said in an unsteady voice.

Hearing her mimic what her husband had often reminded her during her visits to his chamber, with Jared closely observing, made his blood boil. Randall had attacked her once, and he would do it again. His sanctimonious babble was nothing more than a convenient facade which he did not hesitate to flaunt in front of Jared, who knew the full extent of the man's miserable character.

Emilee, however, was right on one point. Time was running short, and Jared feared for her safety once he was no longer living in the parsonage. He resented the delay in his post now more than ever, and he renewed his vow not to bend to Randall's blackmail attempts or to leave her at the mercy of her husband. "God doesn't will injustice," he argued, "and I won't rest until I've proven it.

"Don't," she pleaded. "What we've shared is too precious to be destroyed by bitterness. That's why I wanted to show you my little memory chest. I spent too many years harboring anger toward my mother when I could have chosen to remember good things about her—or to learn them. We must accept God's will and do the same thing for one another. If we don't, every day we spend will be washed with resentment instead of joy, and we'll destroy the future one day at a time."

He gripped the memory chest so hard the edges dug into the palm of his hand. "I have no future without you, Emilee, and you have no future with that man."

She walked over to him and stood beside him to lay her hand atop his. She laced her slender fingers between his. "I love you, Jared, but all I can give you is my heart. Please don't break it by becoming bitter. Remember our love. Find joy in knowing we once shared something very beautiful."

Her arm pressed against him, and he inhaled the delicate scent of mint she used in her soaps. For weeks, he had lived here with her, listening to the sound of her voice, but was unable to speak what was in his heart, yearning to hold her, but unable to touch her or to hold her as she drifted away from him. Unwilling and unable to resist the beauty of her form as well as her soul, he held on to her hand as he stood up. When she did not step back as he closed the very short distance between them, he took her into his arms. He wrapped her in his embrace, and he could feel the rapid beating of her heart as her breasts crushed against his chest.

"You are beautiful." His voice was hoarse, and he nuzzled the side of her neck. Need overpowered reason. Longing replaced the restraint that he had used during their first kiss, and he claimed her lips to satisfy a hunger that came from deep within his soul. Tasting. Nibbling. Tracing the dimple in her lip and teasing the corners of her mouth. Urgently and passionately, he coaxed her sweet lips apart to claim more of her and to brand this memory upon his heart. And hers.

She could not resist him. It was wrong and sinful, but nothing could have felt more right or more loving. She closed her eyes as she weakened and gave in to her heart's desire and melted into his arms to let his strength support her. Her body tingled from head to toe and love transformed the physical intimacy she had once feared into pleasure beyond her wildest imagination.

She clung to his shoulders and welcomed the pressure of his lips. His hand caressed the small of her back, and her breathing grew ragged. He was her temptation and her only love, and she could no sooner deny her need for him than stop the beating of her heart. His chest rubbed against her breasts, as sensitive to his touch as her lips were to his kisses, and when her hips moved against him in a sultry rhythm, she felt the full evidence of his arousal as passion raged nearly out of control.

She loved him, but she could not tarnish their love with a memory that would shame them both. Reluctantly, but quickly, she broke their kiss and turned her face away to rest her cheek against his shoulder. Chest heaving, he held her tight and laid his cheek upon her head. As they stood together, heart to heart, passion ebbed as slowly as a morning glory folded its tender petals against the heat of the sun, but there would be no morning after when passion would ever bloom again.

He toyed with the ribbon that held her hair. When his fingers brushed against her neck, she sighed and pressed a kiss to the cleft in his chin before she eased from his embrace. She captured his gaze and held it. Her heart pounded in her chest, and her cheeks flushed when she saw the depth of his longing still brooding in his eyes.

When she moved to speak, he pressed her lips with his fingertips. "Listen. Please just listen," he urged, exactly as she had asked him to listen to her when she had told him she could not leave her husband.

She blinked back tears and nodded.

He dropped his hand away and smiled. "I love you, and God willing, someday I'll be able to show you how much I treasure you, every day and every night, for the rest of our lives." He picked up her memory chest and pressed it into her hands. "My heart is my memory chest. I do treasure every moment I've spent with you, but I dream of more. So much more."

As his eyes caressed her, she memorized the planes of his face and the way his hair curled at his temple. Beneath heavy dark lashes, his eyes glistened like silver moons promising magic yet to be discovered—magic she yearned to share with him, but never would.

"I won't dishonor our love with bitterness or resentment," he vowed, "but I will never find joy again until we are together as man and wife."

She clutched his gift in her hand and stored his words in her heart. She could not plead with him to try to find happiness in the years ahead because she knew she would not find it, either. She was committed to keeping her marriage vows and fulfilling her obligations as the minister's wife, but the most she could ever hope for was peace—of mind, heart, and spirit. "Promise me one thing?" she asked.

"If I can," he answered, replaying her role on that unforgettable night when they had first declared their love for one another and he had asked her to promise to let him care for her as she recuperated from her "accidental fall."

"When the time comes for you to leave . . ." She paused, unable to keep her voice steady. She took a deep breath and tried again. "When you leave, you mustn't come back or try to see me here. We both need time. . . . It wouldn't be fair to Randall."

"If I leave, I'll make you that promise," he said firmly.

Before she could argue her point further, chaos exploded. The study door flew open and banged against the wall. Olivia burst into the room. Apparently frightened awake, Troubles leaped up and raced across the room, taking a shortcut through Emilee's skirts, and disappeared in the well of the desk. The echo of Randall's voice calling her name as he pounded on his bolted chamber door, a not-uncommon occurrence as he demanded more and more of her company, filtered downstairs and blended with male voices coming from the front of the parsonage.

Too shocked to move or to sort through the cacophony of sounds and motions, she stared at Olivia. Visibly trembling and short of breath, the older woman was as pale as the white hair on her head, and her eyes were wide with confusion and hurt.

Jared reached her in several quick strides before Emilee recovered her wits. "What's wrong? What's happened?"

"What hasn't?" she groaned. "I was just tidying the parlor after my friends left when . . . when Randall started calling for Emilee." For the first time, Olivia looked away from her son and directly at Emilee. "I thought you were with him, but once he started calling your name, I started down the hall to look for you. That's when there was a knock at the front door."

Emilee flushed with guilt. She had completely lost track of time, abandoning her husband in the process. Before she could apologize, Olivia turned back to Jared and wrung her hands as tears misted her eyes. "You . . . you have callers."

Emilee should have left immediately to see to Randall's needs, but she was too alarmed by Olivia's distress to leave. Who had come to the parsonage to upset Olivia to this degree?

Fortunately, she answered Emilee's question in her next breath.

"Ezra Traymore is here with visitors. He . . . he insists on speaking with you privately. He's so upset, he . . . he yelled at me when I asked them to wait in the parlor."

Jared hugged his mother, but his eyes blazed with anger. When he spoke, his tone was soothing. "Ezra and I have been discussing several investments. He's frustrated because I've been dragging my feet and probably just brought some of the other investors along to convince me to loosen up my purse strings. I'm sorry if he upset you. It won't happen again."

Appearing much calmer, she sniffed. "I ought to go outside and fill a pitcher with snow to dump on his bald head," she snapped. "He acted like it was a matter of life or death."

"For Ezra, profit *is* life or death."

"Then I'm going to Hester's to speak to Reverend Shelton right now. I have a good suggestion for tomorrow's sermon." She huffed her way out of the study. Emilee was set to follow her out of the study, but before she had taken a single step, Ezra Traymore stormed into the room just ahead of a young couple she did not recognize. She could not leave discreetly now, with five people crowded into the small room, and Ezra made escape even more difficult when he slammed the door closed and blocked it with his body.

"We have a problem," he snapped and glared at Jared and Emilee. Encased in a thick black overcoat, Ezra looked like a bear ready to attack a rival for invading his territory, an odd image since the truth was quite the reverse.

Jared stepped forward, partially blocking Emilee in a protective move she welcomed. "The only problem here is your unconscionably rude behavior. You've frightened and offended my mother and barged in here like a runaway freight wagon. If this is any indication of how you conduct business, I was wise to be cautious about participating in the investments you recommended."

"This is not about commerce."

Calm, but hoarse, the voice that rang out belonged to the man beside the young woman and riveted all attention on the couple who stood together near the fireplace. Of average height, he wore thick spectacles spotted with melting snow-flakes that also covered his heavy overcoat. A dark muffler wrapped around his neck was unusually high and covered the man's chin and mouth. He gripped a cumbersome package with one gloved hand and held the petite woman's hand with the other.

Snow had laced an intricate design on her dark blue bonnet and cloak, which matched the color of her eyes. Limp blond ringlets, wet from the snow, curled around a face with cheeks reddened by the cold. She did not speak, but despite her di-minutive form, she had a solid presence.

"I apologize for our . . . our . . . intrusion," he rasped. His weather-flushed cheeks turned deeper red, and he seemed fully embarrassed.

Jared's body remained tense, and he accepted the man's apology with a stiff nod.

While Ezra struggled out of his overcoat, the man helped his companion remove her cloak first. Once he was bereft of his own coat and muffler, he looked uncommonly thin, but his features grabbed Emilee's complete focus. It was no great stretch to assume the man had survived a fire that must have nearly cost him his life and possibly accounted for his low, raspy voice.

Thick, braided scars on his neck thinned as they rose up-ward to his chin and reached as high as his lips, which ap-peared to be normally sculpted. A few scars along the sides of his face were mostly concealed by dark brown hair, but were more severe near his eyes, which were hard to see behind his spectacles.

Suddenly aware she was staring, she dropped her gaze from the man's face, but only got as far as the man's collar before her eyes widened. Her heart thudded once and then skipped a beat, but she could not take her gaze from the Geneva bands of lace that graced the lapel of his waistcoat.

He was a minister!

She glanced from the minister to Ezra, and finally to Jared, who rose quickly to accept the package the minister offered to him. She noted he had not removed his gloves and assumed his hands were also badly scarred.

"I believe . . . this . . . this is . . . for you," he managed. His whisper was hoarse. His words were uneven, and he looked frantically around the room as he loosened his collar.

From where she stood, she could only see the side of Jared's face, but he looked as shocked as she felt. The only rational explanation for Traymore's urgency and obvious distress and the minister's presence turned her body to stone. A feeling of dread pooled in the pit of her stomach. Despite the temporary leave of absence granted to Randall, the Board of Elders must have secretly decided to replace him. Obviously, the new minister had arrived earlier than they had planned and well before they had notified Randall of their decision.

Her heart began to race, and Jared's insistence they would be together suddenly made sense. His promise to find away for them to be together echoed in her mind, and she recoiled. Would he have encouraged the board to replace her husband to satisfy his promise to her? Did he think she would leave her husband if he had no pulpit? Hadn't Jared understood a word she had said about honor and commitment?

No wonder Randall had been calling for her. He frequently kept his curtains open now and observed callers when they approached the parsonage. He must have seen Ezra and his guests, recognized the minister, and surmised what had happened. Since Randall was still locked in his chamber at Jared's insistence, he was probably in a state of utter panic.

She looked at the minister again. He had removed his spectacles and was dabbing a handkerchief at puffy, red-rimmed eyes. His breathing had become short and irregular, and it was clear he was experiencing some sort of severe physical distress. When he began to cough and wheeze, the woman hurried to his side.

"We have to leave. Immediately," she urged.

Her words seemed to snap Jared out of a trance. Within seconds, he had the curtains yanked aside and the window fully opened. He guided the minister to stand in front of the window for fresh air. "The cat," Jared snapped as he began to stalk around the room. "Find the cat!"

Ezra stood frozen in place with a look of total stupefaction on his face, and Emilee's mind reeled with confusion. "Troubles? Why—"

"Find him and get him out of here," he ordered as the woman helped the minister to undo the lacings on his shirt. "Unless I'm mistaken, this man is suffering from an allergy to cats."

Stunned into action by the harsh tone of Jared's voice, Emilee pulled the chair away from the desk. She bent down, found Troubles where he had hidden earlier, picked him up, and took him into the hallway. Ignoring his hiss of protest, she slammed the door closed before he could bolt back inside.

When she turned around, the minister was still facing the window. His breathing had returned somewhat to normal, but Emilee's heart was still racing. How had Jared known about the cause of the man's distress? She met his gaze, and he answered her question with a troubled look. Before he could offer an explanation, the minister turned around and readjusted his clothing before he put on his spectacles.

Jared extended his hand. "It's good to finally meet you."

The minister accepted Jared's handshake and put his arm around the woman's shoulders. His face was solemn, even sad, when he looked at Emilee. "You must be Emilee."

She swallowed the lump in her throat, and tears welled in her eyes. The minister and Jared must have been corresponding, and his betrayal stung badly.

"I know you have a whole host of questions. We'll try to answer each and every one of them, and I want you to know how truly sorry—"

"It's not your doing," she said quietly. "The board apparently has made a decision to replace my husband, and you have every right to accept their offer." She aimed her anger and disappointment at Ezra for the moment, and squared her shoulders. "The elders may have the right to hire a new minister to lead our congregation, but they should have done so without misleading me or my husband. You've unfairly led him to believe—"

"Absolutely not," Ezra insisted without any trace of anger. Only sadness. "You have no idea what's happening here, do you?"

Totally confused, she looked at the minister and the woman she assumed to be his wife. Jared moved to Emilee's side and took her hand. She pulled it away and glanced up at him. He had the same look of sadness in his eyes as everyone else in the room. It was more than sadness, though. It was . . . pity? They felt sorry for her? She took a step back, as though she could flee the room and pretend this was not happening to her or to Randall.

The minister and the woman took both of her hands to hold her in place. "Please don't be afraid," he murmured in a voice so choked with emotion he touched her heart. "This is my wife, Beth. My name is Greene. Reverend Randall Greene."

TWENTY-SEVEN

His gloved hands were warm. His gaze was compassionate, but his claim was beyond outrageous. It was ludicrous. Emilee pulled her hands away. "That's impossible!"

"I'm afraid it's not only possible, it's true. There's a great deal we need to discuss," Beth said. She placed her hand on her husband's arm and looked up at him. "You really shouldn't stay here. Even with the cat out of the room, you're still going to have difficulty breathing."

He sighed and looked at Emilee. "Is there another room, perhaps? One where the cat hasn't been recently?"

"Only the parlor," Emilee responded, then thought better of her hospitality. "Perhaps it would be best for both of you to leave. I really don't have anything more to say. You're obviously trying to—"

"We'll wait for you in the parlor," Beth said when the minister began to wheeze. The minute she opened the door, Troubles ran back inside and the couple hurried out of the study

"Emilee."

Jared's voice rang out, and she stiffened as he approached her. He caressed her with his gaze, but he had a determined glint in his eyes. He shifted the package from one hand to another and took her arm. "Reverend Greene and his wife have traveled some distance to come here as a result of an investigation I requested. I've been expecting this documentation to arrive by post, but I had no idea . . . Please. At least give the man an opportunity to explain himself."

Eyes wide with disbelief, she pulled away from him. "You had Randall investigated? When? What could you possibly hope to find? Why didn't you tell me?"

"Because I wasn't sure anything would come of it, and I didn't want you to worry . . . or to hope . . ."

Ezra puffed out his barrel chest. "For the Reverend's sake, I don't recommend we keep them waiting. If you don't intend to listen, I do. You two can settle your differences later."

"I'll listen," Emilee said firmly, "if only to prove you all wrong." Refusing Jared's arm, she swept out of the room and went directly to the parlor. The house had become eerily quiet, and all she could hear now was the pounding of her heart and the quick tap of her footsteps as she hurried down the hall.

Within minutes they were all assembled in the parlor together. With the windows cracked open to allow a flow of fresh air to accommodate the minister, Jared stoked the fire and added extra logs to combat the chill in the room. The cold in her heart, however, would not be so easily warmed. Ezra stood near the doorway like a sentry posted to keep guard. The man who had the audacity to call himself Randall Greene sat on the settee next to the woman who ridiculously claimed the name of Mrs. Randall Greene.

Seated in a chair facing them, Emilee held her spine stiff and folded her hands on her lap. When Jared finished his chore, he handed the package back to the minister before positioning himself behind her chair. When she felt his hands brush her shoulder as he gripped the back of her chair, she edged forward to sit on the edge of her seat.

Her foot tapped impatiently on the carpet. The fire crackled to life, and the paper on the package rustled as the minister opened it. He discarded the wrapper and leafed through the sheaf of papers on his lap, withdrawing several, which he handed to his wife. He moistened his lips and drew several deep breaths. "Several weeks ago, I was approached by Alexander Dumars, who is the investigator Mr. Burke hired. Once I learned the nature of the investigation, I insisted he allow me time to secure the necessary documentation to confirm my identity. I also asked to deliver this report personally. Beth, would you give those papers to Emilee? When you're finished reading them, please let both gentlemen peruse them as well."

His wife handed the papers to Emilee, and she scanned them quickly before studying each one very carefully. The first document was a diploma from Yale inscribed with the name Randall Greene and dated for 1828, the same year her husband claimed to have graduated. The second, equally impressive, confirmed his ordination as a minister. A marriage certificate, dated only last year, had an embossed seal for a church in New York City and showed the names Randall Greene and Elizabeth Johnson.

"As you can see, they're all original documents and quite official," he said.

She chewed on her lower lip and handed the papers up to Jared. When he immediately walked them over to Ezra, she knew Jared had been reading them over her shoulder. "Documents can be forged. With the exception of the marriage certificate, the other two documents belong to my husband," she insisted. Her foot tapped faster. Randall had never shown her either of these documents, but since Reverend Burke had never displayed his credentials, she had not questioned Randall's decision to follow suit. She wondered if Reverend Burke had seen them, but decided it did not really matter. The documents were forgeries, and this man was an impostor, and she was too smart to be taken in by him.

"Understandably, you're doubtful and defensive," Beth said. "I would be, too, if our positions were reversed."

"They're not reversed at all," Emilee countered. Try as she might, she could not be angry with the woman. She seemed far too sweet and innocent to be involved in any form of chicanery. Even the man who tried to claim Randall's identity as his own had an aura of goodness about him that defied logic in light of his fraudulent claims. What motive could he possibly have? The congregation in Surrey was as poor as it was small, by eastern standards, which made it a ridiculous thought to think he might covet her husband's ministry.

Only two other people seemed to be involved in this man's claim: Ezra Traymore and Jared. What motives would they have to try to destroy her husband? As an elder and the head of the board, Ezra would never stoop to such a low trick and embroil the church in scandal or controversy. Jared was the only one left who might possibly have a motive. He had already admitted to hiring an investigator, but she knew him far too well to consider him as suspect for more than a heartbeat. He was an honorable man in every respect, and he would not try to fool her with mistruth.

Stymied in her own mind, she twisted her hands. "I don't understand," she confessed. "This makes no sense."

Ezra handed the papers back to the minister. "I'm not fully convinced myself. Emilee is right. And I need more proof before I accept your claim to be Reverend Greene."

Whatever his faults, Ezra Traymore was a man who took his many positions and his responsibilities seriously. Whether it was conducting the business of commerce or the church, he was extremely conscientious. As justice of the peace, he was known to be fair. She had never looked to him as her ally, especially since his wife was so bitter against Emilee, but she did so now. Jared, however, offered no comment, and she resisted the urge to turn and look at him.

The minister remained unflustered. "I don't blame you for being skeptical." He rifled through the papers again, pulled one free, and handed it to Emilee himself. "One of the reasons I delayed my trip was to make sure I could prove my identity to you. I'm certain this will satisfy any doubts you might have. Actually, it's not very long, and you might read it aloud for Mr. Burke's and Mr. Traymore's benefit."

She nodded and swallowed hard. She braced both feet flat on the floor and looked at the letter. "The letterhead reads the Eastern Bible Society, and the letter itself is dated October 24, 1834. It's addressed to Jared." She cleared her throat, already on guard, since the man sitting on the settee had gotten a letter from the same Bible Society that had sponsored her husband at Yale. "It is with a great deal of concern that I write to you. I have known Randall Greene for over ten years, having served as his mentor during his training at Yale for the ministry. I was under the assumption he had taken a position at Surrey to replace your father several years ago. I was disappointed Randall failed to keep in contact with me, but my disappointment is now explained away, and my assumption has been proven wrong."

She paused, unable to continue speaking. Her hands began to tremble, and tears blurred the words on the letter. Jared reached around her and held her hands steady as he continued to read in her place. "Randall Greene met with me today in my solicitor's office where this letter is being prepared. His appearance has been altered by the injuries he sustained in the fire while doing the Lord's work in New York City, but upon my oath as a minister of the Gospel, I am certain beyond any and all doubt he is the Randall Greene with whom I am closely familiar. I am willing to testify to that truth in any formal deposition you might require. I also remain hopeful you will determine the name of the man who has apparently assumed Randall Greene's identity for the past several years and see he is brought to justice for perpetrating a dastardly fraud on the members of the First United Church of Surrey. Signed, the Reverend Mr. Matthew Wooden and attested to by James Brett, Esquire."

After Jared handed the letter back to the minister, there was not a sound in the room. Like deadly arrows, Jared's words pierced through her denial and struck her heart on their way to the truth: The man she had married was not Randall Greene.

Her mind flashed back over the past two years and selectively chose clues to support the letter: Randall's lack of confidence, his need for help writing and delivering sermons, his obsession for privacy, and his absolute refusal to go to New York City. All pointed to a man who had been proven to her to be an impostor.

Bile soured her mouth. Anger flowed through her veins, flushed her cheeks, and pounded in her head. Fighting for every breath she took, she defensively launched a counterattack in a rush of bitter, angry words. "If you're Randall Greene, who is the man I married? How could this happen? Why didn't you come here for the position yourself? Why did it take all this time for you to show up?" Chest heaving, she turned to Ezra. "Why didn't you check the man's credentials more closely? Why didn't the elders know?" she pleaded.

"You should have known. *Someone* should have known!"

Jared laid his hands on her shoulders and gently massaged them. "No one knew. It's not anyone's fault. Try to relax and stay calm. Don't let yourself get so upset—"

"Upset?" She snapped her shoulders away from him, got to her feet, and swung around to face him. "I have every right to be upset. "I'm . . . I'm married to a man, and I don't even know who he is!" Tears streamed down her cheeks, traitors all. "I've been stripped of everything! My home, my position in the community, my pride, even my name!" She tore off her wedding ring and threw it to the floor. "I have every right to be upset and you can't tell me otherwise because I have nothing left! Nothing!" she cried, venting every fear and pouring out the anger that made her heart race and her mind reel so fast she was dizzy.

Jared's gaze remained steady, holding her fast in a sea of fury. He walked around the chair and wrapped her in his arms. "You have me." He whispered so low only her heart could have heard him. "Always and truly. I never wanted to see you hurt so badly. Never. Cry, Emilee. Let everything go until you only have room in your heart for me. For our love. For our future. Please, love," he crooned.

His soft words relaxed her rigid muscles. His body warmed her. Without anger, she had only tremendous pain, and she clung to him as heavy sobs tore through her body. He rocked her gently from side to side, holding her and supporting her until her sobs subsided into weeping. Her sides and stomach ached. Her eyes swelled. Her throat burned. Still he held her until the well of her anguish had gone dry, for now, and she lay limp in his arms.

When her heartbeat was once more steady, she wiped her tears with her hands and accepted the handkerchief he offered with a grateful smile. Too mentally and physically drained to think, she could not look any further into her future than taking full breaths of air. Mortified by her emotional outburst, she was surprised to have any semblance of pride left.

When she turned around and looked at Reverend Greene and his wife, she found their expressions nonjudgmental and understanding. She sank back into her seat, and Jared stood beside her holding her hand.

"I know this is a terrible shock," the minister offered. "It was to us, too."

He continued to speak just above a raspy whisper, and she had to strain to hear him, which kept her fully focused on his every word. At best, she found herself in a very tenuous situation, but he did, too—a bond between them that allowed her to consider him as well as herself. "How could this have happened?" she asked. "Where have you been these past several years?"

"Start at the beginning," Beth urged her husband.

He nodded. "Unlike my compatriots at Yale, I had no family or influential friends. I struggled academically and I was also particularly mediocre in the pulpit, even before the fire that damaged my vocal cords. The only offer I received to begin my ministry was in New York City as a prison chaplain. The position paid very little, but I didn't have to preach rousing sermons. I only had to listen and counsel, which served my limited talents."

He took his wife's hand. "I was content for several years, but from time to time, I would contact Reverend Wooden. No other positions became available until Reverend Burke requested recommendations for his replacement. We corresponded, he extended an invitation for me to visit, and I accepted."

Ezra spoke up. "But if you accepted, why didn't you arrive, and how would someone else know your plans? You must have some idea who took your place."

The minister turned to his wife and smiled sadly before he spoke again. "I severed the few ties I had, but several days before I was set to leave, I received a request to visit one of the inmates I had been counseling. The night I visited changed my life forever."

For the first time, emotion choked off his words, and his wife took over telling his tale. "A little more than two years ago, there was a disastrous fire at Moorville, one of the New York City prisons. Forty inmates died in the fire, and scores of keepers and volunteers fighting the fire were killed or injured. Perhaps you remember reading accounts of it.''

She looked to each of them, one at a time. Ezra nodded. ''From what I recall, one of the convicts set the fire in an attempt to break out of the prison.''

Jared stiffened and shook his head as he tightened his hold on Emilee's arm. ''I only returned from Europe several months ago after an extended absence,'' he explained, and Emilee heard the regret in his voice.

''I don't recall anything about it,'' she murmured, but she did picture Randall's scarred shoulders and his fear of fire, and her mind latched onto a thought too frightening to voice.

Fortunately, she was distracted when Beth began to talk again. ''My father is a man who prides himself on using his wealth to help others, and he opened our home to three men who were severely burned. Besides myself, my mother and two sisters nursed them under the supervision of a physician. Only two men recovered, including Randall.''

She gazed lovingly at her husband's face and smiled. ''As you can see, he was very badly burned. In addition to the scars you see, you've heard the damage to his voice. The doctor held out very little hope, but Randall is a strong man whose courage and faith defied all the odds. We didn't even know his name until he had recovered the use of his hands and could write again. His voice box was terribly damaged, and he's had to learn to talk all over again. It's only been within the last few months he's regained any clarity in his speech.''

As if on cue, the minister cleared his throat to end the tale. ''God has worked two miracles in my life. The first is obvious; the second, of course, is Beth. She stayed unfailingly by my side and inspired me to fight for life every day I was ill. She inspires me still. The happiest day of my life, after my ordination, was the day she became my wife. We've tried to focus on the future rather than the past. After all the time that had passed, I just assumed the position here had been filled by someone else. When Mr. Dumars tracked me down, I realized . . . well, you know the rest.''

Jared spoke up for the first time. ''Are you saying you can't help us to identify the man who's been using your name and your credentials?''

Once more, Emilee found herself on the edge of her seat, and her heart began to race. The minister's face grew solemn.

Ezra stepped farther into the room. ''You must have some idea who he might be,'' he said. ''He was looking out the upstairs window when we arrived.'' His eyes widened. ''Of course. No wonder he was highly agitated when we first arrived. I thought it odd at the time, but . . . he recognized you, didn't he?''

Reverend Greene frowned. ''I suppose he did.''

Jared's grip on Emilee's arm became almost painful. His voice was cold. ''And did you recognize him?''

''Yes. I did.''

A sudden, very loud thumping noise followed by scrambling sounds outside interrupted the minister, and Jared bolted past Ezra, ran into the foyer, and out the front door. Emilee glanced out the window with horrified fascination and watched as Jared pulled on her husband's legs, which were dangling from the roof over the front porch, and hauled him to the ground. After a brief scuffle, Jared subdued her husband and held him by the scruff of the neck as he marched him back into the parlor.

All heads snapped to face the man who now stood gasping for breath after a foiled escape attempt. Jared quickly turned his charge over to Ezra and returned to Emilee. He urged her to stand, and put his arm protectively around her shoulder.

She refused to look at the man who had completely betrayed her, and kept her gaze on Reverend Greene and his wife. Whatever the man's crime that had landed him in prison, he had committed far worse against her and the members of the congregation. As a woman now branded by scandal that far exceeded, in shock value alone, anything her mother might have done, she waited with the others for him to offer some insight into who he really was.

She caught her breath as her heart lurched in her chest. Even though Jared had been willing to risk his own reputation by offering to marry her if she divorced her husband, the scandal associated with her now made it impossible for them to ever make a life together.

She stepped away from him, crossed her arms, and gripped her waist. Pain sliced across her chest and stole her breath as the future exploded into one vast universe devoid of respectability or honor or love.

Her husband glowered as he pulled out of Traymore's grasp and attempted to right his disheveled clothing. "How any of you can justify this . . . this abuse is beyond comprehension," he spat.

Jared's hands tightened into fists. "Abuse? You were trying to escape!"

Indignation flushed her husband's cheeks bright red. "Of course I was trying to escape—from a locked room where I've been kept against my will even though I'm nearly fully recovered from my illness! You've overstepped yourself, Burke, for the last time." He narrowed his gaze and glanced at the minister. "Are you behind this . . . this abomination?"

The minister did not flinch. His gaze was steady, his features unbelievably kind. "It's been a long time since we've talked, Oliver," he murmured.

Her husband's eyes widened. "That's impossible, since I'm quite certain we've never met. You unquestionably have me confused with someone else."

Traymore puffed out his chest. "This is Reverend Randall Greene. The *real* Randall Greene, and the only question begging an answer is just exactly who you are."

"You know very well who I am," her husband protested as he raked his hair with his hand. "Is that what this is all about? This man just walks into my home, makes outrageous claims, and you . . . you simply take his word?"

The minister shook his head. "It's serves no purpose to hide the truth. Not anymore. It's over, Oliver."

"My name isn't Oliver. It's—"

"Farley. Oliver Farley," the minister said quietly.

Jared stepped over to the settee and picked up the papers the minister had laid aside. He held up the sheaf of papers and waved them toward her husband. "Don't waste our time trying to convince any of us you're Randall Greene. This man brought proof to the contrary,'' he gritted.

"Irrefutable proof," Traymore added boldly. He looked directly at the minister. "Since he refuses to face reality, perhaps you should tell us exactly who this impostor is."

"His name is Oliver Farley, an inmate I counseled at Moorville Prison where I was chaplain."

Her husband paled. "That's a lie! A preposterous lie!"

Before Emilee's mind could even register the horror of truly being married to a prison convict, Ezra lashed out at him. "What was your crime? How much time did you have left on your sentence? As justice of the peace, I'll make sure you serve even more time for the crime you've committed here!"

With her senses numb and her mind a vacuum, Traymore's voice sounded hollow as he sputtered with indignation.

The minister smiled sadly. "The last time we were together, Oliver had less than twelve hours left in the prison. That's when the fire broke out and he managed to escape."

"You mean he was about to be released?" Emilee felt the blood drain from her face.

"No, I'm afraid he wasn't about to be released. Oliver had sent for me to stay with him that night because at dawn he was going to hang . . . for murdering his wife."

Murdering his wife. Murdering his wife. The room started spinning. Out of control. She was out of breath. Bright lights popping like exploding fireflies. Pain. Hurt. A black hole. Deep. Safe. Hurry!

Emilee leaped, quite willingly, into the peaceful abyss of unconsciousness, and the last thing she heard was Jared's voice calling her name.

TWENTY-EIGHT

Seven days singed by the flames of hell on earth. Seven nights lost to cold, horrific nightmares. By now Emilee had spent enough tears to create an eighth ocean saltier than the Dead Sea. Her spirit had been reduced to a parched and barren desert where happiness bloomed out of reach atop cactus plants spiked with betrayal, scandal, and notoriety.

There was no oasis of faith or love. Only relentless winds of misery and endless stretches of hopelessness in the shifting sands of pain and self-doubt that would not settle into firm ground until the man who had destroyed her life was far from Surrey.

Sequestered in self-imposed exile, she had not left the guest room in the widowed twins' home since leaving the parsonage. She had refused all visitors, including Jared, had eaten only enough to keep Olivia from harping, and had slept only when exhaustion forced her to leave her chair by the window where she sat, day and night, to watch out over the village that had been her home and her focus as the minister's wife.

What a farce.

The minister had turned out to be an escaped convicted murderer, and she had been held up to the world as a total and complete fool.

From her vantage point on the second floor, she had been able to see the town square, where the villagers had gathered more frequently than usual after the scandal had broken. When they had occasionally turned and looked in her direction, she had dropped the curtain back into place.

Heavy snow had fallen a week ago, and she had watched the pale winter sun glisten on the snow-crusted bronze statue of George Washington just across the new site for the meetinghouse and studied the statue for hours on end in an exercise bordering on obsession as she asked the same questions over and over again. Was it hollow inside, as empty as the shell of her heart? Was it solid metal, like the pain in her breast that left no room for a heart at all? Or like her role as the minister's wife, was the bronze only a veneer that would wear away much more slowly than the facade of her life had been ripped away?

She woke at dawn the following morning, dressed, and resumed her vigil at the window while the rest of the village still slept. Like veins that carried blood to sustain life, dark wagon ruts in the snow crisscrossed Main Street as commerce continued, but it was still too early for the business day to begin. With curiosity she again eyed the stack of lumber delivered to the town square late yesterday and with no small measure of hesitation anticipated watching the meetinghouse get set into place.

The meetinghouse held far too many memories turned bitter. With only a few hours before the workmen would arrive, forcing her to drop her curtain, she focused her gaze on the statue again. Lost in thought, she barely heard the rap at her door. Olivia had come once again to deliver the morning meal. She finally had abandoned her efforts to engage Emilee in conversation, so Emilee kept her back to the door, impatient for Olivia to leave the tray and resume an isolated existence.

Especially today. She had slept fitfully. She was uncommonly restless and on edge. Brittle enough, she feared, to snap into pieces given the slightest provocation.

"You have a beautiful view from your window."

She recognized his hoarse, raspy voice, and her heart began to pound. She stiffened, and her sense of violation was profound enough to shatter her isolated world and rattle her numbed senses back to life. "I'm not accepting callers. That includes you."

"Yes, I know."

"Then please leave."

"Why?"

Growing impatient, she gritted her teeth. "Because I asked you to go."

"Why?"

She clenched her fists and dried-up emotions welled to life. "It should be fairly obvious, especially to you."

"Why?"

Her impatience stretched into anger. "I'm not going to explain why because I'm not going to speak with you."

"Why?"

Anger simmered into a boil. "You're being rude! I don't want to talk to you or anyone else."

"Why?"

Explosion! Chest heaving, she leaped to her feet, spun around, and glared at him. "Why? Why! Is that all you can say, Reverend Greene—*why*?"

"You must ask yourself why a hundred times a day, Emilee. So do I." He paused, his face serene, his voice a hoarse whisper. "Why has God forsaken me? Why must I hurt so badly? Why have I been chosen to be humiliated? Why, blessed Lord, do you let Your beloved suffer so? Why?"

From the dried well of her anguish and despair, tears appeared to wash away her anger and flood her with grief and sorrow. "Can you tell me why?" she sobbed.

He shook his head. "I don't know the answers to your questions or to mine, but I'm certain of one thing. God loves you. He's surrounded you with people who love you, just as he's done for me. Let Him help you now. Let them help you. Let me."

"It . . . it hurts too much," she cried, crossed her arms, and clutched her waist with her hands as a band of pain tightened around her chest.

"Let us share the hurt and give you comfort."

"Why bother? I have no future. I can't ever go out again in public. People will whisper about me wherever I go, even though it's not my fault."

He sighed. "Yes. I know."

With her vision blurred by tears, she looked at the scars on his neck and face and noted the gloves on his hands. He did know, more than anyone else, what it would be like to be subjected to inquisitive stares and gossip. She dropped her gaze, ashamed of herself for even thinking her situation could compare to his. Her scars were inside where they could be hidden from strangers in a new town or a new place. He carried his scars for all the world to see every day for the rest of his life. How did he handle the pain and still manage to smile?

"I feel . . . very selfish," she murmured.

"You're not selfish," he admonished. "I've had the opportunity to meet many of your friends and neighbors, and not one of them has described you as selfish." He chuckled. "Perhaps a bit rash and headstrong at times, when you rush into the thick of things before thinking about the consequences."

Her nervous giggle ended in a set of loud hiccups. "Jared told you that, didn't he?"

The minister smiled. "That and much more."

"Why?" she asked, surprised to find herself enjoying the opportunity to turn the tables on him.

He grinned. "I asked him."

"Why?" She started to smile.

"Because I care."

"Why?"

He laughed. "He should have told me how bright and quick you are, as well." He extended his hand to her. "Everyone else has left to do errands which will keep them occupied for several hours. There's a wonderful breakfast waiting downstairs just for the two of us. Let's eat while we talk."

With trembling hands, she wiped the tears from her cheeks. "Jared put you up to this, didn't he? And his mother and the twins. This has been one grand conspiracy, hasn't it?"

"Absolutely."

"Do you . . . do you often go to such lengths to rescue a lost soul?" she asked as she self-consciously smoothed her skirts.

"Absolutely."

"I suppose it would be senseless for me to argue."

"Absolutely," their voices chimed together, and she smiled, truly smiled. For the second time in her life, she slipped her hand into his, but this time she held on for dear life, hoping he would show her the way home—to joy and laughter and, above all, love. There would be many difficult days ahead, particularly until Oliver Farley had been sent back to New York City to face punishment that was long overdue, but she would fight through the pain for the rest of her life—if Jared still would be there waiting for her.

"You said this wouldn't happen. Couldn't happen," Jared snarled.

Ezra mopped his brow and swept a handkerchief across the top of his bald head. "The county judge issued the order, and I have to see it carried through. I don't like it any more than you do, but the law is clear. The man has his rights."

Rigid with fury, Jared needed every last ounce of his self-control to keep from leaping over the desk that separated them and strangling Ezra, even if he was only the messenger. "When?" he gritted.

Ezra averted his gaze. "Thursday."

"That's the day after tomorrow!"

"I know that," Ezra grumbled as he rolled his body out of the chair and stood up. "I stopped in here as a courtesy, not to be harangued. Before you have another point you'd like to drive home with such gracious tact, I'm leaving. There's work to be done to meet the court order."

Jared rubbed his forehead, but his efforts did little to relieve the pounding in his head. "I apologize. This hasn't been easy for any one of us."

"No," Ezra admitted with a weary sigh. "And it's going to get a whole lot worse." When Jared went to rise, Ezra waved him back into his seat. "I'll see myself out. I have to stop upstairs before I go and tell Farley he's won his legal battle. Sniveling bastard!"

Jared sank back into his seat and listened as Traymore's footsteps mounted the stairs to the second floor of the parsonage, where Oliver Farley was guarded twenty-four hours a day, since Surrey had no jail. Troubles had been exiled to Jared's property so the real Reverend Greene and his wife could move temporarily into the parsonage after they had offered to stay until a permanent replacement could be found.

Jared still had his old chamber, but spent little time sleeping. When he had ordered his investigation into Randall Greene's background, he never anticipated the actual results. Since the real Reverend Greene's arrival, however, things had gone from bad to worse and now—the incredible.

On top of his own guilt, Jared worried day and night about Emilee. Would she ever forgive him for his role in exposing Farley and the pain she had suffered as a result? Would he have forgiven himself if he hadn't investigated the man and something had happened to Emilee?

He would know soon. She had agreed to meet with him this morning for the first time since he had carried her limp body out of the parlor. He had spent the last week in a haze of meetings with lawyers and Ezra, in Ezra's dual role as head elder and justice of the peace, and Jared had looked forward to giving her news today that would cheer her. Through Ezra, Jared had obtained an official annulment of her marriage to the alleged Reverend Mr. Randall Greene, although technically an annulment wasn't really necessary. Jared had hired a crew of men to finish the cabin Robert Walters had started, and as soon as Emilee would agree to marry, Jared would be able to take her home to his property, where they would be far enough away from the village to be left in peace until this whole ugly episode had been put to rest.

Now he would have to give her the news Ezra had delivered today—news that was bound to break her heart again and made his property useless as an escape.

He checked his pocket watch and got to his feet. He had just enough time to walk to his mother's to arrive by ten o'clock as promised. He donned full cold-weather gear—hat, coat, muffler, and gloves—and left through the front door.

The cold air bit into his face, and he hunched in his coat as he stomped through the snow. He had already decided to answer each and every question Emilee would ask as honestly as he could, but honesty alone would not be enough. The minister may have paved the way for Jared today, by breaking through Emilee's self-imposed exile, but he had to walk this last mile alone and convince her he loved her, despite what had happened. To do that, he would have to bare his soul, tell her about Farley's blackmail attempt, and warn her the worst was yet to come.

Above all, he had to make sure she knew he loved her and wanted her. Truly.

TWENTY-NINE

Mercy Traymore passed Emilee as she crossed the town square and gave her no acknowledgment beyond a vacant nod. Emilee smiled to herself and said a quick prayer to the good Lord and the late Howard Shale, whose wardrobe had proved to be the perfect disguise, just as she had hoped. After skirting the lumber piled near the foundation for the meetinghouse, she hurried down Main Street with lots of apprehension and a small twinge of guilt.

Olivia and the widowed twins meant well, but Emilee did not need or want three chaperones when she met with Jared for the first time since learning the man they had all known as Reverend Mr. Randall Greene was an escaped murderer. The note she had left simply told them there had been a last-minute change in plans and she was going to take a walk with Jared instead of visiting in the drawing room. Since the three women had all been urging her to get some fresh air, they should not object overmuch. Unfortunately, Jared had no idea of her plans, and unless she quickened her steps, she would not intercept him and her ruse would be uncovered.

The cold air felt good on her face. The hat, muffler, and overcoat were old, but substantial enough to keep her warm. She held the man's trousers up with a sturdy pair of suspenders, and she had used fresh cleaning rags to stuff the boots to keep them on her feet. She actually maneuvered over the snow-packed ground much easier than if she had worn a gown and cloak, and soon passed the general store. Again, no one paid her much attention, and in her anonymity she found freedom that gladdened her heart.

When she was several squares away from the green-shuttered parsonage, her apprehension grew. She kept her gaze averted from the structure where Farley was being held under guard until the paperwork for his transfer back to New York City could be processed.

She had not seen him since the day his identity had been revealed, and she had no intention of seeing him again. Ever. Reverend Greene had broached the subject over the past few days, but she remained adamant in her refusal and closed her mind and heart against the man who had been her husband. Instead, she focused on Jared and how they might somehow still find a way to be together. It might not be soon, but someday seemed a lot closer now than it had only a few days ago when Reverend Greene had used great kindness and a bit of humor to break through her shell of despair.

The moment she saw Jared turn onto Main Street, she slowed her steps. With a backdrop of dazzling white snow, his tall, dark form was even more distinctive. As the distance between them closed to several feet, she could see his beloved face clearly. When he passed her with bold, determined strides and a curt nod, she spun around so fast she slipped and nearly lost her footing. "Jared," she whispered.

He braced to a halt, turned around, and cocked his head as he looked at her oddly.

"Jared." A little louder.

He took a few steps back toward her and stared. "I beg your pardon. Do I know you?"

She pulled down her muffler and tipped back her hat. "I thought we might take a walk."

His mouth dropped open. His eyes widened with recognition and disbelief, and a slow grin grew into a smile that stretched from ear to ear. "Emilee! What in the name of creation are you doing dressed like—"

"I wanted a chance to see you alone, but I didn't want anyone to recognize me. Your mother and the twins had other ideas, although their concerns about my reputation at this point seems a bit ludicrous."

His eyes glistened. "What an absolute treasure you are." He held out his arms to embrace her, apparently thought better of it, and dropped his arms. "For appearance's sake, I suppose that will have to wait."

She shivered and jostled her legs and arms. "Can we walk somewhere? It's freezing standing still. I've got a blanket stuffed under my coat in case we can find someplace private to talk."

"In the snow?" He frowned for a moment, then shaped half a smile. "I've got an idea where we could go. It's a bit of a walk, but if you're sure . . ."

"I'm sure."

He led the way, and she walked by his side, backtracking over the route she had taken through the center of the village. They drew little attention from the few people who had ventured out into the cold, but did not risk any conversation. By the time they reached their destination at the northern end of the village, her feet were numb, but he quickly settled them inside the lean-to the Walters family had abandoned for the cabin on Jared's property.

The three-sided building provided privacy and protected them from the wind. Jared built a fire in the hearth which would keep them warm as long as they left on their outerwear. He spread the blanket she had brought on the wooden floor in front of the fire and helped her to sit down beside him. The flames gradually leaped to life, bathing the lean-to with warmth, but it was the woman by his side who gave him the greatest comfort.

He took her hand and broke the silence first. "I've missed you. Why wouldn't you see me before now?"

She kept her gaze focused on the fire, as though the answers danced in the flames. "I'm . . . I'm not sure. I guess I just needed time to be alone. Or I thought I did, until you conspired with Reverend Greene to convince me otherwise." She sighed. "It still seems odd to call him that. Lots of things feel strange. Or awkward. I feel empty and hollow one minute and heavy with despair the next. When I think of you, my thoughts get twisted up in knots. I worry about what will happen to us . . . if we'll ever be able to put this behind us, or if the scandal will drive us apart."

He put his arm around her shoulder and held her close to his side. "Sweet love of my life," he murmured. "I wish I could make this all go away for you, but I can't. Just remember you don't ever have to be so alone. I'm here for you. Always.''

He handed her the annulment papers he had stored in his pocket. "I had Ezra draw these up for you, to set your mind at ease and to give you concrete proof your marriage to that monster no longer exists, even though technically it never did. Keep them in a safe place, and when you feel doubtful, you can look at them. You're free, Emilee, and when you're ready, we'll make plans for our future together. Time is a great healer, but love is far stronger. We're lucky to have both.''

"I know," she whispered and secured the papers inside her overcoat. She dipped her head as she curled against him. She gripped the front of his coat and cuddled closer. "Tell me what happened. How you knew about . . . about *him*.''

"Oliver Farley?" Jared spat his name. "It's a good thing he's under guard or I'd kill him in a heartbeat." When he felt her stiffen, he hugged her. "I've had the opportunity, and I certainly have motive, but I wouldn't give him the satisfaction of winning in the end." His chest tightened, and he deliberately kept his news hidden, if only to share a little more time with her and make her feel safe . . . for a little longer.

He diverted his thoughts back to her question and answered her as completely and honestly as he could. When she asked a number of questions, he realized how carefully she had been listening and how quickly she grasped details, particularly when she connected the information in his letter from Will Cooper and the real Reverend Greene's allergic reaction to Troubles.

"There's one thing I don't understand," she said after he had given her an accounting that left out only one thing: Farley's blackmail threat. "When Dr. Pounds asked you and your mother to stay with us while I recovered, why did you insist on remaining until Ran—Farley's treatment had run its course? And why did he allow it?"

No last-minute reprieve. No more time to delay. He held on to her hand and hoped she would not pull away from him and retreat into another shell when she learned the truth. "After Dr. Pounds told me you had been hurt and we talked later that night, I also spoke to Farley. I set the terms for the rest of his recovery. At least most of them. Unfortunately, he didn't take it kindly when I informed him he had to resign as the minister.''

Her body tensed, and she looked up at him. "You tried to force him to resign? Why?''

He kept his gaze steady, but his heart started to pound. "Because I knew your injuries weren't accidental, and he didn't deserve to be in the pulpit after what he'd done to you.''

Confusion danced in her eyes. "But he asked the board for a leave of absence, which they granted. He didn't resign,'' she argued.

"No.''

"Why?''

He did not care a whit about tarnishing her image of the man who had nearly strangled her to death, but Jared did care about her perceptions of him. Would she see him as weak and ineffective or worse because he had bent to Farley's demands, only to stall for time? He took a deep breath. "Unless I agreed to remain silent about your alleged accident and backed down on my insistence he tender his resignation, he threatened to use the pulpit to expose my father's sins and to charge me with stealing your affections.''

"He knew?'' She gasped and covered her mouth with her hand.

Jared recounted his conversation with Farley and left nothing to her imagination. "I had no other choice,'' he said with resignation that still bristled his ego. "Since I had already hired the investigator in New York City, I could only bide my time and pray he would uncover something I could use as leverage against Farley to protect my mother and to protect you.''

"You should have told me what he'd done.''

He shook his head. "Your recovery was utmost in my mind, and there was nothing either one of us could have done about it. Not until the results of the investigation arrived. As it turned out, Farley's blackmail attempt became a moot point. At least for a while."

She furrowed her brow and moved closer to the fire. "He can't hurt anyone now. He's being sent to New York City to face his sentence. Your mother told me Ezra expected Farley to leave under armed guard. He won't be allowed to speak to anyone. Not here. Not anywhere. The officials in New York City are anxious to carry out his sentence very quickly and without delay. They were embarrassed enough to learn he hadn't died in the prison fire—"

"He's not going back to New York City."

When Jared reached out to hold her, she arched her back and resisted. Her dark green eyes snapped with disbelief and alarm. "Of course he is. He killed his wife and he's been sentenced to die!"

"He's hired a lawyer and filed an appeal."

She paled. "That's outrageous! On what basis? That he's reformed?" She placed her hand on her throat, and her chin began to quiver. "Why didn't anyone ask me for a statement? I would have told them the truth, that he tried to kill me."

His heart lodged in his throat, but he was glad she no longer tried to defend the man by pretending her injuries were accidental. "He didn't appeal his sentence. He appealed extradition back to New York City." He ran his hand across his brow. "There's no easy way to tell you this . . ."

"Just . . . just tell me! Is he going to hang or isn't he?"

Jared nodded. "The court order arrived today. His execution will be at dawn on Thursday. Here, in the town square. And he'll have one last opportunity to speak publicly before he hangs."

Tears filled her eyes. She crossed her arms and gripped her waist. A low keening moan escaped her lips, and she began to rock back and forth, staring into the fire and breaking his heart. The court order had granted Farley's request by ordering that he be hung in Surrey, but it had also sentenced Emilee to be part of a historic public hanging—the first ever in Surrey— and one the villagers would never forget.

Surrey had no public jail because it did not need one. The

worst crime ever to rock the small village happened years ago when Jared had been a child. Stories continued to be told about a farmer, Thomas Motley, who had stolen a horse. Rather than be hung, he had committed suicide. Since then, crime had been pretty much limited to failure to pay a debt or a boundary dispute, although the influx of laborers on the canal had inspired a number of disorderly conduct charges resolved by stiff fines.

No words he could say would take away the scandal or the pain she would have to endure for the rest of her natural life and probably beyond, known forever as the woman who had been married to a murderer who had been hung in the town square.

All Jared could do was protect her by taking her away so she did not have to witness the gruesome event or hear tales about it from gossipmongers. He moved closer to her and pulled her stiff body into his arms. For now, he could offer her comfort and love. By this afternoon, he would have her safely away from Surrey and the sound of the workmen as they built the gallows within view of her window.

Despite all that he had done to resolve the past since his arrival home, he faced the same burden he had carried all these years: his father's secret sins. A far more paramount issue for him was how to protect the woman who had claimed his heart. Short of murdering Farley in his sleep, or abducting Emilee, as well as his mother, to force them to live the rest of their lives in Europe, Jared was not at all sure how he was going to stop Farley from making one last public statement and shattering not one world, but three.

He had less than forty-eight hours.

This time, he would not fail her.

This time, he would protect her before she got hurt.

This time, she would not have a choice.

Neither did he.

THIRTY

"Y̶ou're absolutely not going in there."

Jared blocked the door to Farley's chamber. He crossed his arms over his chest and braced his feet. "I won't permit it."

Shorter in stature and pressed for time, Emilee stiffened her spine. "Reverend Greene got permission for me to have one visit. You don't have the right to stop me. And just where did you send the guard? He's the only one who should question me. Not you."

Fire crackled in his gray eyes, turning them into smoky pits of stubbornness. "The guard is taking a break."

"Then I'll wait for him to return."

"A very *long* break," he warned with a sardonic smile.

She huffed. "You don't intimidate me."

"Obviously," he quipped. "If you had any sense at all, you'd have listened to me and been miles away from here by now. You're as stubborn and short-sighted as my mother. She doesn't have any idea what's going to happen tomorrow if I don't come up with a way to silence Farley, but you do, don't you?"

"Of course I do. I've spent the past full day and a half listening to workmen build the gallows with one eye on the window and the other on the clock," she said. She deliberately kept her voice low, even though her stomach was doing flip-flops and her knees were shaking beneath her skirts. "It's nearly midnight. There's very little time left. I have to speak to him and persuade him not to say anything to hurt your mother."

The fire in his eyes began to smolder. "I spoke to Reverend Greene and told him about . . . about my father and Farley's threats. He spoke to Farley, then tried to reason with Farley myself, but—''

''You spoke to Reverend Greene about your father?''

A sad smile. ''He's a good man, Emilee. I thought he could help, but Farley refused to say a word to either of us. Even if I'm fool enough to let you inside, what makes you certain he'll talk to you?''

''Why are you so certain he won't? He's been asking to see me ever since we learned his true identity. I was the one who refused to talk to him, not the reverse. I won't stay long.''

His smoky eyes softened. ''It doesn't take long to strangle someone. Or have you forgotten?''

Involuntarily, her hand went to her throat, and she dropped it as soon as he noticed and rewarded her with a knowing frown. ''I won't ever forget that night,'' she murmured. ''Just as I'll never forgive myself if I don't try to convince him it would serve no purpose to hurt your mother now. I love her, too. Do you want to see her humiliated in front of the entire village? Unless you're prepared to see that happen, you'll let me see him.''

He slowly dropped his arms to his sides. ''I'll go inside with you.''

She shook her head. ''He won't talk to me if you're there.''

He crossed his arms again. ''Then we're at a stalemate.''

She let out a deep sigh. ''You're right. You're also twice my size. I can't overpower you or push you out of my way, but the man I grew to love has never once resorted to using his strength against me. He's a gentle man. A caring man. He has always shared his strength and his courage. You are that man, Jared. Why won't you do that for me now when I need your support more than ever?''

She paused and closed her eyes briefly. She held her hands out to let him see how they trembled. ''I'm not a fool. I know he's a dangerous man. I'll even admit I'm afraid to be alone with him, but I'll be able to conquer my fear for your mother's sake if I know you're here, waiting to protect me if I need you. You've loved me enough to stand by me when I've been weak or afraid, but can you love me enough to let me stand alone?''

Her heart pounded in her chest, and she searched his eyes to look beyond his fear and concern for her and the anguish of his own failure to resolve the dilemma that had stymied them both to see the depths of his devotion shine through. He placed his hands on her shoulders, slid them up to cradle her face, and pressed a kiss to her lips. ''Love is still too new for me to think beyond protecting you. Forgive me?''

She kissed the palm of his hand and glanced at the door behind him. ''You won't go far in case . . .''

''I'll be right here,'' he vowed. He smiled and put his hand to her heart. ''And here. Promise me you'll be very careful.''

When she nodded, he turned, slid the bolt free, and opened the door. Without saying another word, she slipped inside the candlelit chamber and closed the door behind her. Oliver Farley stood looking out the window on the far side of the room. He ignored her entrance, but the moment she started walking across the room, he turned to face her.

Her shock was so great, she stopped as if stuck to the floor, and she stared at the man standing before her. He bore such little resemblance to the man who had been her husband, she had to blink her eyes and look around the room to make sure he was not elsewhere. Disheveled clothes hung on his frame, and his hair was knotted and unkempt. A bristly beard covered cheeks sunken in their sockets, and even in dim light, his eyes looked red and puffy.

She had often wondered how she would feel if she ever saw him again or what words she would use to castigate him for his cruel betrayal. She had planned the words carefully and had even written down all the mean-spirited things he had done that ranged from verbal humiliation to physical abuse. The most horrific thing he had done, however, was use her faith and the vows she had taken on the day they married to manipulate her and subject her to his will, a vile and despicable mockery that warranted no mercy or forgiveness.

She had wanted to scream at him, pound on his chest, and pummel his face with her fists, and she even had pictured his broken body sprawled at her feet. Faced with the opportunity that had only come in her nightmares until this moment, she found reality far different from what she had expected.

She had no desire to yell or flail at him. There was no fury. No thirst for revenge. Only a hollow emptiness inside of her, and she held as still as a bronzed statue—invulnerable to destructive emotions or pain and incapable of more than disinterest.

"Emilee? Is . . . is that really you? You've . . . you've come?"

A familiar but shaky voice. He ran his hand through his hair and tucked in his shirt. "Reverend Greene said you wouldn't come to see me, but I knew you would."

The all-too-familiar arrogance had crept back into his voice, and he cocked his head. "You came alone. I'm surprised Burke allowed you to—"

"Jared is not my keeper. He's my friend."

Farley sneered, and his face twisted into an ugly mass of pale flesh. "And your lover. He's just like his father—a slave to lust and devoid of honor."

She recoiled from his charge of adultery. "Honor? You dare to speak of honor when you used blackmail not once, but twice, to hold on to a ministry you had no right to claim?"

He swatted his hand at her, and his eyes glittered with a maniacal glow. "I had every right. God forgave me for my sins and spared me to do His work. He led me here."

"He spared Reverend Greene for the ministry, not you," she argued, amazed by his twisted logic.

"That's not true! You've seen the man and heard him speak. He's grotesque to look at, and he couldn't deliver a sermon from the pulpit and expect anyone beyond the first bench to hear him. The devil's work! Satan destroyed the minister because he was saving lost souls, but the Prince of Darkness did not prevail over God, who chose *me* to spread the Gospel in Reverend Greene's place."

Chest heaving, he pointed his finger at her. "You were chosen by God to be the handmaiden of my redemption, but we have both displeased Him. And now . . . ." His voice trailed off to a whisper, and his gaze grew distant. "Now He is calling me Home to share in His glory, but first I must prove my worthiness."

Frightened by his self-serving religious fanaticism, she went along with his irrational notions, if only to find a way through them to protect Olivia. "How will you do that?"

He looked at her like she had just crawled up from the underworld. "By suffering the humiliation of public execution, just like His Son. And like you've done for others, you must do watch with me tonight and be there to sustain me tomorrow at my last moments and bear witness to all who have betrayed me that the power and glory of God has no end."

She pressed him further, horrified by the very thought of attending his execution. "Who betrayed you?"

"Reverend Burke and his son. The elders, especially Ezra. Even you. And I will destroy all of you before I die. Just as the Father's Son destroyed the temple, I will destroy the church here." He paced around the room, mumbling and muttering to himself. "Heathens and infidels . . . all of them . . ."

The intensity of his fanaticism frightened her to the depth of her soul, and she struggled through her frazzled thoughts to find a way to thwart him. It was pointless to argue against him using any sort of logic that demanded he hold himself accountable; instead, she would have to follow his own perverse thinking.

She closed her eyes. Tears streamed down her face. Above the pounding of her heart and the ramblings of a madman, she prayed for wisdom and courage. Nothing she had ever done as the minister's wife had been as challenging or rewarding as being a watcher. She had shared the last moments of the dying to ease their fears and give them courage to face their Maker, but she was the one now filled with fear and doubts. Could she watch with him, comfort him until dawn, and then watch his execution? Would she be able to change his mind about vilifying the entire church and village, or would time run out for all of them? The horror of failure was unimaginable, and she shuddered.

Help me, Lord. I cannot walk this road alone.

She opened her eyes and approached Farley. "I'll be here and watch with you," she promised. "But if you want to share in His glory, there is something you must do. I will help you to prepare."

He eyed her suspiciously. "I know what I have to do."

"You let me help you before. Remember the sermon on the Miracle at Cana and how well that was received? Remember how I sat in the first bench at meeting and helped you when you'd forgotten the words to your sermon? How can I be the handmaiden of your redemption if you won't let me help you now? There isn't much time."

As he hesitated, his gaze darted around the room and settled on the door. "How do I know you'll keep your word and stay with me till the end?"

She held her head high, but her knees were shaking and her heart was racing. "Because I will walk with you to your destiny, and when it is time, I will stand beneath the gallows until you draw your last breath."

"Burke won't allow it."

"Yes, he will."

She walked over to the door and opened it wide. With the light behind him, Jared was a dark silhouette that filled the doorway and his presence renewed her courage. She quickly told him about her plans in a loud, clear voice Farley could also hear. She answered the anguish in Jared's eyes with a small shake of her head. "I'll keep trying," she whispered, "but you should prepare for the worst. Convince your mother not to attend the execution so she won't have to hear him herself. Stay with her. If I fail, you'll know quickly enough and you can speak to her privately before anyone else can tell her about your father." She paused. "Farley's so bitter, he's going to attack everyone. The elders, even other members of the church."

"Don't ask me to let you go alone. Not tomorrow," Jared pleaded.

Her eyes filled with tears. She pressed her fingertips to his lips before she held his hand to her heart. "You'll be here with me," she murmured, then stepped back and closed the door.

Jared fought against his first instinct—to tear through the door and end Farley's miserable life here and now—by slamming his fist into the palm of his hand. He stared at the door, picturing the image of her precious face. Her words echoed in his mind. *Protect your mother. Don't let her hear him. Protect your mother. . . .*

He paced the hall, his steps in rhythm with the soft echo of her words that faded below the loud pounding of his heart, the sharp rap of his boots on the wooden floor, and the murmur of voices inside Farley's chamber.

Jared stopped abruptly and listened to the whisper of an idea that came from his heart and grew louder in his mind, shaping an idea that roared with potential he had almost missed because he had failed to follow his own strategy: When faced with an implacable enemy, launch an attack from behind.

"I've been such a fool!" He checked his pocket watch. Twelve-thirty in the morning. The guard was due back in half an hour. Time enough to sound the alarm and assemble the troops, but not enough time to do it alone. He strode to Emilee's former chamber, where Reverend Greene and his wife were resting, raised his hand, and knocked on the door.

At dawn, Oliver Farley would meet his well-deserved fate, but not on his terms. On Jared's. God willing, by this time tomorrow, Farley would be burning in a hell of his own making. And so would his last words.

THIRTY-ONE

The church bell tolled once, and then again, sounding a death knell that carried far and wide through the dark and eerie night to wake the sleeping and send shivers of desperation through Emilee's body and spirit.

She fought the wave of despair flooding her soul. Her mind scratched and clawed through her thoughts for a lifeline, just one single thread of hope, one that would hold her fast only long enough to find one last plea that would not fall on deaf ears before she drowned in her own failure.

The chamber door opened. When Reverend Greene, his face solemn and much paler than usual, entered Farley's room, the last thread of her hope snapped. Near exhaustion from lack of sleep and numbed by her long, unsuccessful watch, she sank down into her chair.

''It's time,'' he rasped.

Overwhelmed by her inability to convince Farley to admit to his sins and seek forgiveness through prayer before he died, Emilee barely had the strength to stand up and don her dark green cloak. When she did, her movements were awkward, even clumsy, and her fingers fumbled with the closing on her heavy garment. Her hands shook so badly she could not tie the ribbon on the hood, and she cast it back.

Still seated in his chair near the bed, Farley kept his gaze on Emilee and refused to acknowledge the minister's presence or his announcement with more than a sneer. He had dressed in formal attire, but refused an overcoat. Even by candlelight, the Geneva lace bands on his shirt were a brilliant white mockery, and she wondered what people would say or think when they saw he had worn the very symbol of the ministry he had used to betray them all.

As the minister crossed the room and approached her, she

tried to keep her composure. Physically, he was not a strong or attractive man, but his inner goodness and quiet faith gave him a compelling presence that pervaded the very air she breathed and helped to soothe her battered spirit. When he searched her face, tears welled in her eyes, and she answered his unspoken question with a slow, sad shake of her head.

He nodded. His shoulders slumped, but he quickly straightened them and put his gloved hand on her shoulder. "You will not be alone. Now or ever," he whispered before he turned away to approach Oliver Farley.

With the minister's words echoing in her heart, she watched the two men with bated breath, praying the minister would do what she had failed to do: Save both Farley and the congregation.

When he spoke, his voice was a strong but plaintive whisper. "Would you like a moment to make your peace with God? I can ask Emilee to wait outside."

Farley brushed him away. "I made my peace with Him long ago," he snapped. He stood up, straightened his waistcoat, and smoothed the collar he had no right to wear. Without a moment's hesitation, he closed the distance between himself and Emilee and took her arm.

She cringed, but she did not resist him as he led her to the guard standing in the open hallway, with Reverend Greene walking behind them both.

The church bell tolled once again, but the minister's promise rung hollow in her mind. She was alone. God had abandoned her and had not answered her prayers. Reverend Greene was here for the condemned man, not for her. At her request, Jared was with his mother. There was no one to stay by her side—except the very man who had betrayed her.

The guard stepped aside and followed the three of them down the front staircase, onto the outside porch, and into destiny. Argentine light, husky with the last remnants of night and the promise of a quickly approaching dawn, guided her steps. She held her head high and her body rigid, barely tolerating the pressure of Farley's hand on her elbow. Too numb to think or to feel the cold air lash against her face, she had to quicken her steps to keep up with him.

When they reached the end of the walkway and turned onto Main Street, her eyes widened and her heart began to pound. Starting just ahead at the corner, men, women, and even some children lined the rest of their route to the town square. With their bodies pressed shoulder to shoulder, they formed a frightening human fence between the walkway and the roadway.

Even though she was walking beside Farley to his left, she still would have to pass by the villagers to reach the town square.

The church bell tolled one time again.

Once the official entourage had been sighted, the villagers grew restless. Murmurs grew into jeers and shouts that became shockingly more distinct, and the people became more frightening as Emilee and Farley began to pass by them.

"Murderer!"

"Sinner!"

Faces and words were skewed with venomous hatred. Hands and fists pummeled the air to accompany a spontaneous chant that grew into a mantra: "Hang the brute! Hang the brute! Hang the brute now!"

Emilee shook from head to toe and barely withstood a violent wave of nausea that swept her to the verge of collapse. She chanced a look at some of the villagers, searching for one kind, familiar face. Some were laborers and their families, people she had seen around the village but did not know. Strangers, mostly, who had probably traveled from other towns and villages just to witness the gruesome event. No one she knew.

Not yet.

"Sinners all!" Farley hissed, and glared at his tormentors. "Repent and seek forgiveness."

Once Emilee and Farley had passed this section of people, they fell in a boisterous crowd parading behind the guard and Reverend Greene, chanting and shouting until Emilee's ears ached from the noise. The closer she got to the town square, the larger and more unruly it became, yet Farley became even more stoic. Like a martyr of old, he did not fight back. Neither did he try to protect her.

Hands reached out, grabbed the Geneva bands and ripped them away until no trace remained. A young boy, no older than ten, aimed a stone at Farley and missed, hitting Emilee's skirts instead. The boy tried again, but his aim had improved only slightly. The stone pelted Emilee's head, and she gasped at the sharp, instant pain accompanied by immediate tears. She clutched at her head, but Farley grabbed her hand back and yanked her along with him. She was too stunned to resist, even when they reached the town square, where the gallows loomed just ahead, stark and forbidding in the first rays of the dawn. She slipped on a patch of ice and gripped Farley's arm to keep her balance.

"As clumsy as ever," he grumbled. "At least once in my life, I had hoped to see you summon up a modicum of grace or dignity."

The church bell tolled again.

She clenched her jaw, and bit back an angry retort—for the last time. Through blurred vision, she quickly scanned the execution site. The villagers had spread out to form an angry sea of human faces around the foundation prepared for the meetinghouse. In the middle, the lumber she had mistakenly assumed to be reserved for installing the meetinghouse had instead been used to construct a wooden platform approximately five to six feet above the snow-covered ground.

The hangman, his face covered by a mask to conceal his identity, waited at the top of crudely built, steeply angled steps. At the bottom, the sheriff waited to escort Farley to his ignominious fate.

The most harrowing sight, however, was the thick serpent of rope swinging overhead, coiled into a noose prepared to strike justice.

Gooseflesh covered her skin. Her heart knocked and thudded in her chest, and she swayed on her feet. Reverend Greene came to her side to hold her steady when the sheriff stepped over the foundation and grabbed Farley by the arm. Reverend

Greene acknowledged the sheriff with a nod, and he led Farley away.

She watched and listened as their footsteps crunched across the snow and up the rickety stairs. Shaking uncontrollably now, she scarcely managed to remain on her feet even with Reverend Greene's help as the drama continued to unfold.

The sheriff checked the sky, caught his prisoner's hands behind his back, and tied them together with a bit of rope. After tying the condemned man's ankles, the sheriff read the charges against Oliver Farley and the court order authorizing his execution.

Cheers from the crowd practically drowned out the sheriff's voice. Shockingly, Reverend Greene stepped away, and the crowd of people facing the gallows with her pressed closer to her. Some stepped in front of her until she was surrounded on all sides. Close to panic, she could not take more than shallow breaths, and her heart practically burst through her chest.

She could not stay here to listen to Farley vilify Jared and Reverend Burke as well as the rest of the congregation and then witness the execution. She just could not! The sights and sounds would haunt her for the rest of her life, and nothing Jared could ever say or do would erase this grisly event from her mind or the minds of the villagers.

Her heart nearly stopped beating with the very sure knowledge that she and Jared would never be able to overcome this scandal and realize their love together.

Never.

The church bell tolled again.

The crowd grew eerily silent.

Her heart skipped a beat. Her vision blurred, this time with tears, because she knew the bell tolled a death knell for Farley even as it announced the end of any hope for herself and Jared.

When a strong arm went around her shoulders, she fought and tried to pull away. She snapped her head to the side and froze. "Jared!" Her heart and soul rejoiced, but her worry for Olivia took precedence. "You should be with your mother."

He held her gaze and took her hand. "We'll face life together. Good or bad," he murmured. "Have faith."

"I'm here with you, too, dear."

Emilee snapped her head to the other side. "Olivia! You . . . you shouldn't be here."

Olivia's warm blue eyes moistened with tears. "We're all here," she said quietly and turned aside so Emilee could see the others: The widowed twins. Ansel and Hester Woerner. The church elders. Even Mercy and the rest of the choir, dressed in their special robes!

Wide-eyed, Emilee turned back to Jared and saw others she knew. Paul Leary, so recently a widower. Robert and Nancy Walters. The town council and some of the members of the Ladies Benevolent Society.

Thoroughly confused, she looked up at Jared. He caressed her with a gentle smile and brought his other arm around her to create a cocoon with his body that kept her focus on him. Only him. His presence. His strength. And his love.

"Have you anything to say before you meet your Maker?"

The sheriff's voice rang out over the hushed crowd. Dawn broke wide over the horizon, and Jared tightened his arm around her shoulders.

Farley's voice rang loud and clear. "Before I die . . ."

Out of the corner of her eye, Emilee noted a sudden shift in the crowd. She glanced to the side and watched as Mercy stepped forward, as though Farley's words were some sort of cue, and turned around to face the other members of the choir, who waited expectantly, their faces set in grim expressions. Mercy's choir gown rustled softly as she raised her hands, nodded once, and signaled the choir to begin. Their voices joined together and rose in familiar, precious melody.

"A-ma-zing grace . . . how sweet . . . the sound . . ."

Within a heartbeat, the rest of Farley's words were lost to her as the very air around Emilee resonated with the sound of voices raised in prayerful song while the church bell tolled incessantly in the distance.

"th-at saved . . . a wretch . . . li-ke me . . ."

The strong, powerfully loud voices obliterated Farley's attempts to slander and destroy the people she loved and the congregation he had betrayed! Miracle of all miracles, she could hear nothing but the words to the hymn that had long been her favorite.

Now it was her salvation.

She glanced up at Farley. Already blushed with cold, his cheeks had turned scarlet with rage. The tendons in his neck stood out as he yelled and shouted to be heard above the din that surrounded them all. The voices grew louder. The words to the hymn became more meaningful.

"... Tw-as grace ... th-at taught ... my heart ... to fear ..."

Farley bucked his body, struggling against the restraints that tied his hands and the hangman's strong arms that held him. His face set with determination, the sheriff slipped a hood over the condemned man's face and head. She looked up to Jared and saw him smile at her reassuringly. Even though he dipped his head to her ear to speak, she had to struggle to make out the words: "You are not alone. Now. Or ever."

When Emilee closed her eyes and sank against him, Jared folded her into his embrace. He cradled her tenderly, but kept her from watching the execution as it proceeded to its grisly end. She wept gently, and he absorbed each tremor that shook her body, vowing never to see her suffer so again.

After the sheriff gave the order to begin, Jared watched Oliver Farley die without dignity and without his wicked scheme fulfilled. Emilee's heart, however, pounded in a weak but steady rhythm, and Jared knew his plan to enlist the choir had worked so well she had not even heard the snap of the rope or the choking and gasping as they continued to sing and Oliver Farley paid the ultimate price for his sins—just as she had heard none of Farley's vindictive, fanatical diatribe that would have echoed in her mind every hour of every day for the rest of her life, sentencing her to a lifetime of nightmares.

By the amazing grace of God and the good people who had responded to Jared's call to sing His praise, neither had anyone else.

Even if they had caught more than a few ugly accusations, they would not trust a single one of Farley's spiteful words and would dismiss them as the ramblings of a religious zealot who finally had gone over the edge and plunged into the same madness that had driven him to murder his wife.

"Praise God . . . Praise God . . . Praise God . . ."

The refrain continued, and before Farley's body could be cut down and carted away, Jared lifted Emilee into his arms and carried her through the crowd, which had already begun to disperse. The church bell tolled again. The members of the congregation ended their hymn. As he passed by his friends and neighbors, Jared's heart filled with gratitude, which he offered to each of them in a sober but heartfelt smile.

Not one of the church members had hesitated for a single moment to answer his call for help. Reverend Greene had proven himself, once again, to be far more capable than he had appeared at first glance. Even his wife, Beth, as tiny and petite as she was, had helped by remaining at the church to ring the bell which signaled the call to duty for the members of the church this dawn, just as it would call them to meeting every Sunday when the new church opened.

After a harrowing night-turned-morning, he kept the image of only one person in his mind: Emilee.

Earlier, he had been unable to get through the crowd, and he had waited for Emilee at the town square, relying on Reverend Greene to keep his promise and bring her to Jared. At his first sight of her, his heart nearly stopped beating. There, standing before him, had been the very image of his dreams, an image which bloomed in his heart and shook his very existence.

Standing in white snow with her deep green cloak pulled close and her cheeks blushed a bright shade of pink, she was an awe-inspiring sight to behold. She stood alone, in the midst of chaos and tragedy, more resistant to life's travails than anyone he had ever known. She had struggled against incredible cruelty to survive before, and she fought against it now—a vision of loveliness and goodness as incredibly beautiful and uncommon as a rose in winter and twice as precious.

He held his dream-come-true in his arms. His grip was firm. His heart was full of love. He would help her to heal, from as close by or far away as she needed, until one day—soon—he would stand by her side and say the vows that would bind them together as man and wife.

With love. With joy. And most of all, with honor.

Someday.

Epilogue

Hand in hand, Emilee and Jared entered the vestibule of the new church and approached the wide oak doors that led to the sanctuary. Sunshine filtered through the paned windows, bathing the outer room with light and splaying crisscrossed shadows across the bronze plaque now hanging on the inner wall, which had been freshly whitewashed for tomorrow's long-postponed dedication.

Taking advantage of an unexpected opportunity to view the plaque together privately, Emilee tugged on Jared's hand and led him to the side until they stood directly in front of the plaque.

DEDICATED TO ALL THOSE WHO ARE ALONE
AND ENTER OUR HUMBLE HOUSE OF WORSHIP.

"THAT YE ALSO MAY HAVE FELLOWSHIP WITH US:
AND TRULY OUR FELLOWSHIP IS WITH THE FATHER
AND WITH HIS SON . . ."
1 JOHN 1:13

REV. MR. RANDALL GREENE, PASTOR
FEBRUARY 1835

The board's decision to change the plaque from one honoring Jared's father to one that would honor them all touched her heart. The inscribed words would offer poignant testimony to all who entered the church of the healing power of fellowship and faith, a lesson brought to life on a cold December dawn by members of the congregation who had joined together to chase away darkness and fear, but it was the man by her side who had branded that message on her heart and soul with his unfailing love.

Her pulse quickened, and she squeezed Jared's hand. Smiling, she looked up at the very precious man who had helped her these past few months to find peace in the aftermath of Farley's public execution. Ever patient and faithful, Jared had stayed by her side as she struggled to find her way through a confusing maze of emotions in which raw despair and soul-devastating shame eventually gave way to the stunning power of love, giving her spirit the courage to rebound, victorious and strong, from tragedy, shame, and betrayal.

Although Farley had mocked the ministry he had claimed by fraud, even in death, Jared had helped her to see that she had fulfilled her role as the minister's wife with honest dedication and faith. He had been giving and loving, sustaining her in her darkest moments of doubt with the promise of a new life—one that would be filled with selfless, abiding love and mutual devotion.

She gazed into his eyes and saw the same hunger and longing that filled her soul. The journey they each had made to reach this day had been wrought with many painful detours, but each and every one had led them straight back to one another, where the love they shared had grown even stronger.

In just a few moments, they would be joined together as husband and wife in a ceremony to be witnessed by many of the villagers who had gathered together on that fateful morning to turn tragedy into triumph and who waited now in the sanctuary for their arrival.

Joy bubbled in her soul, and her heart beat with anticipation. Anxious to begin her new life, one she could claim with endearing love and blessed honor as Mrs. Jared Burke, her eyes misted with tears. "The dedication tomorrow will be even more special now," she murmured.

His eyes glistened as he brought her hand to his lips and pressed a gentle kiss to her fingertips before placing her hand over his heart. "Every day and night will be special, as long as we're together. I love you, Emilee. Truly."

She swallowed the lump in her throat. "As I love you,"

she whispered, honored to be able to enter the sanctuary and stand before the congregation to pledge her love, her life, and her troth to the man who held her heart captive and who graced her life with his very presence.

Amazing grace.

An amazing love.

A most amazing man.

How truly sweet life could be.

Haywood Smith

"Haywood Smith delivers intelligent, sensitive historical romance for readers who expect more from the genre."

—*Publishers Weekly*

SHADOWS IN VELVET

Orphan Anne Marie must enter the gilded decadence of the French court as the bride of a mysterious nobleman, only to be shattered by a secret from his past that could embroil them both in a treacherous uprising...

_____ 95873-0 $5.99 U.S./$6.99 CAN.

SECRETS IN SATIN

Amid the turmoil of a dying monarch, newly widowed Elizabeth, Countess of Ravenwold, is forced by royal command to marry a man she has hardened her heart to—and is drawn into a dangerous game of intrigue and a passionate contest of wills.

_____ 96159-6 $5.99 U.S./$7.99 CAN.

Start a love affair with one of today's most extraordinary romance authors...

HER SECRET AFFAIR

BARBARA DAWSON SMITH

Bestselling author of *Once Upon a Scandal*

It is Regency England. Isabel Darling, the only child of an infamous madam, is determined to exact revenge on the scoundrels who used her late mother—and uncover which one of these men is her father. As she sets her sights on blackmailing the Lord of Kern, his indignant son Justin steps in to stop the headstrong Isabel—and start a passion from which neither can escape...

"Barbara Dawson Smith is an author everyone should read. You'll be hooked from page one." —*Romantic Times*

HER SECRET AFFAIR
Barbara Dawson Smith
0-312-96507-9___$5.99 U.S.__$7.99 Can.